
SHOCK OF FATE

Anchoress Series Book One

D. L. ARMILLEI

Diamond Cove
Publishing

Second edition, February 2019

ISBN 978-0-9986720-0-7 [Mobi]
ISBN 978-0-9986720-1-4 [ePub]
ISBN 978-0-9986720-2-1 [Softcover]
ISBN 978-0-9986720-3-8 [Hardcover]
Library of Congress Control Number: 2017901625

Diamond Cove Publishing, LLC,
P.O. Box 2292, Palm Harbor, FL 34682-2292
DLA@DiamondCovePublishing.com

Shock of Fate

I-Ching #51

"The shock of disturbing events creates terror and trembling. Seek a higher truth and you will find success."

—The I Ching or Book of Changes

Prologue

Thursday Night:
Latitude 44.8542° N,
Longitude 93.2422° W, Earth World

MICHAEL CROSS SCANNED the restless crowd but couldn't find the demon.

Families—humans of the Earth World—lined up, waiting for the Mall of America to begin its Midnight Madness sale.

Filthy terrigens.

They had camped in front of the mall for days. Crisp pop-up tents dotted the crowd like a virus, along with a clutter of beach chairs, blankets, and pillows. Most of them had food-and-drink-stocked coolers. Toys and trash littered the ground. Their need for *more,* the *greed,* oozed from the crowd.

Yeah, this place would definitely attract a demon.

Michael continued to survey the terrigens, wondering what had possessed him years ago to take a job requiring him to spend time in the Earth World hunting demons.

I guess I had ideals back then. And earning a spot in the elite sector of the

Lodian military impressed the ladies. His chest tightened as he remembered the exact moment when his life went bad.

Michael's rookie partner, Tilly Hopewell, caught up to him, interrupting his thoughts.

Tilly stared at her palm. A dot flashed on her multi-track. "I'm picking it up over there." She pointed through the crowd to an area dense with shadows.

Clusters of adults bundled in bright spring jackets held cups of hot coffee on the chilly June night. They chatted with one another like old friends, oblivious to the danger lurking nearby.

Michael snapped his hand over her multi-track. He had no need for terrigens to see something resembling the newest smartphone, which they'd ask about and want to buy. "Terrigens can't see demons. But they can see us." *Does she think wearing hot, heavy pea coats to hide our uniforms is for fun?*

What he'd told Tilly wasn't exactly true. Terrigens *could* see demons. They just didn't know it.

Demons liked to appear in a form that enabled them to hide and move easily in the darkness. They usually camouflaged themselves to the point of invisibility, but occasionally terrigens glimpsed their movement as a wisp of smoke, the flicker of a shadow, or a blur. All of which the Earth World's humans brushed off as a trick of the eye.

Tilly looked away, abashed.

"Rookies," Michael mumbled with disgust. They came charging into the field fresh out of training, high on adrenaline, ready to be a demon hunter. They never seemed to grasp it takes years to become a competent Grigori. A protector.

This last thought made his stomach clench. Reflexively, he ran his fingers along the scars on his jaw and neck.

Tilly glanced at him, mistaking his movement for a command.

Irritably, he moved forward, motioning for her to follow him.

Demons were too cowardly to appear in their true form to terrigens, which gave the Grigori an advantage. Demons feared if they were seen, the Earth World humans would try to kill them, and the

Grigori would target them for exhibiting aggressive behavior by showing their true selves.

Demons were also lazy. It took a tremendous amount of energy and strength to hold their true form on the same higher vibrational frequencies as terrigens.

And showing themselves proved not as effective as *seeping*. Michael shuddered. Demons found seeping easy.

Michael and Tilly dodged as several kids careened by, laughing and playing. Lights from a massive storefront cast a forbidding glow over the crowd. That, along with the light of a near-full moon, created many hiding places in the shadowy gaps among the crowd.

As Michael and Tilly edged across the line, the terrigens tensed and shifted their bodies, as if preparing to defend their spots. The terrigens calmed after realizing the interlopers had only crossed the line, not cut in, and again became entranced by the mindless vigil of the sale.

Tilly wrinkled her nose as they inched their way down a delivery alley between the towering yellow brick of two mall walls. The air stunk like week-old garbage.

And sulfur.

"The demon is near," Michael whispered.

A faint rustling sound came from behind the trash bin ahead. His hand snapped into a halt position. He nodded to Tilly, who understood the unspoken command to use her multi-track to anchor the demon.

Tilly hesitated and whispered, "It smells like sulfur, and the demon is holding itself at one of the highest terrigen frequencies. That's odd, right?"

"Stronger demons sometimes emit sulfur," Michael replied. "And can hold at higher frequencies."

"Don't they usually lower their vibration to try and slip away from us?" Tilly asked.

"Usually," Michael said. "Could be a Class II."

Tilly tensed.

Grigori classified demons by their behavior. Class I demons were weak and cowardly. Class II demons were strong and aggressive. All demons were cunning and evil but had no interest in killing terrigens. They needed terrigens to produce negativity that generated new demons and to feed the ones already here, allowing them to become stronger, to become Class IIs.

The Grigori aimed never to let Class I demons linger long enough to become Class IIs.

"I gave you a command," Michael growled. He hated training rookies. "Anchor the demon."

He scrutinized Tilly's fresh, young face to see whether the demon's whisper had influenced her. Demons used silent words to seep into the subconscious of any unsuspecting human's mind, causing the person to succumb to "brain rot," as Michael liked to call it.

Brain rot corrupted the mind of the victim, prompting unsettling, negative thoughts that led to depression, intolerance, anxiety, and ideas of violence. Eventually, the thoughts became so disruptive people acted on them and performed atrocious deeds, committed violent or immoral acts, harmed others, or harmed themselves. This created an environment of fear, terror, and darkness—an environment where demons thrived.

Grigori referred to this process as *seeping* and underwent training to be unaffected by it. Still, Michael wondered about his rookie.

He pulled back his pea coat to grab his own multi-track when a wisp of smoke, swirling like a tiny tornado, emerged from the shadows.

Tilly sprang to life and thumbed the switch on her multi-track to secure their own and the demon's vibrational frequency and lock it in. Then she pressed a button that took both demon and hunters to a lower vibration and out of the terrigens' sight.

"Use the net," Michael commanded.

Tilly swiped her finger on the multi-track, and a web-like net shot forward, trapping the swirling demon.

Stronger demons could change frequencies after being locked in, taking both themselves and the Grigori on a changing frequency ride. The net provided extra insurance the demon would be held at the Grigori's desired frequency and not the other way around. This allowed the Grigori to hold the demon steady so they could kill it. Killing was protocol. Their job required them to keep the demon population under control.

Sometimes, due to fear, demons "popped" back into their true form when confronted by a Grigori. If not, Grigori had been trained to force demons into their true form using the multi-track so they could get a visual description to put in their reports.

But staring at Michael from under the net wasn't a horrible creature.

It was a little girl.

She stood alone in the alley, trembling from fright. A ray of moonlight draped her, highlighting the girl's white-blond hair, flawless porcelain skin, and pretty blue eyes.

Horror tore through Michael and twisted his gut—the demon had replicated his daughter at age five, right down to Van's favorite outfit at that time—red bowtie shoes and a white-ruffled, tailor-made dress.

"I snagged a terrigen. I'm so sorry." Tilly shook her multi-track and slapped it against her palm. "Is my MT broken?"

The little girl sobbed. "Daddy! Let me out of the net," it said, in a sickening echo of Van's sweet voice. "Daddy, don't you love me?"

Michael's shoulders tightened. His stare remained on the daughter-like demon as he grasped the hilt of his ritualized, mini-scythe.

"Grigori Cross, sir, it's one of the kids waiting for the sale," Tilly said. "She's mistaking you for her father. The demon slipped away. I screwed up."

Michael answered by unsheathing his scythe.

Tilly's eyes grew wide. "Remember our Grigori oath?"

Michael understood her nervous tone. He had been back in the field only a short time, and with his sordid past... *well, no wonder.*

"To protect the terrigens at all costs?" Tilly said, an octave louder.

Michael grunted. That was only one of their oaths. And this was no terrigen. He had never seen a demon take human form, and he didn't know what class they were dealing with, but it didn't matter. It had to be killed.

"It's a demon." Michael raised his scythe.

"Demons can't take human form." Tilly darted over to the child.

"Stand down!" He marched forward, ready to elbow Tilly out of the way and strike the demon.

But, as Tilly tore off the netting, the demon-girl looked at Michael. Its stare flashed a phosphorescent violet sheen just like Van's.

Michael paused.

Tilly swiveled to block his attack, turning her back on the enemy.

"It's a terrigen gir—"

A dull, wet sucking sound cut Tilly off as the demon's stick-like appendage pierced her torso. Its tip dripped with blood and chunks of tissue.

The demon-girl retracted its spiked arm and placidly watched Michael with eyes now so dark and empty, they made his soul shiver.

Michael held onto his scythe as he grabbed hold of the rookie.

Tilly clasped his arms. Bits of blood dribbled down the sides of her mouth as she attempted to speak.

She slid from his grasp, slumped to her knees, and crumpled to the ground.

Michael didn't blame the rookie for her mistake. Demons were more interested in humans' suffering than in their death, and demons in their true form usually appeared the size of a small dog with a deranged combination of reptilian-goat features. Given enough time, Michael knew Class II demons could develop the potential to kill a human. But he had just witnessed an unclassified behavior.

Holding the form of a human took a tremendous amount of strength for a demon, way beyond the ability of a Class II.

Tilly's training manual hadn't covered demons taking human form, because Grigori commonly believed it wasn't possible. But Michael had recently uncovered information in a hidden ancient scroll that a demon appearing in human form was not unprecedented. It had happened a thousand years ago, during the Great War between the Lodians and the Balish.

Not everyone can be saved. Michael staggered backward, away from his rookie's body.

He couldn't go back in time and change things. *Life is for those who can be saved.*

His attention returned to the demon-girl. He wondered why it hadn't yet attempted to kill him.

Its eyes had returned to a beautiful warm blue; its spiked appendage transformed back into a child's arm. It swiveled its ankle back and forth and smiled coyly at Michael, like Van had as a child whenever anyone confronted her for doing something wrong.

Michael kept his stare on the Van-like doppelgänger as he unsnapped a salt bomb from his belt.

He smashed it at the demon's feet, hoping it would have a paralyzing effect, despite the demon's strength.

The demon squealed. It lunged and growled at him like a rabid animal, forcing him to dart and dodge.

Terror filled Michael as he realized it was a rare Class III, one with the ability to raise its vibration high enough to reach the Living World. His world.

He struggled to remain composed as the demon-girl paced and snarled, assessing his weaknesses before pouncing again.

Michael unhooked the multi-track from his belt. "Screw protocol." He pointed his MT at the demon-girl. Rather than attempting to net it again, he toggled a button and raised only the demon's vibrational frequency—a dangerous, unauthorized way to kill a demon.

The demon-girl let out an ear-shattering shriek of pain before it exploded into a fit of vaporous black rage.

The smoky mass didn't dissipate as he had expected. Instead, it took the form of a human-reptilian chimera.

"Damn." Michael stepped back and craned his neck to get a full view of this newest demon as it stretched its quasi-female body high and spread its reddish-brown wings wide.

None of his Grigori killing tools would be any match for this.

The creature snorted, lowered its angular head, and perused Michael as if wondering whether he was worth eating.

Michael dropped his multi-track, gripped his mini-scythe, and met the creature's eyes.

The demon snorted, so close to Michael's face its hot breath ruffled his hair.

He braced, ready to fight to the death.

Instead of attacking, the demon grinned at him like a friend, raised its glabrous body, and then seeped soundlessly into the earth.

Michael loosened his grip on the scythe. He stood there, stunned by the understanding of what had just happened.

He urgently needed to get back to the Balish palace to fulfill his secret plan.

Class III demons appearing in the Earth World signaled the first stage of Dishora, a prophesied time when darkness would rise to oppose the light. It would start with another Great War between the Lodians and the Balish. Everyone would choose a side.

With dread, Michael knew this day would come.

Darkness always seeks to destroy the light.

Chapter 1

Saturday Night:
Providence Island,
Earth World

"SORRY YOUR FATHER never showed up for the placement ceremony today, Van." Ken Rose shook his head in disappointment. The flickering light from the bonfire picked up the dusty blond highlights in his hair.

Van shrugged. "Who cares?"

It was near midnight and they'd both shown up at an after-party in the woods, far from the prying eyes of adults.

"A sophomore's never won an All-Grades Trophy like you did," he said. "And for Capture the Flag. That's the toughest event in the games."

"Whatever." Van inhaled the heady scent of the pine forest. She leaned back against a giant oak, hands behind her, anticipating a romantic moment with her boyfriend.

Ken nodded, satisfied with her answer. "Catch you later." He bounded off to hang with his friends.

The rough bark dug into Van's delicate skin. She sprang forward, angry at messing up her new dress, all for nothing. She brushed off the dirt and bark as Ken and his buddies gathered around the "Reservation Boundary: Off Limits" sign at the edge of the clearing.

I handpicked this outfit for tonight, she thought irritably. A long-sleeved, off-the-shoulder, form-fitting, blood-red mini dress with red tights and black thigh-high boots. The dress played up her smooth, shoulder-length white-blond hair and highlighted her fair complexion.

Van thought the outfit made her look older than her fifteen years, and she hadn't been sure her step-mother would let her wear it out of the manor. Genie had commented that Van was dressed "like a trollop," but her step-mother said it with a closed-lip grin of approval and let her go. Genie understood Van's appearance played an essential role in her top social standing at Canterbury Bells Charter School.

After a few playful punches, Ken and his pals started throwing stones at the sign and daring one another to cross the boundary line. The latter act would get any one of them permanently banished from their small island off the coast of Massachusetts.

The Native Island tribe owned and partly occupied Providence Island. Ages ago, the tribal Elders petitioned the U.S. government to declare the island a sovereign state with the ability to govern itself and won. Now, the Elders controlled and regulated everything on the island.

There were two sides to the island: the townie side and the tribal reservation.

Van and her father had been tribal residents from birth, and Genie by marriage, but they lived just outside the boundary line on the townie side, along with the non-tribal residents and the other Native Islanders who had children.

Childless Native Islanders, including the Elders, occupied the reservation. Children and all non-tribal members needed permission by an Elder to enter their land.

Ken and his friends knew this. The idiots.

Now that Van thought about it, she didn't care for the tone of Ken's remark concerning her father. Everyone on the island knew Michael Cross worked long hours at an important job with the Elders in a division of Homeland Security called the Grigori. This special unit worked with the mainland's government and often took her father away from home.

Van didn't understand her father's work. No one outside the reservation did. She only knew what her father told her: the Grigori made up "an elite tactical unit of safety enforcement." Her father had been reassigned to the field in the last year, which kept him away from home more than ever. As usual, his job had probably made him miss the Placement Ceremony.

Van stood within the bonfire's illumination.

Ken caught her eye and smiled, his white teeth flashing through the dark night. "Loosen up and have some fun," he yelled.

Van caught herself frowning, something she tried to avoid; she didn't want to get frown lines. She ran her fingers over her hair and smiled back at Ken. He had a good point. Tonight marked the beginning of Jaychund, a thirty-day celebration of the moon particular to the Native Islanders.

The first night of Jaychund meant school had let out for summer. The games—sporting events accounting for the last part of final exams for kids in high school—were over. Earlier in the day, during the Placement Ceremony, students had received the trophies they'd earned during the games, and teachers assigned the undergrads their placement tracks for the next school year and awarded seniors their permanent career placements.

The best part of the tradition happened at night, after the ceremonial formalities, when all the teenagers met secretly at Astrid's Hollow to party around a bonfire. Tomorrow, the islanders would continue the celebration with a two-day festival.

Van always looked forward to the island's annual celebration of Jaychund. She found comfort in the ancient tribal traditions but felt awkward admitting this to her friends, who thought all celebrations organized by the Elders were lame.

Suddenly, a group of freshmen buzzed around her.

"Oh, Van, I love that dress," one girl said. *Named Jade, maybe?* "Is that from Ropa Moda?"

Van had a cool reputation to maintain and forced herself to be unenthusiastic over their arrival. Though she loved the attention.

"It's from off island," Van said. "Genie buys all my clothes in downtown Boston." She felt better after reminding them—or herself?—that she could afford to shop there. Well, her parents could, anyway.

"Your hair looks *amazing*, Van," another girl said. "Gotta love Miss Nutting and the Naked Ape, right?"

Van eyed the girl up and down, sure she lived in Community Gardens, a place the islanders nicknamed Hide-a-Way and Genie considered a shantytown.

"How long have you been going there?" Van asked, knowing perfectly well the girl couldn't afford the Naked Ape. Then she felt an immediate pang of regret that worsened as she acknowledged the girl's weak chin and split ends.

"Did you hear the rumors?" a third girl asked, eager to please.

Van felt so distracted by this girl's mismatched nightmare of an outfit—*Genie would never let me out of the house in that*—she almost didn't catch what the girl had said.

However, the words registered, and Van perked up. Gossip was like currency on the small island. She raised one of her perfectly sculpted eyebrows.

Thrilled at the show of interest, the girl babbled on. "The Elders are looking for some kids to help with a project off island."

"Away for the whole summer," said another girl, who had an upturned nose.

"Pernilla won every event in her own year *and* every All-Grades event, except Capture the Flag," the girl from Hide-a-Way said. She grinned, acknowledging Van's achievement, then continued. "Pernilla will get chosen for the project, for sure."

"I heard she was sick for months before the games," the girl with the mismatched outfit said. "Almost wasn't able to compete."

"She obviously got better." Van didn't appreciate how no one ever seemed impressed with her accomplishments. She had placed first in her year and had won the All-Grades Trophy for Capture the Flag as a sophomore—that was something too.

"I overheard the Elders call Pernilla a 'special case,'" the girl from Hide-a-Way said. "What do you think it means?"

Van shrugged. "It's the first time a junior has placed number one overall in the games."

Or it could be Pernilla always seemed different, being a strange ethnic mix of Native American and Native Islander. Her light blue eyes, courtesy of the Native Islanders, combined with the naturally tan skin of the mainland's Native Americans and thick, wavy, light brown hair. All these features made her a striking contrast to her predominantly fair-skinned, blond, blue-eyed peers. She attracted all the boys, and she was Van's biggest competition for their attention.

"Who cares about Pernilla?" Jade gushed. "Oh, Van, you will *so* get chosen."

"The Elders love you," said the girl with the nose, whooshing her hand in a gesture that said, "No worries."

The other girls bobbed their heads up and down like marionettes in a most irritating way.

Van looked down her nose at Jade. "Not interested. I have other plans for summer."

They acted like Pernilla had earned a place on the project and Van hadn't, but would get the placement anyway because of her family's high status.

Well, Pernilla could have the project. Van had no desire to leave the island. She had been off island as required for school field trips and had found the mainland crowded with angry, violent people. Ignorant too. They often referred to Providence Island as "that cult."

Just because the Elders restrict our use of the internet and TV, and the island doesn't get smartphone reception, doesn't mean we're a cult.

Van didn't care for any of the newest technologies, anyway. She believed the gadgets took people away from nature and limited their human interaction.

Besides, she looked forward to bumming around on the beach all summer with Ken and her best friend, Paley Ash. Van shivered with annoyance at the freshman even suggesting she *work* during break.

Ken appeared, jarring Van from her thoughts. He'd evidently overheard their conversation.

"You'll get chosen for the project, Van, like it or not," Ken said. "The Elders favor kids in the reservation program. Which means you."

Van belonged to a group of kids selected for extra classes that took place on the reservation, in addition to regular classes at Canterbury Bells. The kids in the special classes were superior athletes and the only students allowed to compete in the Jaychund games before entering high school. Pernilla excelled in athletics but, oddly, had never been placed in the reservation program.

"Hey, guys," said a superficially cheery voice.

Arriving like a bad rash, Pernilla intruded into their circle, attached at the elbow to her best friend, Maren.

"Flotsam," Van greeted Pernilla, then nodded at Maren. "Jetsam."

"Van's in the reservation program because she needs special attention," Pernilla chided, "being a bit slow in the head and all."

"*Excuse me?*" Van raised her brow.

"That's why they never placed me in the program," Pernilla said. "I was too smart."

"Take it easy, Pernilla," Ken said, then turned to Van. "Let's go."

"I was here first. I'm not going anywhere." Van crossed her arms. "Tell *her* to leave."

"No way," Pernilla snapped.

Ken grasped Pernilla's elbow. "Come on." He pulled her away.

Van heard him whisper, "Why are you bothering Van?" It seemed a bit too intimate a question for casual friends, causing her curiosity to pique as her stomach tumbled.

Maren stood firm and glared at Van.

Van scowled back. "I think it best you go take care of your friend."

Maren tossed her head and left to rejoin the party.

"Don't listen to Pernilla," Jade said. "*Special* doesn't mean remedial."

Van never thought it had until now.

She remembered being a slow learner as a kid, but she'd struggled due to frequent illnesses. The special classes made her feel better, healthier. They helped her gain physical strength and enabled her to be as smart as everyone else.

"Have you seen Paley?" Van asked, missing the company of her best friend since nursery school.

"She's probably out trolling for guys," the girl with the nose said, smirking.

The other girls giggled unkindly.

"Paley is still your favorite charity case, huh?" Jade asked Van.

Van could barely hear Jade above the rising human howls echoing throughout the woods. Tradition dictated the islanders howl at the moon at midnight during Jaychund.

Once the noise quieted, Van said fiercely, "Paley got a job at the Naked Ape. Got special permission from the Elders. She's a contributor, just like the rest of us."

Van's schoolmates saw Paley, an orphan, as a drain on the island's resources because she didn't have a family to contribute to the island's economy and therefore deserved nothing. But Van never felt that way about Paley.

"Ah-woo!" *Whump*.

Van became smothered by pudgy softness, hyacinth scent, and clouds of highlighted blond hair. She grinned and hugged her friend back. "Paley!"

After they disentangled, Van looked over Paley's outfit. "You look great!"

Jade eyed Paley's bolero jacket, silk shirt, ankle boots, and beautifully manicured hands. "Van's right, you do look good. How come?"

Paley's shoulders slumped.

The girl with the mismatched outfit asked, "Van picked it out and bought it for you, didn't she?" She and her friends turned up their noses and wandered back to mingle at the party.

"They're just jealous." Van's heart bled for the pain these jerks caused Paley. She was glad to see them go.

Paley shrugged and hung her head.

"Let's go find Ken," Van suggested, hoping to break Paley's sullen mood brought on by the disrespectful freshman. Van had last seen Ken pulling Pernilla away, followed by Maren. Now, Maren chatted with a few other girls from her own year and Pernilla wasn't with her.

Paley agreed, and they meandered into the thick of the party.

In the woods alongside the clearing, they saw Pernilla making out with some guy, not even troubling to move out of the moonlight.

The two figures separated; Van gasped.

Ken, hearing her involuntary reaction, looked over with the expression of a thief caught in a searchlight.

Van snorted in disgust and stormed away through the crowd, clipping anyone in her way.

"Hey!" Ken shouted as he jogged to catch up with her. He grabbed Van by the arm and twisted her toward him. "I can explain!"

"Ouch!" Van cried. "Let go of me!"

Ken relaxed his grip, but held firm. "It was an accident."

"What happened? Did you fall on her face?" Van yanked her arm out of his grip.

"I, uh—"

"Does anyone else know? Did anyone but us see you?"

Ken's lips formed a stern line. "You care more about what other people think, not that I kissed another girl?"

"I—I'm mad at both," Van said confused. "I don't want anyone to know because it's *embarrassing*."

Pernilla appeared next to Ken and butted in. "*I* want people to know."

"Nilla, please," Ken said in a strained voice.

"Nilla? Nilla?" Van wanted to puke. "You have a cute little *nick-name* for her?"

"No. No!" Pernilla stomped forward. Ken grabbed at her, but

she jerked free and stuck her face in Van's. "I'm sick of pussyfooting around her."

"Oh, you better get out of my face, girl," Van warned.

Paley watched the altercation, nervously shifting from foot to foot, her face pale even for someone with a booth-made tan.

Ken stood like a lump, looking terrified.

Pernilla's face contorted. "No one likes you or that weird flash of violet you get in your eyes." Her hands curled into claws. She raised them, settling into the familiar fighter's stance. "Your family is rich. That's your only skill. No one wants to be friends with you. Our parents *make* us be nice to you under orders by the Elders."

Maren edged her way behind Pernilla, her eyes wide. "Pernilla, let's go."

Pernilla ignored Maren and continued to glower at Van. "You're a pathetic waste of space. Being in special classes doesn't even help you. You're such a baby. Still slow and weak. Everyone but you grew out of that."

"Your reasoning's flawed, just like your skin." Van's nostrils flared. "I get good grades. I'm placed on the reservation track."

"Even Paley has started to earn what she has," Pernilla hissed. "But you—you get special treatment from the Elders because of your *mother*!"

Pernilla startled Van by using the word *mother*, rather than *stepmother*. The Elders forbade the islanders to talk about Van's birth mother, Aelia.

"Leave my family out of this," Van snarled. She bent down and snatched a stray branch off the ground.

"Take it easy, Van," Paley said.

"Don't tell me what to do." Van's knuckles turned white as she gripped the branch like a weapon and held a steady gaze on her nemesis.

Pernilla took a few steps back, still crouched in a defensive stance. "You're *handed* everything because of your family name. You never *earned* a thing. Not your placement. Not your grades—"

"I won an All-Grades Trophy in the games this year!"

"The games are fixed."

"Nilla!" Ken spurted.

Pernilla's only saying that because she wants Ken. It doesn't make it true. Van gave the branch a menacing twirl.

"Hey, Van, put that down." Ken's eyes widened.

Van ignored him and whirled the branch with savage satisfaction, taunting Pernilla. Knowing how to fight came from Van's special classes. It was something she never thought she would use in real life.

Everyone at the party crowded around Van and Pernilla. Not a peep came from the onlookers.

Ken moved between them, his arms spread. "Pernilla," he said in a serious tone, "you need to leave *now.*"

"Oh, how cute. Your other trophy is trying to help," Pernilla said. "You didn't earn him, either."

All of Van's classmates in her year, including Paley, came forward from the crowd of onlookers and surrounded Van, ready to aid in her defense.

Pernilla hesitated, but didn't stand down. She glared at Van, curling and uncurling her hands. Several of her friends, including Maren, gathered behind Pernilla in a show of solidarity.

After a long moment of strained tension, Pernilla lunged forward.

Woot! Woot! A siren from a Providence Island Security buggy tore through the night.

The noise stopped the altercation, and the crowd scattered.

Van dropped her stick as a spotlight lit the darkness of the woods like the morning sun. *Oh, this isn't good.* Unauthorized party in a restricted area, potential fight—both were against the rules.

A security guard leaped from the buggy and hollered, "Vanessa Cross! I need to see Vanessa Cross! *Now!*"

Chapter 2

D ay 1: 12:45 a.m., Earth World

PALEY RAISED her hand to shade her eyes from the light and whispered to Van, "There's no way security would've known about the fight unless they were monitoring us the whole time."

"Break it up," blasted a gruff voice over the buggy's loudspeaker, although the crowd had already started to disperse when the jeep-like vehicle erupted from the woods.

Only Van, Paley, and Ken remained in the clearing.

A stocky man jumped out of the buggy and approached Van.

"Vanessa," Chief Mumford said with a sigh of relief. "You okay?"

"Yeah. Why wouldn't I be?"

All the people on the townie side knew one another, and Van had grown used to the adults being hyper-protective of her. She figured it was out of respect for her birth mother, who had been loved by all. The community considered Aelia's death a tragic loss.

The chief mumbled into his shoulder speaker microphone. "Confirmation, visual. Butterfly is unharmed."

He wrapped his arm around Van's shoulders and let out a relieved chuckle as if his primary aim was making sure Van remained safe from harm, rather than dishing out disciplinary action.

"Come on, I'm taking you home." He shuffled her toward the buggy as two other vehicles screeched to a stop in the clearing and flicked on their rooftop spotlights. The chief yelled to the other security guards, "Sweep the area. Make sure no kids are lingering. We'll deal with punitive measures tomorrow. There's no place for these kids to hide on the island." He turned toward Ken and motioned him to the buggy. "And you, Kenan. In. You too, Paley."

Paley settled into the front to ride shotgun. Van slid into the back seat. Ken slipped in next to her.

Van glared at him and slid out the other side.

Chief Mumford twisted around from the driver's seat. "Vanessa! What're you doing?"

"Van, we need to talk." Ken attempted to follow her out of the buggy.

She snapped her palm at him. "Don't."

Van walked around to the passenger side and opened Paley's door. Her insides jittered as she gripped her friend's arm and tugged her from the passenger seat.

"We're going to walk," Van declared, knowing the adults on the island were soft on her and usually let her have her own way. At least, she hoped this was still the case.

After her altercation with Pernilla, everything she had thought about herself and her place on the island had become jumbled. She needed the walk to sort out what had happened with Pernilla and was still furious with Ken.

"We'll go straight home. Promise." Van jerked her head at Ken, who sat like a forlorn puppy in the back seat. "He needs a ride, though."

"Straight home, both of you," the chief said. "No detours, or I'll know about it." Chief Mumford stepped out of the buggy and scanned the clearing, searching for stray partiers to take home.

Van and Paley entered the path through the woods. The full moon cast some light but deepened the tree shadows, making it difficult to see. Thankfully, having grown up on the island, they knew the woods better than they knew each other.

"It must be bad if *you* wanted to walk home." Paley side glanced at Van. "For a reservation program athlete, you sure are *lazy*."

Paley was trying to cheer her, but Van was in no mood. She felt like burrowing deep into the earth and never coming out.

"I wasn't worried about you fighting Pernilla," Paley said. "I know you can call on your imaginary friend for help."

"Jacynthia's *not* imaginary." Van huffed and strode ahead of Paley, wishing she had made this a solo trip. "Just 'cause you can't see her," Van muttered as she ducked under some low-hanging branches. "This better not mess my dress *or* my hair."

"I loved the twirly thing you did with that stick." Paley dodged a branch and caught up to Van. "Didn't look like rhythmic gymnastics to me."

"Twirling is used for combat too."

Paley's round eyes turned toward Van. "I wish they taught regular kids that stuff."

Paley changed her eye color as often as the wind changed directions. Right now, even in the moonlight, her contact lenses glowed an unnatural bright green. Her gel fingernails gleamed, painted to match. Both courtesy of her job at the Naked Ape.

"I'll teach you." Van's Casadei boots had a low heel. Still, her feet were killing her. "I haven't broken in these boots yet. I don't think they were made for walking."

"I don't think *you* were made for walking," Paley teased.

Van remained silent, lost in her own thoughts.

Paley persisted. "Can you believe—"

"Is Pernilla right?" Van asked, interrupting. "No one gives me credit because they think the Elders fix my grades and rig the games? Which means I…" Van could barely bring herself to say it. "… never earned my placements." This news would devastate both her step-mother and her father. Unless they already knew her high placements were a scam.

Paley scrunched her face. "You can't listen to Pernilla. Winning the games went to her head. She's gone crazy with power."

"I have no desire for power."

Paley shrugged. "It's easy to say you don't want something when you have it."

The path in the woods ended, and they turned onto the well-lit, paved Honeybell Road.

Van snorted. "If I had any power, I'd keep you here. You still plan on leaving the island when we graduate?"

"Yep." Paley skipped, emphasizing her joy. "I can't wait to leave this rock."

It was two years away, but Van already felt an uncomfortable tug in her chest. "Stop talking like that. You're the one who's crazy. If you leave, the Elders won't ever let you return."

"I don't want to come back." Paley's light steps stopped. "Out there, I can discover what happened to my parents, where they came from, where *I* came from." She glanced over her shoulder at Van. "You can't possibly understand."

"You're right." Van faced Paley. "I love my little island. I'm so… *connected* to it. The sugar maples, the salty sea air, the ocean lapping against the shore…"

Paley glanced left and right and whispered, "The Native Islanders worshipped your mother. They would have considered Aelia tribal *royalty* if the Elders used those kinds of titles." Her normal volume returned. "It makes sense for you to feel that way. You're a legacy."

And a burden. Van always knew she was different, but now Pernilla had exposed her as remedial, and Van realized she must be a constant humiliation to her family.

She hadn't even come into the world right. If Van hadn't been born, her real mother would be alive, and her father wouldn't have been forced to give up field duty to raise her. At least Aelia wasn't alive to see her daughter become a colossal failure. Van wrapped her arms around herself as if bracing against a chill.

Paley didn't know how lucky she was not to be bogged down by family tradition. She had the freedom to do whatever she felt like doing. She could act as smart or as dumb as she wanted, as ladylike or as unrefined, as good or as bad. Nobody had any expectations of her.

"How long are you going to be mad at Ken?" Paley asked.

"Well, he is my *permanent placement*." Van forced a chuckle. She and Paley had a running joke about Van being Ken's wife as a career track.

Van and Ken had dated since the sixth grade. Van wouldn't throw away their history together over his brief lapse in judgment with Pernilla. Besides, her step-mother would be furious if she and Ken broke up. It would reflect poorly on the family. But Van would make him pay by not speaking to him for a week.

"Right." Paley grinned. "Your dream of marrying Ken and having eight sniveling little brats running up and down the waterfront."

"And shopping all day, and beach hopping, and going to the salon…"

Paley groaned and rolled her eyes. "Ugh. You'll be as useless as Genie."

"Oh, real nice." Van giggled, genuinely this time. Paley always improved her mood.

They arrived at the intersection where the island's six main roads met, unofficially called the crossroads. This undeveloped, treed-in area stood dead center in the narrowest part of the hour-glass-shaped island.

"See ya later." Paley turned south onto Reservation Road, heading in the direction of the Gables Orphanage.

"Yup, bye," Van said. She veered north onto Sandy Cove Lane toward Mt. Hope Manor, a house she hadn't earned and therefore didn't deserve.

Chapter 3

Day 1: 1:32 a.m., Earth World

For such a promising start, Van's night had gone downhill fast. She welcomed the solitude of the walk home, despite the painful blisters swelling on her heels.

Things aren't handed to me. I earned my grades and my trophy.

Visions of Pernilla's snarling face haunted her thoughts.

Pernilla! Of all the nerve. Seducing Ken. Saying the Elders force people to be friends with me. She's such a—

Van halted. She saw something scurrying up the road toward her.

"What the—?"

A small furry animal stopped under the glow of a nearby street-light and sat upright on its hind legs. Its round eyes locked onto Van's. It had the face of a kitten, but with ears too long, like a rabbit's, and white fur, though much whiter than any animal should be. It almost glowed.

"Whatever."

It wasn't the first time Van had seen a strange animal running loose on the island. Besides being a protected tribal reservation, it was also a national wildlife preserve. Rumors abounded of a scientific research facility on the reservation. The critter had probably escaped from that facility or from the preserve. Either way, island security would take care of it.

She swept her hand. "Shoo!"

As it scampered into the woods, Van glimpsed a coiled tail. She rubbed her eyes. "I'm going to need a pair of Paley's contacts soon."

A soft rumble of vehicles in the distance grew louder and louder.

Not security again. She'd had enough of people messing with her tonight.

She ducked behind the nearest tree as three Grigori military buggies careened past her. Van hoped they'd continue on to Sweet Bay Drive, which led to the back of the reservation. Her stomach sank as the buggies instead bore down on Manor Road, which led to one place. Mt. Hope Manor.

It's not about me. I'm going straight home, just as I told Chief Mumford.

It wasn't unusual for Grigori to congregate at the manor at all hours of the night. While growing up, Van felt as if her father was more dedicated to his job than to his family.

Moments later, Van reached her yard and strode past the creepy stone jaguar gargoyles guarding the entrance. She saw the black military buggies in the U-shaped driveway, their shadowy outlines emphasized by lights shining from every window on all four floors of the sprawling colonial manor house. Van glimpsed movement through the cathedral window of the first-floor sitting room.

She had no desire to run into anyone, so she walked around to the back, slipped through the servant's door, and entered the kitchen. Even here, every light had been turned on, making Van wish she had a pair of sunglasses. Once her eyes adjusted, she noticed items askew and out of place in Genie's obsessively neat and orderly kitchen, as if it had been searched.

Heated voices from the sitting room echoed down the hallway.

Van's stomach knotted. She figured Genie was ripping into her father for missing the Placement Ceremony today, and in front of other Grigori too. Van cringed. She didn't want to be the cause of her father's trouble.

Hoping to slink upstairs to her bedroom, she opened the door to the servant's staircase off the kitchen and paused. Muffled voices, the sounds of moving furniture scraping the floor, and drawers opening and closing reverberated down from the second story.

Van panicked. She whipped around, ran back through the kitchen, and out the servant's door, then skidded to a stop on the dew-covered lawn.

Wait a minute. Why is the manor being searched? They'd better not be rifling through my bedroom. Maybe I can find out what's going on. Besides, this is an island. Where can I run to?

She crept along the outer perimeter of the house until she reached the side yard, then crouched under an open window of the sitting room.

"—few nights ago when his partner was killed in the field under his supervision, which is suspicious enough on its own," a gruff male voice said. "Now, tonight, Grigori Cross has gone missing on the same night the Balish crown prince was assassinated. Coincidence? We don't think so."

"Grigori Fynn, easy," warned a familiar-sounding female voice. "The problem is, with Michael—Grigori Cross—unaccounted for, the Balish will use this as evidence the Lodians' Grigori are responsible for the death of Prince Devon. You may feel safe hidden here on Providence Island, but the tension between our two tribes in the Living World is already strained. This situation will make it worse. *Much* worse."

Van could place this voice now. It was Uxa Huxatec—an Elder and her father's boss.

"You two were close enough to be on a first-name basis. Why don't you know where he is?" The voice that answered Van would've recognized anywhere. She'd heard it constantly nagging her for the last fifteen years. It was her step-mother, Genie. "Last I knew, he missed the ceremony yesterday because he got called into work by *you*."

Uxa sighed. "He is my first assistant, Iphigenia. Nothing more."

My father is missing? This was news to Van. *Who are the Balish? The Lodians? Where is the Living World?* She figured they were using code words and became more interested. Gathering her courage, she peeked in the window.

Uxa stood in the center of the sitting room, dressed in the customary attire of the reservation Elders: a tunic-styled, sky-blue uniform with silver edgings and exaggerated shoulders, with a matching cape. Van had met Uxa a handful of times and had always felt intimidated by the imposing black woman who wore her dark blond hair scraped back into a long, straight braid.

Uxa's sharp blue eyes focused on Genie, who sat on the Edwardian-style sofa with her arms crossed and a pout on her full pink lips.

"Grigori Cross has a pattern of blatantly disregarding the rules," accused Fynn, a young man with curly blond hair and a nose that looked like it had been broken at least once. "Like transporting to the Living World without authorization. While there, he travels outside the boundary of Salus Valde. Which, might I remind you, is an *illegal* act. And we believe he's done it again tonight. His mysterious absence has put us in a precarious position with the Lodian Consilium—the oversight committee for the Grigori."

"Stop talking to me like I'm an idiot." Genie leaped from the sofa. "You're insinuating Michael snuck out of Lodian territory to go plot with someone in the Balish royal family who wants the throne? The *Balish?* Really? The tribe that wants to snuff the Lodians out of existence? I can't believe you're questioning my husband's integrity again. Didn't we go through this fifteen years ago?"

"Cross weaseled out of a conviction back then, but not now." Fynn narrowed his eyes. "He's a disgrace to the Lodian people. A traitor!"

Genie shrieked.

"Grigori Fynn!" Uxa scolded the young officer. "Watch your words."

"How dare you! You stand in *my* house, saying *my* husband's a traitor!" Genie's voice rose, spurred by fury. "Fynn—you call yourself a Grigori? You're nothing but a lost little boy. Uxa's lapdog. I won't take this disrespect from any of you. Get out! *Ohhh!*" Genie swept her arms into the air and fell back onto the sofa in a dramatic semi-faint.

Uxa slid onto the sofa and took Genie's hand in hers. "It is just —we are expecting trouble with the Balish royal family," Uxa said in a placating tone. "They have called for a formal meeting later today."

"Devon's twin sister, Princess Solana, is now the heir," Fynn said, careful to use a neutral tone. "She's only twenty-two and ambitious. She'll be looking to prove her worth. It means we can expect trouble."

Van started and half-ducked as a brutish man stormed into the formal room and addressed Uxa by her official title, HG, or Head of the Grigori.

"The yard is clear, and we've finished searching the manor's upper floors," he said.

Van sighed in relief at her lucky timing, arriving in the yard after they had swept it.

Three other men and four women followed the loutish man into the room.

Van recognized their midnight-blue military uniforms—the same uniform her father wore to work, now that he was back in the field. The same uniform Van had said made him look like a member of a SWAT team. Now that she knew about her father's trouble at work, the memory tugged at her heart.

"And?" Uxa asked.

"We found nothing."

"Happy now?" Genie crossed her arms.

Van wondered whether Genie had caused this mess by misplacing something. Van had become skilled at finding things for a reason; she had to, with Genie being such a ditz.

Yet Van couldn't help but gaze at her step-mother in awe. The yellow-and-white-lace trim of Genie's silk nightgown peeked out from under a white cotton bathrobe. The robe clung to her body, complimenting her toned figure, curvy in all the places men seemed to care about. Her natural silky white-blond hair, a trait valued by their community, appeared uncharacteristically disheveled, but added to her allure. Van figured her step-mother's breathtaking beauty was the reason women on the island disliked Genie and the reason her father created a scandal by marrying Genie so soon after Van's mother had died.

A rustling noise next to Van startled her, and she hurled herself to the ground.

She half-expected a head to pop out of the window and accuse her of spying. Instead, she heard a soft chirrup. She glanced over to see the small white animal she had encountered earlier. It sat on its hind legs, staring at her with large, soulful eyes.

Van calmed her heart rate while still on all fours by breathing deeply.

"Mrrwp?" asked the little thing.

She raised an index finger to her lips, hoping the little animal would get the hint and be quiet. Van could've sworn she overheard Uxa say they planned to search Michael's private rooms in the basement but couldn't be sure, so she turned her attention back to the window.

"Mweep rwp!" the animal chattered even louder.

Van glowered at the little thing. "*Shush.*" Yet it had her attention and began turning in half-circles, glancing from Van to the far end of the house. She ignored it and looked back at the window.

This increased the creature's agitation. It twittered louder and bounced back and forth, swiveling to face Van, and then the far end of the house.

Terrified its noises would draw attention to the window, Van crept close to the little animal to shoo it away. But when Van moved nearer, it stopped making noises and scurried forward. When Van stopped, so did the animal, and then it incessantly chirruped again.

Intrigued, Van trailed the eager little critter around to the back of the house. It scampered past the servant's entrance and stopped just before the far corner, where it sat on its haunches and pointed its whiskery nose to a spot on the exterior of the house.

"Sorry, little guy," Van said. "There's nothing here." To prove her point, she reached out and rested her palm on the white wooden shingles.

Under her touch, an outline of a door appeared. Van, who had passed by this part of the house a million times, had never noticed the camouflaged door on the house's exterior. "It must lead to my father's private rooms in the basement," she murmured. "I bet it's locked."

She ran her hands over the spot where the doorknob should be and felt a rough edge. Then her eyes adjusted, and she saw a small, concealed disc with a horizontal bar. Using the tips of her fingers, she grasped the bar, turned the door handle, and pushed. To her surprise, it opened.

Van hesitated, not sure she should go in. Her father prohibited anyone from entering his private rooms. She didn't want to upset him.

A streak of white fluff zipped inside.

"Oh, great." Now Van had to go inside to get this thing out of the house.

She stepped through the doorway, used her hand to feel along the wall for the switch, and flicked on the lights.

The door snapped shut behind her.

Van gaped at the intricate stone carving covering the far wall. Embellished with ivy, bursting stars, and varying cycles of the moon. It depicted two men and two women in togas enjoying a celebration. Unfamiliar writing lined the carving's edge.

She scanned the windowless room. A mess of loose papers, maps, pens, odd paperweights, quills, and scrolls were scattered everywhere. A piece of scrap paper stuck out from the middle pile on the coffee table, bearing the same writing as the wall carving.

Van tugged at the scrap. Something slipped out of the pile, pinging noisily as it bounced off the aged mosaic tile floor. She bent down and snatched it up. It was a gold coin imprinted with a fancy crest and the words *Royal Balish Mint.*

Balish again! She tucked the coin into her mini dress's pocket, along with the scrap of paper. Her father would never notice their absence, not with all this junk strewn everywhere. She glanced around the rest of the study.

A worn, oversized, leather-bound book lay open on his no-nonsense solid oak desk. Van perused the yellowed parchment pages. It was a Native Island Legends storybook, opened to a page about a tribal warrior named the Anchoress.

Van knew this silly story from childhood. The Creator of All Things had brought the warrior into being. The Anchoress passed down her magical powers to the first female in each generation. The heir remained dormant until called upon to help fight during Dishora, a time when evil would rise to destroy all light.

This book contained realistic illustrations of horrible mud crea-tures rising from the earth Van had never seen before. One picture showed a slimy, fanged mud-demon clutching a female warrior with its claws while it breathed fire, burning its victim to death.

Van slammed the book shut, sure it would give her nightmares.

Turning, she noticed the wallpaper adorning three walls of the study. Its repetitive yellow coin pattern stood out against a sepia-toned background. The design reminded Van of her birth mother. Van knew little about Aelia, except she had collected coins.

The wallpaper, along with the Balish coin, gave Van an over-whelming sense of guilt. She was trespassing and being in the study gave her the jitters. The faint scent of bleach made the room even creepier. She glanced around at the clutter.

Whoever cleaned the room didn't do a very good job. Or has it been searched?

Uxa said they hadn't searched the lower level of the manor yet. Maybe whoever had turned her father's study upside-down had also accidentally left the outer door unlocked.

Van moved toward the door and paused. *The little animal.* Her eyes darted around the study.

She saw it rummaging in the fireplace, sending dust and ashes spiraling into the air.

Van sneezed. "Stop it, you're making a mess."

She bent to scoop up the ash-coated animal and noticed an object lying among the charred logs. She squinted.

It was a diary-size, partly burned book.

Chapter 4

Day 1: 2:15 a.m., Earth World

VAN PLACED the little animal to the side of the fireplace and plucked the charred book from the still-warm ashes. She flipped the ancient hand-bound text from front to back.

Footsteps pounded in the hallway startling Van, making her almost drop the book.

Uxa and her Grigori were coming to search the basement. They probably had gotten the key to her father's study from Genie.

Van clutched the book and rushed toward the door she had used to enter the room. She yanked it open, then hesitated.

Where's that little animal? It was nowhere in sight. She opened her mouth to call for it but didn't know its name. Cat? Bunny?

The knob rattled on the study's inner door.

Van was out of time.

She dashed outside. The door snapped closed behind her. Afraid to be seen passing the windows of the other basement rooms, she wedged herself into the immaculate shrubbery lining the perimeter of the manor. She sat on the cold ground, no longer worried about dirtying her dress, and securely settled in to outwait Uxa and her Grigori, knowing they had already searched the yard.

The window above cast enough light for her to see, and she examined the charred book. *Hm.* Van held it between her palms and closed her eyes.

Sometimes, when Van touched emotionally charged objects, she could pick up thoughts of the owner or get impressions of events that had happened around the object.

Van opened her eyes and huffed. She got nothing from the book. Frustrated by her lack of control over this ability she'd had since childhood, she used her wrist to brush ash off the singed cover. It revealed part of the book's title: ****ridicus Lib***lus.**

"Never heard of it," Van muttered to herself, but she wasn't alone.

"Mip?" The little animal had returned, white and fluffy as ever.

So relieved the cute little puff had made it out of the study, Van felt tempted to scoop it up and give it a big hug. She didn't, though, because dangling out of its tiny mouth hung a ragged piece of material.

The animal flicked its head, waving the piece of cloth at Van.

She used the edge of her dress to protect her fingers and took the dirty fabric from the little thing's mouth. She held it up to a beam of light. Jagged pieces of black material—most likely, a cotton-poly blend—surrounded a triangular black patch with a red-and-gold insignia. Above the patch, in red block letters, was the name "Rogziel." It looked like it had been torn from a military uniform. Something dark and crusty rubbed off the patch onto her dress.

"Ugh!" *Dried blood!* She tossed the repulsive patch aside and warily eyed the innocent-looking animal.

"Brwwp meep eerp," it replied.

Is it… scolding me?

The creature scurried from the hedge.

Van didn't care. It had been a long day, and her feet throbbed from walking in her new boots. She laid the book on the ground next to her, then rubbed her arms, warding off the night's creeping chill. She sank down into a comfortable position and closed her eyes.

Her father stood alone in his study, holding the ancient diary. Blood-soaked, he wore an unfamiliar black military uniform.

He stumbled to the fireplace and mumbled, "Let us hope… no Lodian… ever lays a hand on this."

He tossed the book into the fire.

Van woke with a start. One of her hands lay face-up on the charred text. The patch peeked out of the binding.

"What the—?" She wiped drool off her mouth with the back of her hand. Protecting her fingers with her dress, she pulled the patch out of the binding and dropped it to the ground, grabbed the book, and slipped out of the hedges.

Someone had turned off the light from the window above, making the shrubbery dark. All was quiet. Uxa and crew had long gone.

Van entered the manor properly, through the front door, thinking she wouldn't run into anyone. She glanced into the sitting room, startled to see Genie there.

"H-Hi." Van reflexively hid the text behind her back.

Her step-mother sat on the sofa, motionless as a statue. "Go to your rooms," Genie said, without looking at Van.

"What about—"

Genie turned her incredible blue eyes toward Van. "Vanessa," she said as if issuing a threat. "It is *unladylike* to ask questions. And look at you. You're covered in filth, and that horrid hair. You're a ghastly mess, not fit to be seen. Now, *go to your rooms!*"

Van stomped up the main stairway, nostrils flaring. She stormed down the third-floor hallway and into her bedroom. Her stuffed animals, pillows, and books lay askew, but the Grigori did a good job of hiding they had searched her rooms. Still, the idea of strangers rummaging through her personal belongings didn't sit well with Van.

She slammed her bedroom door, not because anyone would hear it, but because it made her feel better. She chucked the text onto her white, hand-carved desk and headed toward the master bathroom.

Van noticed a dark spot on an oversized pillow on her queen-size bed. She looked at it closely and gasped.

The blood-stained patch! Again.

The window next to her bed was ajar. It had to be that little animal. She scanned her bedroom and tensed at seeing a ball of white fluff atop her *Beowulf* textbook. For a second, she thought it was the critter, but it was only Twinkle Toes, the stuffed bunny her father had given her for her fifth birthday, the last birthday he had ever spent with her. The living ball of fluff was nowhere in sight.

Apparently, the little animal wanted Van to keep the patch. She grabbed a tissue from her vanity and tucked the patch back into the binder lining of the text, along with the coin and the piece of scrap paper from her pocket. On the way to the bathroom, she tossed the "contaminated" pillow onto the floor. Luma, the greatest house-keeper in the world, would take care of it. Van could always count on her to stack the linen closet with fresh lavender-scented towels and to keep Van's pink-and-white bathroom glistening-clean.

Van turned on the shower, peeled off her boots, and shimmied out of her filthy mini dress. As hot water steamed the bathroom, she twisted her backside toward the mirror and grimaced at the fat, worm-like scar running down the lower right side of her back.

Ken would never be attracted to her if he saw that ghastly thing. To make matters worse, whenever Van asked her father how she had gotten the scar, he would say, "It's a birthmark." Van knew this wasn't the truth, but when she persisted, he got angry. As she got older, she stopped asking.

After showering, Van blow-dried her hair and changed into a matching cotton tank-and-shorts pajama outfit. Outside, the sky remained black.

Van grabbed Twinkle Toes and lay on her bed, hoping to fall asleep. Yet too much of what had happened during the night kept spinning in her head. She slid out of bed, sat down at her vanity, and picked up her enamel, boar-bristle hairbrush. She started brushing her hair ninety-nine times, as Genie had taught her.

Humph. Genie. Why won't my step-mother tell me anything? Where's my father? Is he a traitor?

What did all those code words mean—Living World, Lodians, Balish? Maybe the *Balish*, the word imprinted on the coin from her father's study, were real people. Too bad the Elders restricted internet use, though she doubted code words used by the Grigori would pop up on any Google search.

But, the answers might be in that charred text.

Van put down her hairbrush at stroke eighty-eight and picked up the book. She plopped back onto her bed and flipped through the pages, some singed, others outright burned. She skimmed over the crudely drawn pictures and strange writing that, at first, seemed to be Latin. This would've been great because she could read Latin. Instead, the writing appeared to be some kind of Latin-based language, one Van had come across twice. Tonight, on the stone carving and on the scrap paper she had found in her father's study.

Her mother popped into her mind. Everything Van's family possessed—the manor, money, status—came from her mother's side. All of it belonged to Aelia. Not to Genie, not to her father, and not to Van. But because of Van, Aelia wasn't alive to enjoy any of it. Sometimes, Van wished she had never been born. She suspected her father felt the same way. He rarely paid attention to her and had spoken to Van about her mother only once, at age eleven, on the day he had taken her quahogging.

Her father had rented a rowboat and paddled them to the nearest sandbar off Buzzard's Bay, then dropped anchor. The sky looked bright and cheery, the water calm and inviting. Van breathed in deeply. From that day on, she would never forget how the salty scent of the blue-green ocean filled her with peace and contentment.

"It's low tide," her father said.

Van didn't understand what that meant, but smiled anyway, thrilled to be spending time alone with him.

Her father hopped out of the rowboat into the shallow water, and Van did the same. She thought it odd to see her father in swim trunks and not in his work uniform. But signs of his job remained on his body: the distinct markings of the Grigori—black tribal tattoos on the nape of his neck, bands around both upper arms— and long, thin scars along his jaw, neck, and chest.

He handed her a tool that looked like a spade, except with three claw-like prongs. He showed her how to use it to scoop up sand, sift it in the water, and then check whether it contained a clam with a hard shell, called a quahog. They used a rusted metal ring to measure its size. If the quahog was too small, a "baby," it fell through the ring, and they tossed it back. If the quahog didn't go through the ring, into the bucket it went, to be eaten later.

Sometimes they found a scallop. Large enough scallops went into the bucket. One time, Van's father pulled up a spider crab, sending Van screaming back into the rowboat, nearly capsizing it.

Deep creases had formed around the corners of her father's eyes, so dark blue, Van could've sworn they were brown. He "saved" her from the scary creature by flinging it far away into the water.

It was the only time she had ever seen her father smile.

With morning fading into noon, they'd climbed back into the rowboat to head home, but her father didn't start rowing. Instead, he stared at Van with a strange expression on his face.

When Van caught his eye, he said, "You look just like her."

She knew who he meant.

"I see her every time I look at your face… your eyes. You have the same eyes," her father said in a shaky voice.

Until that time, Van had no idea she looked like her mother. She held still, afraid if she breathed, her father would clam up tighter than the quahogs in their pail.

His cropped, rich brown hair glimmered in the waning after-noon sun as he looked past Van. "She loved this island. Your mother did. Never wanted to leave."

Van's mother had felt the same deep connection to the island she did. Even this tiny scrap of information helped close the huge desperate gap inside her, one that could only be filled by learning more about Aelia.

Her father focused on some distant point on the horizon. His eyes glistened. "I loved her very much. Remember that… remember that."

Van almost cried for him. She wanted badly to apologize for killing his beloved wife, her mother. Even before this day on the water, Van had never questioned her father's love for her mother. Not even after she was old enough to understand the rumors about him being a womanizer and how people wondered whether his relationship with Genie had started before his wife's death.

As far as Van was concerned, her father had been a widower with a newborn baby to raise. He needed help and thought it best for his child to be raised with a mother figure in her life. Enter Genie.

"I wish I had something of your mother's to give you. There's… nothing left."

Van wanted to ask if this was because Genie felt jealous of anything that had to with Aelia but chickened out.

Her father hesitated, as if wanting to say more, then reached out and grasped the oars.

Hoping to keep him talking, Van worked up the courage to ask him about his scars. "Do they hurt?"

He paused and again stared off into the distance. "Well, princess," he sighed, "even old wounds still hurt sometimes."

"H-How did you get them?" Van desperately wanted to hug him, to take away his pain. But she didn't dare touch him.

"They're the result of going someplace I wasn't supposed to go," he said briskly, then continued rowing.

In hindsight, Van knew he hadn't given an actual answer, only a veiled warning for her not to wander into dangerous, off-limits places.

Bang! Bang! Bang!

Van shot upright, torn from her memories.

Paley rapped at her window, perched on the bough of the giant oak.

Van slipped the text under the covers as Paley crawled in and dumped her worn backpack on the floor. Paley slept over whenever she wanted to escape the confines of the orphanage, which was often.

She made herself at home, unselfconsciously changing into her bedtime T-shirt and shorts. "My bunkmates were making too much noise, still excited over Jaychund. I had to sneak out again, just to get some sleep." She stared at Van. "Something wrong?"

"No." Van felt too confused about everything she'd learned over the last hour and wasn't ready to share it yet. She shrugged. "I found out my father is in some kind of trouble at work."

Paley unrolled the sleeping bag Van kept in her bedroom. "Pfft. He's always in trouble. People love to hate on him."

"For sure." Van wanted to continue reading the book and hoped Paley wouldn't feel like staying up and talking.

"You get any flak about your brawl with Pernilla?" Paley asked as she fluffed the contaminated pillow Van had thrown on the floor.

"Nope. But there's always tomorrow."

Paley rolled her eyes in solidarity.

"I wouldn't use that pillow," Van said. "It was on the floor."

"It's fine." Paley yawned. "Night."

"Night."

Within moments, Paley had fallen asleep.

Van went back to skimming the text. She flipped through the pages, trying to make out any of the words. Finally, she gave up.

Yawning, she leaned over to shut off her nightstand light, saw the time on her clock, and gasped. She had spent an hour mesmerized by a text she couldn't read. Van flicked off the light, snuggled under her sheets, and squeezed Twinkle Toes to her chest...

She drifted into dreams filled with toga-wearing people she felt she should know, who spoke a language she didn't understand.

Chapter 5

Day 1: 6:37 a.m., Earth World

VAN JERKED awake as Genie's muffled, angry voice drifted in from the hallway, followed by indistinct voices responding to her stepmother's drama. Van tensed. No one else occupied the third floor, which meant they were headed for her bedroom.

Paley popped up from a sound sleep and gaped at Van with eyes full of terror. For all her casual flouting of the rules, Paley knew if a Grigori discovered her away from the orphanage without permission, she might lose her hard-won employment at the Naked Ape. Genie and Van's father were okay with Paley sleeping at the manor, as long as no one complained. After being caught at the bonfire last night, Van and Paley didn't want to push their luck.

Blankets and pillows flew.

Van leaped out of bed to help hide Paley, who sprang up, grabbed her backpack, and scrambled for cover in Van's oversized closet.

Van tossed the sleeping bag in behind Paley and had settled back into bed when she noticed the burned book on her nightstand. She grabbed the text, dashed across the room, and tucked it into the neat pile of clean clothes Luma had left on her bureau.

She dove back into bed and tried her hardest to look nonchalant as the door to her room burst open.

"Oh, good. You're awake." Genie marched into Van's room.

Her step-mother had changed into a sharply pressed knee-high dress, styled her hair in a chignon, and expertly applied her natural-looking makeup. She looked like her usual self again.

"Put on your bathrobe. There are some Grigori here to talk to you. I directed them to your sitting room."

Genie sounded irritated, so Van obeyed. She slid out of bed, grabbed her pink-and-white bathrobe from a hook on her bathroom door, and followed her step-mother into the adjacent room.

"Sorry to barge in like this, Vanessa," Uxa said.

"They're not sorry." Genie's high cheekbones flushed pink.

"Would you prefer to talk downstairs?" Uxa asked Van.

Van's L-shaped walk-through bedroom closet extended into the sitting room. Paley could hear their conversation through the slats in the closet door. Van shook her head. She wanted Paley to listen to what Uxa had to say, so she wouldn't have to repeat the conversation later.

Fynn shifted his weight from foot to foot. His eyes darted around the room. When he caught Van staring at him, he turned away as if trying to hide the fact he was searching for something.

Van got the shivers. She had an inkling he and Uxa suspected Van had found her father's text after the Grigori had swept the manor last night. She rested easy, knowing she'd securely tucked the book inside a pile of clothes in her bedroom.

Van sat on the edge of a red velvet chaise lounge. "What do you want?" Her words had come out more harshly than she'd intended, but they sounded better than, "Get the hell out of my rooms."

"Vanessa, do you remember me?" Uxa asked. "I work with your father."

"HG Huxatec, my father's boss." Van pulled her bathrobe

tighter. "I've seen you when I'm on the reservation. You stop in our classes sometimes to talk to the teachers."

Uxa seemed pleased. "No need for formalities. You can call me Uxa. This is Tussel Fynn, an associate of mine from the reservation—"

"They came to take you away!" Genie shrieked.

Van's stomach lurched. "W-Why? Did I do something wrong?"

Uxa was an enforcer of rules. A strict woman, obviously here to deliver news of Van's punishment for last night's fight.

"No, no, not at all." Uxa held her unwavering gaze on Van. "You may have heard the rumors. We are forming a team of children to work on a project this summer."

Van sighed in relief, then got angry.

You barged into my bedroom at 7 a.m. to tell me this? Why?

She suppressed her harsh words and kept her cool. She knew acting out would affect her placement and reflect poorly on her family.

"Yeah. I've heard about that." Van couldn't hide the disappointment in her tone. She knew where this conversation was going. Instead of enjoying the beach, she envisioned her summer filing papers in some boring satellite office on the mainland of Massachusetts.

"*Special* children," Fynn said. "For a *special* project."

His attempt at a smile made Van suspicious, rather than reassured.

"An internship, if you will. It's a great honor," he continued. "You're the only one chosen from the island."

"Vanessa's not *special*." Genie harrumphed. "She's slow. That's why she's in remedial classes. She's not summer project material."

Van flushed and looked down, twiddling with the robe's cotton sash. Genie had known all along Van hadn't earned her placements, the Elders had fixed them in her favor.

"Your placement tests showed you have certain abilities," Uxa said. "Abilities no one else has."

"You got the results mixed up." After what Pernilla, and now Genie, had said, Van wasn't sure she had any abilities at all.

"No, no. There is no mistake." Uxa waved her hand dismissively. "We need *you,* and we need for you leave right away. You will spend the summer away from home."

Van's anxiety flared. "I don't want to leave the island." *Or my clothes or my bedroom or Paley or even Ken.*

"She's not going anywhere!" Genie stomped her exquisite foot on the floor.

For once, Van appreciated her step-mother's interference.

"It is a short while," Uxa said. "Only thirty days."

"Twenty-nine, not counting today," Fynn cut in.

"She doesn't want to go! She'll be useless," Genie screeched. "She could never survive away from her hairdresser for that long."

It astounded Van how much noise could come out of someone so petite.

"This is not optional," Fynn said to Genie. "The results of Van's placement tests assigned her to this, er… *project.* She's required to abide by the island's rules."

As abrasive as he was, Fynn was right. Van had no desire to be permanently banished to the mainland. She sighed. "Only twenty-nine days?"

Uxa nodded.

"No," Genie said. "Not unless you tell me *exactly* what she'll be doing over there. My husband is missing, maybe even *dead.* Now you want to take my daughter? Isn't anything enough for you people?"

Van welcomed Genie's concern, but became disturbed by her step-mother's mention of her father possibly being dead.

"Over where?" Van asked. "The mainland?"

"I'm sorry, Iphigenia," Uxa said to Genie. "All I can tell you is Vanessa will be working with the Grigori. The rest of her mission is classified."

Van's back stiffened. "Mission?"

Genie persisted. "Does this have something to do with Michael's disappearance?"

Strained silence followed.

"Can you at least give me *any* news about my husband?"

Uxa threw Fynn a look.

"Come with me," he said to Genie. "I'll give you the most up-to-date information we have." He clasped Genie by the elbow and led her from the sitting room.

For the first time in Van's life, she hated to see Genie go. Left alone with Uxa, she realized what she would miss by being placed on the project. The beach, the boardwalk, the parties. Her eyes welled up, thinking of the unfairness of it all.

Van swallowed hard, then asked, "Does this have something to do with my father?" Her voice came out squeaky from the tightness in her chest. "Why did you call it a mission?"

"I will give you all the details once you arrive at the reservation. For now, you must pack."

Van used the back of her hand to wipe her eyes before they spilled over and embarrassed her. "Can Paley come with me?"

"Sorry, no. She did not place for it."

"Is Pernilla going?" Van asked, practically spitting her nemesis's name.

"It does not matter that Pernilla placed number one overall in the games." Uxa shifted, as if trying to get comfortable. "This is a special situation. We did not assign her to this project."

Van let out a sigh of relief. The project would be easier to tolerate without Pernilla there.

"Vanessa… did you see your father last night?"

Van remained outwardly calm as her internal alarm blared. She shook her head no.

"Did you find… did he… leave you anything yesterday?"

The charred text. Uxa was asking about the book. Again, Van shook her head. "Nuh-uh."

Technically, Van *didn't* see her father last night, and he didn't give her anything. She'd *found* a text in his fireplace, a book he'd apparently tried to destroy. Genie once told Van white lies were okay if it meant protecting the family, and Van started to think her father might need protecting.

Uxa gave a curt nod. "Get packed and be ready by six o'clock tonight. Fynn will pick you up here and bring you to the reservation. I have a meeting to attend, along with many things to do before briefing your team tonight, so I must be going."

Uxa walked across the room. She grasped the doorknob, then paused and glanced back toward Van with a solemn expression. "The wheel of fate has turned upon you, Vanessa. You have been called forth to do a great deed. You are standing on the threshold of a legacy."

Van gulped as Uxa left, closing the door behind her.

Chapter 6

Day 1: 7:43 a.m., Earth World

THE SECOND THE sitting room door closed, Paley burst from the closet. "You got chosen! How cool is that?"

Van cringed at Paley's loud voice. "*Shh!* Someone could be lurking."

"Doubt it," Paley said. "I would love to see the reservation and go on an off island adventure. I wish they picked me too. Thanks for trying."

"You lucked out." Van led Paley back into her bedroom. "I'm not looking forward to being support staff for the Grigori. Shuffling papers around instead of going to the beach." Van took off her bathrobe and re-hung it on the bathroom door. "From going to my classes on the reservation, I can tell you, there's nothing to see there."

"But you get to find out what the Grigori actually *do*. Uxa called it a *mission*. That's *exciting*."

"Not exciting. I have nothing to wear." Van fanned her fingers and frowned. "Is the Naked Ape open today? I need to get my hair and nails done before I leave."

"You'll be on a team." Paley gave her a huge smile. "There'll be boys from off island."

"Mainlander boys? Ick." Van shuddered elaborately. "Our guys are just fine."

The ringing of the Inter-Island Connect landline intruded on their conversation.

Van tore out of the bedroom, practically decking Paley on the way. She ran to the wall phone in the hallway. "It's probably Ken calling to apologize," she said in a rush. "Not that I care." She picked up the receiver.

It was Miss Nutting.

"I heard about your placement on the summer project," she said. "I called to say goodbye and offer you a complimentary blowout and polish change." Miss Nutting understood thirty days was too long to be away from the salon.

"Paley's here with me," Van said. "It's okay if we both come, right?"

Miss Nutting hesitated.

"We'll be there in a bit," Van said before Miss Nutting answered, then hung up.

Paley scrunched her face. "What?"

"She sounded… upset." Van shrugged. Miss Nutting's hesitation showed she didn't want Paley tagging along. Definitely out of character for the good-natured hairdresser.

"Oh." Paley let out a breath. "Well, you're there all the time. She'll miss you."

Van rummaged in her closet for a backpack. "She'll miss my money, you mean."

"No. That's not what I mean." Paley gathered her things and shoved them into her worn backpack.

Van tucked a clean pile of clothes into a brand-new pink-and-red backpack. She grabbed her favorite hairbrush, and then Twinkle Toes.

"Why are you bringing that?" Paley asked.

"I can't sleep without Twinkle Toes." Van tried to smush the stuffed animal into her backpack. It wouldn't fit, so she left it on her bed.

"I meant your backpack."

"Depending on how long our appointments take, I might not have time to pack this afternoon." Van pulled off the sales tags. "These are just the essentials. I'll have Luma send the rest of my things."

The girls changed into capri pants, summer tops, hoodies, and flat sandals. Van searched the first floor for Genie but couldn't find her step-mother. Luma had taken off for the long holiday weekend, and Van's father was MIA.

Van grabbed the nearest IIC to call for a taxi.

"Why don't we walk?" Paley asked, full of pep.

"No way." Van's blistered feet still hurt after walking in her boots last night. She dialed Providence Island Taxi.

Ten minutes later, a classic yellow six-seater buggy pulled up.

"Our glorified golf-cart is here," Van said.

She and Paley slid into the back and slammed the door.

"Put it in on my family's account, Urvi," Van said.

The driver grumbled his acknowledgment, stepped on the accelerator, and they zipped away. The buggy bumped and bounced as Urvi took them over a "shortcut" on an unpaved roadway.

"Don't you think it's a little strange you were the only one chosen from the island?" Paley asked. "I know you get picked for everything, but you're only a sophomore. It's weird. Just saying."

"Why are you saying anything at all?" Van snapped. Paley's usually well-hidden envy showed in her comment, implying Van hadn't earned her place on the project. She glanced at Paley, ready to blast her, but saw Paley's defeated face, and Van's resolve crumbled. "I'm sorry. I'm a little stressed. We only have a few hours, so let's make the most of it."

"Maybe Miss Nutting will know how I can sneak off island and meet up with you." Paley's mood shifted to cheery. "I can give you updates on what's going on."

"Okay! Then I won't miss anything." Van gripped the seat to keep from being expelled from the buggy as Urvi careened around a corner.

"Miss Nutting will know a way," Paley said, also holding tight. "Trust me, working in *that* beauty salon, most of her clients are Grigori and Elders. She knows *everything*."

Van kept her grip on the seat and breathed in the fresh, salty air. She gazed out the opened window, admiring the white birches with their curls of peeling bark, the massive trunks on the courtly beech trees, and the shimmering pines. All of which faded into picture-perfect sand dunes dotted with spiky green beach grass as Urvi zoomed down Boardwalk Way. Within minutes, they skidded to a stop outside the door to the Naked Ape.

Miss Nancy Nutting, the proud owner of the jungle-themed salon, wore a fern-print smock, with her curly, butter-yellow hair swept up in a tiger-striped clip. She offered her usual greeting when they walked in, but today her smile seemed forced and her shoulders tense.

Was it because I brought Paley?

Paley plunked her backpack down next to the colored contact lens display and dug into the newly arrived merchandise.

"Tell me everything Uxa told you about this *project*," Miss Nutting said, guiding Van into the shampoo chair. "Spill."

Van and Paley told their story, while Miss Nutting washed Van's hair. Afterward, the hairdresser seemed even more agitated and combed out Van's wet hair with painful jerks, rather than her usual flowing motions.

"Ow! What's going on?" Van asked irritably.

"Is that all Uxa told you?"

This serious side of Miss Nutting disturbed Van. She wished the carefree, graceful hairdresser she knew and loved would return. "Yeah. Why?"

"I've known you both since you were babies." Miss Nutting dashed over to the salon's door. "Paley, you're like a daughter to me, kindred souls, both of us being from the Gables, and since you're here, you can hear this too...and Van left to be raised by that rotten step-mother of yours…there are things you need to know before going over there."

Miss Nutting clicked the lock, flipped the "open" sign to "closed," and turned her back to the door.

Patting down her apron, she faced Van and Paley with an expression so commanding it would've stopped an avalanche. "I need to tell you girls the truth about the island."

Chapter 7

D ay 1: 8:52 a.m., Earth World

AFTER MISS NUTTING suggested they "act natural," she whipped out the Whisperer, a low-noise, cordless hairdryer, along with an enormous round brush, and began styling Van's hair. "Do you know why our Native Island tribe has blue eyes, blond hair, and skin pale as the moon?"

"You mean, versus the Native Americans who're darker skinned, with black hair and brown eyes?" Paley's own hazel eyes were now aqua blue and had a yellow star surrounding each black pupil.

Van grimaced at Paley's newest choice of colored contact lenses and answered, "We learned in school the Native Islanders have an altogether different ancestry. We're the only ones left of our tribe in the entire world. That's why our island is private and basically kept hidden from the mainland."

"And why there are so many rules," Paley added, checking out her newest eye color in the wall mirror.

Miss Nutting continued to blow out Van's hair; their eyes met in the hair-dressing mirror. "Ever wonder why the Elders allowed your step-mother Native Island resident status, despite her not being a Native Islander?"

"Not really," Van answered.

"Why she goes on shopping trips off island at least once every month?"

"Genie is from the mainland, and she likes to buy expensive things so she can look nice." Van shrugged. "The island shops don't have what she wants."

"No." Miss Nutting shook her head. "No." She shut off the hairdryer. "I'm just going to come out with it. Genie is not from the mainland. She's from the other world."

"You mean… like an *alien*?" Paley asked, mouth agape. She dropped into the salon chair next to Van as if her body had gone limp from shock.

Van narrowed her eyes at Miss Nutting. Of course, Genie was a piece of work, but to claim she was from another world? *Come on.*

"She's from a different tribe than your father and you, Van. She's not a Lodian by birth. That's why she's not liked by many here."

Mention of the word *Lodian* made the hair prickle on the back of Van's neck. Both Uxa and Fynn had used that word last night while Van eavesdropped through the window.

"Wait—what?" Van's head spun. She closed her eyes to get a grip.

Miss Nutting sighed. "I thought I'd made myself clear. Van, you and your father—and all the Native Islanders—are from the other world. The Living World. Some live there, some live here in the Earth World, on the island, mostly on the reservation. Your father obviously lives here, but he commutes to the Living World when the need arises. Though, as a Grigori in the field, most of his work is on the mainland."

"Hold up." Van raised her palm as if to stop this flood of information from drowning her. "You're trying to tell me I'm from some other world called the Living World? And so is my father and step-mother?" She felt numb.

"Sure am." Miss Nutting nodded so vigorously, ringlets popped from her hair clip. "And Aelia, your birth mother, she was Lodian too. You're all Lodians, you, your father, all the Native Islanders, including the Elders, and all the Grigori. All from the Living World. The Elders offered Genie asylum, so she's considered a Lodian, which is why she was allowed to marry your father. Genie tells you she's going shopping on the mainland as a cover for when she travels to the Living World, sometimes to visit your father when he's working at Lodestar, which is Grigori headquarters. She's not *always* shopping."

All Van could muster was, "M-My parents didn't go to Canter-bury Bells?" Her world as she knew it was falling apart. She rubbed her throbbing forehead.

"I'm afraid not, hon." Miss Nutting anxiously glanced at the salon's window, then resumed styling Van's hair. "Here on the island, townies live their lives same as any other Massachusetts resi-dent, but they're bound by the rules of the Elders, unaware another world exists, as you and Paley were." Miss Nutting finished Van's hair with Jungle Mist hairspray. "Uxa and the other Elders are bigwigs. High-level politicians. They're part of the Lodian Consil-ium, the ones who make our rules here on the island, which is their Earth World outpost, and in Salus Valde, which is Lodian territory in the Living World."

Van glanced at Paley, sitting in the adjacent hairdressing chair, to see if her friend was buying it.

Paley's slack jaw and lack of movement indicated she was sold.

Miss Nutting pulled over a swivel stool. "The Elders require all the Grigori here to take an oath to keep knowledge about the other world a secret." Miss Nutting glanced at the door, then whispered, "The island holds things that need protecting from both worlds."

"Protect *what?*" Van asked.

Miss Nutting's hands trembled as she removed Van's old nail polish with a cotton wipe. "Well…" she hesitated. "The portal, for one thing."

"Portal? You must be kidding." But after overhearing Fynn, Uxa, and Genie last night, Van knew Miss Nutting wasn't kidding. Her numbness gave way to anger at being lied to her whole life. During Van's childhood, she had overheard adults using strange words but figured they were whispering about boring adult problems. She never gave the "code words" another thought. Until now.

"That's why the reservation is off limits, because of this portal?" Paley asked.

"One of the reasons." Miss Nutting finished rubbing off Van's polish and picked through the nail polish bin. She found Van's specially formulated for her hot-pink-colored nail polish called *Twinkle Toes* and rolled it between her palms. "Grigori are a select group of the Lodians' military who take an oath to protect the portal, terrigens, and Salus Valde from enemies. They vow never to pass the secrets of the portal to anyone other than another sworn Grigori."

"Why once a month?" Van asked. "You mentioned Genie's shopping. What do her trips have to do with this?"

"I don't think Genie is a Grigori," Paley said. "Is she?"

Miss Nutting shook her head; her curls bounced back and forth. "People of the Living World are born with a component in their blood called *ichor*. We call these people *vichors*. If you have no ichor in your blood, you're called a terrigen." Miss Nutting set aside the unopened polish and began shaping Van's nails. "Vichors can't spend more than one moon cycle in the low vibration of the Earth World without getting, well, dopey… *weak*. They have to go back to the Living World to recharge. If they don't, they'll get sick and die."

Paley leaned forward. "Tell me more about these *vichors*."

"All the Native Islanders are vichors, including the Elders and everyone else who lives or works on the reservation side of the island. All of them need to recharge. They travel back and forth constantly. That's why no townies are allowed onto the reservation, to keep the portal a secret. The orphans in the Gables were all born in the Living World—"

"I *knew* it!" Paley leaped out of her chair and bounced up and down like Miss Nutting's curls. "I *knew* I was special. My parents are Lodians! I'm supposed to be in the Living World!"

"Calm down." Van reached out and shoved Paley back toward the chair.

"Do you know who my parents were?" Paley asked.

"Sorry, Paley. I know nothing about your parents. Please, let me finish. All the orphans—"

"Why are you telling us this?" Van asked, putting it all together. "Is it because my project isn't on the mainland? It has something to do with traveling to the Living World?"

Miss Nutting stopped filing and grasped Van's hands with such sincerity, it made Van squirm. "If Uxa told you to pack, then… yes, I'm afraid so, hon."

"Does it have to do with the death of…," Van fumbled for the memory. "Um, some Balish guy named Prince Devon?"

Miss Nutting froze. Her expression looked comical. "H-How do you know about that?"

"Yeah, how?" Paley asked, dumbfounded.

"I overheard Uxa and Fynn talking to Genie last night," Van confessed.

"You know it's not polite to eavesdrop, Van," Miss Nutting scolded. "There are severe consequences for loose talk. All three of them could get into serious trouble if they knew someone had overheard their conversation." She resumed filing Van's nails.

For a moment, Van feared she had gone too far.

Then Miss Nutting opened up. "Death? That's putting it mildly." She gripped Van's hand a bit too tightly. "Prince Devon was attacked outside the Balish Palace in the woods of Tipereth. Burned to death. Nothing left of him but ashes, I heard." She briefly raised her eyes to Van's without stopping her aggressive filing. "It was the work of demons."

Paley gasped as Van frowned.

"Demons? Oh, come on," Van said. *Miss Nutting is apparently taking drama lessons from Genie.*

"What's a demon? They sound dangerous." Paley wiggled close to the edge of the chair as if to hear better.

She seemed more excited than terrified. As if the whole story was make believe, like the Native Island myths told to children.

Miss Nutting finished filing Van's nails and began smoothing on a bottom coat. "The demons are gone from the Living World," she said. "But beware. It's still a dangerous place to be right now."

"Oh! This is *so cool*!" Paley popped out of her chair again.

"Not cool," Miss Nutting said. "Something is happening with the Balish over there. The Moors—the Balish royal family—have supreme power in the Living World, and Lodians are their sworn enemies. I hear the Moors are up in arms over the death of Prince Devon. They're sure his death was an assassination by a Lodian. I think they're planning an invasion of Salus Valde."

"What if I turn down the placement?" The pit in the bottom of Van's stomach told her this was all too much.

Miss Nutting's curls jiggled again as she shook her head. "Uxa will manipulate you into accepting." She began painting color on Van's nails.

Van took pleasure in watching each pink stroke of *Twinkle Toes* cover her otherwise unsightly bare nails. "Why hasn't anyone ever told me any of this?"

Miss Nutting waved her hand at the locked door. "People here are cautioned against speaking of that which should be kept secret," she said, as if reciting someone else's words.

"Uxa would never risk Van's life with anything dangerous," Paley said.

"Paley's right." Van held her hands steady for Miss Nutting to finish polishing. "You adults are always so overdramatic. I'm sure my project has more to do with filing papers in a boring office than with this 'Living World' and its problems."

"I agree," Paley said enthusiastically. "We'll probably be doing office support for the Grigori while they sort this mess out. Still, it's going to be exciting!"

"*We'll?*" Miss Nutting glanced at Paley, lifting one eyebrow.

"Forget about sneaking visits. I'm *so* going with." Paley glanced at Van as if expecting an objection, and then asked Miss Nutting, "Can you get me through the portal so I can go over with Van?"

Miss Nutting paused and raised her eyes to Van.
"Well?" Van asked. "Can you?"

Chapter 8

Day 1: 11:37 a.m., Earth World

"No way am I traveling to the Living World by myself," Van said. "If it's possible for Paley to come with me, it's going to happen." *Forget about Uxa and her placement tests.*

It was close to lunchtime and Miss Nutting worried they wouldn't eat, so she ordered wraps, a side of fries for Paley, and diet iced teas from the Boardwalk café.

Van treated them by putting lunch on her family's account.

While they munched on their wraps, Miss Nutting finally said, "There is a way to get Paley over, but it's risky bringing a terrigen through the portal."

"Terrigen? Who's a terrigen?" Paley asked with a mouthful of the steak-and-cheese wrap.

Miss Nutting tipped her head toward Paley.

"Who says I'm a terrigen?"

"Your blood tests do," Miss Nutting said. "No ichor, none. Same as me."

"Tests aren't always right," Paley said with a pout.

"You told us Paley was born in the Living World." Van scrunched her brow. "That means she's a vichor."

Miss Nutting shook those curls again and started talking before she finished chewing a bite of her tuna salad wrap. "The orphans placed in the Gables are known terrigens, no ichor in their blood. It's possible for other kids on the island to develop ichor by the time they begin kindergarten. On rare occasions, it comes out later. The Elders are always on the lookout for this." Miss Nutting swallowed, then sucked iced tea through her straw. "People in the know can tell which kids have ichor. They're the kids who are a bit *slow*. They're put into the reservation program. Van, you have ichor."

Van paused, cucumber salad wrap halfway to her mouth. "You mean my special classes were really…?" She put the wrap down, appetite gone.

"Were really wha—?" Paley asked, shoving french fries into her mouth.

"In the Living World," Miss Nutting answered. "So you could recharge. The elevator to your classroom took you through the portal to a floor in Lodestar Station. That's why you had to continue with your classes even after you got smarter—um, older."

If Van came from the Living World and had ichor in her blood, why weren't her father and Genie proud of her? Why did they make a big deal over Van being born slow? Maybe Pernilla was right. Van remained stupid despite being recharged. Had the Elders fixed her placement status to cover it up? If so, why?

A more depressing thought occurred to Van. Was this the reason her father always seemed so disappointed in her?

"Whoa," Paley said. "I kind of figured only adults would need to recharge."

"How could I not have known my classes take place in another world?" Van asked, worrying this confirmed her lack of intelligence.

"Oh, the Elders and the Grigori go out of their way for the kids not to know," Miss Nutting said, chomping away. "And their parents. If their parents are terrigens, that is. It wasn't just you, Van. No one is supposed to figure it out. The program is designed to make the kids, and the parents think it's simply another class in a different location. One better equipped for athletic training."

"How can we get Paley over?" Van's mouth felt dry. She grabbed her iced tea.

"First things first," Miss Nutting spoke with half-chewed food in her mouth, again. "You can't get through the portal without being attuned, usually by a Grigori."

"My father's a Grigori." Then Van remembered he was already in trouble at work. And missing. And possibly a traitor.

"That's no help." Paley rummaged around for the last french fry. "Where can we find a Grigori who'll help us?"

"The reservation is filled with Grigori. Not one of them will help you."

"Why not?" Van asked, affronted.

"They took an oath to keep the portal a secret from terrigens. Another problem is the Grigori monitor the portal. I'm sure there'll be a transport record. Grigori also take an oath to protect terrigens. Sending you through the portal is not protecting you, Paley." Miss Nutting, her pretty face now pale and tense, stood up, leaving the rest of her wrap. She walked over to the shampoo bowl and fiddled with the faucet.

"Keeping me from transporting will protect me?" Paley halted her last fry midway to her mouth.

"Van can travel through, no problem. It's you, Paley, who we have to worry about." Miss Nutting stopped fiddling, and her expression grew grim. "Bad things happen when a transport goes wrong."

Van resisted rolling her eyes. *More adult drama.* "Just tell us what to do, and we'll do it."

She could use Paley's help over there, especially if her father was in trouble. With Paley watching her back, it would be easier for Van to cover up her father's mistakes. Van would do whatever it took to protect the Cross family's reputation.

Miss Nutting motioned Paley over to the sink. She chewed on the inside of her cheek, considering whether to tell them.

"I'll take the chance." Paley plunked herself down in the shampoo chair. "I really want to see where my parents came from, what their life was like. Maybe… even… find out what happened to them."

Miss Nutting, always a sucker for a sob story, turned on the words like water coming out of her shampoo faucet. "They're called the Twin Gemstones. They're not used for transport anymore, considered too unstable." The shampoo foamed as Miss Nutting massaged Paley's scalp. "We don't know which terrigens will transport successfully and which ones won't."

Paley wrinkled her brow. "If I can't transport through, so what? Wouldn't I just stay in one spot?"

"It'll seem like you can go through, but you'll bounce back. What you'll get for your efforts is an addled brain, memory loss at best, brain damage or death at worst."

"It sounds risky," Van said. *And like something I would get in trouble over.*

Paley raised her wet head, nostrils flaring. "I have a chance to find out about my parents. I'm not letting it slip by me. I'm doing this with or without you, Van."

"No. You won't. You can't, actually." Miss Nutting pushed Paley's head back into the sink and continued to rinse her hair. "The Twin Gemstones have to be used in pairs. The holders of the gemstones must travel through the portal together, and one must be a vichor."

Miss Nutting sat Paley up and wrapped a towel around her head. "The vichor's energy, along with the energy of the gemstones, is what makes the attunement high enough to transport the terrigen." She sat Paley down in a hairdressing chair. "Each gemstone will automatically attune to each traveler's vibration—their unique energy pattern—and then combine into one vibrational signal. Once you're attuned, the portal's vibration will change to match your vibration. This allows for transport."

Paley grimaced. "Huh?"

"Like a lock and key," Van said. Thanks to her cellular biology and physics classes at Canterbury Bells, she understood the concept.

"Exactly." Miss Nutting pulled a wide-toothed comb from the salon cart and began detangling Paley's hair. "Both of you will have to carry a gemstone. Keep it on you at all times. Although I'm not sure how you plan to get around Uxa and Fynn."

"I've already worked it out." Paley winced at the detangling. "I'm an expert at skirting authority. It's my training from being at the Gables. Will I be able to stay for a month?"

"Possibly," Miss Nutting said. "Depends on how strong Van's energy draw is. She'd be channeling the energy of nature through her connection to the gemstones. That's what would keep you there."

"I *have* to tell Ken all this," Van said, forgetting she was still mad at him.

Miss Nutting's eyes widened. "Oh, no! You can't tell anyone, or I'll get banished from the island." She picked up the dryer and began styling Paley's hair.

"Van's energy is strong," Paley said, over the whirr of the hairdryer. "Let's do it."

Van appreciated Paley's vote of confidence. But according to Pernilla and Genie, she wasn't strong at all.

"I told you this to discourage you. Even if you managed to get through the portal, the Grigori would notice within minutes an unauthorized transport had occurred. You'd never get away with it."

Van prickled over being told she couldn't do something. "Paley's proved herself to be a contributor with her job here at the salon. I can talk Uxa into letting her stay in the Living World and help with the project. That way, Paley would earn a higher placement." And get the naysayers off her friend's back, once and for all.

"It'll be fine," Paley said lightly. "Van can grease some palms to get me on board. Money grows on trees—"

She glanced at Van, grinning, and they finished the old joke in unison, "Family trees." Both of them chuckled.

"This isn't funny." Miss Nutting bobbed her brush at them. "There's a serious risk to Van's health using the gemstones and a danger to your life, Paley. The gemstones might not get you safely through the portal. If they do, Van might be too compromised to complete her project."

Ugh. Adults always made things more difficult than they had to be.

"Where are these Twin Gemstones?" Van asked.

"They're impossible to get. I don't even know where they are." Miss Nutting put the final touches on Paley's hair.

Van scowled. "You sure?"

Miss Nutting twitched. "As far I know, only three sets of Twin Gemstones existed. Two were destroyed. The third... well, the third is rumored to be here, on the island."

Paley yelped in delight.

"If they're anywhere, they'd be on the reservation," Miss Nutting said. "Stored in one of the buildings in the complex, I expect."

"That place is super protected," Van said, her sudden hope deflating. "It's where I go for my special classes." She wondered whether Miss Nutting had told them about the Twin Gemstones only because she thought they'd never be able to get them.

Miss Nutting was an orphan, like Paley. Most of the Gable's kids had a tendency to challenge authority. Van could tell Miss Nutting felt conflicted about helping, but respected them enough to answer their questions honestly. However, Van also knew Miss Nutting had used the information to convince Van and Paley their idea was misguided, ensuring they wouldn't do anything reckless that would never work.

Miss Nutting frowned. "Even if you could get into the complex, expensive pieces of equipment like that... they'd be vaulted away in a secure place, same as any valuable set of jewels."

"*Jewels?*" Van perked up. "Do they look like jewels?"

"Like two sparkling gems, about the size of eggs, like the essence of the ocean captured in a prism, or a fiery dawn... a brush of clouds gathering before a storm..." Miss Nutting drifted away into her own world.

Paley stared blankly.

To Van, the description couldn't be any clearer. Miss Nutting often overheard insider secrets from her clients at the Naked Ape, but the details of this description made Van wonder if Miss Nutting's past included a personal experience using the Twin Gemstones.

Van threw back her shoulders and declared, "I know *exactly* where they are."

Chapter 9

Day 1: 12:43 p.m., Earth World

AFTER VAN and Paley promised Miss Nutting they wouldn't do anything stupid, they left the salon and headed back to Mt. Hope Manor. To their relief, the house remained empty. If their plan was going to work, they had to move fast.

They needed to steal the Twin Gemstones, stash Paley in the Living World, and for Van to return to the manor in time to meet Fynn at six p.m.

Van zoomed up to her bedroom and grabbed her backpack. She grinned, knowing she had made the right decision to pack her essentials earlier. She had no time to gather her suitcases and had already planned on Luma packing the rest of her clothes and sending them to her.

With Twinkle Toes crammed into her overstuffed backpack, she could barely zip it closed. Van thought about ditching the stuffed animal, but couldn't bear parting with it. She heaved on the overstuffed backpack, did a quick check of her hair and makeup in the mirror, and then dashed back downstairs.

Although they had never attempted it before, Van and Paley already knew the best way to sneak onto the reservation—through the manor's backyard. They shot across the grounds and disappeared into the trees, then jaunted through the woods to the water's edge. They climbed down the seven-foot storm wall onto slimy beach rocks.

Van's feet throbbed, still sore from last night's walk. "I'm not cut out for this," Van said, as she and Paley maneuvered across the slippery rocks.

"And you think I am?" Paley held out her arms, trying to keep her balance.

They stepped off the rocks onto the squishy sand of low tide. As the cold mush oozed into Van's white Bottega Veneta sandals, she considered ditching the whole idea and sprinting back to the sanctuary of her bedroom.

They slogged onward, trapped between the lapping sea and the jagged rocks. Eventually, they passed the boundary markers indicating the restricted reservation area. The reservation wasn't difficult to sneak onto; only the consequences of getting caught—getting banished from the island—kept unauthorized islanders away.

The Elders strictly controlled who could enter onto their sacred land. Despite being a tribal descendant, even Van wasn't permitted to enter the reservation, except to attend her special classes. Paley, a townie, was never allowed on the reservation.

Neither of them worried about this, being too focused on executing their plan. They felt relieved when the wall of rocks ended, and they could walk on the dry beach sand that bordered the woods.

According to Van's teachers, three-quarters of the reservation comprised a nature preserve, which would give them cover as they searched for the complex. While sneaking through the woods, they stopped once to rinse their muddy feet in a puddle.

They continued on, and although they tried to be quiet, every step crackled with crunching leaves. They expected security guards to come crashing through the woods at them, but the area seemed deserted. Only the occasional bird reacted to their presence, taking flight at the noise of the interlopers. Without incident, they located the complex.

Van and Paley crouched in the wild brush overlooking the three interconnected buildings that housed the island's government. Van knew nothing about the farthest away, a flat rectangular structure called Providence Island Research Facility. The middle and tallest building, called Marble Hall, was full of offices. The smallest and closest, a domed building called the House of Lacus, accommodated Van's special classes.

"We need to get in there," Van whispered. "But we have to be careful. It's guarded."

"I don't see any guards," Paley said in a low voice. "Must be short-staffed for the holiday weekend."

"It still has to be locked." Van eyed the main doorway.

"Why would someone lock it?" Paley asked. "Every day is a workday on the reservation."

"What if someone's in there?" Van had begun to reconsider the whole idea. "If we get caught, we'll be banished from the island."

"We'll be careful. We can hide in the shadows."

Van remained skeptical.

"Uxa needs you for her project, so you'll just get a slap on the wrist," Paley coaxed. "If anything, I'll get kicked off the island. I want to leave anyway. What's a few years earlier? It's worth the risk to me. I have to find out about my parents."

They had come this far. They needed to do something. "Let's go," Van said.

Dried twigs snapped under their feet until they reached the grassy, manicured lawn surrounding the House of Lacus. Van's stomach tightened from fearing security would nab them, but they arrived at the door without being caught. In fact, the entire area was clear of people.

Despite the warm June day, Van shivered. "Weird."

Paley shrugged and tried the door. It opened.

"Even weirder," Van said.

"Right? Don't they believe in security?" Paley smirked as they slipped inside. "I mean, they'll let anyone transport these days."

"Where are all the Grigori?" Van asked as they tiptoed down a cool, white-and-gray marble hallway, dimly lit by wall sconces.

"Who cares?"

"It's over here." Van's voice came out louder than she had intended, and the hallway's acoustics amplified her words.

Paley mouthed, "We're dead."

They stood paralyzed, expecting island security to descend on them at any second. Nobody came.

Van opened her mouth to comment, when Paley whispered, "I know, *weird*."

She led Paley into a circular atrium made of granite and marble with a domed ceiling. Benches carved from the walls and flanked by Doric pillars lined the perimeter. In the center was a fountain with a statue of a toga-clad woman. The expansiveness of the atrium always made Van feel insignificant. Whenever she had passed through for her classes, it bustled with Grigori, island security, Elders, and Native Islanders. Now, all was silent, except for the tinkling of the fountain.

Against the far wall stood a piece of ugly artwork, a dais holding an enormous black disc bordered by a band of granite lined with pictographs and symbols. A set of curved stairways protruded from the wall, one on each side of the disc, leading to the dais. Underneath, at floor level, Van saw the elevator she had taken to her classes.

Van pointed to the elevator. "Miss Nutting said that's the portal."

"Great. So where're the gemstones?"

"This way." Van reached the far archway when she realized Paley wasn't behind her. "Paley," Van hissed. "What're you doing?"

"This fountain… have you ever looked at the statue?"

Van and the other students never had time to look at anything. Her teachers always herded them into the elevator. No dilly-dallying allowed. "C'mon," Van urged. The stress of trespassing on the reservation made her cranky.

Paley didn't respond.

Van stomped back, imagining she would have to drag her friend away by the hair. But when Van reached Paley, she couldn't help but stare at the amazing statue too.

Water poured into the fountain from an urn carried under a beautiful woman's left arm. In her right hand, she held a torch. A sword lay sheathed in her belt, and around her neck, she wore a coin pendant necklace.

"She looks like you," Paley said, not taking her eyes off the statue.

Van grunted, pretending to be unimpressed. After fighting a deep pit of denial in her stomach, she had to admit the resemblance. "Maybe someday."

"I wonder what it says." Paley pointed to an engraving at the base of the fountain.

Van had never noticed the writing before, but now her eyes widened. It was the same language she had seen in her father's study and in the burned text. Only this time, the words became intelligible. She read the inscription out loud. "Queen Amaryl of the Dark War."

The text! Had she left it behind? Then she remembered tucking the book into her folded shirts and let out a breath. The text was in the stack of clothes she'd stuffed into her backpack.

Paley mumbled, "Another cool thing you learned in your classes here, I guess."

"No… I didn't—" Van wasn't sure how she could read the words, and it scared her. "I mean, yeah. We learned some of that language in class," she lied.

Van's eyes wandered to the face of Queen Amaryl. She found herself unable to look away. The statue exuded a lifelike energy, reaching out to Van across time and space. Van squirmed under the scrutiny of the woman's gaze. She felt undeserving of being in the presence of such an honored warrior.

"She looks too young to be a queen," Paley said, breaking Van's connection to the statue.

"Come on." Van hurried back toward the archway. "Stop dilly-dallying."

This time, Paley followed.

Van opened the smooth wooden door, and they entered the control room.

"I was in here once, by accident," Van said, distracted by the control panel stretching along the wall, covered with knobs and dials. Tiny lights flashed, but the screens remained dark. *Probably set to monitor the portal automatically.* Van, again, felt the eeriness of the unattended station.

In the back of the room, stuffed between consoles, they saw a life-size statue of an elderly man with a long beard and dressed in a simple toga. He sat in a cross-legged position with his hands on his knees, palms up. The statue seemed unremarkable, except for the stunning jewels the man held, one in each hand.

"What a strange place to display a piece of art." Paley eyed the statue. "The Elders could use an office decor lesson."

Van smiled at the statue as if she had bumped into an old friend. "Like Genie always says—if you want to hide something, keep it out in the open."

Paley lunged for one of the gemstones. "These must be worth a fortune." She tugged at it, using both hands, then tried the other. "They won't come out. They're stuck."

"Get out of the way." Van grasped one gemstone. She felt a slight vibration in her hand, and, with little effort, out popped the jewel. "Easy peasy." She handed it to Paley.

Her friend gazed in wonder at the gemstone, as if she had fallen in love.

Van removed the second stone. "I'll keep this one. You keep that one."

"They automatically attune us to travel through the portal," Paley said. "That's what Miss Nutting told us, right?"

"I guess so." Just getting the gemstones had seemed like such a far-fetched idea, Van hadn't considered the details. She copied the elderly man statue and held the gemstone in her open palm.

Paley held hers the same way and moved her hand next to Van's.

Both of the gemstones flashed a multitude of vibrant colors until they synchronized with each other. The stones settled on a brilliant golden yellow and throbbed as if sharing a single pulse.

Van smiled. "According to the principle of forced vibration, we are attuned."

"Showoff," Paley teased. "I remember nothing from physics class. For someone who's supposed to be slow, you're kind of smart."

Van giggled and tucked her gemstone into her backpack. "For safekeeping."

Paley did the same. "Let's get to the elevator."

Van planned to take Paley over and get her settled in a bed-and-breakfast. Then Van would return to the manor and meet Fynn. They figured with the terminal being unmanned, it would take at least an hour for the Grigori to notice the unauthorized transports. By then, Van would already be back at the manor and Paley would be safely hidden.

Miss Nutting would've mentioned if the transport showed the traveler's identities. If questioned, Van could deny she had gone anywhere. When Van returned to the Living World with Fynn, she would talk Uxa into letting Paley stay and help with the project. If Uxa made Paley go back to the island, at least her friend would've had the chance to experience her parents' birthplace. It was a perfect plan.

Soon after they stepped back into the atrium, the granite stone band with the ancient symbols surrounding the disc moved clockwise, rotating faster and faster until it became burning yellow-orange. A thin strip of ocean-blue water filled in the layer below the fiery band and rotated counterclockwise.

Within the blackness of the disc, waves of silver sparkles twinkled; its darkness held an unfathomable depth. The sparkles began to swirl.

"I guess *that's* the portal," Paley quipped, though she sounded breathy and excited.

"The gemstones remotely activated it." Van gaped at the spectacular disc. "The portal never did that when I went to my classes. The Grigori must've waited until all the students got on the elevator before turning it on."

The elevator had taken a bit of time to get moving, but with Van's limited elevator experience, she'd never thought twice about it. No wall existed behind the "artwork" as Van had imagined. In that space, the elevator went straight into the portal.

As they walked up one of the marble stairways, Van's legs felt wobbly. She took deep breaths with every step, unsure of herself. *Do I have the guts to go through with this?*

They stood side by side in front of the swirling portal.

Paley raised one hand and crossed her fingers. With the other, she clasped Van's hand and squeezed.

Van returned her grasp, and together they stepped into the blackness, into the unknown, into the Living World.

Chapter 10

Day 1: 2:43 p.m., Living World

Coolness washed through every cell in Van's body. Air rippled over her bare skin, yet her hair and clothes remained still.

She wasn't afraid or uncomfortable. The sensation felt refreshing. It seemed different from transporting through the elevator, where she had felt nothing. Then Van saw light, and the portal expelled her onto a platform.

Paley landed next to her. It surprised Van they were no longer holding hands.

The writing on a granite stone relief indicated they had arrived at Lodestar Station. It reminded Van of the House of Lacus, except this atrium appeared long and rectangular, rather than round, and more embellished: the columns were Corinthian; white stone benches encircled flourishing green flora; and on the far side, above one of several high-arched exits, hung a colossal clock with roman numerals. The clock had four hands and varying phases of the moon on its face.

"Wow! What a ride." Paley patted her hands up and down her body. "Yup, everything's still here."

"Let's go while the station's deserted." Van nervously glanced around the atrium. Oddly, it also seemed empty of people.

"Where is everybody?" Paley grinned. "Doesn't anyone *live* in the Living World?"

"I don't know, but it's creeping me out. The elevator to my classes opened into a hallway. Our room looked like a regular classroom, except it had no windows. The gym had high walls with windows near the top. All I could see was the sky. I thought we were close to the domed roof of the House of Lacus." Van raised her eyes toward the rows and rows of windows on the floors surrounding the atrium. "Now I know my classes were here, on one of the floors above us."

"The elevator must be a direct route to the floor of your classroom," Paley added. "The swirling disc is probably the public crossing route. If the Grigori took your class through the main portal, I'm guessing you would've suspected something strange going on."

"Yeah. None of us would've been able to keep it a secret."

Van took in the enormous oil paintings of important-looking people set in decorative silver frames lining the walls. Some were depicted in light blue robes, others in fancy togas.

"Uh, I hope nobody is looking out any of those windows." Paley glanced up at the rows of floors surrounding the atrium. "I doubt the Grigori allow kids to use the public portal."

They hurried off the landing and rushed toward the archways. Each had an engraved stone sign with a destination.

Van pointed to the one under the clock. "Lodestar Village. Sounds like a good place to hide out."

They had just reached the archway when they heard pounding footsteps coming from the landing behind them.

"Grigori!" Van said.

"People!" Paley said at the same time.

Van and Paley raced down the exit ramp and burst onto the sidewalk. Eventually, they slowed to a jog.

Van glanced back at Lodestar Station. The monumental structure towered over the village and reminded Van of her class trip to the White House. But no Grigori stormed after them. They slowed to a walk, giving Van time to catch her breath and scan the panorama.

She took in the village's beauty and joy poured through her, so profound her past seemed as if covered by an oppressive film of gloom. Each breath cleared away the murkiness she never knew hid inside her.

She loved the dazzling village. The rows of fairytale cottages lining cobblestone streets, the spectrum of green trees that seemed to wrap the town in a blanket, the surreal blueness of the sky, the grassy rest areas with their gorgeous array of colored flowers and inviting stone benches. A mountain rose in the distance, so magnificent Van had trouble believing it was real and not a constructed backdrop.

"Look at all the cute shops," Paley squealed, gaping at the quaint cottages. "One of them has to be a restaurant. I'm starving."

They meandered down the winding stone sidewalks of the bustling village, hoping to blend in and evade any snooping Grigori.

Van inhaled jubilant scents of rose, jasmine, and cypress. Her heart opened to the plethora of people before her. Some chatted while taking an afternoon break on the benches. Others sipped sparkling water from eye-level fountains. Most moved along in their colorful, stylish clothing with fabric-made store bags dangling from their hands and elbows. The women's clothes varied between dressy pants and pencil skirts; most wore stunning calf-length capes over their outfits. The men wore casual tunic-styled shirts with tight-fitting trousers tucked into calf-length boots. They all appeared well-dressed, even the children and the women sporting jean-style pants.

Not wanting to gawk at them, Van directed her attention to the shops' display windows. She and Paley passed handcrafted jewelry stores; a candy shop flaunting specialty fudge; a place that sold archery equipment, camping gear, and other sporting goods; and another that displayed upscale dresses.

Van gazed at a red A-line dress she recognized. Genie had worn a similar dress to yesterday's Placement Ceremony. Her step-mother must have bought it on one of her "off island" shopping trips.

A man swept out of a shop called Lodestar Village Apothecary, jostling Van out of her thoughts. Her heart skipped a beat as she took in the midnight-blue uniform of the Grigori.

A blond woman wearing tan skinny jeans and a matching tight-fit tee under a tan cloak with an elaborate silver clasp followed him. The couple, engrossed in their conversation, didn't notice Van.

"What does HG Huxatec say?" the woman asked. "Michael Cross was her first assistant, after all."

Van's stomach did a flip. *They're talking about my father!* People treated him like a celebrity on their small island. Still, Van was surprised to discover his popularity in this world too.

While Paley busily drooled over fudge in a candy shop's window, Van trailed behind the couple. She walked close enough to hear their conversation, yet far enough away not to be noticed.

"She's still in the meeting," the Grigori said. "With President Sterling, the rest of the Lodian Consilium, and the Grigori, at least, the ones who didn't get stuck watching over the Station, like me." He made a grunting sound. "Along with the entire Balish Council, including King Nequus."

The woman grimaced. "The Balish are always looking for ways to cause trouble with us."

"Cross has put us in a precarious situation. HG's worried about the outcome of the ruling."

"I'm sure she has a plan to fix this mess, no matter the ruling." The woman glanced behind her as if sensing someone listening.

Van zipped into a nearby shop, waited a few seconds, and then continued to follow the couple. Thankfully, crowds bustled along the sidewalks, and Van blended into the rest of the pedestrians.

"Do you have to get back to work?" the woman asked the man.

"Yeah, my break's almost over. We've got a couple of guys watching the station, but they're probably spying on the meeting instead." He chuckled. "Like I will be when I get back." He continued in a serious tone, "The Balish have gathered enough evidence this time for the repeal of Manik's law. If we lose the protection of that law…" He shook his head in trepidation.

"The Balish will invade Salus Valde," the woman said.

"HG doesn't want to cause mass hysteria, with the public thinking we're on the brink of Dishora," the Grigori continued. "It won't be long, though, before people hear about Class III demons killing Prince Devon—"

"Harrus, shush!" The woman cringed.

There can't be demons here. This world is way too peaceful for that. And Miss Nutting had told Van demons had vanished from the Living World. Then she remembered the mud-like demons in the Native Island Legends storybook she saw in her father's study. A chill of truth rippled through her skin, causing her to shudder.

Harrus lowered his voice, "—and notice the simultaneous disappearance of a high-profile figure like Cross. The rumors about his past will resurface."

"Alleged disappearance," she said.

"If Cross was rotten enough to murder his first wife all those years ago, he's rotten enough to be involved with a takeover of Salus Valde. He was guilty then, and he's guilty now. What? Don't give me that look, Fiona."

Harrus's words shook Van to her core. Her father hadn't killed her mother. Van had when she was born. This was common knowledge on the island. Besides, her father worked in security, protecting Salus Valde. He would never be involved in a takeover. This guy had it all wrong.

"He's involved all right," Harrus continued. "He's been sidling up to that Balish princess. What's her name? Solana. That power-hungry, money-grubbing—"

"Aelia was a star—loved by all Lodians," Fiona said. "What happened to her was a national tragedy." Fiona shook her head as if to emphasize the waste of a life cut short. "We all felt emotionally invested in her future, even people like you who didn't know her personally. Except you're still holding a grudge against Michael for marrying her, aren't you?"

"Me and the rest of the Lodian community," he said. "Since when does a dirty commoner get to marry into one of the purest Lodian bloodlines? Maybe sixteen years ago, but not anymore, thank-the-light-and-all-that-is-good." Harrus straightened his right hand and made a sideways figure-eight gesture in front of his chest. "And then keeping Aelia's last name after her death. And giving it to that… that… *Balish* replacement wife of his."

Van's jaw dropped. *Genie is Balish?* Miss Nutting had said Genie was from another tribe, but *Balish?* No wonder the women on the island hated her. They must have sensed Genie was the enemy, or perhaps they subconsciously absorbed the tension exuding from the Grigori who knew Genie's history. This must be why Miss Nutting used the word *asylum* when she told Van about her step-mother.

"His current wife is Antares-Balish," Fiona said. "Not Balish-Balish."

"Humph, no difference." He wagged his index finger at Fiona. "Being banished to live on Providence Island for marrying Aelia wasn't a high enough price for Cross to pay."

"He confided in me once, you know," Fiona recalled. "One night, after his wedding to Aelia, we worked late and went down to the pub for a drink—"

Harrus glared at her.

"Of course, this was before I met you," Fiona quickly added. "He was distraught and had one too many mugs of mead. Told me deep in his heart he regretted marrying Aelia. It was the day he found out she was pregnant."

"So, eight months later, he lured his pregnant wife into the woods of Tipereth to kill her off? The lousy scoundrel. What were you thinking, having a drink with him?"

The woman trembled. "Michael left poor Aelia's body behind in the woods. Destroyed all her belongings when he got back, I heard. Didn't want to leave a single trace of her behind. Their baby was lucky to have survived."

"Did it? No one has heard hide nor hair of the child for fifteen years."

"They say it's a girl who lives on Providence Island. You know what it means if she exists, don't you? If the child survived—"

Someone roughly grabbed Van's arm, spinning her around.

"Van!" It was Paley. "Has this world turned you deaf? I've been calling after you. I want some fudge."

The couple twisted around at Paley's outburst.

Fiona eyed the two of them. "Are you okay?"

"We're fine," Van muttered, still stunned by the conversation she had overheard. According to them, Van's power-hungry, money-grubbing, wife-murdering father lurked out there somewhere, hanging around with the Balish Princess Solana, plotting against the Lodians. *Against me.*

"Why are you looking at us like that?" Paley said to them. "Am I not allowed fudge?"

"We're fine." Van nudged Paley's elbow. "Come on."

Thankfully, the couple was too busy to make any further inquiries and went their own way.

Deep in thought, Van followed Paley back to a candy shop called Serendipity. Van's father and mother had been banished from Salus Valde and forced to live on Providence Island for *marrying* each other? It didn't make sense, although it explained why her parents hadn't gone to Canterbury Bells.

Paley picked up some rocky road fudge, and candy coins the shopkeeper called chocolate "stips."

In a daze, Van went through the motions of being impressed with the vast, mouthwatering selection of petits fours decorated with tiny flowers, mini pies piled high with whipped cream, and a variety of handmade chocolates: dark, white, milk, in cubes and barks, with nuts, without. Finally, she grabbed a box of rock candy off the shelf, just so they could get moving.

Van had no appetite for sweets or anything else. She felt torn between running home and hiding under her covers forever and staying to discover the truth about her father.

I always thought I had killed my mother when I was born. Van chewed on her lip.

Being free from this guilt came with the price of knowing her father had murdered her mother, which was no better.

That couple is wrong. Van concluded her father hadn't killed her mother. She had. Then she buried the conversation in a dark corner of her mind.

Paley slapped their candy down on the counter.

"This together?" the cashier asked. His thick white mustache blew out at the ends when he spoke.

Paley snickered at the man as Van nodded. Any another time, Van would've found the cashier's resemblance to a walrus funny too.

"That'll be a quarter pec."

Van paused, confused.

"Don't look so shocked," the cashier said. "The Balish raised prices on everything. It costs me a fortune to have my ingredients shipped into Salus Valde. Besides, my confections are worth every pec."

"*Pecs?*" Paley asked. "What the heck is a pec?"

"Um—" Van looked at the money in her hand—*dollars!* Earth World money. She snapped her hand closed. "Ah, hold on a sec." Van slipped off her backpack and ruffled around until she found the burned text and pulled out the coin she had found in her father's study. "Here you go."

"A bagoc!" The cashier narrowed his eyes at them. "Don't you have anything smaller?"

"Uh, no." Van shifted uncomfortably under his scrutiny. "Sorry."

The man gave her change, and Van shuffled Paley out of the shop.

"Where'd you get that weird money?" Paley popped a large piece of fudge into her mouth.

"Found it in my father's things," Van said.

"Awesome." Paley's smile showed fudge smears on her teeth. "It never crossed my mind this world would have different money. Good thinking."

They continued strolling down the main road in the village center. As Paley entertained Van with a running commentary about every shop they passed, Van noticed people glanced their way a little too often. Suddenly, it dawned on Van no one else wore shorts and sandals or carried backpacks. She and Paley didn't exactly blend in.

Van pushed Paley down the nearest side street. "It's getting late. We need to find a place for you to hide and wait for me to get back."

"How about there?" Paley pointed halfway down the shaded cobblestone street at a hanging wooden sign that read *Three of Cups*. On it, a faded painting depicted three medieval-looking maidens merrily toasting with gold chalices.

"I don't know, it doesn't look like a bed-and-breakfast to me." The sign made Van think of a medieval castle.

"I won't need a bed-and-breakfast after Uxa accepts me on the project. Besides, I need proper food."

"But what if—"

Paley grabbed Van's elbow and pulled her toward the Three of Cups. "We can ask about local bed and breakfasts while we're in there *after* I eat."

Paley opened the heavy wooden door without hesitation.

The crowded, noisy eatery had an aged stench, which caused Van's nose to stuff up. The exposed beams and stone hearth worked with the eatery's tavern decor. Van glanced down, expecting a dirt floor and heartened to see wood planks.

They weaved their way through the crowd, passing a table of women dressed in bonnets and puffy-sleeved dresses, chit-chatting and nibbling from small dishes of cooked meats and bread. Some patrons sipped funny-looking drinks. One had a spiky plant sticking out of a tall glass; another drank from a fluted glass filled with a clear liquid with a red candy heart floating on the bottom. Most of the men sipped from tin mugs brimming with froth. The crowd seemed content, giving the eatery the feel of a local hangout.

Van nudged Paley toward a table in a corner, and they sat down.

"How cool is this?" Paley's eyes darted every which way.

"Keep your eyes on the clock," Van said. "I don't want to lose track of time."

A bouncy barmaid with wavy, canary-yellow curls appeared at their table, looking like one of the maidens from the sign outside. "Hey, girls. My name's Plexa. What can I get for ya?"

"Do you have a menu?" Van asked.

"Menu? All's we got is the board." Plexa bobbed her head toward a massive blackboard scrawled with messy chalk writing, displaying the day's fares. "Just say what you want, and I'll fetch it."

They both gaped at the board, overwhelmed.

Plexa eyed them more closely. "You girls don't look familiar. Where're ya from, anyway?"

Van drew a blank. She searched her mind for a plausible explanation for why two obvious outsiders were in the eatery and couldn't come up with one.

"From that giant white building down the road," Paley said.

Plexa drew her eyebrows together. "You came from Lodestar?"

"Sure, that's right," Paley said. "We came from Lodestar."

"We'll have two—" Van hoped to stop the conversation as she searched the blackboard. "Sassys, please." As far as Van could tell, the drink contained lemon, ginger, mint, cucumber, and something called Gabba Grain.

It worked. The bar-maiden stopped scrutinizing them and bounded away to get their order.

"Paley, we need to leave. The waitress is suspicious."

"Oh, calm down. As long as we don't run into Uxa, we'll be fine." Paley flipped her hair repeatedly as if hair-tossing were an event in the Jaychund games.

"What is wrong with you?" Van glanced in the direction of Paley's interest.

A tall boy about their age, with sunflower-blond hair and a cute button nose, leaned against a wall. When Van's eyes locked with his royal-blue ones, she felt a jolt, as if her heart had been restarted after a long sleep. His thick lips curved upward into a crooked smile. He had mistaken Van's ogling as a cue to come over. Van couldn't help but stare as he made his way across the crowded eatery.

His lean build was accentuated by his tailor-fit, brown and tan tunic-style clothing. He had innocent, boyish looks but moved with the sleekness and majesty of a lion as if he knew the lay of the land. Which meant he knew she and Paley weren't supposed to be there.

Oh, this isn't good.

Van's eyes remained locked on the boy's until her line of vision became eclipsed by a bursting corset.

Plexa plunked their sassys on the table, then went off to serve other thirsty patrons, clearing Van's line of vision.

At their table stood the handsome, button-nosed stranger.

Chapter 11

D ay 1: 4:26 p.m., Living World

"Haven't seen you girls around here before," the boy said. "Need help deciphering that crazy menu?"

Van suddenly hated everything about him. His arrogance, his smug tone of voice, his stupid blue eyes.

"Sure," Paley cooed.

"No, thanks," Van said.

"You sure? Because that drink is—"

"We're *fine*," Van said, ignoring Paley's angry stare. She snatched the tall, cool glass in front of her, took a defiant sip, and nearly choked to death.

Van, along with Paley, had sneaked tastes of liquor from her parents' cupboards in the past, but she had never tasted anything this strong.

"Sassys are made with Gabba Grain, grain alcohol. Very

potent." His eyes twinkled as Van used her fingertips to wipe her watering eyes. "There's no drinking age here."

"Yay!" Paley yelped, then took a deep sip from her drink.

"What do you mean by *here?*" Van asked, over Paley's grain alcohol induced gasps. "You make it sound like we're supposed to be someplace else." Van suspected he knew they came from the Earth World.

"That's not it at all," he said with a lopsided grin. "I'm pretty sure you're supposed to be here, all right."

"What do you mean?" Van snapped.

He looked flustered for a second and then collected himself. "If you weren't here, then how would I have met you?"

His words rang insincere to Van, though she supposed most girls would find him charming. Case in point, Paley audibly sighed, causing him to turn her way.

"Nice eyes."

"Thanks." Paley strained over the table, trying to wriggle closer to him.

Van fidgeted over his comment. Most new people commented on Van's beautiful blue eyes, not on Paley's obvious colored contacts.

Paley giggled for no reason and batted her "nice" eyes at him, although they still watered from the harshness of her drink.

The boy made Van uneasy, and she wanted him to leave. She worried Paley's flirting would keep him at their table, and she was right. He pulled out a chair and sat himself down as if he'd been invited.

"My name's Brux." He held out his hand to Paley. "Brux Lake."

Paley's hand zipped out in a flash. "Paley." She shook his hand, holding it for an inappropriate amount of time before setting it free.

Brux stretched out his hand to Van.

His lack of boundaries made her want to punch him in his button nose. But manners overrode her annoyance, and Van gave his hand an obligatory shake. "Vanessa—Van." His touch made her skin tingle with exhilaration, which infuriated her.

"Hang on a sec." He slipped a hand-held gadget out of his pocket.

Van's father used a similar type of device for work, although this one reminded Van more of the smartphones she saw visitors to the island carrying around, trying to get reception which, of course, they couldn't get.

"What's that thing?" Paley lifted her drink and took a careful sip.

Van winced. If Brux hadn't already figured out they were outsiders, he would now.

"It's one of the new MTs—multi-tracks." He held the device in his hands and used his thumbs to type a message.

Van relaxed a bit. She had expected Brux to stand up, point at them, and scream at the top of his lungs, "Intruders!"

"I'm telling my friend I met some great girls and to come meet us." Brux laid the MT on the table in front of him and looked at Van. "If that's okay with you."

"Too late now, isn't it?"

"It's okay, for sure," Paley said with an affable grin.

"Seems like someone could use another swig of her sassy," Brux said to Paley as he nodded toward Van.

Van fumed.

Paley snickered and took another sip of her drink.

The glassy panel on his MT flashed. Brux picked it up and read the incoming message. "A better idea. How about we go meet my friend? It'll be fun. Trust me."

"Sure," Paley said. "Let's make like trees and leave." She giggled and took another sip of her sassy.

Brux rewarded Paley with a broad smile. "Excellent."

Van squirmed in her seat. "I don't—"

"It's settled then. We go." Brux stood up and tossed some bronze coins onto the table.

If Van's head felt fuzzy from one sip of her sassy, then Paley must be on her way to oblivion. "Okay, let's go." Van couldn't help smirking at their stunned expressions. Little did they know, she planned on ditching Brux, grabbing Paley, and getting them both back home, where they belonged.

The trio left the eatery. Brux and Paley chattered nonstop as he led them away from the village center and down a winding cobblestone street that eventually turned into a dirt road.

Van didn't have a moment's silence to think of a way to get her and Paley away from Brux and back to Lodestar. If she didn't get back in time to meet Fynn, she would be in big trouble with Uxa, which would definitely affect her placement and reflect poorly on her family.

"Are we almost there?" Van asked.

"Almost."

The road got darker, with fewer houses and more trees. Van tried to keep all of the twists and turns in her memory but couldn't. At this point, she wouldn't be able to find her way back without Brux. Having to depend on this immature stranger for their survival triggered a massive fit of anxiety.

Van said, "I have to be back home by six—"

"It's right here." Brux pointed ahead.

A house came into view, the likes of which Van had never seen before. It was a cottage integrated into a tree. Red slat shutters framed arched windows, tangles of ivy grew along the outer bark walls, and it had a red wooden door with a silver half-moon knocker.

Paley's forehead crinkled. "This is a strange place for a tavern."

"I never said we were going to a tavern." Brux rapped on the door. "This is my friend's house."

"I thought we were going to a public place." Van prepared to grab Paley and run at the first sign of trouble.

The red door swung open.

Van gaped.

"Well, look what the cat dragged in," Uxa said.

Chapter 12

Day 1: 5:56 p.m., Living World

"Right time, wrong place, Vanessa." Uxa led Van, Paley, and Brux into the living room of the tree-cottage.

Uxa wore her usual tunic-style clothing, although this outfit appeared less formal, giving Van the impression of a casual-wear uniform. Usually, Van would find this idea funny, but she was too furious at Brux.

Van whipped around to face him. "You set us up? You *lied* to us?"

"Technically, I didn't lie," Brux said. "I told you we were going to meet my friend. Uxa's my friend."

"You said it would be *fun*." Paley pouted.

"Oh, it *is* fun. For me." Brux sniggered.

"*I... you...*" Van could feel her cheeks redden as she struggled to find her words.

"Enough!" Uxa barked. "Brux—go to your assigned quarters. You two, follow me."

The cottage, much bigger on the inside than it initially seemed, had several split levels. Circular walls confirmed the house had been hollowed out of a tree trunk. The decor appeared fittingly rustic with handsome oak furniture. Gorgeous hand-woven rugs accentuated the solid-wood floors. The room was inviting and orderly. Van suspected she wouldn't find a speck of dust anywhere.

Uxa led them into a nearby room she used as a study. For someone with such a tidy home, her office-away-from-the-office was downright cluttered. Mounds of papers, made mostly from parchment, covered her large hardwood desk. Ancient-looking maps and strange instruments lay scattered here and there. She had timeworn hardcover books stuffed into wall-size oak bookcases or strewn about the room, open and dog-eared, on various pieces of furniture. The place reminded Van of her father's study, prompting an unexpected pang of homesickness.

Uxa took a seat behind her desk and motioned for Van and Paley to sit in the two worn leather high-backed chairs facing her.

They slipped off their backpacks, dropped them onto the floor, and slunk into the chairs.

Van felt ashamed for getting caught breaking the rules, but held her head high, ready to defend herself.

Uxa rested her elbows on the desk, touched the tips of her sturdy fingers together to form a pyramid, and silently glowered at them.

Paley burst out, "I'm so sorry, we were only—"

Uxa held up her palm for Paley to stop.

Silence stretched to eternity, intensified by a soft, rhythmic ticking coming from a grandfather clock lodged between two bookcases. The clock's face had an outer and inner circle with roman numerals, strange symbols, and four hands.

At first, Van couldn't tell what time it was, but after a few seconds, the numbers, the hands, and the symbols made sense. The hand in the inner circle of the clock's face indicated *day one* of thirty. Two large hands on the outer ring showed the 702nd hour and 47th minute. The third hand moved counterclockwise, like a reverse stop-watch, and when it ticked to the top, the minute hand clicked to number 46. The thirty-day clock counted down backward to zero.

Van shuddered and shifted her attention back to Uxa.

"Time is of the essence." Uxa slapped her palm on the desk, startling the girls. "I have decided not to waste it by lecturing the two of you on not only breaking the rules but also endangering both of your lives. Am I correct to assume you used the Twin Gemstones to travel here?"

They both nodded glumly.

"Miss Nutting, I presume?"

It wasn't a far leap for Uxa to pinpoint Miss Nutting. Paley worked at the Naked Ape, and it was Van's favorite salon.

"Leave her alone," Van said. "She was only trying to help."

"Only a Grigori can remove the gemstones from the statue of Orgone," Uxa said. "Which one helped you?"

"No one did," Van answered. "I took them."

Van could've sworn Uxa's lips turned slightly upward. As if she were proud, rather than mad.

"I'm not staying here without Paley." Van felt tired. She half-hoped keeping Paley here would be a deal breaker and Uxa would send them both home.

"There is no time to send Paley back," Uxa said. "You would have to go too, Vanessa, because of the gemstones."

"Good, I don't want to go back," Paley said. "I want to stay and help."

Uxa gave a curt nod. "I'm sure Miss Nutting told you, but I want to reiterate—you must keep the gemstones on you. If you separate from each other in this world, the gemstones won't work. How far a separation depends on the strength of Vanessa's energy draw. If you exceed the distance, Paley will be expelled back to the Earth World, weakened, perhaps permanently damaged. Vanessa, you will die a painful death from energy depletion."

They faced each other with guilty looks of terror. Miss Nutting never told them any such thing.

"You weren't thinking of separating, were you?" Uxa asked,

alarmed. "Vanessa, were you planning on keeping your appointment with Fynn and leaving Paley here?"

They both lied, giving Uxa a wide-eyed, innocent shake of their heads.

Van cringed at what might have happened if Brux hadn't found them and they had separated as planned. She wasn't so mad at him anymore, but quickly noted he was still a jerk.

"How did you know where to find us?" Van asked.

"The portal recorded your transport, and a couple of my associates reported running into two oddly dressed teenage girls in the village."

Harrus and Fiona!

"I figured you'd stay there," Uxa said, "and I sent Brux to discreetly find you."

Van curled her lip. "Why *him*?"

"Who better to find two teenage girls than a teenage boy?"

Paley piped up. "So, I get to work on the project with Van?"

"You will go on the mission with Vanessa and her team."

"Yay!" Paley clapped her hands. "Ohhh, *mission*! So exciting!"

"You will meet the others at dinner tonight, and then you will be briefed," Uxa said, with none of Paley's enthusiasm. "Fynn will take you to your quarters."

"Ladies," said a voice from behind. Fynn had entered the study without a sound. "This way, if you will."

Fynn led them back into the living room.

None of the three spoke as they walked up an open, curved staircase spanning the wall of the circular room. On the second floor, they went down a hallway that conformed to the shape of the tree trunk. Fynn dropped them off in a room with two twin beds and small matching desks.

The room appeared cozy until Van realized it had no windows. Then her chest tightened, and she found it hard to breathe.

"Dinner bell will ring at seven-thirty, sharp," Fynn informed them. "Don't be late."

With a click, the door closed behind him.

Van's claustrophobia flared at the sound of the click. *Did he lock us in?*

"This is so cool." Paley chucked her backpack onto the closest desk. "We both get to stay."

"Great." Van tried to sound enthusiastic as she forced each of her leaden feet, one after the other, deeper into the room, although she always felt calmer being near the exit.

"Do you think we can explore?" Paley glanced at the closed door.

"Uxa's *house*?" Van asked, wishing they weren't sequestered. "I don't think so. It would be rude."

Van tossed her backpack onto the desk's chair and threw herself down on the bed *farthest* from the only escape route. She tucked herself in and tried to unwind, but found the low-thread-count sheets intolerable. Her attention kept drifting across the room to the door.

Was it locked? Why would Fynn lock it?

After a few minutes, Paley became uncharacteristically quiet. She lay curled up with a pillow on top of her bedspread and, to Van's annoyance, had fallen asleep.

Van wished she were calm enough to nap. Instead, she sprang off the bed and began pacing the room, which felt smaller and smaller by the second. Finally, she worked up the courage, marched to the door, and grabbed the knob. The instant the door opened, every muscle in her body relaxed. She shut the door, went back to her bed, and tucked in.

She'd rested for what seemed like a minute before a chime sounded from a wall speaker.

"It must be the dinner bell." Paley groggily stretched her arms.

"That means it's seven-thirty. We're late," Van said.

They both scrambled to freshen up.

"Uxa should have set the bell to ring earlier," Paley said, washing her face in a hurry.

They finished getting ready for dinner, left their quarters, and rushed downstairs.

Fynn hadn't told them the location of the dining room, but as soon as Van and Paley hit the bottom of the stairway, they heard voices coming from some place off the living room. They followed the sounds and timidly entered the dining area.

A boisterous group sat around a rectangular butcher-block table in an undecorated room with no windows. Some of them glanced over, but, mostly, no one acknowledged their entrance. They were the last to arrive, causing Van to worry she'd already failed her first assignment. The only empty chairs remaining, besides those at the head and the foot of the table, were on the far end, facing the entrance.

Van took a seat next to a thin girl with droopy, white-blond hair that fell to her waist. She counted nine others besides her and Paley, and she tried not to be intimidated by the motley crew around the table. They all looked like brutes, except for one wimpy guy and the girl sitting next to Van.

These people seemed strange to her. Van preferred the companionship of friends she had grown up with and people she knew from the island. How would she ever relate to this crew? She didn't look forward to spending twenty-nine more days working on a project with them.

"Is Uxa going to show up?" asked the wisp of a girl next to Van. "Do you know?"

The girl sat slumped in her chair.

Doesn't she realize manners reflect your upbringing? Her slouching at the dinner table is an insult to her family. "Don't know. Sorry." Van begrudgingly admired the girl's wide, pale-blue eyes and her pure, simple beauty. Still, Van felt too drained to hold a conversation with someone she didn't know and hoped the girl wouldn't talk to her again. She envied Paley, getting to sit next to an empty chair.

"Hi." Paley bent forward and reached across Van, extending her hand to the girl. "I'm Paley."

"Daisy Lake." The girl reached over and shook Paley's hand.

Van feared Paley might break a bone if she squeezed too hard.

Now that Paley had displayed proper etiquette, Van felt obligated to offer an introduction. "Van."

Daisy's hand rested in Van's as delicately as a flower petal. Having someone this lame in the group meant there was no way Uxa would send them to do anything dangerous. Daisy looked as if a strong wind would blow her away.

"Are you okay?" Van asked. "You look a bit tired."

"I had a rough time getting here," Daisy said in her airy voice. "I'm fine now, thanks." She bent forward and said to Paley, "I like your eyes. Are they common in your family?"

"No," Paley said, taken aback. "They're contact lenses."

Van didn't have time to wonder what kind of doofus would think Paley's eyes were natural, because, as Daisy leaned back frowning, the boy seated on the other side of her leaned forward.

"Ugh. Not *you*," Van said.

"Good to see you too." Brux flashed that infuriating smile.

"Ohhh. Brux. Hi." Paley leaned her elbows on the table and twisted her shoulder under her chin. "Brux Lake and Daisy Lake. Are you two related?"

"He's my brother," Daisy said.

Brux gave a proud nod.

"Attention, please." Fynn appeared in the doorway.

Everyone quieted down.

"HG Huxatec is busy attending to the final details of your mission. She wishes for you to start dinner without her and will join you as soon as she is able."

"What about our briefing?" a girl with a dark blond mohawk cried. She was dressed in combat leather and built like a refrigerator.

"You'll be briefed after dinner," Fynn said. "For now, I suggest you eat. The road ahead will not be easy."

This caused some murmuring until Fynn pushed a red button on the wall nearest him.

Behind Van, a panel the length of the room slid open, displaying a buffet-style banquet. Mouthwatering aromas permeated the air. Plates and bowls overflowed with an assortment of foods: roasted turkeys and baked sweet potatoes, spiral hams with clover sauce, sliced roast beef with mushroom gravy, homemade breads, and a variety of fresh veggie side dishes, along with all the fixings.

The brutes stormed the buffet.

Brux stayed back and waited with his sister.

Van and Paley held back as well, for fear of being trampled to death.

Once the others got their meals and sat down, Van, Paley, Brux, and Daisy made their way to the buffet.

Van passed on the meats but shoveled the fire-roasted potatoes onto her plate. "I'm vegan," she told Daisy.

"Me too," Daisy said in her whisper of a voice. "The thought of harming animals makes me ill. I'd rather die than hurt an animal to feed myself."

"Uh, yeah. I love animals too." Van placed a small scoop of mixed vegetables onto her plate along with a half slice of hearth bread.

Paley snickered at Van's response. She knew Van had become vegan mainly to lose weight, not so much for the animals.

People kept the conversation over dinner to a minimum until they finished at least their second or third helping. Except for Van, who was on a perpetual diet, and Daisy, who barely touched any of her food.

The butch girl with the mohawk rose from her seat. She wiped her mouth with the back of her left hand, which Van noticed was missing the index finger.

"I think we should go around the table, introduce ourselves, mention our special skills." The girl jabbed the air with her finger nub for seemingly no reason, except to make everyone uncomfortable. "I'm sure it's what HG would have us do if she was here."

The others grunted their approval while continuing to stuff the last bits of food into their mouths. Van and Paley nodded. Only Daisy sat motionless, as if she'd heard nothing.

"I'll start. Name's Jorie Alquest. Testing placed me as a weapons expert, allowing me into Advanced Studies after I graduate next year. Also placed expert level in tribal customs but prefer hand-to-hand combat and weaponry." She unsheathed a massive war axe scribbled with runic symbols from her leather belt and held it high. "Meet Zachery. To all you dolts, he's a *labrys*. His curved double blades link him with the power of the moon." She glowed as if speaking about her child and then re-sheathed the terrifying thing.

Jorie sat down, and the girl to her right popped up.

She had crazy-curly, short, white-blond hair and introduced herself as Swanhilda. She ran through a list of impressive survival and combat skills and sat back down. The introduction went from person to person.

All this new information caused Van's head to spin. She swore the boy with a strange name—*Yoatl*—said something about being a wizard. She started to sweat. If her placements had been fixed, as Pernilla had claimed, it meant she didn't have any useful skills.

Van knew she was good at twirling and finding things, but neither compared to the proficiency of these beasts. She dreaded her turn. Telling them her skills would only expose her worthlessness to the group.

And what about Paley? Her talent was being Van's friend. Confessing this to the group would probably get them lynched. Brux would likely lead the pack.

Van's turn came closer. A bead of sweat dripped down her back. She regretted eating so much. Her stomach churned, making her nauseated. This triggered tormenting visions of standing to introduce herself and, instead, vomiting all over the table.

"Don't be nervous," Daisy said in her dreamy voice. "Uxa hand-picked each of us. She didn't base her selections solely on our placement tests."

"Oh." Van breathed a sigh of relief. "That's good." Now Van understood why someone like Daisy—and herself—would be there among these brutes. "What else did she base her selections on?"

"Lineage."

That one word left Van feeling worse than ever. She hadn't earned her birthright, and it wasn't a skill.

She jumped when Fynn bellowed, "Everyone! If I could have

your attention." He stood at the door again. "HG Huxatec has decided to meet with each of you individually before giving you a group briefing."

Van felt grateful for the interruption. She let out a breath and sank into her chair.

Until Fynn said, "First up, Vanessa. Follow me, please."

Chapter 13

D ay 1: 8:04 p.m., Living World

Looking grim, Uxa perched on the edge of her desk in the untidy study. She extended her hand toward the worn, high-backed leather chairs, wanting Van to sit.

Fynn stood to the side of the desk, his arms behind his back, as if Uxa had given the command, "At ease, soldier." The odd grandfather clock read: 700th hour, 56th minute.

"Since Miss Nutting filled you in on our world, I'll get right down to it," Uxa said before Van settled.

"Three nights ago, your father encountered a demon in the field. Demons rarely kill humans, but this one was stronger than average, and it exhibited unusual behavior. It killed your father's partner, Tilly Hopewell. Your father managed to escape."

"He wasn't able to kill the demon," Fynn added, as if Van needed clarification.

Their words stunned Van, prompting her to say in a monotone, "It's the Grigori's job to kill demons."

Uxa's penetrating blue eyes surveyed Van as if considering whether she had suffered brain damage from her trip through the portal.

But hearing someone say, "Your father encountered a demon," point blank, jarred Van. It forced her to face the truth. Demons were real. Her father's job was to fight them. Things she had overheard and seen during her childhood began to make sense, such as her father's scars. *Did he get them fighting demons?*

The scar on Van's back tingled, causing her to shift in her seat.

Uxa gave Van a soft nod. "It is the job of the Grigori to protect the Living World by keeping demons under control in the Earth World. We have protocols in place to ensure this happens. Your father, instead of following protocol, which entails lowering the demon's vibrational frequency and anchoring it, *raised* the demon's frequency—"

"Why would he do that?" Van knew about vibrational frequencies from physics class.

"To help it into our world," Fynn scoffed. "If the demon slips away while being held at a higher frequency, it could find its way here."

Uxa frowned at Fynn, and he stopped talking.

Van didn't like how Fynn made it sound, as if her father had done something wrong. She had already heard enough gossip about him for one day.

"Demons have grown stronger over the last several years," Uxa said to Van. "I gave your father permission to go back into the field, something he had not done since you were born. We are short staffed and need all hands on deck, you could say." Uxa forced a smile.

Van wasn't endeared.

Uxa continued, "Grigori are required to submit field reports to the Balish Council—"

"What does this have to do with my mission?"

"It's called being briefed," Fynn said in a tone that implied Van was dimwitted.

"Thank you, Fynn," Uxa said through gritted teeth. Her eyes remained on Van. "With your father's help, I could alter the reports to hide the steady increase in demon activity in the Earth World, to prevent the Balish from getting nervous and claiming our Grigori were not doing their job. But word reached the council's ears, and I needed to know what King Nequus and Prince Devon were up to, specifically regarding Manik's law."

Uxa slid off the desk and leaned against it, appearing relaxed, but it didn't fool Van. Uxa was someone who always remained alert and ready. And if Uxa had made Van's father fix Grigori reports for her, she was someone who could also be shady.

"Once demons gain enough strength," Uxa said, "they can rise into our world on their own and become a threat to the citizenry. This violates Manik's law, one that protects Lodians and their beliefs from Balish rule, and prevents the Balish from invading our land. It gives the Balish Council the right to receive our field reports for review and to inspect Salus Valde on a whim, but they can't interfere with our daily activities, beliefs, or justice system. The Balish have no choice but to abide by this law, since it is bound by the magic of the Elementals."

The law bored Van. The Elementals being magical sounded cool. Van envisioned a group of divine beings whose supernatural abilities gave them power over mortals. Van wanted to know more about them, but she didn't want to appear stupid. So, she kept her mouth shut.

"Balish may repeal the law if Lodians' beliefs cause direct harm to the Living World," Uxa went on. "Basically, we keep the law intact by controlling the demon situation. With hard evidence of stronger demons, well, the Balish Council would not hesitate to call for an Elemental ruling for the law's repeal, which would remove our protection."

"The Balish have wanted control of Salus Valde for a millennium," Fynn said, unable to keep quiet. "They constantly seek ways around the law so they can take us over."

"I sent your father undercover to spy on the Balish royals," Uxa said. "He got a low-level position as a palace guard in Balefire—the Balish palace—and has worked there for the last few months. When he wasn't working a shift at Balefire or taking a rare day off, I assigned him to the field. This way, he could train new recruits and get firsthand information about demon activity. His partner's death validated demons have grown strong enough to reach our world."

"The only other time in history demons have reached our world was during the Dark War," Fynn said. "No current-day Grigori knows how to kill a Class III."

"Vanessa's been hidden away on Providence Island." Uxa turned her head slightly toward Fynn while keeping a sharp gaze on Van. "She doesn't know about the Dark War."

"Oh, right." Fynn bobbed his head. "Okay, a thousand years ago there was a war between the Lodians and the Balish, called the Great War. It lasted *years* and became so violent, it drew demons into our world. It forced the Lodians and the Balish to work together to defeat this greater enemy, and the Great War became the Dark War. Original documents written during the Dark War aren't available to the public, but we all know the Balish version. Well, all of us except Vanessa."

Van resisted rolling her eyes at him.

Unfazed, Fynn continued, "The Balish Prince Goustav saved our world by using magic to create a weapon powerful enough to defeat the demons. Shortly after the war, Goustav destroyed the weapon, claiming it was necessary for the weapon to be returned to the earth elements. We don't know why he did this or why the Lodians' Grigori couldn't handle the situation or what really happened."

"And we needed to find out." Uxa began pacing. The twists in her long plait caught the light, contrasting the beauty of her hair with her tough demeanor. "The Balish confiscated our ancestral records once they took control after the Dark War. They remained concealed to this day in their Hall of Records, the archives of Balefire."

"So we—er, Uxa changed Michael's mission to comb through

the Hall of Records," Fynn said. "To search for unaltered eyewitness accounts of the Dark War, not Balish-translated propaganda."

Uxa stopped pacing and turned to face Van. "He discovered a bit of Balish lore that claimed Goustav had destroyed only the *physical* part of the weapon. He had contained the powerful *magic* of the weapon in an object that still exists. Hidden in a location bound partly in the spiritual realm and partly in the physical. Accessible by a doorway or a window, where it remains untouched, waiting for someone to retrieve it and use it once again."

Uxa sat on the arm of the high-backed chair across from Van. "He needed to do more research, access more untranslated documents that could help us find this object. With it in our possession, we could keep Manik's law intact by proving to the Elementals we can keep the Living World safe from demons."

"Michael claimed to have found a text called the *Veridicus Libellus*," Fynn said, "commonly referred to by the Balish as Manik's text. King Manik's brother Goustav ousted him from the throne shortly after the Dark War ended. This was when Manik wrote the diary. The text recounts what happened during that time, and afterward, including the object's hiding place and the recipe Goustav used to create his weapon."

Van wasn't sure why, but the little white animal she had seen on the island crossed her mind.

"Because of the impending rise of demons into our world, I instructed your father to get the information from that text as soon as possible," Uxa said. "He planned to retrieve the object himself."

"But it wasn't as simple as it seemed," Fynn said. "The text is a valued artifact from the Dark War, preserved by enchantments and protected by an alarmed, sealed glass case. He had to finagle a way to get at it."

"Last night, he succeeded," Uxa said.

Van frowned. Their annoyance at her father made no sense. "It sounds like my father did everything you asked of him, including risking his life." Without caring how Van felt about it or that she had already lost a mother. "So why are you acting like he did something wrong?"

"The problem is, he disobeyed orders," Fynn said in a tone that implied he took pleasure in pointing out others' faults. "Michael was supposed to read the text only. To go in and out of Balefire undetected. Instead, he *stole* the text, triggering a search for the thief. Which lured Prince Devon into the woods, into a trap, where the prince was ambushed and killed by demons."

"So?" Van felt beyond frustrated. "That wasn't his fault."

"Demons *he* brought here," Uxa said.

Chapter 14

Day 1: 8:33 p.m., Living World

VAN SAT with her mouth hanging open, unmoving, and stared at Uxa.

"Vanessa, I am sorry to tell you this. We think your father stole Manik's text because he is working with the Balish Princess Solana to take over Salus Valde." Uxa paused, possibly to make sure Van hadn't gone comatose, and then continued. "He conspired with demons to kill Prince Devon, so Solana would inherit the throne."

"Incidentally," Fynn said. "The prince's death resulted in another tragedy. Earlier this morning, they found Queen Brigid dead in her bed. Died of a broken heart on hearing news of her son's death."

All was quiet, except for the steady tick, tick, tick of the odd grandfather clock.

"Your father had access to demons," Uxa croaked, overcome with emotion. "As a Grigori in the field, he had access…"

Van used all of her might to whisper, "W-Why? Why would he—?"

"He just… he just…" Uxa also seemed struggling to understand. "He just could not resist the temptation." She cleared her throat before continuing. "The Lodian Consilium was upset by his marriage to your mother. Your father had common blood, and your mother was royal with the purest of bloodlines."

"Lodian bloodlines are called 'royal,' despite our government being a democratic republic," Fynn added.

"Given your father's blood, your parents would pass down a diluted bloodline to their children—you," Uxa said. "Our tribe encourages its people to keep our bloodlines pure, based on family lineage. We believe maintaining the purity pleases the Elementals and strengthens our tribe."

"We discourage Grigori from marrying, and from having children," Fynn said. "Their first commitment is to their career. Family always comes second to their oath. Because of this, the consilium took your father out of the field, demoted from being a lead Grigori to the position of third assistant, an office job. They banished him and your mother to live on Providence Island. He had an ax to grind. If he was after power by marrying Aelia, he didn't get it."

Van didn't care about the Lodians' crazy bloodline rules, or her father's Grigori commitment, or Fynn's rudeness. "Demoted? I thought he voluntarily stepped down to raise me." This devastating revelation hinted her father didn't love Van as much as she had hoped.

Fynn opened his mouth to say something, Uxa shot him a warning glare, and he closed it.

"Your father sought his revenge through Solana. He waited, biding his time until the right opportunity came along." Uxa collected herself before going on.

Fynn gladly picked up the slack. "He never checked in after his shift ended at Balefire last night, which is protocol, and now he's disappeared. We placed him at the scene, and he has motive." Fynn grew animated, as if he were telling an exciting story, which made Van feel even iller. "To inherit the throne, Solana needed someone else to take the blame for her brother's death. We believe Michael smuggled demons here through the portal."

"It worked twofold," Uxa said, looking woeful. "Demons removed the block to Solana's ascension to the throne, and demons being on Living World soil jeopardized our protection from Manik's law. Taking over Salus Valde is a great way for Solana to prove her worth to the Balish Council."

"As a female heir, she will have to do ten times more work than her brother would have done," Fynn said.

"We think your father's payment for helping Solana will be ruling Salus Valde," Uxa said.

"Why doesn't my father just attack with a bunch of demons, then?" Van asked. "Is that my mission? Fighting demons?"

"Demons can't maintain a high enough vibrational frequency on their own to stay here for an extended period," Fynn explained. "Unless they get strong enough to rise using their own power. Your father brought demons to our world, and Solana used dark magic to keep them here, to do her bidding only. It would have drained her energy to hold them here any longer."

Uxa stood and began pacing again. "The official stance out of Balefire is the demon attack results from the Grigori not doing their job."

"B-But, she... they...," Van spluttered.

"Yeah. That's right." Fynn bobbed his head again. "Solana and Michael are framing the Grigori."

"The Balish claim we allowed demons to reach our world, and the cost for our failure is the repeal of Manik's law. Excluding Article 57, the section of the law that restricts adult Lodians from leaving the boundary of Salus Valde. It benefits the Balish to keep that part of the law intact because it allows them to track us."

"But my father went out of bounds. How else could he have worked at Balefire?"

"He used a device that allowed him to get around the Balish squawkers—their tracking system," Uxa said. "That device is now missing. This is why I asked if he had given you anything last night before he disappeared. There was no transport record of his return trip back to the island. But he could have left something for you to find later. Did you find anything?"

Van thought hard about it, but her father hadn't given her anything or left anything for her. She hadn't even seen him yesterday. But she had found a singed text in his fireplace. Was that the device?

Van shook her head.

Uxa gave Van a nod in return, accepting Van's answer. "A death of one of our own is something we could not alter or hide. The Balish Council used that particular Grigori report against us in the chamber meeting today. It was especially damaging, since a couple of days after that incident, demons reached our world, which resulted in the deaths of two members of the Balish royal family. This gave the Balish Council more than enough evidence to prove the demon situation in Earth World is out of control and to call for an Elemental ruling to void Manik's law."

"It gets worse," Fynn said.

"The Balish Council asked the Elementals for permanent control over Salus Valde," Uxa said. "Including decommissioning of the Grigori and giving the Balish full access to the ways and means of the portal, to shift responsibility for controlling the demon population over to them."

"Yeah, yikes," Fynn said, wide-eyed.

"As of the meeting this afternoon, we have realized our worst fears. The Elementals have ruled in favor of the Balish. I pleaded for more time, and it was granted. We have until midnight by the next full moon to prove we can control the demon situation, using all methods available to our tribe." Uxa paused her pacing and turned toward Van. "Which brings us to your mission."

Chapter 15

D ay 1: 8:57 p.m., Living World

"WE NEED to retrieve Goustav's magical object," Uxa said. "The same one Michael read about in Manik's text. It is the only way to protect Salus Valde from a Balish invasion. Your mission is to retrieve this relic."

"I'm not qualified to go. I have no skills." Van remembered Pernilla's harsh words. She crossed her arms. "What if I refuse?"

Uxa and Fynn tensed.

The room became oppressively quiet, except for the persistent ticking of the grandfather clock.

Uxa spoke calmly. "I am sorry, Vanessa, but you are responsible for fixing your own ancestral line. You have a family obligation to complete your father's mission."

"That's not a skill," Van huffed.

"You earned an All-Grades Trophy for Capture the Flag this year," Uxa said. "You excel at twirling."

"But you fixed the games," Van accused in a rush of fear. She also didn't know how twirling would help her find a thousand-year-old relic.

"Manik's law was put in place to prevent another Great War between the Lodians and the Balish," Uxa said. "Without it… well, Grigori are sworn protectors. We will never allow the Balish to rule our land or our people. If Solana invades Salus Valde, there will be destruction of our land, dilution of our culture. A war will tear apart families. And the Balish will not stop there. Once Solana gains access to the Grigori's secrets, she will use the portal to invade Providence Island."

Providence Island? What will happen to my friends? To Canterbury Bells? Astrid's Hollow? Mt. Hope Manor! My clothes! Strangers crawling all over my bedroom—touching my stuff—sleeping in my comfy bed! Using the lavender-scented towels in my bathroom!

"If you are successful, Manik's law will remain intact, and there will be no war. You will bring honor to your family and to yourself by knowing you earned your place."

Van liked the idea of putting to rest Pernilla's rumors about the Elders fixing her test results. She knew if Pernilla believed this, then so did everyone else on the island.

"But?" Van said. "I feel like there's a *but* coming."

"But, you will travel undercover far outside the borders of Salus Valde into hostile Balish territory. We must keep your mission secret. I told you earlier the Balish discovered the increase in demon activity despite our efforts to keep it secret. This means there is a spy in Lodestar."

"It's obvious Michael was the spy," Fynn stated.

"That's easy to say about someone not here to defend himself," Van said, irritated at Fynn for appointing himself judge and jury. Yet she had the sickening feeling he might be right about her father's guilt.

Van trembled, holding back tears. She didn't think she could do what Uxa asked of her, but was being forced to try, anyway.

"You and all the children in the reservation program have been in training to become Grigori ever since you started classes. I have overseen your advancement since kindergarten." A worry line appeared between Uxa's eyebrows. "I carefully selected all of you for this mission. If you refuse, your team's skill set will be out of balance, which will decrease their chance of success."

"Uxa won't tell anyone Michael is your father, if that's what worries you," Fynn said.

Van bit the inside of her cheek, stilling her quivering lip. Although Uxa had said she could refuse, Van felt as if her fate had been set in motion, and she had no choice. To comfort herself, she envisioned how jealous her friends would be over her success, how everyone would hold her in high esteem for saving the island by retrieving Goustav's relic, something she had indisputably earned.

She also didn't want her placement lowered if she refused to go. That would embarrass her and her family. Van didn't want her family name—her mother's respected name—to be disparaged because of something her father might have done, either. And, she could learn more about her mother and uncover the truth about her father if she accepted this mission.

"Okay, I'll do it," Van said, with more bravado than she felt.

Van waited to be dismissed after agreeing to the mission. Instead, Uxa summoned her over to a bookcase.

Uxa pulled a small velvet box from a shelf and opened it. "These were your mother's."

The walls crumbled around Van's residual reluctance. Within the box lay a pair of dangling silver earrings. Van lifted one earring to the light. She peered closely at the tiny interconnected white-gold squares. Separately, the squares appeared plain. Together, they were spectacular.

Although overjoyed with the gift, a troubling thought occurred to Van. According to that woman in the village, Fiona, her father had destroyed all of Aelia's belongings. So, why did Uxa have a pair of Van's mother's earrings? Especially when her father had said he had nothing of her mother's to give her? Van carefully lowered the cherished earring back into its box. "How did you get these? You knew my mother?"

"I only knew Aelia in passing. Your father gave them to me for safekeeping after your mother died. I worked so closely with your father in the years after her death, I felt as if I knew her. She would've wanted you to have them."

"Thanks." Van slipped the jewelry box into her pocket. "Can you tell me anything about her? How come people in Salus Valde know my parents—my birth mother and my father—but nobody seems to know about me?"

Uxa had a distant look in her eyes. "We hold pureblooded Lodians in the highest esteem. Your mother's bloodline was the purest of all. She was a celebrity. Your father became well-known when he married her." She cleared her throat before continuing. "On this journey, you will uncover information about your mother. And, I hope, find your father, before it is too late…" Uxa seemed to get choked up again.

Uxa had just sanctioned Van's ulterior motives for the mission, but the woman's behavior made Van uneasy. She wasn't sure what Uxa meant by *too late* and was afraid to ask.

Uxa cleared her throat again and unexpectedly reached for Van. She gently squeezed Van's shoulders and gazed squarely into her eyes. "Walk strong, my little warrior, and without fear. When someone is marked by fate for good fortune, it comes without fail."

Van didn't have time to digest Uxa's words of wisdom. Before she knew it, Fynn had shuffled her through a secret wall panel and deposited her in a stuffy back hallway.

"Go downstairs and wait in the conference room," he said. "You'll be briefed with the rest of the team after Uxa individually meets with each member."

Halfway down the hall, Van turned back. Maybe Uxa should continue to hold on to her mother's earrings for safekeeping until Van returned. She paused at the doorway and overheard Uxa talking to Fynn. She put her ear to the door, hoping to hear gossip about the next candidate.

"The Anchoress-in-waiting's auspicious arrival is a sign from the Creator," Uxa said. "It proves my plan will work."

"Coming here, the way she did, put her at additional risk," Fynn replied. "Her careless disregard is proof she's not ready for this mission. With the unusual circumstances of her mother's death, we're not sure she inherited the ability to access her magical blood-line. The night she was born, clouds blocked the moon, so we don't know what kind of life she will lead. And she's remarkably unskilled."

"Pray to the light of the Creator that her ancestral magic flows strongly in her veins," Uxa said.

One of my teammates has magical veins? And they gave her a code name from a Native Island Legends storybook? Code names were silly… yet she couldn't wait to find out hers. If the Anchoress-in-waiting was someone weak, then Daisy was the most probable candidate. As Uxa had said, Van won the All-Grades Trophy, proving she possessed strength and skill. Relief comforted Van, knowing she wasn't the Anchoress-in-waiting.

She pressed her ear closer to the door and absentmindedly placed her palm on her stomach to calm its queasiness.

"I don't think she'll survive the journey," Fynn persisted. "If she dies, we'll lose her protective bloodline forever. We'll anger the Elementals. Uxa, I hope you know what you're doing."

"The will of the Creator will protected her on her journey," Uxa said. "All the selected children are capable. Testing proved it. We have no time to waste debating the subject. The Alignment began at midnight. My decision about the Anchoress-in-waiting is done."

"The Balish believe the death of a royal twin is a bad omen," Fynn said, "and Devon was the firstborn, a crown prince. Uxa… are you okay sending these children to their deaths?"

An eerie feeling crawled up Van's spine. She didn't want to hear any more of their conversation. She spun around and bolted down the spiral staircase and into the conference room directly under-neath Uxa's study.

The door clicked shut behind her.

Once again, Van found herself closed in a room with no windows. Fighting off waves of anxiety, she sat quietly at the confer-ence table and waited.

Chapter 16

Day 1: 9:21 p.m., Living World

DAISY ENTERED the conference room next. She nodded and glided into the chair next to Van.

Brux followed. He tried not to look disappointed when he saw Van had also accepted the mission and took the seat next to his sister.

One by one, the rest of the group came in and sat down. Everyone in the room remained silent and pensive about the enormity of the upcoming task.

The one person left to arrive was Paley.

Van wiped the back of her wrist across her damp forehead, her nerves on edge. Her heart battered against her ribcage. *Where's Paley?*

Finally, the door burst open, and Paley strode into the conference room, followed by Uxa and Fynn.

Van calmed at the sight of her friend.

"Hey." Paley slid into the seat next to Van.

"What took you so long?" Van hissed.

"They explained everything to me," Paley whispered. "I found out why we had to meet with Uxa alone. We had to accept the mission without peer pressure, by our own free will."

"I bet she used a different angle to sell the mission to each of us." Van remembered Miss Nutting's warning about being manipulated by Uxa. "I guess we all have our reasons for wanting to go."

"I promised to keep your father's identity a secret."

"*Shh*," Van said, terrified the others would overhear Paley's big mouth. "And I promise not to tell anyone you're a *terrigen*."

Paley's eyes widened, and she mimicked zipping her lip.

"Welcome, warriors." Uxa stood at the head of the conference table, her thick braid dangled down the front of her chest. Standing by her side, Fynn held a bulky pile of papers. Uxa leaned forward and placed her palms on the conference table, as if about to whisper.

The others instinctively leaned in, but not Van. She sat straighter, hoping to look attentive, so she wouldn't be called on.

"Congratulations," Uxa said. "You have all agreed to help the Grigori with an important task. Your courage and bravery will not go unnoticed. You are the future leaders of Salus Valde. You have earned the right to walk proud." Uxa pushed herself up from the table. "There is a reason the Balish confiscated all the records from the Dark War and control everything that was written afterward."

Fynn shifted closer to Uxa, as if to lend her support.

Uxa continued, "Ancient passages describe this object we are after as being created in the sun's image—round, yellow, powerful."

"Like a coin?" Brux asked. "A gold coin?"

Uxa gave a curt nod, pleased at Brux's astuteness. "Based on our research, the object able to recreate the weapon Goustav used to defeat the demons during the Dark War is—"

"The Coin of Creation." Brux looked grim.

A stunned silence hung thickly in the conference room.

Paley blurted out, "A coin? All this—for a *coin*?"

Van slid down in her seat.

"This is no ordinary coin, young one," Uxa said, unperturbed. "It is the element of earth embodied in a coin. The Creator formed it with the same force used to forge the lands, made at the same time as our Anchoress warrior bloodline."

"So, it's a coin," Paley muttered.

"Why don't the Balish have it already?" asked Karpos, a massive warrior who resembled a bear. Van couldn't remember his special skill, but it probably had something to do with juggling boulders or crushing things to death.

"The Balish don't have it because the Coin belongs to the Anchoress-in-waiting," Brux said. "And her bloodline was killed off shortly after the Dark War."

Jorie and several of the other warriors shifted uncomfortably over Brux's words.

"Oh, orthodox Lodians, are we?" said one of the smaller but still brawny warriors, smirking at those who squirmed.

Van remembered this one's name. Trey. He oozed good looks and charm. With his swarthy complexion, bole-brown hair, and hazel eyes, he looked unlike the others, who were fair-skinned blonds. His special skills included acrobatics and combat archery. And he was totally full of himself.

"Well," Trey continued. "What do you say to this? Goustav used the Coin to defeat the demons during the Dark War because there was no Anchoress. Didn't exist then. Doesn't exist now. She's a myth, a children's story."

Jorie's lips grew thin, and her eyes popped, looking as if she wanted to clobber Trey.

Uxa held up her palm to stop the chatter. "She exists. Her bloodline survived the Dark War."

"She *exists*?" Yoatl asked with a slackened jaw.

"Where is she?" Swanhilda asked. "Who is she?"

"One person here carries the bloodline of the Anchoress," Uxa said.

"Who is it?" asked several others at once. Their eyes darted around the table, scrutinizing each person. Most of them landed on Daisy, including her brother's.

Daisy continued to sit serenely, like a delicate flower growing out of a crack in a sidewalk.

At least Van was right about Daisy being the Anchoress-in-waiting. It made sense. If the children's fable was real and Daisy had magical powers, they probably emerged after she got her special coin. Why else would someone like her be here?

"For your protection and hers, I have chosen not to reveal her identity," Uxa said. "This way, if you are captured, her existence will remain a secret."

"Hold up," said a cocky brute.

Van recalled his name was Marcus. She remembered his skill set being war strategies and the ability to use two two-handed weapons at once. He claimed his favorites were battle axes, war hammers, and greatswords.

"Trey made a good point," Marcus said. "If the Anchoress existed back then, she would've won the Dark War for us."

"What most know about the Dark War are the stories translated by Balish scribes, skewed to bolster the Balish agenda," Uxa said. "Exact details, Lodian involvement, and what actually happened, especially regarding our Anchoress and the Coin, are vague. My research found the *Veridicus Libellus* is the only document known to recount the Dark War accurately. It also contains a map with the location of the Coin."

"Do you have this text?" Brux asked.

Uxa shook her head. "The official word out of Balefire is demons destroyed the text during the attack on Prince Devon. However, it is in the best interest of the Balish to declare the text destroyed, so others don't go searching for it. Behind closed doors, they haven't ruled out its existence."

Like a rock to the head, Van remembered the text she had found in her father's study. The room shifted and lost all its air. Through sheer willpower, Van expanded her lungs and drew in a breath. The oxygen acted like fuel to the stalled parts of her body.

No, no. Her book couldn't be Manik's text. She had flipped through the entire thing. It didn't have a map.

Uxa continued, "The Anchoress-in-waiting will be drawn to the

Coin like a beacon light. She can intuitively attune herself to its location."

Most of them couldn't help but glance at Daisy again, who remained unaffected by their apparent belief she was the Anchoress-in-waiting.

Van wondered whether Daisy's lack of response resulted from her being too weak, as if she didn't have energy to spare. Van felt uncomfortable at the thought Daisy wasn't fit enough to survive going on this mission. Good thing Brux would be there to watch over his sister.

"Anyone who knows how to read the language of the ancients and had access to the text could've studied the map," said a wiry male warrior named Elmot. "And would have directions to the Coin. There must be others searching for it."

He had a long face and looked like an overlarge elf. Well-groomed, he wore a pressed, spotless tunic. His specialty was navigation and reading maps. He was the smallest of the guys, making him the runt of the warrior litter.

"Many people have searched for the Coin," Uxa said. "None have found it. All have died trying."

"This only serves to validate the presumption that the text is garbage," Trey said. "The Balish think of Manik's text as nothing more than the ramblings of a madman."

"The Balish discredited it because it's full of Lodian folklore and propaganda," Brux said. "Manik was a Lodian sympathizer, even married a Lodian royal, which is why his brother Goustav rebelled and took over his throne shortly after the Dark War."

"Michael Cross obviously stole that text because its information is genuine," Yoatl added.

Van cringed at the mention of her father.

Paley stopped picking at her gel nails and looked up.

"Based on our intelligence," Uxa said, "we can confirm Michael and Solana are going after the Coin."

Van's stomach dropped.

"Having the Coin will ensure Solana's takeover of Salus Valde,"

Trey said. "It'll secure her position on the throne from being challenged by the male Balish royals."

"Solana's soldiers are scouring the countryside," Uxa continued. "Allegedly seeking vengeance against the thief who stole the text and lured her brother Prince Devon into a demon trap. This action by Solana leads me to believe Michael lost the text, and Solana is using her brother's death as an excuse to go searching for it."

"She's after the map?" Elmot asked, his tone high-strung. "Why? She must have the entire text memorized."

Paley stopped chewing on her cuticle. "Do you know how hard it is to memorize an entire book? Or a map?" Her finger zipped back to her mouth.

Van nodded in agreement, thinking about how tough her classes were in school.

"It's about control," Trey said. "Solana's trying to prevent others from going after the Coin. Anyone who finds the text will go after it."

"Makes sense," Brux said. "Even with her father's massive army at her disposal, Solana would benefit from getting the Coin. We know from the Dark War, anyone skilled enough can harness its energy to create a great weapon. She wouldn't risk letting something like that getting into our hands, not with her planned invasion of Salus Valde."

"Michael is probably headed toward the Coin as we speak." Marcus banged his meaty fist on the table.

Van's mouth felt too dry to gulp. She had undergone training in her special classes, mock-battles where she learned twirling wasn't only a beautiful form of dance, but a combat skill. Her classes had been simulations. Role-playing. Not real life. By following the path to the Coin, she would inevitably run into her father—and then what?

"Does this mean the Escalation has begun?" Daisy asked in her airy voice, startling everyone. "Demons in the Earth world. Demons in our world. Sounds like the first stage of Dishora. According to legend, darkness gains the strength to extinguish all light every thousand years. The Anchoress must fight against this darkness to ensure light continues to govern the worlds."

Daisy's interest in the legend made sense. She was the Anchoress-in-waiting. Van could hang back and let the others do most of the work, while Daisy got the Coin, and faced Van's father. Not Van.

Yet Van became saddened for Daisy. She had overheard Fynn mention the Anchoress-in-waiting's mother had died. Van could relate to that. Maybe their mother's death accounted for Brux being a jerk and Daisy so frail.

"The Coin of Creation will help our Anchoress do that," Jorie stated.

"Right now, we need the Coin to prevent a Balish invasion," Uxa said. "Stay focused, people."

"I wish we had the map," Elmot whined.

"We need to look at what we have, not at what we do not have," Uxa said. "Article 57 of Manik's law is still in place, in our favor. Thank the light of the Creator the—"

A few of them, including Jorie, interrupted by using their hand to make a sideways figure-eight motion in front of their chests while they mumbled, "Thank-the-light-and-all-that-is-good," the same way Harrus had done.

Uxa paused, then, after they were done, continued, "—the Elementals would not allow a squawker on children during the creation of Manik's law. You are all under eighteen and can leave Salus Valde without being tracked by the Balish."

"Ho-yeah," Jorie bellowed. "The Balish would never suspect Lodian children to be out of bounds. Lodians are fiercely protective of their kids."

Fynn swooped by and dropped a folded parchment paper in front of Van. It contained a hand-written physical description, a headshot, personal information, and official stamps and signatures.

"Fynn has handed out your forged border passes," Uxa said. "I must warn you, even with papers, it is best to avoid the border guards. Solana had her father put tighter controls on all border crossings and has squadrons secretly searching travelers for Manik's text. She believes whoever stole the text is the thief who caused Prince Devon to leave the palace and is therefore responsible for the prince's and the queen's deaths. She also believes if the Grigori had done their job, demons would not have been there. Solana's acting outraged. But we know she assassinated her brother for the throne. This makes your mission much more dangerous."

The stuffy room made it challenging for Van to keep her breathing steady.

"What's our cover story?" Brux perused his border pass.

"You will travel as marketeers' scouts. For those of you who might not know, they are children from Hod who scour the lands searching for merchandise to bring back to their parents for sale in the marketplace. When questioned, you will claim your parents sent you to search for the Runestar, a brooch of great value dating back to the Dark War. Rumors of it resurfacing constantly crop up, making it a viable cover story. It is not uncommon for the marketeers of Hod to send their expendable children on a high-risk, low rate of success task. It is too risky for you to carry anything marketeers' scouts would not normally have on them. Like communication devices."

Several people groaned.

Someone grumbled, "No multi-tracks? How are we going to contact you if we have a problem?"

Uxa appeared unbothered by the group's reaction. "Multi-tracks are far too valuable for marketeers' scouts to have. Keep in mind, if Solana discovers your actual mission, she will see you as a threat and have you executed."

"Do we have *any* idea where the Coin is hidden?" Yoatl asked.

"Sources tell me the probable location is in the deep south, in the Pusiel region."

Elmot straightened. His eyes shot wide open. "The only way to Pusiel is through Aduro. We're talking Balish territory, not Balish-occupied territory."

Uxa waved her hand to settle the group. "You were all chosen because, collectively, you can succeed. Each team will contribute to the success of this mission in its own way."

"Wait. What?" Van said. "*Each* team?"

"I will break you into two teams," Uxa declared. "Smaller groups can move easier without drawing attention to themselves, and can cover more ground."

Disgruntled muttering erupted around the table.

Uxa raised her voice. "My selections are final."

Van panicked, terrified Uxa would separate her and Paley. Then remembered Uxa *had* to keep them together.

Paley nervously clasped Van's hand under the table.

Van leaned in and whispered, "She won't separate us because of the Twin Gemstones."

Paley gave Van's hand a squeeze. "Maybe Brux will be on our team."

Van hoped for the opposite.

"We will know the first team as Delta. On this team are Jorie Alquest, Trey Catherwood, Elmot Entwistle, Brux Lake, Paley Ash, and…"

Uxa's pause felt everlasting to Van.

"Vanessa Cross."

"Yes!" Paley crushed Van's hand in an excited grip.

Van wasn't sure whether Paley was happy about *her* being on the same team or *Brux*. Van was just glad no one made the connection between her and Michael Cross. At least, not yet.

"On team Echo is Swanhilda Ragge, Marcus Crompton, Karpos Ledo, Yoatl Xifaras, and Daisy Lake."

All the team Echo members, excluding Daisy, leaped from their seats and made whooping noises as they gathered together, clutching one another with rough hand-grabs and slapping the others on the back as if they had just won a prize.

Van could see why. Team Echo comprised the super-muscular beasts of the group. Again, except Daisy, who was most likely the Anchoress-in-waiting and therefore ensured the success of their team.

Jorie, who fit right in with team Echo, fumed at being placed on what she probably considered the losing side. The team with smaller warriors, relying on luck to find the Coin.

Daisy rose from her chair and drifted over to team Echo.

"Wait a minute." Brux popped out of his seat. "Why are you separating me from Daisy? I can't protect her if we're on different teams."

"I'll protect her." With a lecherous grin, Marcus cupped Daisy with his massive arm and roughly pulled her close.

Van inhaled sharply, fearing he might snap Daisy in half.

"Hands off!" Brux roared. He lunged across the table.

Jorie grabbed Brux by the collar and pulled him back.

Team Echo, minus Daisy, laughed at Brux's futile attempt to throttle Marcus.

"Stop!" Uxa shouted.

Fynn shook his head at Brux.

"Another outburst like that, Brux, and you are off the mission, understood?" Uxa seemed more worried than angry. "Now *sit down*! Everyone."

Brux slouched in his seat, still glaring at Marcus.

Marcus goaded Brux with a smirk.

The rest of each team's members settled on opposite sides of the table, facing one another. Team Echo appeared smug. Team Delta, humble.

"The leader of team Echo will be Swanhilda Ragge."

Team Echo let out thunderous grunts of approval and fist-bumped Swanhilda.

Van felt another flash of terror. No way did she want to be team leader. It would be too much work.

"Team Delta's leader… Jorie Alquest."

Jorie's shoulders slumped as if the weight of the worlds had been dumped on them. Even her mohawk seemed to wilt.

As chatter rose around the table, Uxa pulled Fynn aside and spoke privately with him.

Paley leaned close to Van and whispered, "Uxa should've picked you. You always get the top spots on the island. You should be hopping mad."

Van grunted and shrugged, to cover up just how relieved she was not to be chosen.

"What an insult," Paley kept on. "I trust you as my leader more than *Jorie*. That girl scares me."

Van shrugged again and said, "Jorie better not think she's going to tell me what to do."

"Me, either. *Say* something," Paley urged. "*You* should be team leader."

Van wished Paley would shut up, because now that Van thought about it, yeah, she should have been picked, given her lineage.

"Say something," Paley persisted. "Go." She gave Van a push.

Now Van had to go, to save face. With the teams chatting and getting to know each other, the time was right. Van meandered to the front of the conference room.

Uxa stopped talking when Van approached. She turned away from Fynn and stared at Van expectantly.

Instead of complaining about not being team leader, Van said, "I want to go home."

Chapter 17

Day 1: 10:57 p.m., Living World

U̲x̲a̲ ̲l̲e̲d̲ Van to a private corner of the room and said, "Talk to me."

"I'm useless—"

"Afraid," Uxa said. "You are afraid. This is normal. Everyone at that table feels the same way."

In a pause where neither one spoke, the air hung heavy between them.

"It sounds like you would rather not try." Uxa's lips formed a straight line. "But your fate was sealed the moment you accepted this mission. Now, the only way out is through."

"What if I run into my father?" Van's eyes brimmed with tears. "Fight him to the death over some *coin*?"

Uxa grasped Van's elbow and guided her closer to the wall. "Vanessa, your father is in great danger and does not know it."

"W-What do you mean?" Van's anxiety flared.

"Demons are created from the negativity of terrigens, from the lesser part of themselves, yet demons are drawn to higher vibrations, like the light of the Living World. Light is a threat to their 'food source,' because those who worship the light are peaceful, hopeful, and full of love. It is the reflection of the Creator and represents all that is good."

"Okay. I get that." Van wriggled her elbow.

Uxa released her grip. "The demons your father escorted into this world did not survive, but demons have a collective mind." Uxa leaned forward and lowered her voice. "For the first time in a thousand years, they have reached the light of our world. It reawakened the darkness of their nature. Now, they will stop at nothing to get here. Demons seek the light, not to become one with it, but to destroy it."

Uxa shifted her body as if to brace herself against what she had to say next. "As for your father, there is a consequence to the soul when a person conspires with evil."

"Consequence?" Van paled.

"It is much harder to return to the light after being seduced by darkness," Uxa explained. "Evil is tempting. It lies, manipulates, tricks. Your father turned away from the light the moment he entered into a pact with demons. He will do anything to get the Coin. Without it, he will not rule Salus Valde."

"He can still come back." *To me.* "He can be good again."

"Vanessa, the Coin itself has inherent magical properties from which anyone can benefit, but it also has a dark side. If a person accesses the power of the Coin without pure intent, or against the good of the light, then the Coin's energy will magnify the dark part of their Self and cause the person to fall further into darkness."

Uxa placed a gentle hand on Van's shoulder. "Your father has aligned with the Balish agenda of domination and has conspired with demons. If he even touches the Coin, its power will lure him and he will suffer a fate worse than death. Darkness will consume him. His soul will be lost forever."

Van trembled from head to toe. She couldn't go home now, and talking with Uxa made her even more terrified about the mission.

Van slunk back to her seat and didn't answer Paley's inquisitive stare.

Uxa shouted, "Ticktock, people," loud enough to bring the group to order. "The Elementals have given us thirty days, counting today. Your mission is to find the Coin of Creation and bring it back to me at Lodestar before midnight of the next full moon."

Uxa glanced at each of them as she continued, "The Elementals require the Coin as proof the Grigori can fulfill their duties. Obtaining it will keep Manik's law intact so the Balish cannot attack Salus Valde, thus preventing another Great War between our tribes. The negative energy caused by a war of that magnitude would be enough for demons to reach our world."

Karpos cried, "We got this!"

Hoots and cheers from team Echo filled the room.

"My warriors," Uxa called out.

The team hushed.

"Your path will be dangerous and difficult. I ask each of you to walk strong, cling to your inner light, and use discipline to achieve your goal. When you find yourself doubting, remember this: you are the chosen ones. You will succeed. You must. The survival of Salus Valde depends on it." Uxa let her words sink in, then gestured to dismiss them. "For now, you rest. Roll call is at five a.m."

Once Van and Paley were back in their room, Paley chattered nonstop.

"I can't wait to see where my parents came from... Brux is so cute... too bad you didn't get team leader..."

Midnight neared. Van and Paley changed into nighttime t-shirts and shorts and then slipped into bed.

Van sank into her mattress, exhausted. Instead of falling asleep, she stared at the ceiling. The bloody patch with the name Rogziel drifted into her mind. It had to be a clue from the night her father disappeared, which was why the little animal had been determined she keep it.

Van needed to find Rogziel. She felt sure he had relevant information about the attack on Prince Devon. Maybe he'd survived the attack. Finding him meant finding out the truth about her father.

Van jumped out of her skin when a soft chirrup broke through the tranquility of the bedroom. The little animal had returned and sat on top of her backpack, as cute and glowy-white as ever. It bounced on its springy tail. Its long, bunny-like ears arched for balance.

"Brrrup mrpt." Its round eyes stared at Van.

"You again? How'd you get to this world? Or this room, even?" Van eyed the crack under the door, and wondered whether the little thing could squish underneath, the same way kittens did in her world. She flung off her sheets and tiptoed over to the little animal.

It bounded upright off its coiled tail, which then retracted down to a fluffy ball on its backside. Its tiny white paws twinkled like stars as it padded in a full circle.

The funny little thing grew on Van. "Since you keep showing up, I'm going to give you a name. I'll call you… Wiglaf."

Wiglaf pattered around in circles and then stopped to peer at Van. Finally, she noticed what it was romping on. The text! "How'd you get that out of my backpack?"

"Mrruwp eep," Wiglaf answered.

Van flicked on the desk light, hoping it wouldn't wake Paley, shooed Wiglaf away, and picked up the text. The partly burned title still read **ridicus Lib***lus.*

Veridicus Libellus! This book *was* Manik's text!

Wiglaf butted his head against the book.

"Okay, okay. I'll open it," Van said, catching on. "But it's written in a language I can't read. Jeepers. For something so cute, you can be annoying."

She moved her backpack and sat at the desk. Using the tips of her fingers, she carefully turned through the crumbling pages, searching for anything that made sense. Out of frustration, she flipped the pages back and forth, back and forth. She noticed when she fanned the pages… she could see… *yes*! It was a map, hidden throughout the pages of the text.

Van saw a circle with a pentagram in its center. The drawing looked like a coin. She kept flipping the pages and gasped when the strange writing around the circle became clear to her. *Item of Creation*. It was the Coin of Creation! *The* Coin!

Van's stomach churned in anguish. She had the map to the Coin. But she couldn't tell anyone because… because… her father had attempted to burn it.

She wiped her eyes, trying not to get the text wet with her gushing tears. Van hadn't truly believed he had sided with Solana and was conspiring with demons. But now, the burned book was evidence that proved otherwise. No Lodian would destroy a text that described the location of a weapon so powerful, it would protect them from an invasion by the Balish and from demons. Unless he was a traitor.

Van recalled the dream she'd had in the bushes outside the manor when she witnessed her father throwing Manik's text into the fireplace.

He had said, "Let us hope… no Lodian… ever lays a hand on this."

While she was in the bushes, the patch had slid from the binding of the text. Van's hand had lain close enough for her to get a visual impression of her father following Solana's orders to burn the book so their enemies wouldn't have a map to the Coin. Both of them were aware the Lodians' Anchoress-in-waiting could intuitively locate the Coin, but, as Fynn and Uxa had mentioned, the Anchoress heir was weak and unskilled. Something Van had in common with Daisy. Van's father and Solana seemed confident they would find the Coin before the Lodians' Anchoress-in-waiting did.

But why had her father burned the text in his study? He could have gotten rid of the text anywhere. What was so important that he would risk going back to the manor? And what made him leave before he knew the text was destroyed?

With a sense of dread, Van realized if anyone caught her with the book in her possession, it would look as if she were working with her father. No one, not even Uxa, would believe in her innocence. They would accuse her of treason, spying, and conspiring with demons. She'd be blamed for the murder of Prince Devon and the death of Queen Brigid. This text was dangerous.

Her first impulse was to chuck the book out the nearest window, but solid walls surrounded her. The bathroom! Flush the text! She hurried to the toilet, crashed onto her knees, and was about to tear the book to pieces when a shrill "Whurrup!" halted her.

Van raised her eyes to Wiglaf, sitting on the tank.

His ears stood up straight and alert. He rested his paws on the text Van held between her trembling hands and chattered in his animal talk.

The dark blue of Wiglaf's eyes filled Van with tranquility. She felt calm, composed. What was she thinking? She couldn't destroy the text. Her mission depended on its information. Hadn't her father tried to destroy it too? Van shuddered. Maybe she was more like him than she realized. "All I have to do is keep it hidden."

Wiglaf leaned back onto the toilet tank.

Van reached over and scratched the animal behind his ears. "Thanks, little guy."

She left the bathroom, tiptoed past Paley, and tucked the text into her backpack. She slipped into bed and pulled the sheets over her head. A thump landed on the mattress. She heard a rumbling purr and then felt little paws as they kneaded a place to nest on her stomach. Eventually, Wiglaf settled in, and Van fell into a restless sleep.

Her dreams were plagued with images of faceless soldiers dressed in black. They slashed bloody swords, slaughtering innocent toga-wearing bystanders and anyone who got in their way as they relentlessly pursued Van.

Chapter 18

Day 2: 4:35 a.m., Living World

A SHARP KNOCK jerked Van awake.

"Get up, warriors. It's near five a.m.," a voice called through the door. It was Fynn. "Time's a-tickin'."

Despite feeling as if she had gone to bed only seconds ago, Van awoke rested and ready to go. She made a move to leap out of bed but stopped, due to a warm weight on her stomach. *Wiglaf!*

The critter lifted its cute face and raised half an ear.

A moving lump groaned from the other bed.

Van scooped up Wiglaf. "Sorry, little guy," she whispered, getting out of bed. "But I can't let Paley see you." They were in a hurry, and the distraction of showing Paley the cute animal would make them late.

She hurried to her backpack, pulled out some clothes and Twinkle Toes and dropped them on her bed. Then she tucked Wiglaf inside.

Paley rose, and they rushed around the room getting dressed.

"Do these make me look more Lodian-y?" Paley emerged from the bathroom wearing electric-blue contact lenses, probably with Brux in mind.

"Sure," Van said, and then made sure they both had their Twin Gemstones secured in their pockets.

A few minutes after five, they hurried downstairs dressed in jeans and sneakers and toting their backpacks.

On the way, Van recalled last night's dream, the one that had stopped the nightmare of faceless soldiers. A woman had appeared, ghostlike and ethereal, wearing an amaranthine dress that flowed in a mystical breeze. Her waist-length hair, perhaps once blond, had long ago lost its youthful color. The woman's compassionate light-blue eyes held many secrets. Her alabaster skin managed to escape the ravages of time.

Van knew this woman. She had appeared in Van's dreams as a child and still looked exactly the same. Her name was Jacynthia.

Overjoyed to see her childhood friend, Van tried to speak, but the words stuck in her throat.

Jacynthia paid no notice and said stoically, "A time has come when there is a darkening of the light in the external worlds. You must use this journey to build your spiritual Self. Carry peace in your heart, for if you attach to darkness, you will be swallowed by it and suffer great misfortune. Do you understand?"

Van nodded, too insecure to admit she didn't understand.

"When challenges arise during your journey, turn to me for guidance." Jacynthia blurred and flickered. "A person without spiritual sustenance can inadvertently stray from the light during challenging times. Call on me..." Jacynthia faded into the night.

Van wanted to tell Paley about the return of Jacynthia, but they had entered the dining room, the last to arrive. Again.

"Hey, Jorie," Swanhilda bellowed. "The rest of your team finally decided to show up."

Snorts of laughter rumbled from team Echo, whose members were busy throwing the last of their gear together. All except Daisy, who sat on the floor in a corner.

Team Echo had dressed down. Some wore plain handsewn t-shirts with loose-fitting jackets, some had frayed buttoned-down shirts, and all of them wore cargo pants and hiking boots. Although team Echo had finished eating breakfast, some still managed to fling a few hot cross buns at Van and Paley as they joined team Delta.

"We're on time." Van stiffened. "Did we miss something?"

Last night's dinner table and chairs were gone, and the panel in the wall had been opened. Except now the buffet counter was covered with gear—ropes, backpacks, maps, compasses, daggers, and pickaxes.

"It's okay." Jorie sat cross-legged on the floor, sharpening Zachery a little too aggressively. Her tight grip made her nub-finger even more noticeable. "We got here early. Doesn't matter. We're all here now."

"Hey, team Dud," Marcus yelled from across the room. "We're going south through Tipereth Forest."

"Thanks for the notice," Brux said. "I'll be sure to let the Balish know."

"I'm only telling you, so you don't follow us, meathead," Marcus growled.

Karpos sneered. "Your pathetic team won't last one second outside Salus Valde."

"Ignore them," Jorie warned before Brux could retort. She barely glanced at Van and Paley and said, "Grab some breakfast and get packing."

"*Where?*" Paley mouthed to Van.

Van flicked her shoulder and shook her head. There was no food to be found.

"Use the boundless bowl," the lanky warrior, Elmot, said cheerfully. He shoved a worn, wooden bowl at Van. "Sorry, there's only one left, and we had to fight team Echo to keep them from taking it." He sighed and glanced over at the counter. "They took all the best stuff. Must not have slept more than an hour."

"Thanks." Van tried to keep the sarcasm out of her voice. She flipped the empty bowl over and back, wondering where there was supposed to be food.

Paley shrugged, also baffled.

Elmot caught on. "It's enchanted. Hold the bowl in both hands. Ask for what you want to eat or drink. Keep the food pictured in your mind, and it will fill. It takes a high skill level of magic to leave a self-generating imprint on an object. Boundless bowls are very rare. I'm impressed Uxa got five."

Paley leaned toward Van and shouted, "Bacon sandwich!" at the boundless bowl. Nothing happened.

"Let me try." Van held the bowl as instructed and said, "Two tofu scramble sandwiches," while picturing them in her mind. Instantly, two warm tofu sandwiches appeared in the bowl, exactly as Van had visualized.

Paley grabbed one. "Mmm. They smell incredible."

They scurried to a corner to eat.

Yoatl and Karpos walked by, nearly stepping on them.

Van overheard Yoatl say to Karpos, "Michael Cross, he's not worth the dirt he stands on."

"I hope I run into him." Karpos smashed his fist into the palm of his hand.

Van put her sandwich down, no longer hungry.

"Not gonna eat this?" Paley snatched Van's half-eaten sandwich and gleefully took a bite.

"Do the last check of your gear, team," Swanhilda announced to the room. "Time to get moving." Her entire team—excluding Daisy, who carried no equipment—wore enormous backpacks with ropes, picks, and other gear hanging off.

"Daisy!" Brux rushed over to his sister.

Daisy tried to meet him halfway, but Marcus roughly grabbed the back of her shirt, snapping her backward.

"No fraternizing with the enemy." Marcus smirked at Brux. "Don't worry, big brother. I'll take *real* good care of her. I'll personally make sure she's tucked into bed every night."

Brux charged at Marcus.

Jorie and Swanhilda raced over to break up the fight, each pulling back her own teammate.

"Enough!" Jorie cried. She glowered at Swanhilda. "Just leave."

Marcus and the other Echoes ignored Jorie's request, mumbled a few insults about team Delta, and continued checking their gear.

Brux pulled Daisy aside.

They clasped right wrists.

Brux's eyes welled up. "Walk in light, sister." He broke from the parting ritual and pulled her in for a hug.

"Live in bliss, brother," Daisy said, smothered by Brux, her eyes dewy.

"'Cause heaven's right here, *brother*." Marcus pointed to his crotch as he thrust his hips forward.

Karpos and Yoatl guffawed.

Trey and Elmot were on Brux, holding him back.

"Brux! Stop," Daisy pleaded. "Let us live in peace."

Jorie flung Zachery. It cut into the floor, barely an inch from Marcus's feet. "Leave," Jorie said through clenched teeth.

Swanhilda put a calming hand on Marcus's shoulder. She glared at Jorie and shouted, "Echo—we're out!"

After team Echo left, the room seemed strangely quiet. Fighting the unsettled feeling they were already behind, Van grabbed Paley and they hurried over to select their gear. Two used backpacks sat on the table. They each reached for one when Jorie stopped them.

"You guys are too small to carry one of those on your back. You'll have to make do with the backpacks you have." She stared at Van's. "Wish I could dirty yours up a bit, though." Jorie shook her head despairingly, then commanded, "Get rid of most of your personal items and pack some gear from the table."

Van grabbed whatever was smallest: a compass (she wasn't sure how to use it), a detailed map of the northern region (in case the map in the text correctly showed the Coin's location), a book of matches (she tucked them into her pocket), a coil of rope ("Long enough for most purposes," Trey told her), and a brushed leather pouch shaped like a teardrop ("Fill it with water from the boundless bowl," Elmot suggested).

Paley grabbed her choice of gear and tossed the articles into her backpack.

"Pack these." Jorie shoved thick, black sunglasses, wooly scarves, leather gloves, small squares made of silky brown material (Van had no idea what they were), and ugly weather-resistant utility jackets at both of them. "Just in case."

Van carefully packed all the items around Wiglaf as he snoozed in a mesh inner pocket. She took out her hairbrush and began stroking her hair.

"Van, ditch the hairbrush," Jorie said. "It's too fancy to support our cover story. You two need to change into clothes that fit your new role." She pointed to the far corner of the counter at a heap of tattered clothes. "Leave your own clothes here. All of them." She eyed both Van and Paley. "They're a dead giveaway you're not marketeers' scouts."

"You want me to wear *those*?" Van said, horrified.

"And leave anything else that would be incriminating. I'll check your packs in a bit."

Van and Paley dug through the mound of clothes.

Van complained the whole time. "Cheap." "Ugly." "Wouldn't be caught dead in it."

Finally, they found the most tolerable styles and went behind a dividing screen to change. Van decided on worn khaki cargo pants covered with pockets and a ribbed white tank top, which at least looked clean, to wear under a long-sleeved, frayed khaki shirt, again with lots of pockets. She pulled her hair through the opening in the back of a shabby cap.

Paley picked the same outfit, except in tan, claiming it would better complement her blue eyes.

Van went to put her sneakers back on, when Jorie said, "No, they're too expensive-looking." Van was forced to put on *used* hiking boots. She wanted to gag.

She held back tears as she put aside her own clothes and packed several shabby scout's outfits into her backpack. Wiglaf still lay hidden in the mesh pocket, sleeping soundly. She tucked the matchbook into one of the many pockets in her cargo pants and concealed the Twin Gemstone, her mother's earrings, and her hairbrush the same way. Manik's text was too cumbersome for her pants, so she tucked it into a bottom pocket inside her backpack.

"Here." Jorie handed small coin pouches to each person. "It's a few pecs and some stips. Not much, but it's consistent with our cover story." When Jorie got to Van and Paley, she glanced into each of their unzipped backpacks.

"Good." Jorie dropped the coin pouch into Van's palm.

Van was relieved Jorie didn't pat her down or rifle through her backpack. If Jorie had, she would have noticed Van's contraband.

Paley dumped the coins into her palm to get a look.

Van did the same. Several larger bronze coins marked "one pec" were imprinted with a Royal Balish Mint stamp, the same imprint as on the coin Van had used to pay for the candy. Except hers had been gold and was called a bagoc. She figured the imprinted coins were more valuable. The others were presumably "stips." Worn, thin, unstamped coins. Two were silver; the rest, bronze. She added the change she'd gotten from the candy store to her pouch and then slipped it into her backpack.

Elmot tucked the coin pouch into one of the many pockets in his cargo pants. "Which way we headed, boss?" he asked Jorie with a smile.

Trey rolled his eyes.

Jorie replied, "The best way to the Pusiel region is south through Tipereth Forest—"

"No way are we following team Echo," Brux said. "I refuse."

Joire's nostrils flared. "*If you let me finish*—the best way by *land* is through the forest, the best way by *water* is the Fulguro River. Traveling by river, we'll get to Pusiel days before team Echo."

As Jorie droned on about the details of her plan, every fiber of Van's being told her that going south to Pusiel was wrong. Manik's text showed the Coin in a northern region called Fomalhaut, but Van couldn't say how she knew of the Coin's location, and Jorie hadn't asked for their ideas.

In a fit of frustration, Van said, "Heading south is stupid. Team Echo is already doing that. We should do the opposite—head north. I mean, duh, we'll cover more ground, and nobody knows for sure the location of the Coin." Van expected everyone to jump at her suggestion, but she was no longer on Providence Island.

Jorie claimed her own plan was better, and team Delta sided with their leader, including Benedict Arnold Paley.

"Seriously?" Van said to Paley.

Paley shrugged. "You were so obnoxious about it, even if you were right, nobody would listen to you."

Team Delta gathered their gear and, as far as Van was concerned, headed the wrong way. East, toward the Fulguro River.

Chapter 19

Day 2: 6:43 a.m., Living World

They walked for half an hour when Van felt Wiglaf squirm inside her backpack. She stopped and laid her pack on the grassy field.

The team paused and, except Paley, they all looked like they wanted to throttle Van.

"Don't tell me you already need a break," Brux said.

Van threw him a dirty look. "Wiglaf wants to get out."

"What's a wiglaf?" Brux furrowed his brow.

Van unzipped her backpack. The little animal hopped out onto the grass.

Jorie gasped. "That's—that's a *bunfy!*"

Paley let out a squeal, bent down, and gave the creature a scratch behind the ears.

Van beamed like a proud mama. "Is that what he is? Is he a boy? Can you tell? Because I've been thinking he's a boy."

"He's *so* cute!" Paley said. "Why didn't you tell me before?"

"We didn't have time," Van replied. "Once we packed, he was sleeping so soundly, I didn't have the heart to wake him."

Wiglaf peered at them, enjoying the team's attention. He lifted his head so Paley could scratch under his chin.

She happily obliged.

"They're really rare," Trey said, stunned.

"I thought they were extinct." Elmot gaped in awe.

"How'd *you* get one?" Brux asked.

Van didn't appreciate his tone.

Jorie gazed at the critter. "Bunfys are magical creatures native to Altithronia."

"Does that mean Wiglaf can use magic to turn me into a carrot?" Paley asked Jorie, as she gleefully continued petting him.

"They don't *do* magic," Jorie clarified. "They're mag-i-cal. Can change their frequency and travel to different realms. They attach to one person, watch over that person for a lifetime. This one seems to have picked you, Van, as his charge. Glimpsing a bunfy brings good luck. Having one *choose* you means you're blessed."

Brux snorted.

Trey reached down and scooped up the little guy.

"Hey!" Paley protested.

"What are you doing?" Van screeched.

Trey looked underneath the little animal. "Yup. He's a boy." He placed the bunfy back on the ground near Paley.

Wiglaf suddenly took off, trotting north into the woods.

"Aww. Where's the little fella going?" Elmot asked.

"Trey!" Van snarled.

Paley pouted. "Trey scared him away."

"He'll be back." Jorie placed a thumping hand on Van's shoulder, probably thinking to comfort her, but that stub finger hovered too close to Van's face. "Wiglaf will return when you need him most. As a magical creature, his true home is on Mt. Altithronia with Lilla, the Elemental Guardian of All Animals."

"It's best he go," Trey said.

Van noticed Jorie's eyes narrow suspiciously at him.

Trey continued, oblivious. "The presence of a bunfy reveals

someone of spiritual importance is near, and that makes him dangerous to have around, whether Van's the Anchoress-in-waiting or not."

"Not," Brux said. "It's my sister. I've felt a strong protective instinct for Daisy since birth."

"That's because you're her brother," Elmot said.

"I think Uxa screwed up by putting me on a different team," Brux continued. "It's almost like she's sabotaging the mission."

"Brux is right. It's Daisy," Van said. "If I were the Anchoress-in-waiting, I would know it."

"I'm still not sure Uxa told us the truth about the Anchoress's bloodline surviving the Dark War," Trey said. "Why have two teams, then? I think it's a possibility that neither of our teams has the Anchoress-in-waiting."

Trey's comment enraged Jorie, who had made it clear she was an orthodox Lodian. "Our Anchoress is a reflection of the Eternal Light of the Creator. She exists. No more bad-mouthing Uxa. It lowers morale. She's the HG, and she knows what she's doing."

After this exchange, Jorie's squinty side glances at Trey came more often. Van couldn't figure out what made Jorie distrust him.

For the next hour, the team advanced east, traveling over the grassy hills of Salus Valde. The majestic mountain remained firmly rooted in the backdrop. Van's sense of dread heightened with each step. She knew they were going the wrong way. The bunfy gave her a sure sign by scampering north. But she didn't know how to get the team to listen to her.

"Hold up." Trey snapped his hand. "We're getting close to the Salus Valde-Tipereth border. I need to scout ahead, make sure our path is clear."

Jorie grunted her approval.

Trey dropped his backpack on the ground, kept his quiver and crossbow, and slipped away into the woods.

"Oh, good. I could use a break." Paley plopped herself on the grass. "And a snack."

"Great." Elmot took off his backpack and rummaged through it. "I'll re-check my maps, make sure we're taking the best route."

"My feet are *killing* me." Van fell next to Paley. "They were already sore from wearing my new boots yesterday."

Brux fidgeted as if he felt conflicted about wasting time resting. Finally, he slipped off his backpack and sat on a rock a few feet away.

Jorie assumed her favorite position. Sitting cross-legged, fiddling with Zachery. Only this time, she was treating the labrys's handle with some kind of gooey rub. "Van, Trey has some medicines in his backpack. Ask him for some ointment for your feet when he gets back."

The exposed skin around Jorie's mohawk reflected the brightness of the sun. Van wanted to ask if Trey also had sunblock, then decided Jorie's scalp was none of her business.

"We almost there?" Van asked Elmot.

Paley had used the boundless bowl to get a fully loaded hotdog and was stuffing it into her mouth.

Elmot laughed. "If you consider a week *almost.*"

Paley's hotdog caught in her throat.

"A *week?*" Van thought she'd be back in her comfy bed in a few days. *Ugh! This trip is awful.* She crashed back on the grass and gazed at the sky, resigned.

Trey returned, breathless and wide-eyed. "The path—it's blocked by a Balish squadron. A *royal* squadron. They're headed this way."

Jorie and Brux jumped to their feet.

"We're nowhere near the Coin." Jorie's shoulders tensed.

"It's… Princess Solana," Trey explained, catching his breath.

Brux heaved on his backpack. "She's searching for Manik's text."

Van's stomach twisted.

"Elmot," Jorie snapped. "The maps—which way?"

Elmot held a curled, aged parchment in his trembling hands. "To the trees." He pointed in the direction from which Trey had just come.

Brux, Jorie, Trey, and Elmot beelined toward the trees.

"*Toward* Solana?" Van's feet remained rooted to the ground.

Paley waited with her and cried, "Are you guys nuts?"

"Get moving!" Jorie shouted. "That's an order."

Paley tugged Van's sleeve. "We have no choice."

Among the trees, Van scanned the ground, searching for a stick, sickened she might need to use her twirling skills for combat and possibly against her father.

"Here." Elmot stopped in front of an enormous tree with huge knots on its trunk.

"A trunk-a-vator?" Brux hissed. "They shut these down when Nequus became king."

Elmot looked stricken. "TAVs should still be functional. They're powered by the Universal Energy Grid. An energy source that comes from nature. The Balish can't control that, right?"

"But they restrict and monitor the use of magic, you halfwit," Trey growled. "TAVs are magically imprinted trees that work off the grid. King Nequus had one of their government sanctioned wizards block the magic in the system, making the TAVs inoperable."

Jorie pushed them aside. "I may be able to get it to work." She slid her hands up and down the tree.

"What are you doing?" Van stressed over Jorie wasting their time playing with a tree when they should be running in the opposite direction.

"Off the record, I got some low-level magical skills. Self-taught," Jorie said.

"You're untrained?" Elmot asked, startled. "Doing magic incorrectly can drain your energy and attract bad luck."

"Shut it, Elmot," Jorie said. "I need to concentrate if I'm going to connect to the same vibration as the tree." She closed her eyes and mumbled a chant.

"If you're wrong about the TAV," Trey glared at Elmot, "we're all dead."

Jorie found a knot she liked and pushed her palm against it. A panel glided open, exposing a circular compartment large enough for all of them. They rushed inside. The door automatically closed.

It reminded Van of the elevator she took to her classes on the reservation, which always made her feel trapped inside a box, and this one was smaller. An embedded flat panel screen lit up, displaying a map of the landscape.

"A panel map!" Elmot said as if someone had given him a birthday present.

"Neat-o." Paley maneuvered herself next to Brux.

"We're not safe from Solana yet," Jorie said. "Stay focused."

Elmot pointed to an area in the east. "The map is grayed out here, in the Tipereth region, meaning this entire area's not functioning."

"Meaning what?" Van didn't care where they went, as long as they got out of the suffocating tree trunk.

"The TAV will only let us go north, to Altithronia," Elmot explained. "Just shy of the North Alga border."

"The connections to other TAVs are broken?" Brux asked impatiently.

Elmot nodded. "There might be other connections in the forest, but they're not connected to this TAV's network. As for this one, we can't use it to reach the river."

Brux turned to Jorie. "Can you use magic to unblock the route restrictions?"

"I thought the Balish monitored the use of magic?" Van asked. Stepping out of the TAV only to become imprisoned by Balish soldiers wouldn't make her day.

"I don't see any Balish soldiers in here, do you?" Brux answered.

Van felt her cheeks redden and resented Brux for making fun of her when all she wanted to do was get out of there.

Brux softened at her reaction and explained. "A Balish wizard's job is to monitor the squawker system that detects ripples in the energy of nature that happens when people use magic. The spell has to use a large amount of energy to be detected. Jorie's simple magic will create too low a ripple to alert the authorities. Otherwise, a Balish soldier has to catch you in the act."

"She's obviously not schooled in magic, Brux," Elmot said in Van's defense and explained further. "There are energies in nature we can channel for everything in life. Medicines, transport, communication."

Elmot's conversation helped distract Van enough to curb her anxiety, so she encouraged him to keep going. Plus, she was genuinely interested in the subject.

"People with magical skills can connect to the energies of nature to create magic," Elmot continued. "They do this by focusing their thoughts through meditation and chants. More powerful magic can be produced by using tools, natural objects—a tree, a rock, water—that the witch or wizard uses to change their vibrational frequency to match that of the object before casting a spell. Whatever method they use, they harness the universal energy of nature and use this connection to produce results. It's difficult to hold the energy of nature long enough to do a spell without losing your own energy. It takes training."

"That's a no-go on breaking the route restrictions," Jorie said to Brux, ending Elmot's mini lecture. "My magic can only get the TAV to work the way it wants to work. I'm not powerful enough to break the wizard's block. The only other way to break someone else's magical imprint is by fire." She heaved her chest and let out a snort. "I can't burn down the tree we're in." She reached a hand to the panel map. "Let's just go north. We got no time to waste."

Using the full finger next to her nub, Jorie tapped a tree icon on the screen.

Van braced herself for a wild ride, but the compartment anticlimactically hummed and vibrated.

The TAV stopped. The door slid open.

Van was the first one out.

____

Chapter 20

____

Day 2: 10:12 a.m., Living World

Van blinked to make sure she wasn't dreaming.

The trunk-a-vator had deposited them onto a bluff. Rolling hills spread before her in the distance, blanketed with colorful flowers and weepy trees whose purple-pink leaves flickered in the gentle breeze. The cliff stretched for miles and stood so high, the tips of the pine trees seemed to nip at Van's toes. She breathed in refreshing scents of pungent pine and pure air.

A loud, peaceful rushing sound came from behind the TAV.

Van walked to the backside of the tree and gaped across the gorge at a wide, crystal-blue waterfall as it crashed into jagged gray boulders. A gigantic tree next to the top of the waterfall had dug its roots into the earth like big-knuckled fingers, reaching to the collection pond at the base. The majestic mountain loomed so close Van had to crane her neck for a full view, and she still couldn't see the top. It seemed to stretch forever into the clear blue sky.

Paley appeared next to her. "Could anything be more beautiful?"

Van sighed. "Let's hope the rest of the way is just as nice."

Paley glanced at Van with hooded eyes. "You think Brux would want to take a swim with me?"

"He's the last person in *both* worlds I would want to swim with." Van wondered if Ken missed her.

"Isn't she a beaut?" Elmot said, coming from behind them.

Van noticed he enjoyed hanging around with her and Paley.

"Mt. Altithronia," he said.

The mountain made Van feel insignificant against its unabashed beauty and, at the same time, grounded by its constant presence.

"Back a thousand years ago, the borders of Salus Valde were created using her shadow," Elmot said.

Van didn't care about anything that happened a thousand years ago, and she wasn't interested in Elmot's geeky topography infatuation.

"It's the home of the Elementals," Trey added. He had felt drawn toward the waterfall too. "They sit atop Mt. Altithronia, watching over us mortals."

"We're safe here." Elmot's chest rose with his deep breath. "The Elementals don't allow the Balish on their land without permission."

"But they allow us?" Van asked.

"The Elementals favor Lodians." Elmot smiled at the mountain.

"Yet they're repealing Manik's law so the Balish can come and kill us?"

Trey chuckled. "Van has a point. Better get out of here before they smite us."

"That law saved our tribe from annihilation by the Balish." Elmot pushed his eyebrows together. "None of us would be standing here right now if Manik and the Elementals hadn't stepped in."

"Can't we just stay here?" Paley eyed Brux as if he were something she had created from the boundless bowl. "We can camp in the roots of that tree and let the other team find the Coin."

Trey sniggered. "Don't I wish."

Paley's idea irritated Van. Normally, Van was all for lounging around. But she had an inexplicable urge to keep moving.

They rejoined Jorie and Brux by the TAV.

Elmot knelt and pulled several worn parchment maps out of his backpack. "This is the last chance for us to head south by way of the Fulguro River. I would *love* to get my hands on that map in Manik's text."

"Focus on what we have, not on what we don't have," Jorie said. "What's the fastest way to the river?"

Van resisted the impulse to whip out Manik's text, claiming she had found it in the bushes. She knew the team would never buy it. They'd immediately figure out Michael was Van's father, causing trust issues with her teammates. Van imagined them accusing her of being a saboteur and ditching her and Paley in this strange place, with no food, water, or shelter, and no map to get home.

"Any original book is a rare find, thanks to the Balish." Brux shook his head in disapproval.

"The only reason Manik's text survived is because it's a historical artifact written by a Balish king," Trey said. "A king who is the direct ancestor of the Moors—the current-day Balish royal family."

Jorie prickled over his comment, though Trey didn't notice.

He went on. "Solana's younger brother Ferox, King Nequus, Prince Devon, Prince Merloc, and a bunch of other Balish royals could have studied the text. None had any interest in a book full of Lodian beliefs or attempting to translate the language of the ancients, which is apparently laborious."

As Trey spoke, Jorie got more fidgety with every word. Van felt too intimidated by their leader to ask what was bothering her, and no one else seemed to notice. Van shrugged it off, thinking she might have misread Jorie's reactions.

"Tell me about it," Brux said. "My father taught me. It's a nightmare. Only a handful of people are fluent in it. Commoners are banned by law from reading the language."

"The Balish did that for their own protection," Trey said. "They say if commoners read the language of the ancients, their eyes will burn out of their sockets. Which is a load of crap." He dumped his backpack and kept his crossbow and quiver. "I'm going to go scout. Elmot, if you could point me in the right direction."

Elmot pointed east, and Trey disappeared down a dirt path leading off the bluff and into the woods.

Jorie squinted at Trey's departing form and barked, "Elmot!"

He jumped, startled.

"Find an alternate route in case the Balish have the river blocked."

Elmot scrutinized his maps. "Because of the terrain… hmm… if the east passage is blocked… looks like our only choice is to go north through Blackwood Forest."

Jorie ran her hand over her mohawk. "That's way off track."

"Or we'd have to head back using the TAV," Elmot said. "Get out in Tipereth Forest and head south, like Echo did."

"I'm not a fan of going north," Brux said. "But the farther north we go, the farther from Aduro we get. There'll be less of a Balish presence. Rural villagers pass down folklore through story. If they know about the Coin, they'll talk."

Van lit up.

"I'm not saying the Coin is in the north," Brux added hastily. "But if we can find out where it's hidden in the south, then we can send word to Dais—team Echo."

Jorie pushed out her bottom lip, mulling it over.

"What difference does it make which way we go?" Paley said. "No one knows for sure where the Coin is. That's why Uxa sent two teams. It could be anywhere. Even here."

"We're not staying here, Paley," Van said.

Just when Van thought maybe Elmot wasn't so great at reading maps, he said, "Brux is right. If we go north, we can stop in Agerorsa. It was the site of a brutal battle during the Dark War. Looks like a good-sized town, though not too rural. But it is far from Aduro, so the people will probably talk. It will take us a couple of days to get there, and we'll have to pass through a border checkpoint."

Jorie said, "Let's wait for Trey—"

Trey came bounding out of the woods, limping with a dark red stain on his thigh.

"The Balish are set up on the river's bend," he shouted. "I got too close. They caught sight of me, thought I was the thief."

Trey does kind of look like a thief. Despite being good looking, Van thought he had beady eyes and always seemed to be assessing the situation, working out his next best move.

Trey reached the group and put pressure on the bleed. He rummaged in his backpack and took out a long piece of gauze. "We'll never make it down the river, and now this squadron knows we're here. We've got to go. They'll be here soon."

Trey had barely wrapped the gauze around his thigh when Jorie whipped out Zachery and shoved him up against the TAV.

"You seem to know an awful lot about the Balish." She held Zachery to his throat. "Brown eyes, dark hair—you a Bale? You lead them here? You working for Solana? *Tell me!*" The blade dug deeper, cutting into Trey's skin.

"I'm… a… Lodian… convert," Trey said, barely able to get the words out. "Raised… Balish."

Van took a step back from Jorie, wide-eyed. *So that's what was bothering her.*

"Take it easy, Jorie," said Brux. "Uxa handpicked all of us. He's okay."

Jorie released her blade but didn't back down. "Explain."

Voices of soldiers echoed from the trees.

"We're going to get caught." Paley shifted from foot to foot, looking stressed.

Brux glanced deeper into the forest. "We need to get into the TAV, now."

Jorie stood firm. Nobody moved.

"I immigrated to Salus Valde so I could become a Lodian and live in *peace*." Trey angrily rubbed his neck. "I'm the best resource you have. I know the Balish inside and out. Who better to have on your team?"

Jorie relaxed her stance as the first Balish soldier emerged from the trees. "In!" she commanded.

The team dashed into the TAV.

"You okay?" Elmot flittered around Trey's leg.

"Get away from me." Trey swatted at him. "Just grazed by an arrow. I'm fine."

The soldiers stampeded forward, shouting. It was the longest closing of an automatic door in the history of the world. An arrow skimmed the top of Van's head, as several more pinged off the door frame, causing them to duck just before the door slid closed. Van's heart beat so hard, it seemed about to bust her ribs.

Paley gripped Van's arm and whispered in a shaky voice, "What have you gotten me into?"

Van didn't need Paley's stress added to her already abundant load. They had narrowly escaped the Balish soldiers, and now she had to deal with being trapped in a traveling tree again.

Jorie pressed the only illuminated icon on the panel map, located in eastern Kezef. The TAV hummed and vibrated.

"The route opened!" Elmot pointed at the panel map, his finger still shaking from the close encounter. "That route to Agerorsa was restricted before. The TAV is taking us to the northern edge of Blackwood Forest in Kezef. We'll reach Agerorsa by tomorrow afternoon, without the hassle of passing through a border checkpoint. It's the Elementals helping us find the Coin."

"Or maybe you misread the panel map," Trey muttered.

Van took deep breaths to calm her nerves. Were the Elementals helping them because they're Lodians? Or because one of them was the Anchoress-in-waiting? Van glanced at Paley, who nervously clutched Brux's arm.

No one knew the identity of Paley's parents. Maybe her being on the team was secretly orchestrated by the Elementals. Could Paley be the Anchoress heir?

"Agerorsa!" Brux raised his brow. "I knew the town sounded familiar. My father told me about a library there with a secret room packed full of documents on Lodian lore. All either untranslated or translated by Lodian scribes. It's hidden from the Balish."

"Ho-yeah!" Jorie fist-bumped Brux.

"There's a belief that Grigori can connect to Earth World elevators from TAVs." Trey glanced at Van, expecting her to confirm this as truth.

His comment made Van suspect the group knew she and Paley were from Providence Island. She didn't know if Trey's claim was valid or not. "How's your leg?" she asked, forcing a change in subject.

The door slid open, only this time the land ahead appeared barren and bleak. A dim blue sky hung overhead, streaked with silvery clouds, casting a cold gray light over the horizon.

"There'll be no more chances to use a TAV. The traveling trees end here." Elmot pointed to a desolate-looking area of Kezef on one of his maps. "We'll travel by foot through Mesoterra."

"Kezef is mostly undeveloped," Jorie said. "We shouldn't run into any Balish soldiers. But the terrain is rough and rocky. We'll have to take it slow."

The group marched onward over the vast rural landscape. The wind whipped, the temperature dropped, and soft, fine sand blew from the ground into their faces. It got so bad, they were forced to stop and re-gear.

Van and Paley copied the rest of the group and wrapped scarves around their faces to protect their noses, mouths, and ears from the wind and sand. They put on thick, black sunglasses to shield their eyes, and tucked into their weather-resistant utility jackets.

Jorie was right. Navigating the rocky terrain of Kezef was slow going. Even the wind seemed to blow them backward. Now and then, they passed massive rectangular granite slabs jutting out of the earth as if an underground giant had pushed them up from below. As they traveled farther north, the slabs became larger and more clustered, forcing them to alter their route.

By late afternoon, Van could barely see twenty feet ahead from the wind-whipped sand and silently gave Elmot credit for keeping them on track.

Eventually, Elmot announced they had entered Mesoterra.

The sandy wind abated. The team loosened their scarves and removed their sunglasses. Their journey eased, except when they had to wait for a herd of strange animals to pass. They seemed familiar to Van, with their four hoofed legs, brown fur, curved horns, and humped backs. She just couldn't place them.

"Buffalroo." Brux stood next to her. "Part of the buffalo family from your world."

"*My* world?"

"The Earth World, duh," he said.

Van focused on the buffalroo. When Uxa had asked Brux to find her and Paley in Lodestar Village, she must have told him they were from Providence Island. Van just didn't know how *much* Uxa had told him. Like, did he know Michael Cross was Van's father? Did he know Paley was a terrigen? That Van was using the Twin Gemstones to keep Paley here?

Brux didn't elaborate. He watched the herd pass. "Stupid creatures, really. Annoying. Shouldn't exist at all, yet here they are, thriving. At one time, they were near extinction."

"Why are they annoying?" Paley appeared next to Brux.

"You'll see. Later."

The last of the buffalroo passed, and the group moved on.

After what seemed like hours, Jorie called for a break and led them under a natural archway formed by multiple granite slabs.

Surprised at how tired she felt, Van wondered if her exhaustion came from the energy draw of the Twin Gemstones. She pushed the thought away. Paley was with her, so the gemstones were being used correctly. Her achy body simply validated her athletic awards were undeserved.

She spotted a nearby fallen tree and sat on the trunk. The rotted-out tree crushed under her weight, spilling Van to the ground.

Paley giggled.

"Oh, gross!" Van jumped up and wiped off her butt. Needing to get herself together, Van slipped away and kneeled behind a nearby bush to brush her hair, making sure no one glimpsed her contraband hairbrush. Afterward, she sat next to Paley on a granite slab.

Paley put her hands on her stomach. "It's growling."

Van pulled out the boundless bowl and ordered a veggie burger with caramelized onions for herself, then handed the bowl to Paley, who asked for a chicken-and-cheese sub with onions and peppers. Paley passed the bowl to Trey.

Trey put the bowl down and pulled a sparkly ampule out of his backpack. It looked like a jewel. He offered it to Van.

She flipped her hand to say she didn't want it. "I have a boyfriend."

Trey chuckled. "It's colloidal silver, not an engagement ring. Take a drop, then pass it to Paley. It's got immune building properties." He commanded the bowl to create wild boar with beans, which he poured into a metal dish, and then he passed the bowl to Elmot.

"It makes sense for the Coin to be hidden in the north. A thousand years ago, Fomalhaut was neutral territory." Elmot instructed the bowl to make "Auroch and figs." A concoction that looked like beef stew, then continued. "It's dangerous land to travel through, making it a good place to hide something."

Soon after they finished eating, Paley rubbed her knees together. "I have to pee. Van, come with?"

"Yeah, I have to go too." Van grabbed her backpack.

Brux yelled, "Hey! Where are you two going?"

"Van has to pee," Paley said.

Van felt her cheeks flush.

"Oh, uh, well, stay close and hurry up. It's not safe here."

Brux's protective concern made Van's stomach tickle like she had swallowed butterflies. She wondered about her conflicting emotions. She often found Brux intolerable, but her body seemed to get excited about him. Van shook her thoughts away and followed Paley behind a granite slab, not too far from the archway.

"Here's a good spot," Paley said. "You go first. I'll keep lookout."

Van pulled some tissues from her backpack as Paley turned in standard girlfriend-lookout-position.

Van pulled down her pants. As soon as she squatted, she lost her footing and grabbed onto the slab for balance. *What the?* She could've sworn the ground beneath her feet shifted.

"Dammit." A stream of pee had dribbled all over her thighs and spattered onto her pants and panties. "I need more tissues!"

Paley blindly extended her arm backward, tissues in hand. "Got it?"

Van grabbed the tissue. "Got it. Thanks." She cleaned herself and then tossed the used tissues onto the ground, letting them tumble away in the wind. "Paley, you may want to pee in another spot." Van tucked in her tank top. "I think there's something wrong with the ground here."

"Oh *right*. You're all set, so now you want me to suffer? Don't worry. Brux will still be there when you get back. Wait for me."

They switched positions, with Van's back now turned to Paley.

"What do you mean *Brux will still be there when I get back?*" Van crossed her arms. "You're the one who's flirting with him."

"All the boys always like you better." Paley's voice echoed from behind Van. "I see the way you stare at Brux with your googly eyes."

"I do not!"

"You have Ken, from one of the best families, who is the nicest, best-looking guy on the island, and you want more. How much is enough? I—*ah*! Van! *Help*!"

Van turned around.

Paley stood ankle deep in the sand that seemed to have come alive.

Van glimpsed thin black sticks sweeping in and out, rippling the sand around Paley's ankles. She stared in terror as spindly legs sifted through the sand, sinking Paley.

"I can't move my feet!" Paley wailed. "Do something!"

Van yelled for help. She threw down her backpack and tore open the zipper—not sure what she was looking for—something, *anything*.

Paley sank deeper into the sand.

Van snatched a coil of rope. "Grab hold, and I'll pull you out!" She tossed the line to Paley, who reached for it and missed.

The spindly legs kept sweeping.

"Help! Help!" Paley cried as the sand reached her knees. Tears poured from her eyes.

"Hang on." Van leaned forward, aimed, and tossed the rope. Her body shifted. The sand under her own feet rippled like tiny waves.

Paley caught the rope. But it was too late.

Van lost her balance and crashed to the ground.

Sand pelted against her exposed skin as waves erupted around her body. One creature flicked sand into her eyes. Grains caught in her throat. Van coughed and blinked while struggling to breathe. She rolled onto her back and felt her cap slip from her head as her body sank lower.

Little pinpoints pricked into her calves and thighs. She tried to push herself up, but she couldn't feel her legs. A few creatures rose from the sand and scuttled up her body toward her face. They looked like red and black golf balls with long, thin legs and two snapping front claws.

Van brushed them back, keeping the sea of spider-like crabs off her face. But more and more rose from the sand. She sank deeper and could no longer see Paley.

"Hel—eh." Van tried to scream, but grains of sand shot into her mouth, choking her.

Sand trickled into Van's ears. She felt a sharp pinch on her right arm, and it went numb. The spider-crabs crawled under her shirt, scratching her stomach. She felt another pinch near her belly button, and that spot went numb. She frantically swatted the creatures with her good arm, yet the sand continued to cover her.

It was a losing battle. The creatures were burying her alive.

Noxious fumes filled the air. The spindly legs slowed as the creatures became weaker until they wobbled and fell off. The repulsive smell made Van gag. She tried to lift herself, but she couldn't move. Her vision grew fuzzy. A pair of hands reached out, gripped her by the arms, and easily pulled her out of the sand.

"Sand crabs." It was Brux. "Stinkbomb. Clears them out." He held her tight while seeing whether she could stand on numb legs.

Trey propped up Paley, who seemed okay.

Van opened her mouth to thank Brux and, instead, vomited all over his boots.

Chapter 21

D ay 2: 4:37 p.m., Living World

Brux carried Van, while Trey helped Paley back to the granite archway. The guys settled them on blankets.

Some time must have passed because Van woke to find Trey examining her red welts.

"Sand crab bites," he told her. "How do you feel?"

"I can walk." Van tried to push herself up onto unsteady legs.

"Sit down." Brux caught Van in his arms as she collapsed. He placed her back on the blanket next to Paley.

Van noticed his stocking feet and his cleaned boots drying on a nearby rock. Embarrassed about puking on his feet, she snapped her face away before Brux could see her reddening cheeks.

Jorie kept pacing and running her hand over her mohawk. Van wasn't sure whether Jorie felt concerned about her and Paley's well-being or upset over the time setback.

"Trey," Jorie barked. "How long until the paralysis wears off?"

"I'm a combat medic," he said in frustration. "Cuts, breaks, stab wounds. None of the medicines I brought will dilute sand crab venom."

"Van—your neck," Paley croaked, barely having the energy to say the words.

"It's burning." Van ran her fingers over her neck. "And itchy."

Brux pulled down Van's collar and frowned. "You have a rash."

"I'm itchy too." Paley pulled up her sleeve and scratched her arm.

"They're getting worse." Jorie dropped to her knees next to the girls. "No warriors die on my watch. Elmot! Get me the boundless bowl!"

There was no response.

Jorie twisted, searching for him, as did Trey and Brux. "Where's Elmot?"

"He left?" asked Van, saddened Elmot had disappeared with her and Paley sick and in need, especially since he seemed to bond with them more so than anyone else.

Trey rose. "I'll go look for him."

Brux rummaged through Van's backpack, searching for the boundless bowl. Van flinched, worried he might discover her contraband.

Just then, Elmot hastened through the archway into their camp, grasping a bundle made from a spare shirt.

"Elmot! Where were—" Jorie stopped in mid-sentence as Elmot opened the packet on the ground next to Van and Paley, exposing ten dead sand crabs.

Van let out a shriek. She tried to wriggle away but was too feeble.

"Did I forget to mention one of my skills is toxicology?" Elmot grabbed the boundless bowl from Brux, who hadn't indicated he'd seen Van's smuggled items.

Elmot asked the bowl for coconut water. "I'm good with poisons." He took a sand crab, opened its minuscule mouth with a stick, and tore off its bottom jaw.

Van winced.

"Trey, get your medic kit," Elmot said. "Put five drops of ortega-ancha in the coconut water, please. It will bind the mixture, allowing it to create an immune response in their bodies."

Trey hurried to his backpack and rummaged around for the correct ampule.

"Sand crab venom is an efficient killer." Elmot used his thumb to squish the head of the arthropod. A clear liquid dripped from its fangs into the coconut water. "The venom is a complex mixture of toxic proteins and peptides, exquisitely refined to attack the nervous system. It paralyzes the body by blocking communication between nerves and muscles and essentially stops your body from functioning. The only way to counter its effects is by using the same components to cure as those that produced the symptoms."

Elmot mixed the water-venom mixture with a stick. He commanded the situation with focus and clarity, even more so than when he navigated using his maps.

Trey opened the ampule and dropped five beads of ortega-ancha into the coconut water.

"Couldn't we have used the boundless bowl to make the anti-venom?" Jorie asked Elmot.

"Yeah." Van wearily eyed the nauseating mixture. "One that will taste better and is made of chocolate?"

Elmot shook his head. "I can't create the right chemical makeup using the bowl. Boundless bowls produce only food and drink, not medicines. If I had asked for the anti-venom, it would've given me only the food ingredient I needed. Coconut water."

He extended the bowl to Van and Paley. "Drink up."

Both hesitated.

"You go first," Paley said.

Van took the bowl. Though it barely weighed two pounds, she could hardly hold it. Van drank a sip and almost hurled again. She passed the bowl to Paley.

"Keep taking sips until the bowl is empty," Elmot said.

"How long until they're better?" Jorie asked.

"Well," Elmot said, "we'll have to stay the night. If the cure doesn't kill them first, that is."

"*What?*" they all cried at once.

"Kidding." Elmot smiled.

Elmot making a joke surprised Van. Elmot had a cheery disposition, but, so far, out of all the team members, only Trey had exhibited a sense of humor. Van suspected Elmot had a crush on Trey and wondered whether this was Elmot's way of flirting with him.

"So not funny." Paley pouted.

Van giggled. "It was kind of funny."

"Let's settle in." Jorie sat down on a flat rock, unsheathed Zachery, and repeatedly tossed the axe in the air with one hand and caught it with the other.

Trey took a seat on a piece of granite next to his stored crossbow and quiver, pulled out a dry cloth, and began wiping the arrows.

Elmot wandered off to the side and became absorbed in his maps.

Brux took it upon himself to monitor Van and Paley's progress with drinking the anti-venom. Once they had finished, Brux asked Trey for an ointment to soothe their rashes. While his back was turned, Van used her fingers to tidy her hair.

"We saved the rope but couldn't get your caps," Brux told Van and Paley, offering Van a salve-filled hand. "Let me rub this on your rash."

Van pulled down the neck of her shirt, and he rubbed the salve on her skin. His touch tingled, electrifying her whole body, giving her more healing than the anti-venom.

He treated Paley next.

Brux cleaned the boundless bowl and then said, "Salted auroch strips."

He offered Van some strips, which looked like beef jerky. She refused, but Paley opened her mouth like a baby bird.

"I'm vegan," Van said, as she watched Brux feed Paley.

"Why didn't you say so?" Brux coaxed Van into telling him her favorite food, seitan satay kabobs, and he ordered three from the bowl.

"I have no appetite." Van pushed his hand away.

"Open up." Brux waved a kabob at her and made zooming sounds as if feeding a stubborn baby.

Brux looked so cute and caring, Van smiled, despite herself. She took a bite to make him happy, then gobbled down all three skewers full.

After eating, she recuperated on her blanket and watched Brux out of the corner of her eye, snacking on auroch strips. She wondered what kind of life he had in the Living World, how his mother had died (in what Fynn had called "unusual circumstances") and what he thought about his frail sister possibly being the Anchoress-in-waiting.

Van still didn't know what Brux's skills were, and he hadn't yet demonstrated anything remarkable. To be fair, Van didn't have any spectacular skills, either. She didn't know why she'd even been chosen for this mission, other than her family name. Maybe Brux and Daisy were selected for the same reason—lineage.

The boys started goofing around to burn off excess energy.

Van watched them roughhousing, touched by how concerned the team had been about her and Paley. The others could've left them to rot under the archway and continued with the mission, but they didn't. Van's chest tightened.

"Let's not waste time." Jorie clapped her hands. "Consider this a Grigori weapons training session. Van, Paley—pay attention. Maybe you'll learn something."

"Oh, we're not pretending anymore?" Elmot asked. "Like we don't know Van and Paley are from Providence Island?"

"So you do know!" Paley exclaimed.

"I've known since Uxa sent me to find you in Lodestar Village," Brux said.

"How?" asked Van.

"Well, for one thing, she told me." Brux grinned.

Van tilted her head. "How did you know we were the ones Uxa was looking for?"

"By your clothes," said Brux. "But it was your handshake that confirmed it. When I extended my hand to Paley, she clasped my hand, not my wrist."

"The rest of us figured it out pretty quick," Jorie added. "Doesn't matter. Doesn't change the mission." She twirled Zachery from hand to hand.

From under his jacket, Brux pulled a wavy dagger with symbols on the blade.

Trey unsheathed a hunting knife from inside his boot.

"I'm… as you might have figured, not really a weapons kind of guy," Elmot stammered. "Poisons are more my thing."

"We can all learn," Jorie said. "We'll do hand-to-hand combat, assuming all weapons are lost. That way, it'll be even." She gently laid Zachery down on the ground. Hand-to-hand combat was Jorie's specialty. She focused on showing the others defensive and offensive moves.

Enthralled with the session, Van watched them fight in pairs. Jorie against Trey. Brux against Elmot, which was no match. Brux definitely restrained himself.

"To become a Grigori, you have to compete in the games, sporting events," Jorie said as she lunged at Trey.

Trey dodged her.

"In the past, the Elders only accepted one-hundred-percent pureblooded Lodians," Trey said. "Now, times are tough. More demons, not enough warriors. They're more lenient."

"You still have to prove yourself." Brux easily knocked Elmot to the ground. "If someone is a commoner and makes it to the games, he or she has to place first to be accepted into Grigori training."

Van's father was a commoner. He must have placed first. Impressed, Van hoped she had inherited his abilities. *Wait. Games?* The Jaychund games. They're tryouts for the Grigori! The kids in the reservation program actually competed for placement in the *Grigori! Duh!* She truly was slow. She wondered if placing first in one All-Grades event had qualified her. It seemed likely since Uxa had chosen her for this mission.

"Grigori are hunters," Jorie said, as she and Trey prowled around each other. "And protectors. They kill demons generated by terrigens in the Earth World before they get strong enough to rise here."

Brux and Elmot focused on Elmot's lack of combat skills and didn't participate in the conversation.

"The Balish believe terrigens are lesser people in a lesser world," Trey said, as he lunged at Jorie and missed.

Jorie gripped Trey in a headlock. "Is that what you believe, Bale?"

"Of course not," Trey said in a strained voice. "Why do you think I defected?"

Paley glowered. "Terrigens aren't *lesser people.*"

"Lodians believe everyone is equal." Trey had shaken loose of Jorie's hold. "And all things in nature are interconnected and interdependent. That terrigens are sentient beings who deserve respect."

"Why can't terrigens exist here?" Paley asked, feeling well enough to sit up.

"Every living being has a range of vibrational frequencies," Trey explained. "Humans who have ichor in their blood can reach higher frequencies, which allows them to stay here in the Living World. The attuning process for travel through the portal requires adjusting these frequencies."

"Why do terrigens generate demons?" Van changed the conversation before Paley revealed herself as a smuggled-in terrigen. "Can't the Grigori stop them from doing that?"

"The thoughts and actions of humans produce energy," Trey said. "But terrigens have a lower vibrational frequency range than vichors. Whenever a terrigen commits a grievous act against the light—anything violent or destructive that doesn't promote the good of the people—this act generates negative energy that concentrates over time, creating a life form we call a demon."

Van was relieved to hear this. She half-expected Paley to generate a demon every time her friend complained.

"Demons then corrupt the minds of terrigens by attaching to them and disrupting their thoughts. This makes terrigens more agitated and violent, creating a vicious cycle." Trey crouched and kept his gaze on Jorie.

"Demons thrive and breed in negative environments, and most demons are lazy," he continued. "They settle for corrupting lower-frequency terrigens. But some demons are determined to snuff out any spark of light they can find. These stronger, more advanced demons are attracted to the most hopeful, positive terrigens. The terrigens who radiate the brightest inner light."

Trey dodged Jorie, then pinned one of her arms behind her back for a moment.

"These terrigens exist at the highest level of their frequency range, so the demon needs more force and effort to affect them. But the demon's whisper—called *seeping*—can adversely affect anyone." He shuddered.

Van shivered in response. Seeping sounded awful. "Any human, or just terrigens?"

"Any human," Jorie answered, lunging at Trey. "Thankfully, the vibrational frequencies in the Living World are too high for demons."

Jorie caught Trey in her grip again.

"To stop the terrigens from generating demons, you'd have to kill pretty much all of them. It's the only way. And not a workable one," Jorie said, as Trey struggled against her hold. "Doesn't matter because our Grigori would never even let anyone try." Jorie grinned at Trey's efforts, but held firm. "They vow to protect the weak and innocent."

"Terrigens are too ignorant to know they exude energy that creates demons." Trey wrapped his arms around Jorie's waist and swiped one leg behind her knees.

Jorie released her hold as they both fell to the ground.

"Or that demons, Grigori, and another world exists." Trey caught his breath as he jumped to his feet. "That's what makes them innocent."

Jorie and Trey then focused on one-upping each other, ending their conversation with Van. She felt okay with this because the whole time she'd kept sneaking peeks at Brux to see what he did. Now she could fully concentrate on watching him.

Van couldn't take her eyes off Brux and how he maneuvered himself around Elmot. He was so… *masculine.* Like Ken when when he played lacrosse. Occasionally, Brux stopped and taught Elmot the basic defensive moves he had just demonstrated. Brux's patience with Elmot showed he had a soft side.

He'd be good with kids. Van squirmed on her blanket.

Brux caught her eye. "Feel like moving about?" He extended his hand and coaxed Van to her feet. "Take it slow and show me what combat skills you learned in school."

"No real skills, not like yours," Van said. "Just twirling, rhythmic gymnastics. It's a type of dance also used for self-defense with staffs, rods, or sticks." She had him find her a stick, but felt uncomfortable as she performed her lame sequence.

"Tha' was great!" Elmot gushed, with a slight lisp from his swollen upper lip.

"Um. Yeah. Van," Brux said. "You're doing a high-level martial art called koga-clava. It's not taught to many people, and it's difficult to master."

Van's eyes opened wide, dumbfounded by this news.

Exhaustion from her ordeal with the venom set in putting an end to her training. "What happens if demons find some way to get here again?" Van slumped back down onto the blanket. "How do we fight them?"

"Good question." Trey ran his fingers through his mussed-up hair. His training session with Jorie had also ended. "We can't kill them with hand-to-hand combat or by twirling sticks."

"We won't be able to anchor them either," Jorie said. "For that, we'd need a modified multi-track." She bent down and picked up Zachery. "Grigori train for years to kill demons without generating any additional negative energy."

"So what do we do?" Paley asked, still looking wan.

"We do our best. And be fast at it." Jorie twirled Zachery in figure eights. "Listen. Light has a high vibration. By raising a demon's vibration higher than it can tolerate, the demon will explode and die. Light can kill all demons. This means we could use anything infused with light or blessed by the light, known as *ritual-ized*. Like as Zachery here." She gave Zachery a wave.

"How do you know this?" Trey asked.

"Did an internship at Lodestar. I'm on track to become a Grigori." Jorie's whole body glowed with pride.

Brux raised his eyebrows. "Impressive."

Van felt a jealous pang seeing Brux's enthusiasm for Jorie's accomplishment. She tapped his arm to get his attention. "I don't get it. If demons come here, they can't survive because their vibration is too low. So why's it a big deal?"

"If enough demons gain the strength to rise," Brux said, "their presence will lower the vibration of our world. The membrane-like veil between our world and yours will crack and eventually break if they're not defeated. The worlds will crash together, bringing chaos."

"Demons on our soil are a sign the Escalation to Dishora has begun," Elmot said in a shaky voice.

"The only other time in history demons reached our world was during the Great War, which caused that war to morph into the Dark War," Trey said. "Demons are here now, without a war taking place to strengthen them. It's unusual."

"Michael Cross brought them here," Jorie said. "There's nothing unusual about a traitor acting like a traitor."

Jorie's comment crushed Van. No wonder her father's soul was in jeopardy. He had taken an oath to protect both of their worlds from demons and instead brought them here. The father she knew would never do anything like that.

Van felt more determined than ever to find the Coin and fix this mess. She knew Manik's text could help her locate it, but she couldn't translate the passages on her own. She wished Paley's special skill was reading ancient languages. Although, it was just as well Paley didn't have this skill since her friend had trouble keeping anything a secret. Who else could Van trust?

Night crept in, cloaking the landscape and cooling the air. Everyone huddled near the campfire. After they used the boundless bowl and ate dinner, Trey passed around a wineskin of steaming acorn-honey water. Van and Paley refused. After choking down the anti-venom, neither of them had any desire to drink anything ever again. Trey assured the others the water had many nutritional properties.

"You sure?" Brux teased. "Maybe we should ask Elmot."

Van knew he'd referred to the earlier incident when Trey, the team's medic, couldn't treat her and Paley's sand crab bites, and Elmot, the navigation expert, had cured them.

Trey laughed and punched Brux in the arm. Still grinning, Trey turned to face Van and Paley. "So, Providence Island, huh? You two must have some badass skills to be brought here. I mean, I know dozens more kids in Salus Valde who are better qualified for this mission."

"Thanks a lot," Paley huffed.

"Just my opinion." Trey shrugged. "No offense."

"I know what your skills are," Van said to Trey. She turned to Brux and asked, "What are yours?" She hoped to draw attention away from herself and Paley, plus she was dying to know.

"Language expert, mostly." Brux took the wineskin from Trey. "Translation skills. My specialty is the language of the ancients." Brux sipped from the wineskin and reached around Van and Paley, extending the wineskin to Elmot.

"Of course!" Trey cried. "I remember you said your father had taught you, but to be *fluent*! Excellent. It makes sense, with you being pureblooded."

Jorie snatched the wineskin from Elmot's outstretched hand. "I'm classified as pureblooded too." She squirted a sip into her mouth, then wiped her lips with the back of her hand. "So's Elmot." She passed the wineskin to Trey by smashing it into his chest. "I assume Uxa chose Van and Paley for this mission because they are too. None of us can read the language, though, I'll bet."

"My father's a professor of philology at the Royal Lodian University," Brux said. "Teaching is in his nature."

"And he's a consultant to the Lodian Consilium," Jorie said matter-of-factly. She shrugged at the blank stares. "I saw him hanging around with Uxa during my internship."

"Oh, I would love to work as a professor at the Royal Lodian University," Elmot said.

Trey rolled his eyes.

Jorie scowled. "You don't want to be a warrior?"

Elmot shook his head. "With multi-tracks, the Grigori have little need for navigators in the field. I'd like to teach cartography and work behind the scenes, using my skills to help develop new, better multi-tracks."

"Why not teach toxicology?" Brux asked.

"I have no interest in studying poisons," Elmot said. "I love maps."

"How about you, Brux?" Paley asked, batting her eyelashes. "Do you want to be a Grigori?"

"It's important to my family I become a warrior," Brux said. "It's my birthright."

"And you don't want to?" Trey asked.

Brux shrugged. "I'll do whatever it takes to protect Daisy."

The group chatted until, one by one, they grew tired.

Elmot and Jorie pulled out their silky brown squares and tugged a string that "inflated" their sleeping bags. Then Paley did the same. They nestled in and retired for the night.

Trey, a history buff, kept Brux talking.

Every inch of Van's body ached as if a boulder had rolled over it. She longed for sleep. However, an idea kept poking at her, keeping her awake. Brux, a *language* expert? She needed to show him Manik's text. But could she trust him? After a headache-provoking internal struggle, she decided yes. If the text would help Daisy, she felt sure he'd keep it a secret.

To Van's annoyance, Trey monopolized Brux, debating the differences in translations of the ancient language.

"—because they've misinterpreted the ancient word for *worthy* to mean *royal*," Brux said heatedly.

Trey snorted in disgust. "The Balish had something to do with that. I can't wait to get into that secret room in the library tomorrow and comb through all those authentic documents. I heard plural nouns are often mistaken for singular—"

Snore! Van wished Trey would shut up and go away. But Trey hogged Brux's attention far into the night, and Van's heavy eyelids

won. She inflated her sleeping bag, succumbed to its snuggly softness, and fell into a deep sleep.

Chapter 22

Day 3: 5:14 a.m., Living World

VAN STIRRED, not fully awake. "What's that *horrible* noise?" It sounded like a crowing rooster on steroids.

"It's the crack of dawn." Paley's muffled whine came from inside her sleeping bag.

"Now you know why buffalroo are so annoying." Brux leaped out of his sleeping bag, wide awake and ready to go.

"Some tribes believe if the buffalroo don't crow, the sun won't rise." Jorie deflated her sleeping bag. "Just wait. After the alpha male starts, the rest of the herd joins in."

As if on cue, more buffalroo began crowing.

"There we go," Jorie said.

Trey emerged from his sleeping bag, scratching his head and looking scruffy. "Now I know why some tribes kill them for food. It's the only way to shut them up."

"Better not kill them," Jorie shouted over the screeching.

"They're a protected species. Against Balish law. Anything related to sun worship, the Balish protect."

Elmot also rose. His clothes remained pressed and clean, as if he had a secret dry cleaner hidden away in his backpack. Van felt disheveled in comparison.

"That explains why there's so many," Elmot yelled. "Buffalroo, not Balish." He chortled.

"I thought we were out of Balish territory," Paley said in a grouchy voice.

"The Balish rule extends throughout most of the Living World," Trey said loud enough to be heard over the noise. "Salus Valde and Altithronia are two of the few exceptions."

Elmot showed Van and Paley how to deflate their sleeping bags. "Made with Balish-approved magic," he said. "Bought in the markets of Hod. They allow for easy storage, so they're great for travelers." Elmot folded his into a neat little square in the same precise manner he folded his maps.

Van figured his neat mannerisms accounted for how his clothes stayed so immaculate.

The buffalroo finally stopped crowing, to everyone's relief. But besides Van's aching body from yesterday's walk and the sand crab attack, her ears now rang. Her grumpy mood persisted as she folded her sleeping bag.

The group ate a quick breakfast, geared up, and headed out for an all-day trek to Agerorsa.

By late afternoon, the landscape changed. Loose sand became compact and rocky, and tree-strewn flatlands replaced the giant slabs of granite.

"We're in northern Kezef, close to the border of Fomalhaut," Elmot said.

They picked up the main road leading into town, walking in the open as marketeers' scouts would do.

About a quarter mile from Agerorsa, Trey abruptly halted, knelt down, and placed his palm on the dirt road. "You feel that?"

They stopped and listened.

"Take cover! Quickly!" Jorie roared.

Van heard it. The pounding of horses' hooves coming their way. The team dove into the thick shrubbery lining the road.

Van gasped as a squadron of massive black horses stampeded past, headed toward Agerorsa, blowing up a cloud of dust. Their riders wore black balaclavas, black gloves, and black capes that flailed in the wind. A red-and-gold insignia embellished their left upper chests.

"Balish soldiers." Brux grimaced as he crouched between Van and Paley.

After the riders had passed, the team re-gathered in the brush.

"Not just Balish soldiers," Trey said. "Royal Balish Soldiers."

Paley bit her cuticles. "You guys told us soldiers aren't supposed to be here."

"They're not," Brux said. "The town's too far north for the Balish to care about having a military presence."

"Royal squadrons are an elite branch of the Balish military," Trey informed them. "They protect members of the royal family. They'll do whatever their assigned royal wants them to do. We should skip Agerorsa. A royal presence here makes it too dangerous."

"But *why* are the Balish here?" Jorie ran her hand over her mohawk.

"I like Trey's idea of skipping this town," Van said. A *royal* squadron had passed them, which meant her father might be there. She got queasy at the thought. She wasn't ready to face him. "I have a bad feeling."

"We came all this way," Jorie said. "We're going in. Keep a low profile, sneak into the library, get what you can, and then leave. I'll find out what the Balish are doing here."

A half-hour later, they arrived in Agerorsa. Elmot told them it was densely populated and wealthy, but the first thing Van noticed was the stench. Then the dirt. Malnourished children, smudged in grime and dressed in shabby clothes, ran unattended on the street ripe with decomposing garbage. Their parents weren't doing any better. They sat listlessly on rotting crates outside their dilapidated shanties. Flies buzzed about, crawling on their skin. Their vacant eyes told of a fight against poverty lost generations ago. They barely noticed as Van and the others passed.

"Elmot," Van said. "You are way off calling this town wealthy."

"We're in the outskirts," Elmot explained.

A small boy with fringy black hair caked with dust ran over to Brux. He reached up and tugged Brux's sleeve. "'Scuse me, mister." The boy smiled pleasantly, displaying yellow, chipped teeth.

The boy's hygiene horrified Van. She expected Brux to shoo away the diseased ragamuffin.

Instead, Brux bent down to the boy's level and smiled. "Hey, big guy. What can I do for you?"

"Do you got any food?" the boy asked. He looked about six years old.

"What's wrong with him?" Van backed away from the boy. "Is he sick? Brux, be careful."

Jorie marched over.

Van relaxed, confident Jorie would share her sentiment about protecting the group from disease and send the boy packing.

"Ares!" A scrappy woman scampered out from the wasteland and grabbed her son. She appeared frightened and close up, much younger than Van had initially thought. "Please, don't hurt him. He didn't mean no harm."

"We're not *Balish*," Brux said, affronted. "Of course, we won't hurt him."

"Give them the boundless bowl," Jorie said. "Give it to them."

"B-but…," Van stammered. *Our food!* "They're non-contributors. Why are we rewarding them?"

"Everyone deserves to be treated with respect." Jorie placed her hands on her hips. "No matter how much or how little they have."

"What'll we eat?" Van's eyes widened.

"Don't worry, Van," Elmot said. "I'll make sure you always have something to eat."

"Will Uxa be mad at us for giving away her bowl?" Paley asked.

"I think Uxa will be mad if we *don't* give away her bowl." Elmot went behind Van and unzipped her backpack.

Paley reached in and took out the bowl.

Van was glad they did. If they left it up to her, she didn't think she could do it. She was too afraid of being hungry.

"We're capable warriors," Brux said without judgment. "We can fend for ourselves. They can't."

"Oh, thank you! *Thank you!*" the woman said tearfully; the boy gave another horrifying grin. "May the light guide your path!" She hid the bowl in her worn shawl. Then she and the boy scurried away before Jorie could change her mind.

The team continued deeper into Agerorsa. The dirt road became more deserted. No one else approached them, and there was no traffic. They reached a paved road, and the houses improved with each block, becoming well-maintained two-story clapboard homes, but people had them shuttered tight.

"Where is everyone?" Paley's eyes darted over the houses and down the street.

"The squadron must have drawn them into the town square," Brux said.

Following Elmot's lead, they turned down a wide cobblestone road leading downtown and to the library. A noisy crowd mobbed the town square.

"What's going on?" Van whispered to Brux.

Paley grabbed hold of Van's backpack to keep them together as they weaved their way through the crowd.

Jorie told them to wait while she went ahead. She returned within minutes. "They have a prisoner. He's accused of consorting with demons."

Van's stomach lurched. Was the prisoner her father?

"On what grounds?" Trey asked angrily.

"He's a townsman," Jorie answered. "They caught him with Manik's text. They're saying he's the one who lured Prince Devon into the woods to be murdered."

Van breathed in relief. The prisoner wasn't her father, and *she* had Manik's text. The townsman was innocent. They'd set him free. Regardless, she didn't want to linger. If someone searched her backpack, she'd be the one on display in the town square.

"Whose squadron is it?" Elmot stretched and balanced on his toes, trying to see over the crowd. "Can you tell?"

"The Corporal Princess," said a heavy-set man standing in front of Elmot. He wore a loose-fitting jersey with a leather belt and brown legging pants.

"Solana Moor," Elmot murmured.

Van gulped. If Van's father was working with Solana, and her squadron had come to town, then it stood to reason her father was there too. Van cowered, hoping to become invisible.

"Good for her," said the man, straining his neck, hoping to glimpse the prisoner. "Neighbor or not, I always knew he was a dirty thief. If not for him, Prince Devon and Queen Brigid would still be alive."

"Get to the library," Jorie said in a low voice. "I'll stay and find out more about what's going on."

The others disappeared into the throng. Paley trailed behind them, until Van grabbed her arm and whispered, "Let's do our own recon."

"I'm in." Paley smiled. "I want to see the town, get a feel for where my parents might've come from."

"Maybe we can find a beauty salon." Van frowned at her chipped nail polish.

They made their way to the edge of the crowd and strolled down the sidewalk, gazing at the impressive commerce buildings. Some were made of marble with stately pillars. Others had A-frame roofs bunched closely together. With all the businesses closed, Van had to give up her hopes of getting a blowout for her hair and a manicure. Paley peered into the window of a closed clothing shop, while Van noticed the townspeople liked to collect stones. Many piles of them lay along the side of the road.

Van lagged so Paley wouldn't hear when she asked people if they knew a man named Rogziel, the name from her bloody patch. Van had no luck, and not until she heard a horse snort and shuffle did she realize she had reached the front of the crowd.

A row of Balish soldiers stood between the crowd and the man they held captive, tied to a post. Her heart wrenched at the sight of the severely beaten man. Her first instinct was to turn and run. But she had come on this mission to find out about her father, and curiosity got the better of her. This presented the perfect opportunity to find out more.

She gathered her courage and edged close enough to see the soldiers' insignia patches. They were like Rogziel's patch, which had been torn from a Balish military uniform, but apparently not from a Royal Balish Soldier's. Maybe the patch belonged to a palace guard who worked with her father.

Van decided she would risk glimpsing her father as long as she stayed hidden in the crowd without him spotting her. Only by setting eyes on him could Van gain absolute confirmation her father and Solana had hatched some villainous plot to take over Salus Valde. Her thoughts broke when the soldiers parted, and one of their own stepped forward.

Van braced, sure she would catch sight of her father. Startled, she instead saw a stunning, dark-haired girl emerge. Despite never having seen her before, Van knew it was Princess Solana.

The princess moved effortlessly, yet deliberately, like a predator. Glossy black hair cascaded down her back. Her full, blood-red lips beautifully contrasted with her smooth, sun-kissed skin. Her unitard military uniform clung to her curvy body with laser precision. She wore matching black elbow-length gloves and knee-high boots. Solana emanated both power and femininity.

Van could tell one glance from this girl reduced powerful men to crumbling piles of dust, which probably accounted for her father falling under the princess's influence.

Solana strode forward, all dark and smooth. Her irresistible charm deeply disturbed Van. The girl's beauty didn't fool her. Solana reeked of *danger*.

As if sensing Van's scrutiny, Solana stopped and turned her sharp, sun-gold gaze in Van's direction.

Van gasped, feeling like a field mouse caught by a feral cat. She shifted her body behind the man in front of her to block Solana's line of sight.

"Our *Sanctus Novus* tells us creatures of evil will rise from the mud!" Solana bellowed. "Seeking to swallow the sun, to consume all light!" She dramatically subdued her voice. "Until nothing remains… but darkness."

She paused with her head down, as if allowing the audience time to appreciate her words.

The audience mumbled.

Solana looked up solemnly. "Sadly, I must concede that evil now infects our peaceful world. Solmor, the time of darkness prophesied in our revered *Sanctus Novus,* has fallen upon us." Solana theatrically paused again, then said, "Evidence of this is clearly demonstrated by the murder of my beloved brother, Prince Devon, by demons."

Solana's tone grew firm and confident. "Death of a royal twin is a bad omen. It signals the start of great troubled times ahead. Terrigen-created demons will ascend from their world to conquer ours. It is the job of the Lodians' Grigori to prevent this from happening. Yet the Grigori are no longer capable of protecting our world. They allowed demons here, bringing Solmor upon us!"

The crowd angrily muttered in agreement with the princess's words.

"I have been called here to deliver justice to this man." She extended her arm toward the trembling man strapped to a post.

"I am innocent!" he cried.

Solana scowled at the man. "I caught this man in possession of Manik's text. A text we thought was lost forever. He is the thief, the reason my brother was in the woods the night of the demon attack. He is responsible for killing my brother *and* my mother!"

The crowd shouted their support and glared at the hapless man.

Van scrunched her forehead, confused. Solana had made a mistake. Manik's text was in her backpack. They should let the man go.

Solana seemed pleased with the crowd's response and continued. "People! The light of the Creator that is within our king, *my* father, is at risk from the dark forces harboring in our land. In the king's name, I have the right to gather, confiscate, and destroy any weapons, lands, or traitors necessary. I will fight evil to protect our king's position and to *protect his subjects.*"

The crowd cheered.

Solana breathed deeply through her nose, as if gaining energy from the inflamed mob. "This man conspired with darkness. Now he must *pay*!"

The people roared their approval.

A shriveled hand roughly grabbed Van's arm. "This here's no place for girls or children," said a repulsive old man. "You best be collectin' your friends and headin' on outta here."

"Hands off, pal." Brux appeared, shoving the old man away from Van.

The old man held Brux in his stare. "There's nothing here for marketeers' scouts, son. Best you be movin' on."

Brux scanned the crowd and stiffened, catching on to the old man's hint. He nodded his thanks and then grabbed Van's arm. "Come on, let's go. You too, Paley."

"Shouldn't we get Jor—"

"No!" Brux snapped. "And stop wandering away."

Van didn't know what made Brux in such a rush until she took a closer look at the mob—made up only of men! She shuddered. "W-What's going on? Where are all the women and children?"

"They're in their houses," Brux said, dragging Van. "We're leaving town."

Paley hung onto Van's backpack, following them.

"We'll rendezvous with Jorie and the rest of the team at the border of Agerorsa," Brux said.

"How will they know where we are?" Van asked.

"Standard warrior protocol." After a heavy pause, Brux said, "If they don't meet up with us, I'll head back and get them. I need to keep you safe."

Paley tsked.

"Sorry. To keep you *both* safe."

"Since when is my safety your priority?" Van scoffed.

"It's my job as your teammate. I hope Daisy's team does the same for her."

"Halt!" A Balish soldier had appeared from an alley between houses and blocked their path.

"Run for it!" Paley shouted as she turned and bolted away.

Although Van had thought of simply talking to the soldier, it was too late.

She and Brux dashed off.

Van heard a wobbly *zwoop*, and a nearby house exploded, blasting fragments close to her head. Bits of wood and dust covered her hair. The soldier used a short rod with a wire pyramid on the tip to fire rays at them.

"Damn!" Brux cried, dodging blasts. "He's using a DEW. Curse the Balish and their technology."

"What's a DEW?" Van asked, brushing debris from her hair as she ran.

"Directed-energy weapon." Brux led them through alleyways back toward the outskirts. "They're really expensive, not many around."

"I think he means we're in trouble," Paley said in a shaky voice.

More soldiers joined the pursuit. They closed in.

"This way," Brux said.

The three rushed around a corner and came to a dead end.

"Dammit!" Brux pounded his fists against the shingles of the building blocking their path as if he could knock it down by sheer will.

Van and Paley jiggled the handles on the doors in the alley. They were all locked.

"We're trapped," Van cried.

A door swung open.

"Come in, quickly." Ares's mother waved them inside. She led them through the basement and down a bulkhead that opened into a secret underground passageway.

She introduced herself as Hertha, and the three thanked her profusely.

"You helped me, helped my family," Hertha said. "I pay back by helping you escape."

"How did you get here?" Brux asked kindly. "We're not on the outskirts where you live."

"I part of secret group who resist Balish occupancy, Balish law,"

Hertha said. "We use underground tunnels to help protect ancient documents from Balish. Others in our movement took your friends to secret room in town library."

They passed through the tunnels, under the outskirts of Agerorsa, and exited the passageway into a wooded area on the edge of town.

"You be safe here." Hertha turned to head back. "I see what I do to help your friends."

"Why would our friends need help?" Brux called after Hertha as she disappeared back into the tunnel.

Van changed the subject, hoping talking would calm her nerves. "I know Dishora from my childhood storybook. But what was Solana talking about… the *Sanctus Novus*? Solmor?"

"The *Sanctus Novus* is the book of Balish beliefs." Brux kept a worried eye on the dirt road for their teammates.

Paley let loose with a giddy laugh, full of nerves. "Sounds like a book that would make Jorie throw you up against a tree."

"The Balish think terrigens will cause the downfall of the Living World," Brux sneered. "That they're a danger, and so are the Lodians for protecting them. Ridiculous." He shook his head in disgust.

"Uh, isn't that what we—um, Lodians believe?" Van asked.

Brux shook his head. "The *Victus Opuseulus* tells of a time when the two principles of good and evil rise and oppose each other. It's a natural phenomenon where darkness attempts to absorb all light, canceling itself and everything else out of existence. An event called Dishora."

"So each book has its own belief system," Van said. "Lodians in Salus Valde believe in the teachings of the *Victus Opuseulus*, and the Balish, who are from Aduro but occupy and rule just about every-where, believe in the *Sanctus Novus*."

Brux nodded. "Both of the ancient books help their respective people understand the world—but they're so different from each other." Brux shrugged as if it were no big deal, though Van knew it was to him, and to the people here.

"The originals are written in the language of the ancients,"

Brux continued, "to prevent the lower classes from having access to the information. Many translated copies exist—sanctioned by the Balish—but I'd love to get my hands on the originals."

A black cloud rose from the town's center, breaking their conversation.

Paley scrunched her nose. "Something's burning."

Brux leaped from the brush to flag someone down.

Van peeked through the branches and saw Jorie, Trey, and Elmot hustling down the road.

Brux sighed in relief when they arrived. He patted Jorie on the shoulder and nodded at Trey and Elmot. "Glad you made it."

"They're destroying their own town," Jorie said, catching her breath.

It was the first time Van had seen Jorie flustered. She and Paley came out of hiding and greeted them.

"Solana convinced them that to prevent Solmor, they must cleanse the town of demoniacal influence," Trey said. "By fire."

He and Elmot had smudges of soot on their faces and clothes.

"Jorie met up with us in the library." Elmot brushed off his clothes. "We barely made it out alive."

"Solana's goons caught us rifling through the documents in the secret room," Trey said.

"They let the prisoner go, though, right?" Van asked.

"We escaped." Trey stretched out his hand, showing bloodied knuckles. "Jorie's training session came in handy."

Brux told them about Hertha.

"If it wasn't for her underground friends showing us the way out, we'd be dead," Jorie said.

"Like that townsman tied to the post," Trey added, finally answering Van's question.

"What?" Paley screeched. "He's *dead?*"

"It's about the Coin," Van murmured.

Solana and Van's father had sacrificed an innocent man to get rid of the library. They both would've known the townsman didn't have the real text. Solana and Van's father had used the man as a scapegoat. They didn't want anyone else doing research on the Coin.

Brux said to Van and Paley, "It was a stoning. I didn't want to tell you before. I was hoping to spare you the details. That's why there were no women or children in the square."

"It's the Balish way." Trey looked grim. "Their justice system."

Jorie shook her head sadly.

Paley stood motionless, appearing stunned.

Van's insides jammed up. The crowd had stoned a man to death for having a text she had in her backpack. If Van got caught with Manik's text, next time, she would be the one tied up in town square. Her knees wobbled. She closed her eyes to steady herself.

"Solana's out of control," Jorie said. "She's gathering supporters to help her take over Salus Valde."

"She's already the heir to the Balish kingdom. They control everything." Van's body trembled. "Why does she want *more*?"

"Greed is like a burning flame," Trey said. "It's all-consuming, suffocating everything in its path until nothing remains."

Van bent to calm her dizziness and gagged.

Brux rubbed her back. "It's okay if you want to throw up on my boots again."

Chapter 23

D ay 3 into Day 4: Living World

BEFORE SOLANA BEGUILED the townspeople into burning down their own town, Trey and Elmot had done some digging at the library.

Based on writings in the ancient documents, they both agreed a town called Dricreek was the team's best chance to find more information about the Coin. Just one problem. The town was too small to appear on any of Elmot's maps.

"I only packed detailed maps of the southern regions." Elmot's shoulders slumped, as if he had failed the group.

Van poked around inside her backpack and pulled out her map. "Maybe this will help."

Elmot perused the map. His face lit up. "Here it is! I can get us there. Van, thank you."

"Ho-yeah!" Jorie yelped. "Good work, guys."

"What made you pack that map?" Brux asked. "Especially after Uxa told us the Coin was in the south."

Van shrugged. Manik's text showed her the general location of the Coin to be in a northern region called Fomalhaut. She just couldn't tell anyone without revealing she was Michael Cross's daughter.

With that, they headed northwest toward the Kezef-Fomalhaut border. Van breathed a sigh of relief as Agerorsa faded into the distance.

During the trek, Jorie occasionally blurted out, "Ticktock!" Even when no one trailed behind, irritating Van to no end.

Van's skin also bothered her. It had improved, but still felt sore from the sand crab bites and the resulting rash. Her feet were killing her, and her back ached. Instead of focusing on how miserable she felt, Van redirected her thoughts to fantasizing about using the Twin Gemstones to transport her and Paley back to her comfy bedroom at Mt. Hope Manor.

Dusk had settled in when Jorie announced, "We're losing light. The moon's not strong tonight. We camp here."

Van dropped her backpack on the ground, thankful the moon wasn't "strong." Otherwise, Jorie would've undoubtedly forced them to keep going, and Van didn't think she could survive taking another step.

Paley appeared clammy, with dark circles under her eyes, her hair limp with grime, and a coating of dust covered her body. She looked like a walking corpse, but Van couldn't spare the energy to say so.

Elmot held the map up to the moonlight. "We're two days away."

Van and Paley both groaned.

Itching to flex his archery skills, Trey wanted to hunt for food, but Jorie told him, "No. Unknown terrain is too dangerous."

Trey begrudgingly agreed. They could eat from their meager supplies, which comprised dried meats.

"Um." Paley scanned the food options. "Van, there's only dried meat."

"I'm too hungry to care." Van ditched her stance on veganism and grabbed several strips.

Exhausted, she and Paley dropped to the ground and gnawed on the auroch, paying no heed to the others.

Elmot, Trey, Brux, and Jorie rolled up logs for seats, collected dry sticks, arranged stones in a circle, and started a campfire. Soothing smells of cedar wood filled the air.

"I'm still hungry," Paley whispered to Van.

They watched the others settle in and begin eating their rations.

Van's stomach rumbled. Her share hadn't been nearly enough, either.

"If they hadn't given our boundless bowl away, we wouldn't be starving right now," Van fumed.

"Yeah, but we'd all be dead. None of us would've escaped Agerorsa without Hertha's help."

Van crossed her arms and huffed. "I just want to go home. This entire mission is a waste of time. We don't even know where the Coin is." Though Van knew. Which reminded her to show Manik's text to Brux. Doing so would end this torture.

Around the campfire, Elmot revealed more about the information he and Trey had uncovered in the library. "We confirmed Goustav used the Coin to create his weapon. We didn't have enough time to find out why Amaryl handed it over to Goustav, though."

"She probably didn't know how to use it." Trey snickered.

In a flash, Jorie whipped out Zachery and, with the precision of a practiced warrior, whacked him across the chest with the flat part of the blade.

"Oooof!"

"Amaryl?" Van murmured. The statue of the woman in the fountain she had seen in the House of Lacus was Queen Amaryl of the Dark War. "She was the Anchoress in her day?"

Brux bobbed his head. "Amaryl's mother was killed during the war before she could pass the knowledge of the Anchoress to her daughter." He sat on the log next to Paley, who miraculously perked up.

"No wonder she had no idea how to use it," Paley said.

Van suspected Paley's concern was more for Brux's attention than for caring about Amaryl. She didn't like the growing coziness between Brux and Paley, especially since Paley knew Van had feelings for Brux. As a friend, Paley should step aside.

"How would someone use a *coin* to create a weapon?" Van asked, changing her focus from Brux and Paley to the task at hand. "Sounds ridiculous." Van visualized Queen Amaryl flinging the Coin like a Frisbee, trying to lop off soldiers' heads, and giggled.

The others ignored her, though Elmot gave her a worried side glance as if she were losing her mind. Then he went on. "We found some new information about Goustav. Could be important, if it's true. We read he fathered a child."

"Goustav had no kids," Jorie said. "He got cursed by a sorceress whose family he murdered during the rebellion. Everybody knows that."

Elmot leaned forward. "Goustav believed he had an heir—a girl —*before* the sorceress cursed him."

"If we didn't get jumped by Solana's goons, we could've nabbed some documents to offer proof," Trey said. "Maybe even traced Goustav's lineage. Now, even if we find someone who claims to be his heir, we won't know if he—or *she*—is legit. We can't rely on the cantankerous Elementals to help us verify the heir's identity."

"Whoa," Brux said. "If Goustav's lineage carried forward, one of his descendants would be the rightful heir to the Balish kingdom."

"And a tremendous threat to Solana's throne," Trey added. "Can you imagine? That heir wouldn't stand a chance."

Elmot held his palms toward the fire. "It's a good thing the Balish think our Anchoress-in-waiting's bloodline died out during the Dark War. That her existence today is a myth carried on by the wishful thinking of orthodox Lodians. Or they'd try to kill her too."

Brux turned to Elmot. "I'm not sure if Solana believes that."

"That's something no Bale would ever believe in," Trey said. "The Anchoress is a Lodian belief."

"The Balish fear our tribe," Jorie said. "With or without the Anchoress-in-waiting."

"The Balish fear Lodians because we're descendants of the Elementals," Brux said, addressing Van and Paley. "Not all vichors can harness the energy of nature to create magic. Our blood connection to the Elementals gives Lodians the genetic capability to be highly skilled in magic, more so than other tribes. Those with the highest concentration of Elemental blood are pureblooded, or 'royal.'"

"Elemental blood gives Lodians the ability to connect to the frequencies of the Elementals to create potent magic," Trey added. "During a war, the Balish could no longer outlaw magic, putting them at a disadvantage."

"They fear us because our Grigori are strong." Jorie beat her fist against her chest like a beast.

Brux ignored Jorie's outburst and said, "The Anchoress is super-powerful because she has the highest concentration of Elemental blood of any human. That, coupled with her innate ability to connect to the moon's energy to amplify her magic, makes her an unbeatable force."

"Keeping the percentage of Elemental blood at its highest is why the Lodian Consilium and the Lodian people encourage royals to marry other royals," Elmot said. "This pleases the Elementals, ensuring their continued favor of the Lodian race."

"Seriously, how come nobody has any clue who this Anchoress person is?" Paley asked. "You all seem to think it's Daisy, but you're not sure."

Trey looked up from the campfire. "Lineages from a thousand years ago are hard to trace. People had just begun to use surnames. Those who believe Amaryl, the last known Anchoress, had a baby refer to her child as the lost baby of Amaryl and Rowen."

"Uxa confirmed the Anchoress bloodline exists, that means Amaryl had a baby," Brux said. "The Lodian Consilium perpetuates the myth that Amaryl *didn't* have a baby to protect her heir from the Balish."

"The baby survived, and her parents didn't," Trey said. "So we have to assume someone adopted her. But who? And what name did they give her?"

"And Lodian tradition evolved into carrying last names through the female's line," Elmot said. "While the Balish carry last names through the male's line."

"Theoretically, the Anchoress heir could live anywhere," Brux added. "Her bloodline makes her resistant to the drain of the Earth World. She can live there without having to recharge."

Van undeniably felt drained when she didn't go to her special classes. The Elders allowed her to stop going when she was in the fifth grade, and Van had gotten sick again. If Van were the Anchoress-in-waiting, she wouldn't need to recharge in the Living World. For her, this settled it. Daisy had to be the Anchoress heir.

"Everyone knows your family's lineage, Brux," Trey said.

"How come?" Paley asked.

"The purest bloodline families are celebrities in Salus Valde." Elmot hugged his knees.

"It's the consensus among those who believe in the Anchoress heir that your family traces back closest to the lost baby of Amaryl and Rowen," Trey said to Brux. "That's what I heard."

"I agree," Brux said. "I think if the Anchoress heir is someone on our two teams, it's my sister."

"Can't there be two?" Van asked. "Two teams, two heirs?"

Elmot shook his head. "There is only one. The firstborn female carries the magic of the Anchoress bloodline. And when she connects to her magical abilities, she'll become so powerful the Balish royal family will feel threatened."

"No kidding," Trey said. "Once she's called forth, the Moors will no longer be in denial about her bloodline. They'll know she exists and send assassins to kill her like there's no tomorrow."

A pained look clouded Brux's face.

Jorie threw a contemptuous glare at Trey. "Not helpful." She stood. "Enough. Time for shut-eye."

After what had happened in Agerorsa, they decided to sleep in shifts.

Van's body weighed heavily, as if her muscles were made of sandbags, so she didn't care what they did. She was out the moment her head hit the sleeping bag.

Chapter 24

Day 5: 6:17 a.m., Living World

Van slept through the night. Yet when the golden light of daybreak shone on her face, she thought the morning had come too fast.

Walking filled her day. Walk, walk, walking. With little rest, except brief stops for water and nibbles from their diminishing food stores.

Jorie kept repeating, "Making good time to Dricreek." Brainwashing them into another forced death march.

By afternoon, Van's sweat-drenched clothes clung to her body. She shuffled her throbbing feet from fatigue, and no longer cared about her chipped nail polish and frizzed hair. Her only goal: survival.

"Are we there yet?" Paley's shoulders slumped. "How much longer?"

Van, a top athlete, kept fit and even she found it difficult to keep pace with the group. Her heart went out to couch potato Paley, figuring the journey proved even more arduous for her friend.

The rest of the team entertained themselves by goading one another.

"You're naive to think it's a coincidence… our mission… coincides with the Alignment." Trey panted from exertion, trying to keep his breath while talking and walking.

"I never… said it was." Brux drew in his breath from the effort of the walk.

Van had difficulty getting the words out of her dry mouth. "Wha-what's the Alignment?" Not that she cared. She wanted the distraction.

"Whaddya live under a rock?" Even Jorie breathed heavily from the challenging trek, though her expertly cut mohawk held up like a trooper.

Van conceded Jorie had simply been born with great hair.

"Every year, there's a specific time in the celestial cycle," Brux said. "When the round calendar… the solar calendar of the Earth World and the linear calendar… the lunation calendar of the Living World… intersect for thirty days. We call your dating system the Calendar Round, and ours, the Long Count."

"Like a wheel rolling on the road." Elmot fared about as well as the others. "The solar calendar goes in a circle like a wheel. The same date comes around every year." He took a breath. "The lunation calendar is one long string of dates. The same date is never repeated—the metaphorical road."

"The ancients called the point of intersection—when the wheel hits the road—Luxta," Brux said. "Today, we use the translation, Alignment."

"The thirty days is now?" Paley asked, red-faced and scuffling to keep up.

Brux and Trey grunted.

"Why's it not a coincidence?" Van asked.

"Folklore says you can only get the Coin during the Alignment," Jorie said.

"If we miss this window of opportunity… the Coin disappears

back into its place behind time and space." Brux paused to catch his breath, then continued. "Still existing but at a higher, unreachable vibration. If someone takes possession of the Coin, it gets anchored here."

Dusk crept over the horizon, and Jorie mercifully announced they could stop for the night. She set up camp, while Elmot and Paley went to search for berries and mushrooms.

Trey scanned the terrain and decided the area was ripe for kopidodens. He darted away to hunt for the squirrel-like creatures.

Brux went to gather firewood.

This time, Van volunteered to help Brux, hoping she could get him alone.

"Can I borrow your axe?" Van asked Jorie. It would be easier to chop, rather than break branches, ruining what was left of her manicure.

"It's a *labrys*," Jorie said. "A weapon of war. If you try to touch it, you'll pull back a bloody stump."

Van couldn't tell if Jorie's reddened face was from being sunburned, or being enraged.

Gathering wood proved a waste of Van's effort. She tried to get Brux alone, yet Paley and Elmot kept intruding by foraging for edible plants in the same area where Van and Brux gathered wood.

People's lack of boundaries on this trip made Van want to scream, as did the stress of trying to find the Coin before her father did. She wanted to fix his mess without bumping into him, so they could both get back to their normal lives. Van would spend her days lounging at the beach, and her father would go back to being a good guy, doing his job as a Grigori.

Right now, with Solana running amok, torturing innocent people and burning down villages, Van's father probably kept getting closer and closer to the Coin. The farther north they got, the more Manik's text would help them. She had to get Brux alone.

The rest of the team ran out of matches, so Paley offered hers.

Brux started the fire, while Jorie prepared several kopidodens caught by Trey. Elmot skewered the meat onto sticks, along with some mushrooms, and cooked the kabobs over the campfire. It smelled delicious, and Van and Paley were starving, so they didn't complain about eating the strange meat.

After dinner, they sat by the fire, drinking rockwine from Elmot's wineskin, one of their few remaining rations. For fun, they went around the circle, each declaring which food they would eat if they still had the boundless bowl.

Van had never experienced wine before. It smelled like musty earth and tasted like flat grape juice with a kick. Her cheeks flushed. The wine warmed her stomach, extending into her fingers and toes. It gave her a sense of groundedness and confidence. After a few more passes, her anxiety waned, and heartfelt affection for the others grew.

They're all pretty great. I'm so lucky to be on this adventure with them.

She laughed at everything Brux said, funny or not. Van had such a good time, her cheeks hurt from smiling.

"Done." Trey whipped the empty wineskin at Elmot.

Van frowned at the wineskin, then fell into a fit of giggles.

"Good thing," Brux said. "Someone's had enough."

To Van's surprise, he tilted his head toward Paley, who slouched on the log with her eyes half-closed.

The others chuckled, though none of them seemed affected by the wine.

"You laff now," Paley slurred. "I'm th' loss baby—th' Anchoressss." She slowly slid to the ground.

Van clung to her seat, staring wide-eyed at her motionless friend. "Is she dead?"

Paley wheezed and then began snoring as loudly as a buffalroo.

This sent Van into another fit of giggles.

"Time to call it a night." Jorie rose from her log. "Who wants first watch?"

"I will," Van and Brux said in unison.

Jorie furrowed her brow at Van. "Okay," she said, as if it were a question. "*Both* of you take first watch. Brux, after two hours, wake up Elmot, then it goes to Trey, then me. It should be close to dawn by then." No one seemed surprised Jorie skipped Paley.

Van had planned to take first watch and, once everyone was

asleep, wake Brux and show him Manik's text. Now Brux had made it easy for her. They would be lookouts together.

She watched Jorie and Trey settle into their sleeping bags, but before Elmot got into his, he jumped up and—to Van's horror—rummaged through Paley's backpack. He grabbed something, and Van panicked. What if it was Paley's Twin Gemstone? Van held her breath.

Elmot pulled out a small brown square and pulled the string. He wrapped the inflated sleeping bag over Paley and then tucked himself into his own.

Van sighed in relief, though now she had a headache.

Brux tossed a wineskin filled with water at her. "Drink. I'm going to get more wood." He pulled a branch from the campfire to use as a torch. "I'll be right back."

Van watched the dark woods swallow Brux and became overwhelmed with anxiety. Her hands trembled, and the forest shifted. The wine that had bolstered her had turned. She closed her eyes and felt both nauseated and giddy. No wonder Jorie had hesitated to let Van take watch. Well, their leader was right. Van wasn't fit for such an important task.

She slid off the log onto the ground and sat in the lotus position. She pressed her sitz bonez into the cool dirt and straightened her spine as she had done many times in her special classes. Her heart pounded against her ribcage, her breathing erratic.

To calm herself, she began a technique called four-square breathing. Deep breath in, one… two… three… four. Hold, one… two… three… four. Let it out, one… two… three… four. Hold again, one… two… three… four. And, again.

She repeated four-square breathing until her heart stopped racing. A calmness filled her, the same tranquility that happens just before drifting to sleep.

"Hello, my little warrior." Jacynthia appeared bright and vibrant, hovering several feet above the ground. Her long white hair flowed in a mysterious, otherworldly breeze.

Jacynthia! Van said without speaking.

"Your distressed mind called out to me. I am here. But have little time."

I have so much I want to talk to you about. The wine got in Van's way and disrupted her peaceful state. Jacynthia became blurry and started to fade.

"Breathe deep. Focus on the light within. Stay calm."

Van struggled to obey. Finally, Jacynthia came into focus again. Van had many questions, one of them being the location of the Coin. However, she asked her most pressing question first. The issue related to the motive behind her father's actions.

Why, in a place where there's so much for everyone, do people commit acts of… evil?

"What is dark seeks that which is light to extinguish it. But by doing so only serves to enhance its brightness. Our own fears and weaknesses create darkness. It gains energy through others because it cannot harness energy on its own. Evil has no power, other than that which we give it."

I—

"Hey!" A hand roughly grasped Van's shoulder and shook it.

She lost her connection to Jacynthia and snapped her eyes open.

Brux hovered over her, smirking. "No slacking on the job." He walked to the fire and threw in some dry branches. "I've never seen anyone sleep sitting in that position before."

"Maybe because your big mouth keeps waking them up." Van angrily brushed dirt off her butt and then plopped down on one of the log seats.

"Nah." Brux turned toward Van with a stupid grin. "That's not it." The campfire roared. He stepped back and sat on the log next to Van.

She jumped up.

"Hey, now. No need to be like that." Brux continued grinning as he watched Van rifle through her backpack.

"I have to show you something," she said.

Brux raised his brow.

"You can't tell anyone. Promise?"

"Promise," Brux said with an even bigger grin.

Van glanced around the campsite, satisfied everyone else was asleep. She sat down next to Brux and handed him the most sought-after text in the Living World.

"What's this? Your diary?" Brux flipped the book back and forth. "I'm flattered." Pieces of the burned text came loose and crumbled onto his lap.

"Careful with that! Read the cover."

"—ridicus Lib—lus? *Veridicus Libellus!*" He strained to keep his voice in check. "How—what are you—where?"

"This is a first," Van mocked. "You, being unable to speak."

"Seriously, Vanessa," he said. "How did you come across this text?"

"I—I, uh… *found* it," Van said, worried by his tone. "Um, in the woods." Maybe she shouldn't have shown him.

Brux opened his mouth to speak.

Van flashed him her palm. "Listen. I know having this on me is dangerous. I don't need to hear it."

"Dangerous on account of it being Manik's text, yeah," Brux said. "And because the Balish regulate all the books in circulation. You need to have papers authorized by the Balish court system proving you have the right to own a book."

"There are no *papers*," Van said. "I didn't show it to you to get a lecture. I showed it to you because I need your help to decipher it. It has information about the Coin."

"Did you have this text the whole time? Is this how you knew we should head north?"

Van gave him a timid nod. "Nobody else knows about it. You can't tell *anyone*."

"Not even Paley?" Brux opened its cover with great care.

"No. Paley is incapable of keeping anything to herself. I need you to look at the map." Van reached over and carefully flipped the pages for Brux. "Make sure I read it right, and see if there's anything else that could be helpful to us or Daisy. Maybe we can get word to her somehow."

Brux remained quiet as he perused the text.

"I know the Balish consider it the diary of a madman," Van

said. His unresponsiveness made her uncomfortable. "Maybe it's nothing. We should just forget about it."

"The Balish discredit it because they discredit Manik," Brux said, his nose buried in the text.

"But he was the Balish king during the Dark War," Van said. "When Goustav defeated the demons and scored a victory for their side, right? So why?"

"Manik intended to share the victory with the Lodians, and he had the poor sense of marrying a Lodian princess, Zurial—Amaryl's baby sister. Hardly worth it. Zurial died during childbirth the same night his brother Goustav rose against him." He flipped through the pages, completely absorbed. "The Balish never forgave Manik for being a Lodian sympathizer. It was the main reason for Goustav's rebellion."

"I can hardly read any of it." Van squinted at the text. "I mean, some of it makes sense. It's weird. Some words I understand."

Brux lifted his nose out of the book and narrowed his eyes at Van. "You can read some of these words?"

Van shrugged. "Yeah, why?"

Brux gaped at her like an idiot.

"Stop it, Brux. My eyes didn't burn out, *obviously*."

"Daisy has a knack for reading the language too." Brux shook his head. "Never mind. I think I can figure this out." He turned to the first page. "The ancient words are hard to translate. The text being burnt doesn't help, either. Here." He pointed to a single paragraph on the first page of the book. "It translates loosely to: *Future generations... don't let history repeat itself... during our time all was lost to darkness... battle not against each other, know thy true enemy... heed my words.*"

"What happened during his time?" Van scrunched her brow. "Demons rose. Goustav destroyed them, then turned around and killed everyone who opposed him."

"Is that the real story? The entire story?" Brux flipped back and forth to various pages. "Manik gives us more warnings. Listen to this: *do not misuse the energies of nature...*"

"The Coin?"

"I think so. Manik says not to use the power of the Coin against each other—that's *an incorrect use that damages the soul,* which will make it more difficult to *cling to the light.* Only use the Coin's power against *true evil.* And here, look." Brux pointed to a different paragraph. "*Under no circumstances must the Anchoress surrender her light.* Do you realize what this means?"

"The Coin is an object of light, and don't surrender it to evil? Darkness? Evil darkness?"

"No. I mean—yes. What I mean is, Manik just confirmed the Anchoress bloodline survived the Dark War. Uxa was right."

"Ooooh. No wonder the Balish don't want anyone reading it."

"Listen. He says there's a heavy spiritual obligation attached to use of the Coin."

"Told you so," Van said. "Don't surrender it to darkness."

"This is incredible. The Coin is a magically charged object in its own right. It has its own magical properties. So someone undisciplined or irresponsible can benefit from its power."

"But you still have to access its energy to create your own magic?" Van asked.

Brux nodded. "Manik says you have to be pure of heart and use it only for the good of the people. *If one accesses the power of the Coin with the intent to use it against other humans, which is an alignment with evil, it will cause the holder to fall into the depths of darkness. Their soul will be lost. One must temper oneself against the constant inner pull, back and forth, between darkness and light. One tip toward darkness and it will amplify this part of the soul.*"

Brux pulled his nose out of the text and stared at Van. "The belief the Anchoress has to be worthy to wield the power of the Coin must come from this part of the text. If she uses the Coin's power against another person, her soul will become corrupted."

"Does he say which spell Goustav used to create his demon-killing weapon?" Van asked.

"No." He turned back to the text. "But here's something about the Coin's magical properties. I can't make out too much of it. Looks like it attracts luck… leads the holder on the correct path… useful for battle strategies, escaping enemies. The negative properties, the shadow side of the Coin—" Brux pointed to a charred area on the page. "Can't read it. The rest is burned out." He flipped the pages. "Manik mentions Luxta here…"

Van leaned in toward Brux and looked at the spot he pointed to in the text. His scent, being that close to him, made her stomach unsettled again, except this time in a good way.

He continued reading silently. "Wait a minute. This can't be right…"

"What is it? Something about the Coin? Are we going the wrong way?"

He ignored Van, turned to a new page, and kept reading. After flipping through a few more pages, Brux stopped and glanced at her. "It's a prolepsis." His jaw slacked. "This text. It's a *prolepsis!*"

"So?" Van didn't know what a prolepsis was, and she wasn't about to ask him.

"Manik wrote this as a warning to the *Lodians*. He's trying to warn against something he predicted would happen in the future."

"How would he know about the future?" Van scoffed. Something Brux had read in the text bothered him, and it wasn't the prolepsis.

"After the death of his wife, Zurial, Manik went insane from grief. He became a hermit and spent the rest of his life living in the hollow of a giant tree, where he spent his time in reflection and meditation and wrote *this* text."

"He was psychic?" Van raised her eyebrows.

"It seems so. At least, Manik believed he could predict the future."

"That's probably why people thought he was crazy. Check this out." Van reached over and fanned the pages to show Brux the hidden map. "That's the Coin, right? In the north? Fomalhaut?" She pointed out the crude drawing of a circle with a pentagram in it.

"It is," Brux said. "We'd need to show Elmot to be sure."

"No!"

"We're the team closest to the Coin. The others need to know, Van. It's selfish of us to keep this from them."

"You can't tell anyone! You promised!"

Brux's tone became even more serious. "The night your father disappeared, did he give you anything else besides this text?"

Van bristled over Brux figuring out her father was Michael Cross, which was exactly why she didn't want to share the text with the rest of the team. "I never *said* my father gave me the text. I *said* I found it." Brux infuriated her.

"Van, as Aelia Cross's daughter," he said, fidgeting, "your bloodline… its purity rivals mine, Daisy's." He paused to see if she had any recognition of understanding.

She didn't.

"It makes you a contender for being the Anchoress-in-waiting."

Van shivered, whether from the coolness of the night or from exposing herself to Brux. She didn't know. Or maybe it was from the realization she might carry the magical bloodline of a legendary warrior.

"None of them have figured out I'm Michael Cross's daughter, right?" Van asked, referring to the rest of the team. Uxa had announced her last name when she separated them into teams, but no one had mentioned the connection so far.

"At first, we debated about it," Brux said. "Then we figured if you were related to Michael Cross, you would've told us." Brux snapped the text closed. "It's time to wake up Elmot."

She reached to take the text from Brux and, for a split second, worried he wouldn't give it back.

Brux threw her a lopsided smile and handed it over. "Keep it safe."

Van slipped the text into a pocket of her backpack while Brux shook Elmot awake.

"Already?" Elmot forced himself up and sat by the fire. His clothes appeared as neat and pressed as ever.

Van and Brux inflated their sleeping bags.

"I'm not sure I can sleep." Van envisioned waking up with Jorie's axe at her throat for being a traitor like her father, all because Brux blabbed. "Are you sure you'll keep this a secret? All of it?"

Brux nodded, the tips of his soft blond hair sparkled in the campfire light. "At least, it explains why you're here." He grinned. "Paley, I'm still not sure about."

Van gave him a wary eye.

"How about this? You can stick close to me." He unzipped his sleeping bag, pulled Van in, and squeezed her to his chest.

"You're sure we're not related, right?" she asked.

Brux chuckled. "Absolutely not. Historians have traced our families' bloodlines back as far as possible. The Lakes and the Crosses do not share ancestry. We're good."

Van snuggled into Brux. He was a perfect fit. Being wrapped in his arms made her feel cozy and safe. Before drifting off to sleep, she felt him gently brush his cheek against her hair.

Chapter 25

Day 6: 5:36 a.m., Living World

THE SUN ASCENDED, throwing peach-colored light across the horizon, waking Van.

The quietness of their camp lulled her. Minor aches in her body throbbed. She smiled at the coziness of being warm and nestled in Brux's arms.

She jolted. What if the others caught them like this? What would they think?

With distress, she realized all her teammates, except Paley, had taken watch and had already seen them. Van wriggled to get out of the sleeping bag, causing Brux to stir.

"What's up?" he asked, groggily.

"I don't want Paley to see us," Van whispered. She climbed out of his sleeping bag.

"Why not?" Brux mumbled, still not fully awake.

"Mornin'," Jorie said with a wide grin. She had taken the last watch and now sat on the lookout log, her mohawk straight and perfect. She stood and tossed dirt onto the fire. "Let's get moving. Everyone, *up!*"

Elmot did a full body stretch in his sleeping bag and yawned. He rose and beamed at Van and Brux. "You two have a good night?"

"Shh!" Van pointed to Paley and then put her index finger to her lips.

"Love secrets. We'll talk later. For now, mum's the word." He mimicked locking his lips.

A groan came from Paley's sleeping bag, which showed lumps of movement from within.

Jorie walked over to Trey, who still lay sound asleep. "Where's a buffalroo when you need one?" She prodded the sleeping bag with her toe. "C'mon, pretty boy. *Up!*"

"Okay, okay," Trey grumbled.

They had no water to wash with, which mortified Van. She desperately wanted to take a shower. For breakfast, they each had half of a dried auroch strip and shared a few sips of water from one of their wineskins. They packed up the campsite, being sure to leave the area the same way they had found it, with no trace they had camped there. Then they began their all-day trek to Dricreek.

By early evening, the weary group trudged down a damp dirt road scattered with puddles.

"Dricreek is just ahead," Elmot announced.

Shoddy, box-shaped houses popped up with more and more frequency. The few villagers they passed tended to their own business and paid no mind to the travelers. The people appeared shorter yet bulkier than those Van had seen earlier on their journey, and their preferred style of clothing comprised linen, wool, and animal furs.

They reached the hub of the small village. It consisted of a handful of rustic rectangular dwellings clustered around an extensive, muddy clearing. The village and its people seemed rudimentary, as if the place had been state-of-the-art a thousand years ago.

"Maybe we can get Beowulf to show us around," Van whispered to Paley.

They both giggled, delirious from exhaustion and lack of food.

"It'll do," Jorie said in a tired voice. "Let's check out the long-house." She led them toward the largest dwelling, which, on closer inspection, appeared sturdy, despite its weathered appearance.

Van and Paley waited on the front porch while the rest of the team went inside.

The handmade wooden sign above the doorway read *Ox's Bunkhouse*. To the side of the entryway lay a lumpy shag doormat.

"Shouldn't that be in front of the door?" Paley asked.

"Leave it alone." Van surveyed the longhouse's exterior. "This place looks slightly better than sleeping on the ground."

Paley nudged the mat with her toe and jumped back, startled, as did Van.

The mat rose onto four legs and whimpered.

"It's a living mop," Van said.

"I think it's a dog." Paley bent down to scratch behind what seemed to be the dog's ears.

"Don't!" Van yanked her back. "It could bite you."

They left the mop-dog and entered the main hall, a wide, one-level hovel. Roughly finished, oversized dining tables lined the two long walls, leaving a walkway down the middle of the rectangular room. Along the back wall ran a bar that, despite its well-worn appearance, looked like a newer addition. Animal skins hung on the walls as decorations, giving Van the willies.

Because they were in Balish-occupied territory, Jorie delegated Brux—a male—to go to the bar and negotiate their stay with the bartender, while the others hung back.

The bartender, a rugged man with a hardened face, cackled at something Brux said. The man flashed a gap-toothed grin and haggled with Brux over the price.

While Brux paid the man, a white bird flew in from the open door. It landed on a rafter. Nobody seemed to notice or care, but it gave Van a chill. She recalled a superstition that claimed a white bird indoors was an omen of death.

Brux returned to the group. "Ox, the owner, wouldn't take s-stips."

Van figured s-stips were the unmarked silver coins, as opposed to the bronze stips, or b-stips.

"He's been afraid to break the law since Prince Devon's death," Brux continued. "He heard the Balish are nearby, may even come here. I gave him one losc for all of us. Pretty steep for this area, but it's better than sleeping on the ground."

"Hardly," Van murmured.

"What did he think was so funny?" Jorie asked.

Brux shrugged. "I told him we were marketeers' scouts in search of the Runestar."

"He appreciates the futility of our journey," Trey said.

Ox ceased his pointless task of rubbing scuffed tin mugs with a grayish dish rag and led them through the back doorway, down a muddy path, and to a bunkhouse he called the "King's Castle."

Van assumed he had spoken tongue-in-cheek when she saw the dwelling before them. In no way could it be mistaken for a castle. The hut, shaped like an oversized tent made of wood, had a sloping thatched roof that reached to the ground. Six doors led to six separate rooms, each able to sleep four people. No other travelers were staying in the bunkhouse and paying with a Balish-stamped silver coin entitled each of them to get a private room.

In Van's room were two cot-sized wood framed bunk beds. She sat on the edge of the bottom bunk and dropped her backpack onto what looked like a sheepskin bedspread—and choked from the resulting dust wave. Van kicked off her hiking boots and massaged her throbbing feet, longing for her pink, fuzzy slippers. She had no sooner lain down to rest when Jorie knocked, summoning Van to join the others outside.

"I just talked to Ox," Jorie said. "He knew nothing about ancient documents in the area or any rumors about *any* valuable artifacts from the Dark War, Runestar, or anything else." Jorie winked at them so they would know she also meant the Coin. "He's not serving dinner until after sundown."

"Ugh!" Paley stomped her foot. "I'm starving *now!*"

"The farmhands must come here to eat after a hard day's work," Brux said.

"Makes sense," Elmot agreed. "The town's size is deceiving. We're surrounded by outbuildings. Small farms sell their food to larger towns like Agerorsa. Some specialize in animal husbandry. This area is also known for its millers and blacksmiths."

"Well, aren't you the book of facts?" Trey said.

Elmot smacked Trey on the arm.

"Ox told me to check out another eatery called the Grotto," Jorie said. "It's just outside of town a mile or so down the road, open twenty-four seven."

Van groaned at the suggestion of more walking.

Elmot scrunched his forehead in thought, probably recalling one of his maps. "It must be where people who don't live here go after their day is done. That location is located closer to the farms, drawing people in from the surrounding rural areas. It's off the main route."

"Take only your coin pouches," Jorie said. "And a carefully hidden weapon, if you have one. We want to blend in as much as possible."

Before Van dashed to her room, she noticed Jorie wasn't wearing Zachery. She snickered, imagining Jorie tucking the war axe safely into bed after singing it a lullaby.

Van grabbed her coin pouch and her Twin Gemstone, and, instead of getting a weapon—which she didn't have—she used a tissue to lift the bloodstained patch from the binding of the text and slipped it into her pocket.

The team left Ox's Bunkhouse and marched down the muddy road toward the eatery.

The Grotto, a large rectangular dwelling, featured exposed wood and was crowded with what must have been the region's entire population. Van could barely make out the mural of feasting lords and maidens covering the far wall.

In one corner, three brawny men dressed in burlap shirts huddled together at a table, deep in conversation as they mowed down trays of what looked like enormous turkey legs. A circle of hearty women with flushed cheeks, wearing worn farm dresses, sat around a stone fireplace drinking from tin cups. A bone-thin waitress wearing an ill-fitted, high-waisted wool dress handed out frothy mugs at a table of men playing cards.

"Spread out, so we're not so intimidating," Jorie said. "Get as much information as you can without being obvious. Afterward, we'll gather for dinner and share what we find."

Paley groaned. "I want to eat *now*."

Van, Paley, and Brux tried to stick together, but Jorie shooed them apart.

"Go make some friends," she commanded.

In a flash, Paley was off in search of food.

Brux wandered away, but as soon as Jorie left, he circled back around to Van.

Her heart whirled.

"Something's up," he said. "What's going on with you?"

How did he know? Van flushed. She reached into her pocket and pulled out the crumpled tissue that held the patch. She told Brux how she'd gotten it. "I'm going to ask around to see if anyone recognizes what uniform this patch came from or knows this Rogziel guy. He was involved in the attack on Prince Devon. He knows something about my father, I'm sure of it."

Brux frowned.

"Oh, I know," Van said. "It's a long shot."

"It's not that—it's just, probably not a good idea to go around asking strangers about a Balish soldier's bloody patch." Before Van could object, he added, "And you don't have to ask around. I know what kind of uniform that patch came from. Van… your father's page name… it's Rogziel."

Van lost her breath for a second, stunned. "The patch is from my *father's* uniform?" She needed to make sure she heard him right.

Brux nodded.

Van's father had taken her mother's last name of Cross in marriage because it was a Lodian custom. Now that her father had sided with the Balish, he had apparently taken his page name back.

"When your step-mother married your father, they followed the Balish custom of Genie taking Michael's last name."

"You're saying he loved Genie enough to ditch the Lodian tradition for his Balish bride?"

"No, Van. What I'm saying is—how is it possible you don't know?"

"Know *what?*" Van glowered at him, ill at ease. "I know people think my father killed my mother. It's no secret everyone, including the Elders, was against their marriage. He was a commoner, and she was royal. I mean, *what else is there? What?*"

"It wasn't simply because of him being a commoner," Brux said. "I'm sorry to tell you this, Van. Your father… he's Balish." Brux sounded as if he were announcing a death.

"Part Balish," he answered Van's questioning gape. "From his grandfather, who defected from Aduro to Salus Valde. That's why the Elders were against Michael's marriage to Aelia. He diluted the Cross royal bloodline—your bloodline. Remember, it's considered a disgrace to dilute a pure Lodian bloodline, an act against the Elementals. It could cause the Lodians to fall out of favor with them. If we fall out of favor… well, the Elementals are the binders of Manik's law."

Tainted blood coursed through Van's veins. Her father had betrayed her. Made her… *contaminated.* "How can I be a contender for the Anchoress-in-waiting, then? I'm… I'm not… *pure.*"

"Pure*blooded*, you mean. The Anchoress bloodline is carried through the female's lineage. You could still carry the magic from Aelia *if* your mother was the Anchoress-in-waiting, which she may well have been."

Van raised her eyes to Brux's. "Did he kill her?"

Brux's lips formed a stern line.

"*Did he?*"

"It's a common belief," Brux said grimly. "No one could prove it, though."

"And the patch?" Van asked, despite feeling sick inside.

"It's from a Balish palace guard uniform. If Wiglaf gave it to you, if it is your father's, Van, I'm sorry. It means he's dead."

"Why would you say something like that?" Van shouted. "You're such a jerk. You know nothing!"

"Listen to me, Van," Brux pleaded. "Uxa told me no one survived the demon attack on Prince Devon. They've accounted for all bodies involved in the ambush, *all* of them."

Van whimpered like a tortured animal.

"And if Wiglaf—"

"You're an ass," Van spat. "Stay away from me!" Van turned from Brux to hide her teary eyes. Several men near them glanced their way as she stomped off.

Brux had pure blood. They could never be together. In this world, purebloods married purebloods. And that was fine. She would never do what her father did—contaminate Brux's child, the heir of a royal bloodline, with her impure blood.

Her father's actions infuriated her, to where she wasn't even sure she wanted to save his soul anymore. But she still wanted to find the Coin. To spite him!

How could he have hurt my mother like that? Hurt me?

He'd never cared about either of them. No wonder he married Genie, another Bale. The rumors about him were true. He was a money-grubbing traitor.

Van refocused on her mission and explored the room. She had no desire to walk up to a stranger and start a conversation. But she wanted to do her part for the team and the mission. She wandered through the crowd, trying to find someone approachable, and ended up in the far corner of the eatery alone.

She doubted Paley had done any better. It disheartened Van to see Paley with two boys who were plying her with food and drink. Van scanned the room for the others, figuring she couldn't be the only loser unable to connect.

But they had all succeeded. Trey had joined the men playing cards. Elmot stood at the bar, showing off his maps to a few patrons. Jorie arm-wrestled with a beefy man, surrounded by a crowd placing bets.

To her dismay, Brux had also done well. He sat at a table drinking with four giggling girls who seemed enamored by his attention.

"Why so glum?" asked a voice behind her.

Startled, Van turned. "I, um, sorry. I didn't see you there."

A thin man with salt-and-pepper hair leaned back in a wooden chair propped against the wall. He wore a full-length leather overcoat, breeches, and calf-length boots. He leaned forward, slamming the chair down onto all fours. "Not from 'round here, either, huh?"

"No, I—wait, you're a traveler too?"

"Yup." He stood and extended his hand. "Len Fleeceman. Traveling peddler. On my way to Nickelbury. Made a quick pit stop here for some food and drink. I've an excellent assortment of merchandise. Top quality." His smile reached his ears, displaying clean white teeth.

She clasped Len's wrist, remembering to do the Living World handshake. "Van."

"So, what brings you 'round these parts, Van? Not much up here for marketeers' scouts. You lost? Or just passin' through?"

It never ceased to amaze Van that their clothes, ages, and mannerisms worked so well with their cover story. "We're staying at Ox's Bunkhouse. Are you staying there too?" As soon as the words came out of Van's mouth, she knew she'd made a mistake. For one thing, she had just told a stranger where she was staying. For another, she already knew the bunkhouse had no other guests. It deflated her ego to realize how bad she was at conversing with new people.

"We're after the Runestar," she said, digging an even deeper ditch for herself. "There's a rumor it surfaced in Fomalhaut." Van hoped for a save by adding this last bit of information, which would get him talking about the Fomalhaut region and maybe the Coin.

Len snort-chuckled, spraying from his nostrils. "Now, where'd you hear that from? Never mind." He used his sleeve to wipe his nose. "Lemme fill you in on a little secret." He leaned closer. "The Runestar's not in Fomalhaut."

"It's not?"

"Nope. I've got the Runestar." He beat his thumb against his chest. "It's out back, in my cart." Len took a few steps and opened a backdoor next to where they stood. "Come have a look-see."

Len seemed like a pretty decent guy, and Van wanted to snag

this opportunity to prove she wasn't so useless after all. Even if Len didn't have the real Runestar, if she bought something, it might get him talking about the Coin. As a traveling peddler who was familiar with artifacts created around the time of the Dark War, he'd have loads of valuable information.

She followed Len out of the eatery and into a dark alley.

Chapter 26

Day 6: 7:35 p.m., Living World

THE DOOR CLICKED SHUT behind Van, locking her out of the Grotto.

She immediately realized the folly of trailing after a stranger into a deserted alley. Now, she could only go deeper into the blackness. She inched forward, barely able to make out Len in the moonlit night.

"This way." He waved his arm at her. "Follow me. Not far."

She kept moving, but lost sight of him. "Len?" A scuffling noise behind her broke the silence. She twisted around, squinting in the darkness. "Le—"

Someone grabbed her from the front and clasped a hand over her mouth, muffling her scream. Van squirmed, but his grip tightened. He shoved her against the wall in the alley.

"Why, in light's name, are you following some strange man outside?" Brux growled. "Do you have a death wish?"

Van figured he must've slipped out the door before it closed.

Brux loosened his hand, but before she answered, Len lit a torch from his cart parked on the street.

"Everything okay?" Len called back. "Didn't lose you, did I? Oh, I see you brought a friend. Good! Good! I've plenty of merchandise to go 'round. Come on. No need to be shy." He waved them over to view his wares.

Van glared at Brux, wriggled out of his grasp, and marched toward Len's cart.

"Any more friends you want to bring over's fine with me." Len opened both sides of the cart, lit torches he had in holders, and then fussed with the arrangement of his merchandise. "You wanna bring high-quality merchandise home to your parents? I got the selection. I'll sell cheap. Wholesale. Make your parents proud."

"Where's the Runestar?" Van threw Brux a smug glance. "He said he has it."

Brux twisted his lips. "Yeah, sure he does."

"Right here." Len handed a piece of jewelry to Brux.

Van wandered to the other side of the cart. Len had mostly junk for sale. Van noticed a book peeking out from under some scarves. Its binding looked similar to the binding of Manik's text. She pulled it out. "Aw. Cool." It was a translation manual for the language of the ancients.

She overheard Brux snarl, "This is a fake."

Van hurried back around the cart.

Brux clutched Len's jacket with one hand and held a dagger to his throat with the other. "What're you trying to pull?" Brux snarled. "Why did you lure Van outside?"

"Brux, take it easy. He might tell us something about the Coin." Van bent down and picked up the fake Runestar. If Uxa hadn't shown her a picture of the real thing, she might've thought it was genuine. Not interested in forged jewelry, she tossed the brooch back onto the cart.

"Don't… know nothin'… 'bout any coin," Len croaked.

"Brux!" Van stomped over. "Let him go!"

She felt it—the tingling in her eyes—*before* Len gasped and Brux dropped his hands. Her eyes had flashed their phosphorescent violet sheen.

"Y-Your eyes!" Len dropped to his knees. "It's my honor, Princess of the Eternal Light."

"What are you doing?" Van asked. "Knock it off."

"As you wish, my princess." Len rose.

"The violet phosphorescence in your eyes is a mark of the Anchoress bloodline." Brux sounded baffled. "It must be some kind of mistake."

Van knew Brux had gone back to thinking his sister was the Anchoress heir.

"There's no mistake, my princess," Len said to Van.

"Why do you keep calling me a princess?"

"You're the descendant of Queen Amaryl," Len said. "After the Dark War, Salus Valde became a democracy to hide the royal Lodian bloodlines from the Balish. Royalty will always be royalty to us devoted Manikists, yes. I *knew* you existed. The Anchoress-in-waiting. I *knew* it, yes."

"What's a Manikist?" Van crunched her brow.

"They're an underground movement of Lodian supporters who live in Balish-occupied territory," Brux said. "They believe the Anchoress bloodline survived the Dark War."

"Like Hertha?" Van asked.

Brux nodded.

"Oh, we're much more than that," Len said. "Much more! Yes."

His steadfast stare made Van uneasy.

"Manikists are anti-establishment," Len continued. "We believe the same as did King Manik Moor. In peace and harmony between the tribes, allowing freedom of beliefs. Queen Brigid petitioned to have the *Veridicus Libellus* destroyed because she believed in the writings of Manik's text. That the Anchoress heir exists and poses a threat to Balish rule. Passed her beliefs on to her daughter, I hear. None of the other Balish royals, including her husband or the Balish Council, would listen to the queen because she got her information from an ancient text written by an insane Lodian sympathizer."

"And because she was a woman," Brux said. "Under Balish rule, females have little power, and virtually no say in policies of the kingdom."

Van could tell he was still trying to figure out Len's angle.

"When Queen Brigid continued to voice her concerns, the other royals accused her of being a Manikist, which she was not," Len said.

"It makes sense the queen would be pro-Manik," Van said. "The Balish royal family are Manik's descendants."

"The Moors only believe in money and power," Brux said. "Nothing else."

Len leaned in and whispered, "There's also an *anti*-Manik underground. Their members are Balish. They believe in the Moor family as the rightful monarchs, but they worship Goustav Moor. These rebels are certain he had a child. They're acting up right now, searching for his heir, who would be the rightful ruler of the Balish kingdom. The queen's death. It wasn't from a broken heart. You best be careful, my princess."

"What?" Van scrunched her face. "What does that have to do with me?"

"Tell us everything you know about the Coin of Creation," Brux demanded.

Len stared unwaveringly at Van. "Is that as you wish, my princess?"

Van nodded to placate Brux, despite thinking they needed nothing from this nutjob.

"Ah, the *Coin*. I understand why you would want to retrieve your weapon, now that demons have reached our world." Len paused, as if deciding where to begin. "The Elementals realized early on the Coin was too powerful for mortals to handle. They took it away, kept in on Mt. Altithronia under their watch until it needed to be retrieved by the Anchoress-in-waiting during a time of great emergency."

Van remembered seeing the mountain while she was in Lodestar Village and again at the waterfall.

"That time came 'round again," Len continued. "During the Great War. Queen Cordelia, who carried the Eternal Light of the

Anchoress bloodline at the time, retrieved the Coin from the Elementals. She planned to use the Coin's power against the Balish. She believed it was her responsibility to end the war before demons gained enough strength to rise into our world."

Van recalled hearing about the Great War between the Lodians and the Balish, which drew demons to the Living World, turning the Great War into the Dark War. She knew Queen Cordelia had failed. Van wanted to know why. Len had some useful information, after all.

"On her way back from Mt. Altithronia, before she learned how to harness the Coin's magic, the Balish attacked and killed Queen Cordelia," Len said. "The Eternal Light of the Anchoress passed to her eldest daughter, Amaryl, who then became the Anchoress Queen."

"And the Coin?" Van urged.

"The Coin made its way to Amaryl, but," Len sighed and shook his head, "she was too inexperienced to use it. As you well know, demons made it to our world. Amaryl relinquished her power by handing the Coin over to Goustav. He stepped in and saved the day. We all know how that turned out."

"The rebellion," Van muttered. "Goustav took the Balish kingdom away from his brother, Manik."

"After that fiasco, Manik and the Elementals hid the Coin," Len said. "It was one of Manik's conditions before handing the kingdom, and his son, over to his brother. That, and putting his law in place."

Brux protectively shifted toward Van as Len's intensity deepened.

"The Coin, my princess. Manik saw firsthand how its power could corrupt. With the help of the Elementals, he made the Coin so difficult to find that to survive the retrieval journey, the Anchoress-in-waiting must prove herself worthy of controlling its power." Len lowered his voice and leaned forward.

Brux held up his hand to stop Len from getting too close to Van.

"If you ask me, I think Manik hid the Coin the way he did, and the Balish confiscated all the Grigori records back then and controlled all written word afterward, even to this day… is because what really went down during the Dark War is not what the Balish say. Something happened back then, something the Balish royal family considers a threat, something that gives the Lodians power." Len hesitated, as if he'd said too much.

"Such as?" Brux said in a forceful tone that intimidated Len into continuing.

"We Manikists believe it wasn't the *Coin* Goustav used to defeat the demons. It was—"

Someone in the distance yelled a warning about Balish troops headed their way.

Len twitched. "It's not for me to say." He hastily closed up his cart.

"Where's the Coin?" Van asked. "I, uh, command you to tell me."

"Go to the Troll's Foot Tavern in Araquiel," Len said over his shoulder as he snuffed out a torch. "Show them your eyes. They'll help you."

"Can I buy this book?" Van waggled the translation manual at him. "Do you have papers for it?"

"Keep it. There's no papers." Len hopped onto the seat of his cart, then glanced down at Van. "Good luck, my princess. May the light of the Creator shine upon your path." He snapped the reins of his horse and disappeared into the night.

Van slipped the book into a pocket of her cargo pants. The part of Len's story about Queen Cordelia dying shortly after retrieving the Coin bothered Van. Cordelia had planned to use the Coin against the Balish to prevent the rise of demons. Manik's text had warned not to use the Coin against one another, only against true evil. Did this have something to do with Cordelia's death?

Van shook her head to remove her worrisome thoughts and told herself Uxa didn't plan to use the Coin against the Balish. She wanted it to preserve Manik's law, to prevent another Great War between the Lodians and the Balish. The circumstances of their mission differed from the events that happened a thousand years ago.

Van longed to rehash everything with Brux, but was still angry with him for being a jerk about her father. "Don't say a word about my eyes." Van rushed ahead of him with her nose in the air.

They went back inside the Grotto by the front door. The rest of their group sat at a back table by the mural.

"Where were you two?" Jorie snapped.

"Yeah. *Where were you two?*" Paley gave them a huge smile.

Paley seemed okay about Van spending time with Brux. It heartened Van, despite Paley's new attitude being directly related to the two boys she had recently met.

Brux snorted. "Van thought it was a smart idea to follow a strange man into a dark alley."

"What'd you do that for?" Elmot's eyes widened.

"I was trying to make my fake parents in Hod proud." Van took a seat. "Okay, so I was trying to get some peddler to spill about the Coin."

"Did you?" Jorie asked.

"Van tricked him into thinking she was the Anchoress-in-waiting," Brux said.

He and Van filled everyone in on what Len had told them. Van relaxed when Brux didn't mention her phosphorescent violet eyes.

"Araquiel, the gateway to the north," Elmot said. "The two men I talked to told me the only way in and out of Fomalhaut was through Araquiel because of the mountainous terrain."

"From what I heard, gold mines are in that region," Trey said. "Owned by—*you guessed it*—the Balish. As far as they're concerned, the only reason for anyone to go up there is to steal their gold."

"Good job, guys," Jorie said. "I didn't get squat. I thought this might've been a waste of time. Thinking of maybe heading back south."

"No!" Van, Brux, and Elmot cried in unison.

"There's no doubt the Coin is in Fomalhaut," Brux said. "We'll have to risk crossing the border."

Van knew his confidence stemmed from reading the map in Manik's text.

"Take it easy. We head to Araquiel tomorrow, first light. For now, we celebrate our good fortune." Jorie ordered platters of food and a jug of honeyed wine, using the money she had won arm-wrestling.

They feasted until only bones and scraps remained. The two guys Paley had met pulled up chairs. One girl Brux had flirted with also drifted over.

Van instantly hated her.

Trey and Elmot stood at the opposite end of the table, chatting with two girls, and Jorie wandered off to hang with her arm-wrestling buddies. Paley jabbered a few inches from one of the boys' faces, ignoring everyone else at the table. Brux seemed preoccupied with the stupid girl, who fawned over him like a trollop.

Van pretended to be interested in the other boy Paley had met. He sat across the table from Van, gawking at her like a hungry wolf. As he droned on about his life as a stable boy, Van's thoughts drifted to the mural behind him.

Something about one of the maidens nagged at Van. The woman had the regal bearing of a princess and raised a gold chalice in celebration. She looked to be in her early twenties, dressed in an elaborate formal gown from an age long gone, and wore a coin pendant necklace. Her delicate cherry-colored lips tilted into a smile, her violet eyes… *her eyes!*

Van's hand shot up as she pointed to the wall behind the stable boy. "That woman in the mural… *her eyes.*"

The boy stopped his monotonous monologue and twisted in his seat. "What about them?"

"They're like mine." *Phosphorescent violet.*

He shook his head. "Your eyes are blue." He used the mural as an excuse to come around to Van's side of the table so he could get a better look. Paley and her guy had scuttled to a private corner some time ago, and the stable boy slid into Paley's vacated seat next to Van.

The girl talking to Brux had maneuvered herself onto his lap, so Van scooted closer to the stable boy in case Brux was watching.

"You do kind of look like her." The stable boy stretched his arm around Van's chair.

She figured he was trying to flatter her until she realized Paley had said the same thing. In the House of Lacus. "That's Queen Amaryl, right?"

"So, I was sayin'—"

"Why couldn't Amaryl figure out how to use her own power?" Van interrupted. "Why did she turn the Coin over to Goustav? Do you know?" Anything was better than listening to him talk about the tribulations of sharing a bedroom with his two older brothers.

"Oh, uh, okay. If that's what you want to talk about." The stable boy shrugged. "Probably because Amaryl and Goustav were having an affair."

Chapter 27

Day 6: 9:52 p.m., Living World

Van shook her head to clear her ears. "They were having a what?"

"An *a-ff-aiir*." The stable boy stretched out the syllables as if she were slow.

"I thought the Lodians and the Balish hated each other?"

Or were they drawn to each other like night and day? Like Van's great-grandparents on her father's side. Like her father to her mother, Manik to Zurial. Both of the latter marriages didn't end well. *Now there's Goustav and Amaryl?*

The stable boy narrowed his eyes at Van.

She realized how her question sounded. "I mean… back then, you know?" She figured it wasn't a good idea to talk about the animosity between the Lodians and the Balish persisting to this day. Especially since her team of undercover Lodians had trespassed on Balish-occupied territory.

His chest puffed out as if he'd stepped onto a metaphorical

soapbox. "Amaryl's husband, Rowen, was gone. Went off to fight in the war. Demons were destroying everything, didn't matter, Lodian or Balish. People lived without knowing whether they would survive from one day to the next. Amaryl, the Anchoress Queen, had the Coin but was too dimwitted to figure out how to use it." He snickered. "So, she copied her mother and went to Mt. Altithronia to get help from the Elementals."

The history buff in Trey drew him to their end of the table, leaving Elmot with the two girls, one of them pouting. "Ah, the affair. Fascinating subject."

The stable boy tensed at the intrusion of another guy.

Trey slipped into an empty seat across the table. "Fable has it the Lodians' Elders don't allow an Anchoress whose powers are dormant to travel outside Salus Valde without her assigned protector," Trey said. "It's always a male, chosen by the Elementals. The assigned protector must devote his life to protecting the Anchoress unless she gains access to her full power. Then she becomes a great warrior and no longer needs protection. But, out of loyalty, he usually stays by her side. Continuing his duties until the Anchoress passes down the magic of the bloodline to her daughter and the Elemental's award a new assigned protector."

Elmot excused himself from the girls too. "So romantic, the very idea of it." He sighed. "The Elementals forbid the protector from becoming romantically involved with his charge. They see love as an inherent flaw in mortals, a distraction that weakens the protector, making him vulnerable and unable to perform his job as her guardian." He looked down and shook his head. "Tragic, though. The Elementals seem to pick people who make great couples."

"Goustav was Amaryl's assigned protector?" Van asked. "How'd the Elementals come up with that one?"

"Amaryl's assigned protector took a dirt nap during the war," the stable boy said with a contemptuous grin. "Died protecting her in battle. Which means someone else can take the vow and become her sworn protector."

"Goustav, a great warrior in his own right, volunteered." Elmot seemed to take pleasure in being lost in the drama of the past.

"Since they're forbidden to get romantically involved with each other, the Elementals had no issues with the swearing in of a Bale as the Anchoress's protector."

"So Amaryl and Goustav weren't allowed to be together?" Van asked. "Same rules apply?"

"Yup." The stable boy bobbed his head. "It angers the Elementals when humans break their rules. Nothin' good comes of it."

"The Elementals don't think of the Anchoress-in-waiting as *one* of their many children," Elmot said. "She is *the* child. The child above all other children. They don't choose her assigned protector lightly."

"Their *alleged* affair began when Goustav accompanied Amaryl on her journey to Mt. Altithronia," Trey said.

Elmot and Trey kept sharp eyes on Van as the stable boy tightened his arm around her.

"Goustav looked and acted like Amaryl's husband," the stable boy said. "So, of course, she was attracted to him."

"She had a type, I guess." Van shrugged as if to emphasize her words, but she actually wanted to shake loose from the stable boy's arm. It remained firmly in place.

"No one knows what the Elementals told Amaryl," Elmot said. "But it's believed she never accessed her full powers, which is why she needed Goustav's help."

"He must've given the Coin back to her," Van said. "She's wearing it as a necklace in the mural."

"Amaryl, pffft! What a hypocrite," the stable boy said. "Amaryl disapproved of her sister Zurial marrying a Bale. The whole time the floozy was secretly knocking boots with her soon-to-be brother-in-law."

"There's no historical evidence supporting Amaryl and Goustav's affair," Trey said, relishing the potential for debate. "It's no secret Amaryl didn't trust the Moors. She sanctioned the marriage of her sister to Manik for the sake of peace, for the good of the people."

"Is that them? In the mural?" Van waved her index finger at the wall. "What are they celebrating?"

Elmot and Trey were used to Van's denseness, but the stable boy's incredulous look made Van feel as if she were back at Canterbury Bells.

"It's a painting of *The Wedding Celebration*," the stable boy said.

Van stared blankly.

Elmot and Trey snickered.

"The four royal warriors celebrating the end of the Dark War. Amaryl, Zurial, Goustav, and Manik." The stable boy looked down his nose at Van. "You know about the Dark War, *right?*"

"Duh, yeah," Van said, although she knew little about it.

"Good thing you're pretty." The stable boy shook his head as if Van were an idiot.

Van didn't care for his comment. By the looks on their faces, neither did Trey and Elmot. Yet she tolerated the boorish stable boy because she wanted Brux to see another guy acting interested in her, hoping he would get jealous, come over, and put a stop to it.

"After the Dark War ended," Elmot said, trying to keep the stable boy out of the conversation, "the wedding of Princess Zurial to King Manik sealed the truce between the Balish and the Lodians. It must've been a beautiful ceremony." He sighed.

Trey rolled his eyes.

"Yeah, beautiful. Until the bloodbath eight months later." The stable boy chuckled.

"*Bloodbath?*" Van wished she dared to shake the stable boy's arm from her shoulders.

"The rebellion," Trey said. "Amaryl's husband, Rowen, survived the war and came home in time for the wedding celebration. Legend says Amaryl chose Rowen over Goustav, and Goustav's ego couldn't take the bruising. He believed Amaryl had cast a love spell on him and Zurial had done the same to Manik. He formed a secret plan to break the truce. To kill Zurial before the wedding, releasing Manik from her spell."

"Sounds like Goustav wasn't right in the head," Van said.

"He never carried out his plan because Zurial was pregnant," Elmot said. "He couldn't murder the unborn heir to the kingdom, someone of his own bloodline. It would have been an unforgivable act against the Creator, which would cause him great misfortune. So he suffered the wedding, allowed the truce, and lay in wait until the heir was born. All the while, gathering resistance fighters."

"Many Bales agreed with Goustav. The Balish were the rightful victors of the Dark War," Trey said. "Goustav defeated the demons, so he and his followers believed the Balish should have all the spoils, not split the win with the Lodians."

"The moment Manik's heir, Mehal, was born, Goustav and his men carried out his nefarious plan," Elmot said.

"Like a butcher, Goustav slaughtered anyone who opposed him." The stable boy's hands swooped through the air like he wielded a machete.

Van thought the grotesque gesture unnecessary, but was relieved he'd moved his heavy arm off her shoulders. She shifted her body to make it harder for him to reach around her again.

"He killed them all, except his brother and the baby Mehal," Trey said. "Goustav's plan didn't involve killing Manik, his own bloodline, only breaking the truce. He was off the hook for killing Zurial. She died during childbirth. The Lodians who came to Balefire Palace for the birth weren't so lucky. They were slain, along with many Lodians in Salus Valde, especially those with royal blood."

"It must've been a terrible time." Elmot shuddered.

"Manik already saddened over the death of his twin sister, who'd been killed in battle before the war ended," Trey said, "became so grief-stricken over Zurial's death he couldn't rule anymore and couldn't care for his baby."

"There was no spell. He was in love." Elmot lowered his eyes, clearly distressed over the heartbreaking romance.

"That's when Manik went crazy," the stable boy said.

"Not so crazy," Trey added. "Before allowing Goustav to take control, Manik established a law protecting the Lodians, *and* he hid the Coin. He sealed the deal with the help of the Elementals, who bound Manik's wishes using their magic. This way, Goustav couldn't turn around and change the law once he became king. Goustav never had a child, and Mehal carried forward the Balish royal bloodline, whose descendants are the present-day Moors."

Van opened her mouth to remind Trey about the information he and Elmot had found in the library in Agerorsa, claiming Goustav had an heir, but she changed her mind after a warning glance from Trey. Instead, Van asked, "So, Manik went insane. Zurial died in childbirth. Goustav ruled the kingdom. What happened to Amaryl?"

Silence hung in the air, each waiting for the other to say something.

"Well?"

Trey cleared his throat. "She was slain in the woods of Aduro before having a child. Those present believed they witnessed the end of Anchoress bloodline."

"Yeah, so?" That much was no surprise to Van. She already knew only Manikists and orthodox Lodians believed the bloodline had survived the war.

Trey hesitated, as if deciding whether to tell Van the tragic details of Amaryl's death.

Finally, Elmot said, "Amaryl was murdered… by her lover, Goustav."

A chair crashed into the wall, barely missing Trey's head. Van saw two of Jorie's beefed-up arm-wrestling buddies yelling at each other, and then the place broke out in a smashing brawl. Van ducked and weaved to avoid fists and flying chairs as she, Trey, Elmot, and Brux scrambled to get out the front door.

They made it outside unscathed and found Jorie waiting for them, pacing. Van was glad the incident had detached that ridiculous girl from Brux's lap. But Paley was nowhere to be found.

"Jorie, who knew your womanly wiles would incite a riot?" Trey said with a lofty smile.

"Ho-yeah, they do." Jorie grinned and fist-bumped Trey.

Van, also surprised, saw Jorie as a rough, tough, masculine warrior and wouldn't have guessed Jorie enjoyed flirting with boys.

Paley appeared out of nowhere, disheveled. The boy she'd been talking to earlier trailed close behind.

"What's going on?" Paley asked, as she zipped her jacket.

A body tumbled out of the Grotto's door, and Paley's "friend" realized a brawl had started inside. Without a word, he dashed in to join the bedlam.

Paley pouted, looking devastated to see him go.

Jorie's grin widened. "This town probably hasn't seen this much excitement since the Dark War."

Chapter 28

D ay 7: 12:18 a.m., Living World

As the group headed back to Ox's Bunkhouse, the sky opened, and torrential rain pelted them the whole way.

Once Van reached her room, she shook off her soaked jacket, then lay on top of her lumpy, mildew-smelling bottom bunk bed. Her body was dead tired, but her mind wouldn't stop spinning. Reading before bed always helped calm her so she could fall asleep. She grabbed the translation manual and huddled with Manik's text. By candlelight, she translated a page Brux hadn't yet read.

Amaryl's story bothered her, especially the part where Amaryl had let her people down when they needed her most. What had made Amaryl so pathetic—so *stupid*—she handed over control of the Coin to Goustav, a man who ended up murdering her? Did this have something to do with Manik's warning for the Anchoress not to surrender her light, meaning the Coin?

Len said Goustav didn't use the Coin to defeat the demons. Meaning what? He used something else? Van turned to another page. She knew the book held the answers.

Frustrated with the difficulty of translating the language, she blamed Brux. How could he read the words so easily? The image of Brux with that girl on his lap intruded her on thoughts, which irked Van. She didn't want to care about that.

Brux is a jerk. He's wrong about my father being dead.

But Genie had mentioned the same thing. Van reached into her pocket, took out the tissue, and carefully unwrapped it. She thought about touching the patch and using her ability to get a reading. She had gotten a vision before, when she hid in the bushes outside Mt. Hope Manor and her hand had touched the patch's edge.

Emotionally charged objects carried an imprint, allowing her mind to see related scenes of the owner's life as if she were there. It didn't always happen... and she couldn't get a reading when she had touched Manik's text... but if it worked this time... she might learn the truth about what happened with her father, at least on the night of the demon attack. Van stared at the patch.

She crumpled the tissue and tucked the patch back into the binding of the Manik's text.

Instead, Van concentrated on translating the words onto scraps of parchment she had found in her room. The process was excruciating. She considered going to see Brux and throwing the text at his head. But the longer she worked, the easier the translations became.

She shot upright, her nose buried in the text. Len was right. Goustav hadn't used the Coin to defeat the demons—he'd used the Anchoress! *Amaryl* had single-handedly defeated the demons and Goustav had done nothing. After reading more of the text, Van concluded Goustav had gotten all the glory while Amaryl got murdered. Yet, another reason the Balish concealed Manik's text.

Fascinated, Van continued reading. The book mentioned nothing about an affair. Amaryl would never have been attracted to a loser like Goustav. *Ugh*—the Elementals had told Amaryl how to access the power of the Coin, but the "how to" part was burned out. Van turned to the next page and translated another passage. She peered at the text, checking her translation for accuracy. Manik claimed only the *heir* could retrieve the Coin from its hiding place.

She took a minute to digest this newest bit of information.

That meant only one heir existed, the Anchoress heir. If only the Anchoress heir could retrieve the Coin, then Van's father couldn't get it. Which was a relief, until Van realized she and her team wouldn't be able to get the Coin, either. Not without Daisy.

Van was willing to bet Daisy, like Amaryl, wouldn't understand how to access the magical power of the Coin. Which was just as well. Daisy couldn't use the Coin's powers to protect herself from the Balish, Solana, or any person because it would be an incorrect use, and she would suffer the consequences. This had to be where the Anchoress's assigned protector came into play. Had the Elementals chosen Marcus as Daisy's assigned protector? *Poor Daisy.*

Unless Len had spoken the truth about Van being the heir. Van couldn't deny her uncanny resemblance to Queen Amaryl. Her eyes flashed phosphorescent violet, and sometimes she could read the ancient language without using the translation manual. But Van had to recharge in the Living World so she couldn't be the heir.

Could she?

Van fidgeted. Did Uxa know only the Anchoress-in-waiting could retrieve the Coin? If so, why send two teams? If Daisy were the Anchoress-in-waiting, what did that make Van's team? Did Van act as a decoy for Daisy? Was that Van's contribution to the mission?

Uxa and Manik claimed the Anchoress bloodline had survived the Dark War. Were they wrong? Was Trey right about there being no Anchoress heir? Van had overheard Uxa tell Fynn she was unsure whether the Anchoress-in-waiting had inherited the magical abilities of her ancestral bloodline. This meant the heir could exist, but might not have access to her magical powers. That would support the claims made by Uxa, Manik, *and* Trey.

Van hopped off her bed and marched outside. She sloshed through the mud and burst into the room at the end of the bunkhouse. "What are you hiding from me?"

Brux leaped from his bed, dagger in hand, ready for battle. "Van!" He lowered his weapon.

"Are you and Uxa in cahoots together? Conspiring against the rest of us?" Van struggled to keep her voice low so not to disturb Elmot sleeping in the next room. "What bothered you when you read Manik's text? Tell me."

"I will if you'll be quiet for a second and let me talk," Brux whispered harshly. He lit a candle, and the room flooded with light.

"Up to this point, I thought our only problem was *finding* the Coin," Van said, blasting her words at him. "We had Manik's text, which has the map, and team Echo has Daisy, the Anchoress, who can find the Coin using her intuition. No problem, right? Now, from what I read in the text, finding the Coin is just one problem. The bigger problem being the only person who can actually retrieve the Coin out of its hiding place is the *Anchoress heir*!"

"Van, I did—"

"Doesn't matter if the Anchoress can connect to her powers or not," Van kept talking. "As long as she exists, she can get the Coin, is that it? Doesn't matter if she dies from being weak and unskilled. I think it's sick why you'd let your sister go on this mission. With Daisy being the Anchoress heir, what does that make our team? Why did Uxa send us out? And why is my father going for the Coin if he can't get it? Why did—"

Brux raised his hand. "Van, just stop talking for a second," he pleaded. "I did read only the heir can retrieve the Coin. I'm not sure how much Uxa knows, or you. But then I read more. Manik confirmed what Trey and Elmot found in the library at Agerorsa. Goustav had a child. This means his current-day ancestors can also retrieve the Coin." Brux's eyes locked onto Van's. "I think each team has an heir."

"Brux, if Goustav had an heir, then Manik's text would say heir*s, with an s*. What I translated is singular, meaning one heir—the Anchoress heir."

"I translated the word in Manik's text to be *plural*—the heir*s* can retrieve the Coin. There are at least two heirs." He pounded his chest with his thumb. "I'm the expert, not you. You're just a spoiled brat, along for the ride. You know nothing."

"The ancient Moors wouldn't have let a secret heir of Goustav's live. Someone who could establish his right to the Balish throne. Mehal, Manik's son, would've seen to all of Goustav's heirs being killed. You're the dumb—" Van froze. Her father had Balish blood.

Brux saw the terror in Van's face. His anger melted. "Your father's not Goustav's heir, Van. When he married your mother, an extensive background check was done. Which means it's not you, either. It's one of our teammates. It must be."

"Do Daisy's eyes flash phosphorescent violet like mine?" She would rather be the Anchoress than Goustav's heir. The Balish will hunt both, but the Anchoress had access to magical power, giving her a fighting chance to survive a Balish ambush.

She took his lack of response as a "no."

"It's got to be Trey. He's a Bale," Brux said softly, apparently still convinced his sister was the Anchoress heir. "Solana must either think she's a descendant of Goustav or has found one to work with your father."

"No wonder so many people died trying to get the Coin," Van said, accepting Brux's expertise on the subject. "I bet none of them knew only the Anchoress-in-waiting or one of Goustav's heirs could retrieve it."

"And none had an heir with them," Brux said in agreement. "It would explain why Solana and her mother petitioned to have Manik's text destroyed. They didn't want to give anti-Manikists any more fuel to feed the rumors of Goustav having an heir, which is a serious threat to their throne."

Van wondered if this was what Len meant when he said Manik's text gave the Lodians power. But she decided, no. Goustav having an heir wouldn't benefit the Lodians. Most likely, his heir would take power, and upon discovering his or her ancestry, would align with the Balish.

"Is that the part of Manik's text that bothered you?" Van asked.

Brux cast his eyes downward. "No. It was the part about Goustav using Amaryl to defeat the demons."

"Goustav was a loser, so what's new?"

"Van, don't you realize?" Brux seemed agitated. "It's not the Coin that has the power. It's the Anchoress. The Coin doesn't give her magic. It amplifies the magic she already has inside and turns her into a super-warrior."

Van had trouble visualizing Daisy as a super-warrior and understood Brux's concern.

"The Anchoress has magical power times three," Brux said. "She can connect to the moon, the Elemental part of her blood, and the power of the Coin."

"Daisy will be fine." Van placed a comforting hand on Brux's shoulder. She felt close to him in that moment, attracted to the heat of his body, his musky sandalwood scent. She slid her other hand up his chest and lifted her chin, drawing her lips toward his.

Brux wrapped his fingers around her hands and gently pushed her away.

Van stepped back, shocked and insulted.

"I don't want to be another guy in your collection," Brux said in a strained voice. His eyes clouded with pain.

Van didn't care about his pain. She stormed out of his room and stomped back to her own. She crashed onto her wretched bed. "Screw them all. I'm done with this mission. Done!" If Brux wasn't interested in her, then he should've said so. He didn't have to use Ken and the stable boy against her.

I'm overtired. That's what triggered my temporary insanity to make a pass at Brux. What was I thinking?

Her muscles ached from the long journey and fatigue set in. She needed rest right now. Then, tomorrow, she'd grab Paley and head home. Mission be damned.

Before Van drifted off to sleep, she felt little paws padding on her abdomen.

"Mllwrp." Wiglaf blinked his large blue eyes at Van and rumbled like a tiny motor.

"Hey there." Van smiled. Jorie had said he would return when Van needed him most. "Don't try to talk me into staying." She reached down and scratched behind his ears. "Why are guys so diffi-cult? Huh?"

Wiglaf responded with a rambunctious purr.

Van continued scratching Wiglaf and gazed into his eyes.

There was no escaping Brux, her father, or the mission. She would face all of them with courage, including Brux's rejection. She sighed.

The only way out was through.

Chapter 29

Day 7: 4:17 p.m., Living World

As the team endured another all-day trek over rocky, uphill terrain, the sky mocked them with its bright, cheery blueness, while the air grew blisteringly cold.

Van's aching feet howled in reluctance with each step. Wiglaf had left during the night. Van reconciled herself to the bunfy's departure by looking at it from his point of view. She figured he had done his job by boosting her resolve to keep on with the mission and was, therefore, no longer needed. Still, she missed the funny little thing.

By the time the Kezef-Fomalhaut border appeared on the horizon, it was late afternoon. Van's legs and lower back throbbed.

"Araquiel is just beyond here," Elmot said.

As they got closer to the checkpoint, they saw a crowd of people making their way across the border. Balish border guards had amassed in force.

Van's knees jittered. "There's so many guards."

"We could go back to Dricreek," Paley said.

Obviously, she suggested this with the boy she'd met at the Grotto in mind.

"Will they search us?" Van asked, unable to keep the apprehension out of her voice.

Brux moved protectively closer.

Van glared at him and stomped toward the checkpoint. Anger over his rejection burned away any fear of being searched.

"What difference does it make if they search us?" Trey asked. "Our covers are sound."

"He's right," Jorie whispered as they approached the checkpoint. "We'll be fine. Just stay calm. Stick to the cover story."

Brux glanced from the adjacent line as Van handed the guard her papers.

She flipped her hair and flashed her best smile at the guard. "So, you been doing this long?" Van didn't listen to his answer. Her only motive was for Brux to see the guard thriving on her attention.

The guard's commander urged, "Move the line!"

They had all crossed the checkpoint without incident, except Paley. With her, there was some kind of holdup.

"She's mouthing off to the guard." Jorie's shoulders tensed. "It'll trigger a search."

More guards rushed over and blocked Paley from view.

Van's gut clenched when one guard raised his hand high, grasping Paley's Twin Gemstone.

"What the—?" Jorie seethed as border guards surrounded them.

"Search them," the commander growled.

Two border guards each grabbed one of Van's arms.

Another patted her down. "Hah ha!" The guard excitedly grasped Van's Twin Gemstone. He continued searching her pockets and found the translation manual, then her mother's earrings.

"Gimme those!" Van wriggled to break loose from the guards.

The guard who'd confiscated her items turned his attention to her. He smashed Van's face with the back of his hand.

The two guards holding Van relaxed their grip, and the force of the blow sent her crashing to the ground. Startled and in pain, Van wondered if the guard had broken her jaw.

Brux struggled free and rushed to Van.

Nearby guards whipped out their batons. The closest one to Brux whacked his legs.

Brux wailed and crumpled to the ground near Van.

The guards hammered him with their batons.

Van screamed, along with Elmot and Paley.

Jorie and Trey struggled against their guards, but not enough to get beaten too.

The guards dragged all of them into the stark compound and threw them into separate rooms for interrogation.

A burly guard pushed Van into a wooden chair. The stuffy room with sickly white walls and no windows caused Van's chest to tighten.

One guard hung behind her as if he were the sword of Damocles. Another threw Van's backpack onto the table, along with her mother's earrings, her Twin Gemstone, and the translation manual.

The chubby commander reclined in a comfortable-looking chair, directly across from Van. "So…" He tapped her border pass on the table. "Marketeers' scout, eh." His face resembled a bullfrog. "We'll see about that." He raised his chin, and the guard next to him unzipped Van's backpack and spilled its contents onto the table.

Van shifted in her chair. The guard behind her pinned his beefy hand on her shoulder as if she were a flight risk.

Van watched the commander rifle through her things. She didn't care when he slipped her coin pouch into his pocket. She focused on her mother's earrings. Her brain whirred with ways on how she could get them back. It didn't take the commander long to find Manik's text.

"Well, what do we have here?" he said.

The other two guards craned to get a better view of the item that would condemn their prisoner.

"Do you have the proper permits to be carrying books?"

Van curled her lip. She glared at the repulsive bullfrog-like man, the one who'd allowed Brux to be beaten. She wanted to tell this scumbag where to shove his permits. Instead, Van forced her throbbing jaw to move, causing pain to shoot through her head. "I came across them at an abandoned campfire. Seemed like they might be valuable, at least worth a meal or two."

"Humph. Likely story." The commander held the charred text, carefully inspecting it. His eyes widened, and he threw the text onto the table as if it were contaminated. "Get the box!"

The box? Van kept her cool, but inside her anxiety raged. *Are they going to stuff me in it?* She hated enclosed spaces. Her shoulder trembled under the guard's hulking hand as the other man disappeared for what seemed the longest minutes of Van's life.

The guard returned holding a polished wooden box, small enough to hold cigars.

Van stared at the container, thinking she'd never fit in there. Unless they burned her to ashes first. The room grew fuzzy. The walls closed in, making it a chore to breathe.

The guard opened the lid.

The commander cast Manik's text into the box, then snapped it shut. "I know better than to read the language of the ancients."

Van exhaled, her shoulders relaxed. The commander noticed only the ancient writing. He wasn't sure whether the book was Manik's text. He was afraid to read it, she thought, for fear of his eyes burning out. Such relief filled Van, she nearly giggled.

The commander narrowed his eyes at her, gauging whether she was royal, insane, or just plain stupid. He slammed his hand on the table and leaped from his chair. "Alert Balefire! Tell them we have recovered Manik's text and captured the traitor, the co-conspirator to demons. The *murderer* of Prince Devon and Queen Brigid. Be mindful, men. She may be a little girl, but we are in the presence of *evil!*"

Still reeling, the guards threw Van into the same jail cell holding the rest of her team. Everyone's tension seemed so palpable, Van felt crushed under the pressure. They had witnessed Paley get caught carrying a Twin Gemstone. Van felt confident at least one of her teammates knew the gemstones were used to transport terrigens here, but they probably didn't know about Manik's text—yet.

Anyway, she didn't care. Her bruised jaw ached. She felt bone-tired. The last thing she needed was drama from her teammates.

Jorie ran her hand over her mohawk, opened her mouth to speak, then clamped her jaw shut, apparently still too fuming to form words.

"Anything you care to share with us?" Trey asked, throwing daggers with his eyes.

"Uh, sorry." Van shrugged, irritated they didn't scream at her and get it over with. She had no energy to fight with them. "I didn't think it would matter how Paley and I got here. You knew we came from Providence Island."

"We thought you came the same way everyone from the Earth World gets here—being attuned by a Grigori!" Jorie's cheeks turned red. "Not by using the Twin Gemstones."

"We thought you both were children of the Grigori stationed at the remote outpost. We didn't know Paley is a *terrigen*." Trey spat the last word.

"It's true." Paley glanced at the floor. "Sorry."

"Watch it, Trey. Your Balish is showing," Van said through gritted teeth. "And, Paley, you have nothing to be sorry for."

"I was born in the Living World," Paley said. "If that makes a difference."

"It's against Balish law to bring a terrigen here," Trey said.

Jorie curled and uncurled her fists like she wanted to punch something, probably Van. "You're Michael Cross's daughter! Aelia's daughter!"

Van whipped around to face Brux. "You told them?" Despite her anger, her heart lurched at the sight of his bloodstained clothes.

"They figured it out when they overheard the guards say you were caught with Manik's text," Brux said. "Don't worry, they're mad at me too."

"For light's sake, Van. You didn't think it relevant to tell us?" Jorie paced the cell like a caged animal. Her four remaining fingers twitched over Zachery's empty holster. "Being caught with a *terrigen* and *Manik's text*. Do you know how much danger you've put us in?"

"They're calling in an inquisition squadron, M-Merloc's crew,"

Elmot said, looking disheveled and pale. "They don't call him Merloc the Merciless for nothing." He leaned over and retched.

"Okay, everybody calm down," Brux said. "Let's look at what we have—the information we translated from Manik's text." He filled them in on everything he and Van knew until they heard footsteps echoing around the corner.

"Someone's coming." Paley jumped to her feet. "I don't feel well. I hope they give us some food. You think they will?"

"Doubtful." Trey grimaced.

"You need the gemstones more than you need food," Brux whispered, looking concerned. "Before you and Van start feeling worse."

The commander arrived, followed by several border guards. "All of you, out!" he barked.

Elmot and Trey propped up Brux so he could walk, and they filed out of the cell as instructed. The guards led them to a large room, and then they waited in the hallway as Van and the others entered.

A horde of massive soldiers dressed in black stood shoulder to shoulder. They glared at the prisoners as they blocked those standing behind them, who were involved in a muffled discussion.

Even before Van heard Elmot gasp, she recognized the uniforms. Royal Balish Soldiers. Merloc's inquisition squadron had arrived.

Van quivered, more afraid of facing her father than of Merloc the Merciless. It made sense Solana's two minions—her cousin Merloc and Van's father—would run about the countryside together, seeking the Coin for their crown princess.

The soldiers in front parted as someone from behind stepped forward.

Van braced, prepared to come face-to-face with her father. She was taken aback when Solana emerged.

"Leave me," Solana's silky, yet venomous voice commanded. "I wish to speak to them alone."

The soldiers hesitated.

A glare from Solana sent them hurrying through the door.

"I know you are Lodians." Solana crinkled her nose. "I can smell Lodes a mile away. Call it a gift."

Paley squirmed under the princess's scrutiny; Van remained alert.

"And here we are, caught red-handed with Manik's text." Solana paced. "Connecting Lodians to the incident that killed my brother. Looks like a conspiracy by Uxa and the Grigori to me. An attempt to overthrow my father and conquer the Balish kingdom. What. Am. I. To. Do?"

Jorie shifted, most likely taking Solana's accusation to heart.

Solana goaded them. "Was my brother's death an assassination, rather than mere Grigori incompetence?"

"Don't pretend with us," Brux growled. "We know you and Michael Cross employed demons to do your dirty work."

Van's injured jaw almost hit the floor. *Is Brux trying to get beaten up again?*

Solana snorted, making even that seem attractive. "I'm confused. Doesn't Michael work for Uxa?"

"Everyone in this room knows the Grigori are innocent." Jorie's knuckles turned white from balling her fists.

"You know this, you know that." Solana flicked her wrist. "What *I* don't know is how you got Manik's text!"

Van realized Solana hadn't expected to find the text. The Balish princess had given Michael orders to destroy it, and now she appeared to be suspicious of Michael's motives. The charred book in Van's backpack had put her father's life in danger too. Which meant Van's father wasn't there, and Solana didn't know Van was his daughter.

Both oversights were fine with her. Van couldn't bear the thought of her father catching her plotting against him, of meeting his gaze and seeing indifference reflected in his eyes. It would validate what Van had always felt deep inside, something she didn't want to be true. Her father didn't love her.

"It will be best if you cooperate." Solana stopped pacing. Her golden eyes turned to Van.

An icy chill spread through Van's body.

"Was it Uxa? Did she give it to you?"

Van held the princess's stare, trying to look innocent.

Paley succumbed to the pressure and shrieked, "Just tell her!"

"I found the text in the woods," Van said.

In a flash, Solana's gloved hand whacked Van across her already injured jaw.

As Van doubled over, she felt her eyes flash phosphorescent violet. She stared at the floor and ignored the raging pain in her jaw. Van used her breath to calm her anger until she was sure her eyes had returned to their normal blue. Then she straightened to her full height and glared at Solana.

"I won't ask a third time," Solana warned. "Did Uxa give the text to you?"

Van feared Solana would hurt her teammates if she didn't answer. So she nodded, though it was a lie.

Solana looked at each of them, and then asked, "Are you sure Uxa told you the truth about the attack on my brother?" She continued her unctuous pacing. "Demons reached our world because she is incompetent. Michael sided with me because he knows the Grigori can't perform their duties anymore. Proven the night my brother was murdered. Now, Manik's law is on the verge of being repealed, and Uxa is scrambling to fix the situation. She is using Michael as a scapegoat because he betrayed her by siding with me, and she is using you to get the Coin."

Solana stopped pacing and faced them. "The information in Manik's text poses a threat to my kingdom. To protect my brother, I asked Michael to steal it and to destroy it. A task he blundered, allowing Uxa to find the text and give it to you. We never expected my brother to chase him and get killed by demons."

Of course, Solana was lying. *But if it weren't for Wiglaf, Uxa would've found the text before I did. Solana must believe Uxa gave our team the text with a map because one of us is Goustav's heir, not the Anchoress-in-waiting, who can use her intuition to find the Coin. Which means Solana believes we're a danger to her throne and will kill us all.*

"After the incident," Solana continued. "Michael no longer wished to hide his allegiance with my family. That's why he never returned to Lodestar. Now I need the Coin to protect my people. It's the only way for me to prevent Solmor."

Van had reservations about Uxa, but Solana was an outright menace. Solana wanted power and glory, just like Goustav. Only this time, she would repeal Manik's law and finish what her ancestor had started—taking over Salus Valde.

"If you join forces with me, I'll protect you," Solana said. "You obviously have specialized skills, or Uxa wouldn't have sent you out. Your team can work with my men to get the Coin."

"Over my dead body," Jorie growled.

"That," Solana turned to Jorie, "can be arranged." She gazed at each of them again as she spoke. "I'm sure you read the text and know the general location of the Coin but not exactly where it's hidden. You also know only the Anchoress heir can retrieve it, which means I cannot." Solana's cool eyes landed on Paley.

Paley looked panicked and blurted, "Goustav's heir can get it too."

At first, Van felt a flicker of betrayal. Then her heart went out to her friend. She knew Paley's knee-jerk reaction was an attempt to avoid being tortured for information.

"Manik's text is wrong! Goustav has no heir," Solana snarled, reminding Van of a rabid panther. Solana inhaled deeply, composing herself. "If my men hadn't already informed me the Anchoress-in-waiting is on her way here, I might be inclined to think she is one of you. Nevertheless, if you won't join me, then I can't have you running about the countryside searching for the Coin, getting in the way of my men."

The team remained silent, but Van could feel Brux tense. He must've been wondering the same thing as Van. Had Michael captured Daisy? Van's father had high-level connections in the Grigori, which meant he would know the identity of the Anchoress heir. Len had told them Solana, along with her mother, believed the part in Manik's text about the Anchoress bloodline surviving the Dark War. That was probably the reason Solana had approached Van's father.

Solana strode to the table with their confiscated items. "Gross."

She flicked away Van's hairbrush, then picked up the jewelry box with Van's mother's earrings, and opened it. "Hm. These are pretty."

Van watched helplessly as Solana slid the earrings into one of the skintight pockets of her uniform. Van didn't think she could despise Solana more than she did already. She was wrong.

Solana gently brushed her gloved fingertips back and forth over the cover of Manik's text, which was laying on top of the cigar box. "Since we caught you with Manik's text, it is reasonable to conclude you are the thieves who lured my brother out of the palace. The fact you are Lodians proves Uxa is the one conspiring with demons. Uxa wanted to make the repeal of Manik's law a possibility so she could sanction retrieval of the Coin. Then use its power to take over *my* kingdom."

"That's a lie!" Jorie snarled.

"Grigori would never use the Coin to harm people," Brux said.

"Sounds plausible, though." Solana stopped stroking the text and looked up. "As spies for the Grigori, you pose a threat to my kingdom. You will be imprisoned, interrogated, and then executed."

Those words jolted Van as if the earth had opened under her feet.

"Commander Hackett!" Solana cried.

The bullfrog-looking man came bursting through the door. "Yes, my princess?" He bowed.

"Take these *Lodes* back to their cell. I will begin interrogations myself."

They headed toward the door when Solana grabbed Paley by the arm.

"Starting with this one."

"*Me?*" Paley gasped.

Van resisted the urge to wrap Solana's long, glossy hair around her neck. But with the Balish soldiers lurking in the hallway, any rash action on her part would lead to all their deaths.

Brux nudged her forward from behind.

The guards shoved Van and the others back into the cell and left them alone.

"Nothing matters now," Elmot said with a long face. "We're all going to be executed. After being tortured first, like Paley and, probably, Daisy."

"Don't attach to the dark part of your Self, Elmot," Jorie said. "We'll find a way out of this."

Van's rage at Solana had caused so much tension to build, her body shook. Like a burst dam, she cracked open, and tears streamed down her cheeks.

"Van, pull yourself together," Jorie ordered. "We're Lodians. Solana will do everything by the book. They'll transport us to Balefire for the execution. Gives us plenty of opportunities to escape."

"W-Why would my father side with Solana?" Van wept. "Why would he bring demons here?"

"We know from Uxa's briefing Michael witnessed a Class III demon kill his partner while in the field." Brux carefully lowered himself to the floor. "He believed it signaled the Escalation, that we're on the verge of another Great War. He chose the side he thought would win."

"The evil side?" Van said, still distressed. Or maybe her father believed the same as the Balish royal family. That there is no good or evil, only power.

Her father's soul had eroded from conspiring with demons. Uxa had warned if her father touched the Coin, darkness would consume him with no redemption. She fumed at the thought. *It's Solana's fault for seducing him!*

Anger took away her tears. Van would die before letting Solana get her power-grubbing hands on the Coin.

"Strategically, it makes sense for Michael to side with the Balish," Trey said. "They had a greater chance of retrieving the Coin because they had Manik's text and probably Goustav's heir."

"The side with the Coin will win when darkness rises," Elmot said. "Just like what happened during the Dark War."

"And history repeats itself," Trey said.

Facing Solana had drained all of Van's energy, and she could barely keep herself composed.

"Michael will stop at nothing to get the Coin," Trey said. "If we get it, Manik's law will remain intact. Solana won't reward him with Salus Valde for helping her kill her brother." Trey eyed Van. "You're looking clammy. Do you feel okay?"

"She's terrified," Elmot said. "We all are!"

"Maybe you should sit down." Brux patted the floor next to him.

"I do feel kinda… dizzy." The edges of Van's vision grayed.

Before everything went black, she heard Brux's stressed voice say, "Solana won't have to execute her. Without her Twin Gemstone, she's going to die!"

Chapter 30

D ay 7: 8:32 p.m., Living World

Van drifted down a shadowy tunnel. Fear faded and a sense of peace filled her.

In the distance, she heard Brux frantically calling her name. But the engulfing darkness enticed her with the promise of eternal rest, and she longed to give in to it.

She couldn't give in. She had things to do.

Wait. Those weren't Van's words, they were Jacynthia's.

I can't give in to the darkness. I have things to do, Van said in her mind, repeating what Jacynthia had just told her.

"Giving in to darkness does not serve you." Jacynthia appeared in the dark tunnel with Van.

What difference does it make? Solana's going to torture and kill me, anyway.

"You will persevere. Trust in your connection to the Creator."

Even if I escape this darkness, I don't have what I need. We gave away our boundless bowl. The border guards stole our money. Solana confiscated my Twin Gemstone and Manik's text.

"Harmony and happiness are states of consciousness and do not depend on the possession of material things. You must trust the Creator will provide you with all you need to fulfill your spiritual destiny."

All this trouble with my father… Van struggled to wrap her head around it. She didn't believe her father, the same man who gave her Twinkle Toes on her fifth birthday, the one who took her quahogging when she was eleven, could turn his back on the light… on his family… on her.

And my mother. H-Her earrings were stolen… Tears dampened Van's cheeks. *I don't know who I am anymore.*

"Your frustration is taking you from me." Jacynthia flickered and began to fade. "Retain your vision… stick to your purpose… maintain your faith and gratitude, and you will find your way."

In one last flicker, Jacynthia disappeared.

A pounding headache infringed on Van's consciousness. Her jaw throbbed as her body regained feeling. She lay stretched across something cold and hard, but her head rested comfy on a warm pillow. She slowly opened her eyes and found herself supine on the floor of the jail cell. Van realized the warm pillow was Brux's lap and groaned.

"You okay?" Brux peered at her.

Van nodded slowly to keep her headache at bay. She wiped the tears from her cheeks and remembered the guards had battered Brux's legs. Afraid the weight of her head might hurt him, she sat up.

"At least we know why you fainted," Brux said gently. "The gemstones are draining your energy to keep Paley here, and being too far from them, for too long… well, your energy gave out."

He glanced at Paley, who had returned to the cell. All of them looked less worried than they should for people about to be executed, although a heavy gloom hung over the cell.

"Paley came back in the nick of time," Elmot said tensely. "Otherwise, we might've lost you."

"How?" Van stared at Paley. "You don't have a scratch on you. Weren't you interrogated?"

"It was easy for me to convince Solana that her men lied, and they didn't have the Anchoress heir. I told her I knew this because I'm the Anchoress-in-waiting." Paley gave Van a proud smile. "I told her Uxa didn't believe in Goustav's heir, either, and she had given me the text because I'm weak and unskilled. Not a stretch, I know."

"Solana bought that?" Van asked.

"It was enough to cast doubt, for the time being." Jorie continued to pace.

Paley nodded. "I told Solana I would help her get the Coin if she promised not to kill us and I needed the gemstones for medicinal reasons. They'll help me stay strong for my journey to retrieve the Coin. She had no idea I'm a terrigen."

"The Balish know nothing about transporting," said Trey. "Solana's never seen the Twin Gemstones before. She wouldn't know what they're used for." He spoke good news, but seemed sullen. "I'm not surprised she fell for it."

"I'm not, either. Solana's an idiot." Van wasn't sure what hurt more, her pounding forehead or her bruised jaw.

"You never like anyone prettier or more popular than you," Paley snapped.

"She took my jewelry!" Van said.

"What a shocker." Paley put her hands on her hips. "You snuck incriminating items into your backpack, and Solana took them. Even after Jorie told you not to."

"I don't care what Solana told you, Paley. But she's going to kill us," Van said, raising her voice. "Just like she killed that guy in Agerorsa. She's *evil*."

Van found it odd no one interrupted them. Her and Paley's squabbling usually irritated someone to the point of breaking it up. The group's glumness set off Van's internal alarm.

"What?" Her eyes darted to each of her teammates.

Elmot met her gaze. She noticed his clothes no longer appeared immaculate.

"Paley might've saved us momentarily," he said, full of despair.

"But Solana's men didn't lie about having the real Anchoress-in-waiting."

Jorie stopped her frantic pacing. "Solana told Paley that Merloc caught another team of marketeers' scouts at the Tipereth-Alga border." She ran her hand over her mohawk. "Merloc was already on his way here to meet Solana when we got caught."

"Echo?" Van glanced at Brux.

He stared at the floor and said in a cracked voice, "He tortured the entire team."

Brux sat slouched, with dark circles under his eyes. He looked destroyed, defeated. Van longed to wrap her arms around him, to soothe his pain.

Trey sighed. "Merloc got what he wanted from team Echo. He knows they're Lodians after the Coin and Daisy is the Anchoress heir. As soon as Michael meets up with them, he'll confirm Daisy's identity. Then, we're history."

"If they caught Echo at the Tipereth-Alga border, it means the team was headed north," Elmot said. "Daisy must've tuned in to the Coin's location."

"Michael will grab Daisy and head for the Coin," Jorie said. "Merloc will take the rest of team Echo to Balefire to continue with the interrogations."

Van gazed softly at Brux. "My father will keep Daisy safe. As the Anchoress heir, she's valuable to him."

"The good news," Trey said, "is these barracks are under attack by the Anti-Manik Rebels."

"How is that *good* news?" Van threw her hands in the air.

"They think Solana has Goustav's heir captured here," Trey said. "We saw Solana and her entire squadron run to fight them, leaving the place with a skeleton crew of inexperienced guards."

"We were waiting for you to wake up." Brux struggled to his feet. He held out his hand to help Van stand.

"Excellent." Jorie clapped her hands. "We've already gone over my plan."

"Now, it's time to implement it," Trey said.

Elmot pulled a pin from the lining of his jacket and held it up.

"What's the pin for?" Van asked, thinking it was too thin to pick a lock.

"For emergencies only." Elmot grinned.

"Paley!" Jorie barked. "You ready?"

Paley stopped gnawing on her cuticles and nodded.

Trey smirked. "Time to use your skill."

Elmot handed Paley the pin. "Careful."

The others hung back while Paley sauntered over to the barred wall.

"Excuse me," Paley said in her most seductive voice.

The guard strolled over. "Yeah, sweetheart?" He gripped the bar and leaned in close as he eyed Paley.

In a snap, Paley pricked the guard's bare hand with the pin. He dropped to the floor.

Van gasped.

"Relax," Trey said. "He's not *dead*."

"It's a sleeping potion," Elmot said. "We have about twenty minutes."

Trey reached through the bars and fumbled with the guard's uniform. He snatched the keys and unlocked the cell door.

The team crept down the hallway. They ducked to dodge a roaming guard and then continued to the main room where Solana had stashed their supplies. They entered with no problems.

Trey immediately rummaged through his items. He grabbed a jar of birch tar tincture and treated Brux's injuries.

"The Balish allow Lodians to use magic for creating medicines," Trey told Van and Paley. "Probably why Solana believed we infused the gemstones with medicinal magic."

Van, Paley, and Jorie hastily stuffed their strewn items into the backpacks, while Elmot stood watch at the door.

After they packed all their belongings, Van frantically searched the floor. "My mother's earrings aren't here. The jewelry box is, but the earrings aren't."

Trey went over to Van and rubbed gel ointment on her bruised jaw.

Van swatted his hand away. "Neither is my hairbrush."

"Neither is Manik's text." Jorie heaved one of the larger backpacks over her shoulders.

Van darted to every nook and cranny in the room.

"There's no time," Elmot said anxiously. "A guard is bound to come by any second."

"I have to find my mother's earrings," Van said.

"They're probably still in Solana's pocket." Trey gathered his crossbow and quiver. He tugged Van's arm and one by one they left the main room.

The team hurried down the hallway, hugging the wall in single file.

Van positioned herself to be last in line and dropped back. With doors every few yards, Solana could've put her mother's earrings in any of these rooms. Most guards had left the building, so Van considered it worth the risk of taking a peek.

Hoping to get lucky, she cracked open a door. It revealed an empty interrogation room, which gave her the creeps. She gently closed the door and turned to rejoin the end of the line. Her heart skipped a beat. *Where are they?*

Alone in the hallway, Van panicked. She tried to sprint, but her pant leg caught on a loose nail in the doorframe. She tugged, yanked, and pulled her pant leg while visions of being captured terrified her. Van heard a floorboard creak from the adjacent hallway and jerked her leg, using all her strength, to no avail. *A guard is coming!*

Footsteps echoed from around the corner.

A pimple-faced guard appeared. He seemed startled to see Van, and then he dashed toward her.

Van struggled to break free.

"H-Halt." The guard raised a DEW at Van.

Van stopped wrestling with her pant leg and raised her hands in the air, demonstrating her surrender.

The guard continued forward and snapped his hand to his neck. His pace slowed, and he wavered for a few steps, then thumped to the floor.

Trey rounded the corner, grinning. "Thank the light I have good aim." He pinched his fingers together and motioned to show he had thrown a dart.

Brux rushed to Van and untangled her pant leg from the nail.

"I would rather've shot him with an arrow, but Elmot's poisonous dart did just fine." Trey rifled through the guard's pockets. "Yes!" He held several coins in his palm and slipped them into his pocket.

Brux glowered at Van. "No more detours." To make sure, he jostled Van, so she walked in front of him, sandwiched between himself and Trey.

The trio caught up with the rest of the group, who waited in a nearby hallway.

Jorie glared at Van but held her tongue. She moved the team on.

At a steadfast pace, they made their way out of the compound. They walked outside, hidden in plain sight under the commotion of the attack between the Balish soldiers and the Anti-Manik Rebels, and disappeared into the woods.

The team headed north, toward Araquiel.

Chapter 31

D ay 8: 1:13 a.m., Living World

Hiking through the dark woods up a mountainside at night proved to be slow going.

Traveling the main road into Araquiel would've been quicker, but Jorie didn't want to risk running into Balish soldiers. They had climbed so high in elevation, Van's breathing became more rapid, and her ears ached. Unfortunately, she could still hear Jorie.

"Get a move on!" Jorie yelled. "You rested enough in the jail cell." She started with her random shouts of "Ticktock" again, getting on Van's last nerve.

As they hiked farther north into the mountainous region of Fomalhaut, the weather grew colder and breezier. The sky turned bright blue with the morning sun, but stringy white clouds soon took over. By mid-morning, even Jorie had lost her pep as Van and the others had hours ago. Finally, Araquiel came into view.

The group trudged from the woods and stopped short once they'd gotten close enough to get a good view of the townspeople.

"Whoa," Trey said.

The town bustled with Balish military. Their harsh black uniforms contrasted with the snow-dusted ground and the gingerbread-style cottages distinctive of Araquiel.

"You think Solana's word about escaped prisoners has reached this area yet?" Brux asked, white puffs came from his mouth as he spoke.

"When we left, she was in the middle of a battle with anti-Manikists," Trey said. "So probably not."

"How long do battles take?" Paley asked. "Do we have enough time to get something to eat?"

Van noticed her friend had bitten her gel fingernails down to the nub.

"We may need to split—"

"Hey! You there!" A harsh male voice interrupted Jorie.

Van cringed and turned to see a Balish soldier standing behind them. The color drained from her face.

The others tensed.

"Keep moving," he growled. "No loitering. Keep the walkways clear. The princess is scheduled to come into town today." He shooed them along.

"Well, that settles that," Elmot said as they hurried down the sidewalk. "Word we're fugitives hasn't reached here yet, or we would've been arrested."

"Can we get breakfast?" Paley pleaded. "It smells yummy." She stopped in front of a place called the Beef Hearth. "I'm starving. And freezing."

Brux turned to Jorie. "We should get off the streets."

"We've got to get to the Troll's Foot," Jorie said.

"We could go in and ask where it is." Paley eyed the eatery.

"We could use some nourishment, even if we just buy some rations," Elmot suggested. "Who knows what lies ahead?"

"I've got money." Trey jingled the guard's coins in his pocket.

Jorie sighed and reluctantly agreed. "Let's make it quick."

Van was happy to eat until she glanced above the door at a stained-glass cathedral window designed with five gold pentagram coins. The image unsettled her. "I don't think we should go in."

The group ignored her and walked through the door.

Van followed and gasped at the sight before her.

The Beef Hearth seemed the go-to place for Balish military. Black uniforms dominated the room, and the team's entrance didn't go unnoticed.

Trey eyes darted around the room. "Uh, Van's right. Maybe this isn't the best place for us to get food."

"Too late," Jorie said in a low voice. "If we leave now, we'll draw attention that'll make us look guilty."

"We *are* guilty," Van whispered.

"We should go." Paley changed her tune. And Paley was not one to pass on an eatery.

A potbellied man with cherub cheeks hustled over to them. "No, no, no!" He wore a crisp, striped jersey under a well-used apron. "We don't serve riffraff like you. Out, out!"

"Riffraff?" Jorie's four fingers wrapped around Zachery's handle.

Half the diners in the place stared at them. Several nearby Balish soldiers fidgeted in their seats.

"Keep your hands in sight," the potbellied man warned as he shuffled Van and the others toward the door.

Back on the street, Jorie fumed. "He thinks we're marketeers' scouts. Worthless unless we bring bounty home to our parents."

Brux snickered. "He thought we were going to rob them."

"We probably couldn't afford to eat there, anyway," Trey said.

"Let's head north, outside the downtown area," Elmot suggested as he consulted one of his maps. "We might have better luck, and we'll be away from most of the soldiers."

They went to another eatery, then another, and another. No one would risk letting marketeers' scouts in.

"What're we gonna do for food?" Paley whimpered as they roamed down a quiet side street.

"Where're we gonna sleep?" Van asked. All of this rejection wore her out, and she'd had enough of roughing it.

"Do you need rest?" Brux asked Van.

He had stayed suffocatingly close to Van since her fainting episode. Already in a bad mood, she found it easy to snub him.

Just when Van thought it couldn't get any worse, sleet poured down on them.

They came upon a handful of small, off-the-path eateries. Ducking under a nearby tree to shield them from the sleet, the group squabbled over which one looked most likely to take them in.

Fed up, Van said, "That one." She pointed to a place that gave her the friendliest vibe.

The team agreed.

When they entered, Roguey, the owner of Rocky Mount Eatery, gave them a wary eye. "What brings the likes of you here?"

Jorie told their story about being marketeers' scouts searching for the Runestar. Roguey agreed to feed and shelter them as long as they stayed hidden in his barn for the rest of the day.

Roguey's barn was less than ideal, being drafty, with a leaking roof, and it smelled like moldy hay and horse poop. But with the team so tired, no one was being picky.

Trey paid several pecs to Roguey, who went off to fetch food.

Brux found kindling in the barn and lit a contained fire in an old metal barrel for warmth. Jorie thought it best to wait until Roguey got comfortable with them before asking him about the location of the Troll's Foot Tavern.

Every so often, the scuffling in the stalls and the whinnying of horses startled them. Nevertheless, they settled in, resigned to stay put until dusk.

Roguey served them dinner in the barn. Being so hungry, Van once again ditched her veganism and ate the smoked sausages, along with the boiled potatoes. Although eating meat disgusted her, she had been so hungry the food tasted delicious, and was the most any of them had eaten in the last week. Although thankful for her full belly and the break, Van couldn't shake the disquieting feeling of losing time.

Roguey came in to clear the dishes and brought them playing cards. The deck comprised seventy-two numbered pictorial cards. Thanks to Jorie's magic, they could play a card game called Swirl. Everyone seemed familiar with it, except Van and Paley.

People called the game Swirl because the cards randomly reshuffled themselves like a swirling wind. The game required the winner to collect a hand containing sets and runs, similar to gin rummy. To do this, the player either had to draw the anchor card—this would hold the player's cards in place during the swirl, while it rearranged the other people's cards—or be lucky enough to assemble a winning hand before the next swirl. The Balish had outlawed the popular Lodian game because it required magically enchanted cards to work. But the team deemed Roguey's barn safe enough to play without fear of being caught.

After tiring of cards, they all wandered off to do their own thing.

Brux tended the fire. "Maybe we should rescue Daisy," he suggested.

Every fiber of Van's being told her they had to keep moving north, but this time, when Brux mentioned going off track, it didn't bother her. She knew it came from a place of concern about his sister's wellbeing and Van worried about Daisy too.

"We're not equipped to do battle against Balish soldiers." Elmot sat cross-legged on a bale of hay, maps in hand. "And we're outnumbered."

"We can use stealth to infiltrate the camp," Brux said. "And our wits to outsmart them."

Trey lay on his back, tossing a stone into the air and catching it. "Michael is holding our Anchoress captive—*before* her powers have manifested. She's basically defenseless."

Jorie sat on a wooden milk crate, repeatedly flipping Zachery into the air and catching it. "And her assigned protector is in the dungeons of Balefire, with Merloc."

Van assumed she meant Marcus.

"How does Marcus know he's Daisy's assigned protector?" Paley asked.

"Uxa probably told him during his briefing," Brux said. "APs are born with a deep desire to protect, which draws them to the profession of becoming Grigori. An AP develops an inner knowledge that he's assigned, but he doesn't know the identity of the Anchoress or whether he'll be needed to serve his role or if he's even right about his gut feeling. Protocol, crafted by the Elementals, dictates the HG tells him of his assignment after he completes training and becomes a full-fledged Grigori. And only after the newest Anchoress learns of her position, which usually occurs after her mother dies, or when her mother passes the Anchoress light down to her daughter, using the Transference of Light spell."

Paley shrugged. "The Elementals are an odd bunch, aren't they?"

Jorie nearly dropped Zachery. "Paley! Watch your words."

"Under the circumstances, Uxa probably told Marcus so he could protect Daisy on the mission," Brux said. "I'll bet it's why Merloc believed he had captured the Anchoress-in-waiting to begin with. Marcus confessed to being her AP."

"Tortured it out of him," Trey said callously. "Probably would've been better to stick to protocol and not tell him."

"Daisy could use our help." Elmot frowned, looking concerned.

Jorie lifted her gaze toward the others as she re-holstered Zachery. "We can't risk crossing the southern border again." She bent her head, deep in thought. Her hand grazed her mohawk, then she looked up. "But we could stay put. Michael and Daisy are headed this way. We could wait for them to catch up to us."

"They'll have to come through Araquiel," Elmot added. "It's the only way to the north."

Paley batted her eyes at Brux. "I vote we rescue Daisy."

Brux grinned at Paley.

Van rolled her eyes. "We need to stick to the plan. Stay focused on getting the Coin." Why couldn't anyone else see they had to keep moving? Van had brought Paley along to have her back. She understood why Brux would want to help his sister, but Paley was her best friend and should support Van, not flirt with Brux.

By now, Paley knew Van and Brux had a thing. Just because

Brux didn't return Van's affection didn't mean Paley was free to go for him. At least, that's the way their friendship worked on the island. Paley's disrespect irked Van, and she regretted bringing Paley with her.

Jorie took their comments under consideration, then decided they'd stay and wait.

"What happened to ticktock?" Van asked Jorie.

"It'll be time well spent," Jorie said, putting an end to the discussion.

Afterward, the conversation died.

Van yawned. Her jaw no longer ached. The ointment Trey had put on her cheek yesterday had expedited the healing of her bruise. She toyed with the idea of heading out on her own, then remembered Uxa had told her as a team all their skills were necessary to complete the mission. Van would also need Trey to retrieve the Coin. And she didn't know how to get to the Troll's Foot Tavern.

Yawning again, she curled into her sleeping bag on top of a bale of hay. She had to persuade the group to continue north, but how? Lulled by the patter of sleet against the roof, a full belly, and warmth from the fire, she racked her brain to recall Jacynthia's words. *Don't fight against the darkness, stick to your purpose, maintain your faith and gratitude.* What did that mean?

The only thing Van knew for certain was they needed to keep *moving*, and right now, they were stuck. She tried to call on Jacynthia for advice but fell into a disturbed sleep.

Grandfather clocks relentlessly tick, tick, ticking filled her dreams, reminding her time was slipping away.

Chapter 32

D ay 8: 4:10 p.m., Living World

VAN WOKE UP, irritated to see Brux in a buoyant mood.

He teased Paley, as she broke through the thin ice in the pig's trough and used its water to wash her face. They playfully flicked the near-freezing water at each other, and Paley giggled at everything Brux said. Not that Van cared.

She tried to persuade the others to keep moving, but this only made her seem as if she weren't a team player and didn't want to rescue Daisy.

"The best thing for our mission is going to the Troll's Foot Tavern as soon as possible," Van insisted. "Get whatever info we can about the location of the Coin and then get moving again."

"Rescuing Daisy and getting her on our team is the best thing for this mission," Brux countered. "And no one said anything about *not* going to the Troll's Foot."

"Afterward, we'll head north," Jorie said.

Van gave up and placed her faith in the light, and if that meant doing nothing, she was on the right track.

Roguey dropped by to check on them and handed Van a basket of salted auroch strips on his way in.

"Thanks." Van feared becoming weak from hunger later down the road and secretly tucked a few pieces in her pants pocket before sharing with the rest of the group.

"What time you heading out?" Roguey asked them.

"Change of plans," Jorie said. "We're going to stay for a day or two."

"No, no," Roguey said. "Can't do that."

Jorie leaped to her feet, Zachery in hand. "You tell the Balish we're here?" She pushed Roguey against the wall and rammed the war axe's handle across his neck.

Trey and Brux jumped into a combat stance, drawing their weapons: Trey, a loaded crossbow; Brux, a dagger.

"How long do we have 'til the soldiers get here?" Jorie asked through clenched teeth.

Elmot stayed back with Van and Paley. "Jorie, take it easy," he said.

Roguey held up his trembling hands. "Y-You don't understand. The border checkpoint's closed. Solana isn't letting anyone cross in or out of Fomalhaut. Balish soldiers are searching everywhere for escaped prisoners. Not leaving any stone unturned. I'm tryin' to help you, is all."

Brux muttered under his breath as he and Trey lowered their weapons.

Jorie released Roguey.

"All's I know is you best head on out of here." Roguey rubbed his neck.

The only direction they could go without running into Balish soldiers was to the north. They were back on track, with no effort on Van's part. *Maybe having "faith in the light" worked after all.*

"How do we get to the Troll's Foot Tavern?" Van asked before anyone suggested a change of plans again.

"Why?" Roguey asked loudly. "How would I know of such a

disrespectable place as that?" His eyes darted back and forth, searching, then settled on a snaggle-toothed stable hand who appeared from the shadows.

Jorie, Brux, and Trey snapped to alert mode again.

Instead of being paranoid like her teammates, Van found her curiosity piqued by the stable hand. She figured he had caused the shuffling noises coming from the stalls. He probably lived in the barn's loft, sleeping on haystacks and tending to the horses as his life's work. He must've been spying on them the whole time. If he'd wanted to hurt them, they would all be dead by now.

"This be Jeb, folks." Roguey waved his hands to calm them. "Nothing to be afraid of. Known him my whole life."

"They be okay," Jeb said. "Been watching 'em all day, listenin'. Definitely not marketeers' scouts. Definitely not Balish spies. Lots of talk about the Coin, Anchoress. Saw them using *magic*." He chortled. "These here kids are Lodians, through and through. Safe to say, they be no friends of the Balish."

With Jeb's seal of approval, Roguey happily spilled his guts. He told them both he and Jeb supported peace between the Lodians and the Balish. Roguey called them "fellow Manikists," which he claimed was anyone who didn't support the current Balish regime, and he professed a love for Lodians.

Van didn't have to flash her eyes to convince Roguey she was the Anchoress-in-waiting. He asked how they had heard about the Troll's Foot Tavern, and Van told him about Len. Roguey was a friend of Len's, and, based on that, he willingly gave them directions and the password to the Troll's Foot.

The "password" was a phrase in the ancient language, "*Sandum ete vultrie.*"

Brux told them, "It translates to 'the Balish are excrement heads.' It's a loose usage of the language and something no Bale would ever utter for fear of persecution."

The only problem, the Troll's Foot didn't open until midnight.

Groans echoed throughout the barn, even as Roguey agreed to help support their cause by keeping them hidden for the night.

Ticking sounds of a grandfather clock chimed in Van's head,

loud enough to echo like a headache. The musty the barn smothered her. Her nose, still stuffy from the hay and mold. She feared she wouldn't be able to keep her sanity trapped there, doing nothing until midnight.

"You're a *vultrie*," Paley whispered to Van and then giggled.

"Ha ha. I'm an excrement head." Van grinned, thankful Paley's joke snapped her out of her anxiety spiral.

Resigned to wait, everyone settled around the fire. The conversation turned to terrigens.

"Why do the Balish hate terrigens so much?" Paley asked. "Solana seemed to like me."

"That's because she didn't know you were a terrigen," Van said.

"And Solana thought she could use you to help her cause," Trey added.

"It's a common Balish belief the Creator made terrigens from the mud, or from *below*," Brux said, answering Paley. "Vichors were created from a piece of the Creator's light, or from *above*. This is where the ichor in our blood comes from and why some people believe terrigens are beneath, or not as good as, vichors."

"Lodians are direct descendants of the Elementals," Elmot said. "That's why they favor our race."

"Does that mean Elementals and vichors mated and *poof*, Lodians came into being?" Paley asked.

Brux flashed Paley a smile from across the fire.

Paley perked up and grinned back.

Trey snickered. "Sort of."

"Back before recorded time, the Elementals were sent down to the world of humans to instruct them in the ways of the light on behalf of the Creator," Brux said. "Instead, they ended up frolicking with and seducing humans. As a result, they inadvertently created the Lodian race and, by doing so, interfered with the will of the Creator. An act for which they were condemned. The Creator cast them down from the Heavens to be forever bound to the physical plane, banished to live on Mt. Altithronia."

"It's obvious they still hold a grudge against us mortals for being so gosh darn sexy," Paley said with a flirty grin.

Brux chuckled at Paley's comment.

Trey picked up where Brux left off and said, "This disruption of the Creator's will caused a ripple in the vibration of the world, making it split in two. The less enlightened humans accumulated in the lower vibration, forming the Earth World. The higher evolved humans elevated here, to the Living World."

"Balish have always hated terrigens," Jorie said. "And they hate us because we're the protectors of terrigens and the Earth World."

"They call us dirt lovers," Elmot said to Van and Paley. "A derogatory label."

Jorie shrugged. "If we don't help those below us, we weaken our own foundation."

"People who like dirt and mud aren't so bad." Van remembered how much she loved digging in the sand at Buzzard's Bay beach when she was a child.

"The Balish are plagued with greed and a relentless desire to conquer, just like terrigens," Trey said. "They hate the people most like themselves." He snorted, then grabbed a stick and jabbed at the fire.

Paley leaned toward Van and mouthed, "Is that how I am?"

Van whispered back, "He means the mainland terrigens."

"Actually," Trey said to Paley, obviously overhearing their conversation. "You're the worst kind of terrigen to be. You were born here but got bounced out."

Paley let out a tortured squeak.

"Trey!" Van wrapped an arm around Paley and pulled her close. "Rude!"

"Oh, sorry," Trey said. "I was just telling the truth. I thought you wanted to know."

"You can say things in a nice way." Elmot furrowed his brows.

"By all means." Trey extended his palm toward Elmot.

Elmot hesitated. "Well, um…"

"A blunt," Jorie said. "Paley, you're a type of terrigen called a blunt. Someone born in the Living World who has no ichor."

"You would've died if you'd stayed here," Trey said, trying to make amends. "Your energy vibration is too low. The Living World spit you into the Earth World for your own protection."

"It's not the terrigens' fault." Elmot squeezed Paley's shoulder affectionately and glared at Trey. "They vibrate at such a low level they don't know any better. Their society relies heavily on man-made creations—electricity, oil-based machinery—which deplete nature to operate, which takes them further away from being able to connect to the universal grid."

"They use science to desecrate nature, rather than connect to its abundant flow of energy," Trey said, causing Van to wonder if he still held the Balish belief terrigens were lesser people. "Even at their low vibrational level, they can connect to nature for renewable energy."

"It would make their world a more peaceful, loving place," Elmot said.

"And they would generate fewer demons," Jorie added.

"We can protect terrigens from demons, but we can't protect them from themselves." Trey shook his head.

The depressing conversation, along with Brux and Paley's flirtatious smiles, worsened Van's claustrophobia. She needed a distraction and turned to the friendliest one in the group. "Elmot, can you teach me how to navigate? What other skills do you have?"

Elmot seemed pleased to give Van a mock-topography class. He began by telling her about land formation based on weather conditions over time, then broached the subject of plate tectonics. He explained the natural opposing element of earth was water and how water erosion formed tunnels and caves.

Jorie interrupted, "Why don't you make yourself useful and teach Van how to use the land to defend herself against an enemy, like a Balish soldier or a demon?"

Elmot loved the idea.

Van suggested Paley listen in, but her friend cared only about fixing her nails. Van's heart fluttered when Brux sauntered over, but it sank when he said he'd rather study the translations Van had transcribed from Manik's text. She gave him the parchments from her backpack without protest.

Elmot continued his lecture about how to use the landscape to avoid, escape, or defeat the enemy, and Van felt let down. She thought he would teach her how to use magic to raise a golem from the earth or something similarly cool, but it turned out to be a standard lecture about the earth's landscape. After a half-hour, Brux joined them.

"Did you translate this from Manik's text?" Brux asked Van. He held a scrappy piece of paper.

"No, I found it in my father's study," Van said. "Why?"

"It's a magical Grigori chant to fight demons," Brux said.

Van shrugged. "Oh, I thought it was a poem or a song."

"You translated it correctly, by the way."

"Gee, thanks." Van rolled her eyes. As Brux turned to walk away, she said, "Wait up," and jumped to her feet. "Did you read the part I translated about the Blood Moon? What does it mean?"

"About Manik's prediction?" he asked. "That the next Anchoress called forth to fight against evil will determine the fate of all worlds? Yeah, I read that."

"No… well, yes. I mean, the part where the next Anchoress would be born under a Blood Moon."

Brux nodded.

"I remember overhearing Uxa. She didn't know what kind of moon this generation's Anchoress-in-waiting was born under."

"Elders read the moon's surface on the night Lodian royals are born," Brux said. "Like reading tea leaves as a predictor for what kind of life that person will live. But I've never heard of a Blood Moon." Pain echoed in Brux's eyes. "My parents told me it was cloudy the night Daisy was born." He braced himself, as if each word cut into his heart. "Couldn't see the moon's surface. But we know it was waning, a weak moon… it cast little light."

The account of Daisy's birth matched what Van had overheard Uxa and Fynn say about the Anchoress-in-waiting. They had said the night was cloudy, which was a bad omen, and predicted the heir was too weak to survive the journey to find the Coin.

Van opened her mouth, excited to share this bit of information, then snapped her jaw shut. Telling Brux would only cause him more pain, and despite being mad at him for rejecting her advances and then flirting with Paley, she still couldn't do it. She realized that by hurting him, she would hurt herself as well.

Instead, subdued, she watched Brux turn away from her and return to the dark corner, where he continued his cozy chat with Paley.

Chapter 33

Day 9: 12:00 a.m., Living World

By nightfall, people were getting on one another's nerves. Being cooped up together in a barn all day seemed like a test of the highest caliber. When midnight came, the group readily set out for the Troll's Foot Tavern.

With Elmot's help, they found the poorly lit road leading to the Troll's Foot. One lone stone hut stood on the road, with no sign identifying the structure, only a piece of parchment nailed to the door that read "Closed for renovations."

Jorie threw her hands in the air. "Oh, great! Just great!"

"Wait a minute," Van said. "It's a fake sign, meant to ward off anyone not welcome."

"How do you know that?" Brux asked as Paley shamelessly clung to his arm.

"It's *obvious*," Van said, determined not to go back to the barn. She rapped on the door.

Someone slid open a small rectangular window. Two sparkling blue eyes stared out. "Sorry," said the voice behind the door. "Closed for renovations. Come back another time."

Before he slammed the window shut, Van said, "Roguey sent us. We're... *friends*."

The blue eyes darted, inspecting each of them. "Password?"

"*Sandum ete vultrie*," Van said.

Paley giggled and clutched Brux tighter.

"That's a sentence, not a word." The blue eyes crinkled at the corners.

Jorie pushed Van aside. "Tough crap. Let us in." She reached for Zachery, ready to bust down the door.

Van shoved Jorie back and said to the man behind the door, "I have a word for you—how about *excrement head!*"

Paley giggled again.

"That's two words," blue eyes said, chuckling. The man swung open the door. "Times are dark. A sense of humor goes a long way." He stood aside as they entered. "The name's Noam." He had a stocky build, a balding head, ruddy cheeks, and a bulbous nose. "Only fun people are allowed into the Troll's Foot. I guess I can make an exception for friends of Roguey, though." He guffawed at his own joke. "C'mon, c'mon. Follow me."

They entered the dimly lit room supposedly under renovation; however, cobwebs hung everywhere. Two scruffy men, with a good view of the door, quietly sat in the corner playing cards on top of a barrel.

Van hesitated as Noam led them into a broom closet and then through a hidden door in the back wall. Her palms got sweaty as they descended a narrow flight of stairs. Then another, and another. With each flight, the walls felt more oppressive, crushing her chest until she had to fight for each breath. She was acutely aware of how to get out and the distance to the exit. When she thought they could go no deeper underground, the sound of a rowdy crowd drifted up the stairway.

Noam led them through a thick wooden door painted with a severed troll's foot.

Van winced at the repulsive logo and followed the others into the tavern. The ambiance of the establishment overwhelmed her. One word came to mind: speakeasy.

Although the dress and the design didn't match the Earth World's 1920s, this was definitely where the oppressed secretly came to flaunt their resistance to the current rule. The place roared. A band played fiddles, bongos, and fifes and patrons danced everywhere. Full mugs and good cheer were the spirit of the night.

"Enjoy," Noam said as he left, closing the door behind him.

"Wow," Paley said, wide-eyed. She disappeared into the wild crowd, pulling Brux along with her.

Jorie glowered as she watched Brux's back vanish. "Try to stay focused, guys. Location of the Coin. Go."

"C'mon in," slurred one partier. "Don' be shy."

"We love people who hate the Balish regime!" screeched a tipsy woman at the bar.

Several people held their mugs high and cheered in solidarity.

"Merry meet and merry part, bright the cheeks and warm the heart!" shouted a trio of sloppy men raising and clinking their mugs.

The noisy drunkards and the windowless walls agitated Van's fear of being in enclosed places. She felt light-headed and exhausted. Determined not to succumb, she moved farther into the steamy tavern.

Elmot also seemed uncomfortable with the crowd and stayed close to Van. He navigated to an open space at the bar.

Van scanned the crowd, looking for Brux and Paley, then scolded herself for caring about what they did.

"Hey, folks," said the grinning bartender. "The name's Zane." He appeared a little older than Van.

"Two mugs of mead, please," Elmot said.

"You bet," Zane replied.

Van watched him pour, controlling her breath, trying to relax. She distracted herself from her anxiety by studying the details of the tavern.

Someone had painted the upper borders of the wall with various phases of the moon. Behind the bar hung a huge oil painting of two smiling young women from another time. They stood arm in arm, wearing simple, yet elegant, toga-style dresses. Their wavy golden hair flowed long and free. One raised a gold goblet, the other wore a simple gold coin pendant necklace, and stared out at Van with violet eyes—*Amaryl*. The other woman was her sister, Zurial. Van's attention returned to Amaryl's necklace. The sooner she found the location of the Coin, the quicker they could leave the stuffy tavern.

Zane slammed two foaming mugs down on the bar. "Two b-stips."

"Uh-oh." Van patted her pockets, though she knew she had no money. She couldn't put it on her family's tab in this world. She glanced at Elmot, who had a deer-in-the-headlights look, and shrugged.

"Trey didn't give me any money," Elmot said. "I thought you had some."

"I'll take a stip, pec. Can even make change for a losc. Usually don't take coins with the Balish stamp, though—just for the point of it—but if that's all you got, it'll do." Zane chuckled.

Van shook her head.

"Down on your luck, eh?" Zane placed his hands on the bar and leaned in, conspiratorially. "Well, anyone who hates the Balish is a friend of mine. We can work somethin' out. Tell you what, for a kiss, you get a mead. One kiss, one mead. Looks as though I'm lined up for two kisses." He puckered.

Van turned to Elmot and said, "Well? He wants a kiss. What are you waiting for?"

Zane guffawed.

It sounded like Noam's laugh, and Van noticed his features appeared similar. No doubt, they were father and son.

Zane good-naturedly took a kiss on the cheek from Elmot and a quick one on the lips from Van, then zipped off to sling more drinks. Every time he zoomed past Van, he said, "Let me know when you need another mead. I could use another kiss!"

She smiled, and the next time he flew by, Van shouted, "I guess my luck would be better if I had some *coins*."

Zane stopped short. "Ho! Ho! You bet it would! You've an interest in coins, then?"

Van turned on the flirt. "Oh, *yeah*." She batted her eyelashes. "My mother used to collect coins."

"Oh, she was a numismatist?" Zane squinted at Van, then glanced at the portrait behind him of Amaryl and Zurial. "Who exactly was your mother?" He stared at Van.

"My mother's dead. Let's talk about something else."

"She didn't leave you on purpose," Zane said earnestly. "I'm sure she didn't want to die."

Van fidgeted. No one had ever spoken to her about her mother's death before.

"The connections we have to our family, living or dead, make us who we are. If you don't reconcile your feelings for her, your ancestral line will remain broken." Zane shrugged, then grinned. "You look like Amaryl." He tipped his head at the portrait.

Van flipped her hair, hoping to keep him talking. "What's she wearing around her neck?"

Zane leaned in and said in a low voice, "That's the *Coin of Creation*."

Van felt Elmot tense next to her, though she already knew Amaryl was wearing the Coin.

"Oh! I'm *fascinated* by the Coin." She gave Zane her best smile. "I would love to hear any stories you have about it—like, where it's hidden." She flipped her hair again. She had never tried so hard in her life.

Elmot whispered in Van's ear, "Take it easy, or he'll think you're having a seizure."

Merry patrons at the other end of the bar riotously called for Zane to refill their mugs.

Zane screamed back at them, "Shut it, you fighorns! Can't you tell I'm busy?" He leaned on the bar, closer to Van. "Now, where were we? Oh, yeah—the Coin."

It surprised Van when, instead of getting angry, the patrons roared and laughed. A man, half in the bag, hopped behind the bar and refilled his mug, and then the mugs of his pals. Van guessed money was not an issue at the Troll's Foot because wealthy Manikists secretly funded the tavern.

"See them, over there?" Zane nodded toward several men in the crowd who looked as if they belonged to Robin Hood's Merry Men. "Thieves from Cortica. Also after the Coin."

Van inwardly groaned and added them to the list.

"They hate the Balish, which got them in. But they're dirty scoundrels, the whole lot of 'em. Won't tell 'em a thing. But…"

"You'll tell me," Van said coyly. "For another kiss."

Zane's wide grin puffed his cheeks.

Van obliged, hoping Brux was watching.

"I have it on good authority the Coin is hidden in a place called Yesod," Zane said. "There, it lies deep in the Caves of Wolfenden."

The guy sitting on the barstool next to Van overheard the *Wolf*enden part and started howling like a wolf. Others joined in, howling. Wolf calls echoed throughout the tavern.

Zane rolled his eyes; Van could tell he enjoyed every minute.

"Go on," she urged, glad dangerous information flowed freely in the Troll's Foot.

Zane's brow furrowed. "Sounds simpler than it is. Yesod is the most dangerous, unsettled area of Fomalhaut. It's loaded with roaming troll tribes. Even heard Tarcs are in the area—"

Elmot gasped. "The *warlords*?"

"Shh." Zane waved them closer. "The Coin lies deep in the Caves of Wol—" His eyes darted to the patrons, not wanting them to howl again, he continued, "—in the caves. It's guarded by the Elemental Loka and her wily tricks and traps. A monster roams the labyrinth of tunnels leading to the Coin, ready to destroy any trespassers."

Van's mouth went dry. If Brux knew this, he would be even more worried about Daisy.

"You believe the heir exists?" Elmot asked.

Zane's head bobbed. "Oh, yeah." He stared directly at Van. "The heir survived the Dark War, but her bloodline… it's *cursed*."

Chapter 34

Day 9: 1:32 a.m., Living World

THE ROWDY CROWD called for refills.

Zane turned and yelled, "Shut it, you meat sacks!" He smiled at Van. "I gotta take care of these animals. Stay put. I'll be back." He winked and was off.

Van and Elmot zipped away to tell the others their news. They gathered the team and shared the information Van had "seduced" out of Zane.

Van felt irked when Brux and Paley stole her thunder by adding they not only found out about the Caves of Wolfenden but also how to *get* there, and it had nothing to do with following a map. To which Elmot took offense.

"We have to pass through troll territory," Paley said as if she were an expert.

"We need to bring gnome guides with us to navigate around the roaming troll tribes," Brux explained. "Otherwise, we'll never make it through alive."

"Let's grab us some gnomes!" Trey said, ready to go.

Jorie shook her head. "We'll have to coax the gnomes into helping us. They have to come of their own free will. They're not guide animals."

Van sighed. "How do we do that?" It sounded like more work.

"We have to gain the gnomes' trust," Jorie said. "We'll need to bring their leader a gift. Did you find out what that should be?"

"Nope," Brux said.

"I could give them a pair of my contact lenses," Paley said brightly.

Brux frowned. "Gnomes are earth creatures. They don't value material possessions."

"What would they want, then?" Van said, her mouth agape.

Jorie clapped her hands. "Okay, guys, back to working the crowd."

Van turned to Elmot. "Let's go talk to Zane again. He probably knows." They weaved through the crowd back to the bar.

"Ho! There you are." Zane held an elegant gold goblet.

Van sidled up to the bar, with Elmot close behind. "What's *that?*"

The drunk on next barstool leaned toward Van. "You mus' be pretty special for Zaney to whip that out."

"It's beautiful!" Elmot said.

Zane held the goblet high. "This here's one of the goblets used at Zurial and Manik's wedding feast. The real deal. See." Zane held the goblet up to the oil painting behind the bar. It was identical. "It's a thousand years old. Amaryl commissioned five to be made in the likeness of Zurial's favorite family heirloom, a gold chalice. One replicated for each person at the head table. Zurial toasted using the original gold chalice. Never let it out of her sight. Rumors say she was obsessed with it. But this isn't Zurial's gold chalice. It's the replica used by Amaryl." Zane lowered the chalice, leaned over the bar, and said to Van, "You seemed interested in the ancient royals and their things, so I thought you'd like to see it."

"Yes, I would." Van gawked at the chalice. She didn't feel comfortable touching something so revered and treasured.

Zane held the chalice high and shouted, "Now, let's get ripped!" Then he banged the chalice down on the bar, startling Van.

He crouched below and came up holding a dusty bottle. "Nothin' but the best goes into my precious here." He winked.

For a second, Van thought he meant he would allow her to drink nothing but the best. Then she realized he meant the chalice, not her, and smiled to take the sting out of his words.

Zane gleefully popped the cork and filled the chalice with an iridescent, bubbly drink.

Regulars nearby heard the pop and cheered, causing others to gather around, including Jorie, Trey, Brux, and Paley.

Zane stood on a stool behind the bar. "Take one sip and pass it on!"

The crowd responded with hoots and shouts.

He took a showy sip, then bent down and passed the chalice to Van.

The instant Van's fingers touched the chalice, she felt uneasy. The room shifted, people blurred. She brushed it off as anxiety and lifted the drink to her mouth. The chalice had barely touched her lips when she collapsed…

SHE FOUND HERSELF AT A CELEBRATION… the people dressed oddly… the women wore elaborate toga dresses. The men, loose-fitting tunics with cloaks. Masks hid their faces.

It was the Masquerade Feast to celebrate the end of the Dark War. People all around her rejoiced.

Her mind's eye watched as an unmasked, beautiful woman flowed through the colossal, yet simple sandstone room. The architecture spoke of a different time. A thousand years ago. The woman was Amaryl.

Van felt Amaryl. She was Amaryl.

Yet she saw Amaryl as if peering through a dream.

Amaryl showed Van a scene in her life, using Van's language so she would understand.

It was important that Van understand.

This, the second night of her sister Zurial's five-day wedding celebration, marked the truce between the Balish and Lodian tribes. Despite the joy of the occasion, Amaryl's heart hung heavy with dread. She feared the Balish could not be trusted, but her responsibility as the Anchoress Queen was to do what was best for her people. Her sister's happiness pleased Amaryl, and she believed Manik, despite being Balish, was a good man. So, the wedding of the Balish king to her little sister proceeded as planned.

A sudden rush of love and delight overwhelmed Amaryl as she glimpsed a male warrior enter the palace. He arrived dressed in the traditional celebratory costume of the warrior—a leather pteruges, a hooded red cloak, and his representative animal headpiece. The unique eagle mask covering his face identified the man as her husband.

He headed straight for Amaryl.

"My love," Amaryl said in a soft whisper, afraid if she spoke too loudly, she would awaken and the warrior would fade away, leaving her alone once again.

The man wordlessly grabbed Amaryl's hand and led her through a side door into a lush garden.

Outside, barely hidden by the trees and garden vines, he impatiently pushed Amaryl against the wall. The man reached to touch Amaryl's necklace, a gold pentagram coin hanging off a simple gold chain.

She grasped his hand and brought it to her lips instead. He smelled like earthy musk.

Amaryl smiled tenderly and reached to remove his headpiece.

The warrior clasped her hands and shook his head no.

"You cannot touch my necklace. I cannot touch your mask. I guess we are even." Her laugh echoed like wind chimes tinkling in a lazy summer breeze.

The warrior's capable hands roamed Amaryl's quivering body. She trembled as the warrior touched every sacred part of her. Amaryl's heart savored every stolen moment.

"We should not be doing this here," Amaryl murmured. "We could be caught."

Neither could wait any longer.

Amaryl grew warm from the closeness of their bodies... from the anticipation... a frantic intensity welled inside her, and satisfied as the warrior took her with both passion and desperation.

Van tried to turn away, to disconnect from the vision, but Amaryl held her there, forcing her to watch, and to feel.

It was important she understood.

Van understood just fine and considered it none of her business what Amaryl did with her husband. The lush green trees and vines withered as Van used all her effort to pull out of the vision.

Amaryl tugged at her, trying to keep Van grounded there. She showed Van one last image before the vision faded—of her removing the mask of her lover...

VAN JOLTED back to the present, but not before she had seen the warrior's face.

Her eyes snapped open.

Brux hovered over her, wild with worry.

Why was it every time she regained consciousness, she was on the floor with her head in Brux's lap?

"She's waking up!" Paley's glistening, electric blue eyes stared down at Van.

Brux's brow crinkled. "You're all sweaty and flushed."

His comment made Van blush deeper. She sat up a little too fast, making her lightheaded. She noticed they weren't in the crowded tavern anymore.

"We were so worried," Elmot cooed, clucking around her like a mother hen.

"You okay?" Jorie's concern echoed in her eyes—about Van's weakness as a warrior and how she might have to compensate for it.

"You'll stop at nothing to get into Brux's lap," Paley said, smiling.

Although it was a joke, Van swore she heard a subtle tone of resentment.

While Van lay unconscious, they had moved her upstairs to the room supposedly under renovation. The two sentinels were still playing cards in the corner, with the recent addition of Noam.

"Diamonfitz. Strong stuff," Noam said when Van caught his eye. "Don't know what Zaney was thinkin' giving that to you. It's for heavy drinkers only. Though no one usually faints after one sip. That's a first."

"It's the damn gemstones again," Brux growled.

"There's nothing we can do about that now," Jorie said.

Brux stood face-to-face with Jorie. "Is there any way to fix this?"

"I'm fine," Van said feebly. She remained sitting on the floor.

"Paley being here is killing you," Brux said to Van.

"Oh, thanks a lot!" Paley wailed.

"It's not Paley," Van croaked, sure the gemstones had nothing to do with her vision of Amaryl. She had passed out from receiving impressions from touching the chalice, but she felt too weak to explain this to the disgruntled group.

Paley threw Brux a smug glare and plunked herself on the floor next to Van.

"There's no possible way to send Paley back. She's staying," Jorie said. "We're all going back to the barn. Now."

"What about the gnomes?" Elmot asked as they left the Troll's Foot. "What will we offer them?"

"We'll come up with something," Trey said. "Jorie, keep praying to the light." He said it in a mocking tone, though, deep down, he probably meant it.

The others agreed it was time to move onward, gift or no gift.

Relieved to be back in the damp, smelly barn, Van tucked into her snuggly sleeping bag by the fire. Brux lay next to her, continually sneaking glances under hooded eyes, waiting for her to fall asleep.

But Van couldn't sleep. She had too many questions, and Brux's worried energy disrupted her thoughts so she couldn't call on Jacynthia.

Amaryl had taken Van back a thousand years to show her something important. For the life of her, she didn't know what, other than a lesson in sex education. Van's cheeks flushed again.

Van knew two things. First, she felt confident the vision Amaryl had shown her was real. Second, the man with Amaryl in the garden that night was not her husband, Rowen… it was the Balish Prince Goustav.

Chapter 35

D ays 9 and 10: Living World

VAN'S CHEEKS reddened every time she thought about Amaryl's vision.

"Do you feel okay?" Brux asked, still concerned about the effect of the Twin Gemstones on her.

Van knew she would never get to sleep with Brux fussing over her, so she told him about the vision she got from touching Amaryl's goblet, minus the more intimate details.

He lifted his brow. "You had a memory engram. It means someone from the spirit realm reached across time and space to tell you something. It's a rare ability. Van!" He seemed excited. "That's your skill!"

Thrilled to finally become aware of her skill, she realized she had possessed it for as long as she could remember. Too bad she didn't know how to use it.

Neither of them could figure out what message Amaryl had

tried to pass on to Van, but, after fessing up about the vision, Van found it easy to fall asleep alongside Brux.

When morning came, Van reluctantly awoke. Every muscle in her body ached, and she had a raging headache. She wished she could go to sleep for the night all over again.

Roguey brought them a breakfast of eggs, various meats that looked like bacon and ham, and toast smothered in homemade butter.

Hungry, and with no choice, Van ate the eggs and toast.

They drank fresh yak's milk, to which Paley commented, "Yuck! It makes me want to yack." She giggled hysterically at her own lame joke.

Van wasn't in the mood for Paley's sense of humor, though she silently agreed with her friend. The milk wasn't thick and sweet like cow's milk, but, as Jacynthia had advised at their last meeting, Van "maintained her gratitude" and drank it, anyway.

She dug deep into her well of gratitude after realizing the only place to wash was in the pig's trough. Van held back tears and longed for her bathroom in Mt. Hope Manor, pink and clean with fresh running water and fluffy, lavender-scented towels.

Roguey okayed them to leave the barn but warned against lingering in Araquiel.

They heeded his warning and stopped only once, quickly, to pick up food and supplies. At Elmot's insistence, they spent most of Trey's remaining money on a square of gray honeycomb paper called graphene that projected a holographic map of Yesod, including the Caves of Wolfenden.

With no money left, enough food to last a few days, and one really cool map, they headed north toward the wild land of Yesod.

As they traveled, the terrain steepened. The air turned bitterly cold, reminding Van of the harsh Massachusetts winters. She wrapped a scarf around her face, wore gloves, and pulled a hood over her head. As the afternoon progressed, the sky turned gray and threatening.

"Storm's coming in." Elmot closed one of his paper maps. The sky rumbled, making him peer upward. "Thundersnow."

"We need to find shelter," Jorie said. "Your maps show any caves, Elmot?"

"My holographic map is of Yesod," Elmot said. "We're still in Fleelmulf. I don't have a topographic map of this area."

"I'll scout for some caves," Trey said. "Find one we can make camp in."

"The terrain in this area is too unstable for you to be climbing around," Elmot warned. "Acrobatics champ or not."

Jorie shook her head. "No. No way. Stay put, we'll—*Trey*!"

He was already scuttling up the jagged boulders on the mountainside.

Van and Paley settled onto a rock for a much-needed snack. Used to meat-based food being the only option, Van grabbed one of the smoked boar sticks, along with Paley.

While Van and Paley ate their snack, Trey reappeared on the precipice of a stone cliff.

He called down, waving his arm in a wide arc. "I found a cave! It's close to where you are."

"Watch your step," Elmot shouted nervously.

Van wished Elmot would stop being everyone's mother when she felt her butt vibrate. The rock beneath her shimmied. The trees trembled as small stones tumbled down around them.

Trey, caught off guard, lost his footing and plummeted down the rocky mountainside.

"Trey!" Jorie screamed as the ground shook. She held herself steady, clutching a nearby boulder.

Once the quaking stopped, Van and the others rushed to search for their teammate.

Within minutes, they found him. He lay on the ground at the foot of the mountain with his crossbow and some arrows scattered around him.

"Hey, guys." Trey heaved himself upright with some strain. "What took you so long?"

Van could tell his amicable tone was intended to mask his pain.

Trey's forehead glistened with sweat, and, at first, Van thought he appeared to be in okay shape, except for some minor cuts and scrapes. Then she noticed his right leg sticking out at an unnatural angle.

"It was a frost quake." Elmot knelt beside Trey. "The ground is shifting and cracking as it freezes."

Jorie cursed as she surveyed the situation.

The sharp rocks had split Trey's backpack during his fall. Its contents had spilled, lost forever in the crevices and the gaps between the boulders. Everything was gone. Including most of their food supply.

"Dammit!" Trey lowered his head as he took in their loss. "All my medicines…"

"Including painkillers." Jorie eyed his broken leg.

"I have some drops that might help prevent infection," Elmot said.

"I don't want any of your poison drops!" Trey cringed from the pain of speaking so passionately. Then, he instructed Brux, Jorie, and Elmot on how to make a splint from branches.

Van and Paley wanted to help, but Jorie shooed them away.

Jorie and Brux supported Trey as they made their way into the nearby cave Trey had seen before his fall. Brux and Jorie went in first and checked it out for any lingering creatures, like bears or AWOL Balish soldiers. With Trey's injury and the impending storm, Jorie decided they would spend the night in the cave.

Van was secretly relieved it had forced them to stop. The burden of time slipping away was no match for her fatigued body. They made camp inside to protect them from the cold northern wind but not far enough in to set off Van's claustrophobia.

Trey sat propped against the wall, looking pale and sweaty, his breathing shallow.

"Too bad your bunfy's not here," Jorie said. "Their purrs heal the soul. He could help Trey right now." Jorie stared expectantly at Van.

Van scowled. "I can't pull him out of a hat. He's not a magic trick."

Jorie shrugged and cast a pain-reducing spell on Trey's leg. "Medicinal magic is complicated and not my specialty. I'll try to connect to the energy of the boulders to do the spell." Jorie held her palms over Trey's leg. "I'm not sure if it will work."

"Don't, Jorie," Trey said meekly. "It's not worth the risk to your health."

"If she messes up the spell, there'll be a cost," Elmot nervously explained to Van and Paley. "Casting a spell that doesn't work is draining. It will make Jorie susceptible to minor illnesses like head colds or will give her bad luck. The more complex the spell, the worse the repercussions will be."

Elmot attempted to give Trey his drops, admitting they were poison, but a small diluted dose would help ward off infection and reduce his pain. "Don't be a hero," Elmot said.

Trey was in so much pain, he opened his mouth and let Elmot administer several drops of his medicine.

After Jorie's and Elmot's efforts, Trey felt better, but they were starving and their rations were negligible. Van was so hungry, she feared she might die from food deprivation. She remembered her secret stash of salted auroch strips from Roguey's barn and tossed around the idea of taking them out when Trey confessed to feeling guilty about losing his share of supplies. He talked Jorie and Brux into propping him up and taking him outside to bow hunt for their dinner.

A couple of hours later, they returned in a light snowfall. Brux had collected bundles of dry branches for the fire, and Jorie carried several fat rabbits Trey had speared with his few remaining arrows.

"Couldn't you have at least caught a wild turkey or something?" Van complained, despite her hunger shakes. She and Paley were distraught over Trey killing the poor bunnies. Any of them could've been Wiglaf or one of his friends.

"They're northern buttertail rabbits, not bunfys," Jorie said as she prepared them for dinner.

Elmot cooked the rabbits on an improvised spit over an open fire. The roasting rabbit smelled so good, Van and Paley lost their qualms about trying it.

"Tastes like chicken." Paley chuckled and helped herself to more.

After dinner, Van's stomach became queasy. She wondered whether she was coming down with something, or had overeaten on an empty stomach. Or maybe keeping Paley here with the Twin Gemstones had drained her energy. Van decided to go to bed. She inflated her sleeping bag and slipped inside.

Brux's watchfulness annoyed her, so she pulled the sleeping bag over her head and fell into a deep, dreamless sleep.

SHE WOKE at the crack of dawn to Jorie's cursing.

"Dammit!" Jorie kicked the dirt. "We're snowed in."

As Van stretched her arms, she became aware of an intermittent whirring, like a mini-motor. She lifted her head. A fluffy white mound lay curled up in the crook of her knee. Her heart soared in delight. "Wiglaf!"

The bunfy lifted his head, along with half an ear.

Seeing his cute whiskery nose and fluffy fur, Van couldn't resist reaching down and scooping him into her arms. She felt so hopeful and confident, her aches and pains seemed to fade. She hugged the little animal close to her chest. "You *do* make people feel better."

Wiglaf purred even louder.

"Look who's back!" Paley scratched Wiglaf under the chin.

Van resisted the impulse to pull him away. Paley had been all over Brux, and now she wanted Van's bunfy too. Van shook away the thought, knowing it was ridiculous.

Being so distracted by Paley, she had forgotten about Trey. Van got up and placed Wiglaf on Trey's lap. "I hope he helps."

Trey grunted thanks and feebly patted the purring animal.

"Is he using magic to heal?" Van asked, concerned the little critter might drain himself of energy and get sick.

"Bunfys exist at a higher vibrational frequency than we do," Brux said. "Their purrs range even higher. They give us an attitude adjustment, which makes us feel better, so we have more positive thoughts. They don't heal physical wounds."

"The purring doesn't hurt Wiglaf, does it?" Van persisted.

"Of course not. The—"

"Enough chatter," Jorie said, cutting off Brux. "I'm going stir crazy being cooped up again. We need to get moving. Figure out how to get around this snow!"

Van wanted to keep moving too, but she had no idea how Jorie thought Trey was in any shape to walk. She envisioned Jorie ordering Brux and Elmot to drag Trey along, his wounded leg dangling behind. However, Wiglaf's purrs worked like magic. Trey's color looked better, and he breathed normally, despite no reduction in his injuries. During the night, Trey had whittled a sturdy branch into a cane.

"Ready to go." Trey winced as he lifted the bunfy and struggled to his feet.

Elmot pondered the holographic map alongside one of his paper maps. "I think I've found a way." He sounded excited. "We're close to Yesod. I think we're in this mountain, here." He pointed to an area at the edge of the paper map. "It looks like we could go deeper into this cave, which will lead us to this pathway." He showed a tunnel system inside the mountain displayed on the holographic map. "We'd come out on the other side of the mountain *in* Yesod, closer to the Caves of Wolfenden. That would save us time."

Jorie glanced warily at Elmot. "But?"

"But I can't be exactly sure where we are. This paper map shows Fleelmulf, but it's not detailed. And from the looks of the holographic map, we'll have to go through the center of the mountain. I'm not sure what lies in wait for us there."

"Sounds like a plan," Trey said, looking pale. "Let's do it."

While Jorie beamed at Trey's dedication, Brux said, "We'll need light."

"And food," Van added. She panicked at the idea of going deep into a mountain. It made her incredibly anxious, and she gauged how much work it would be to dig through the snow wall blocking the exit to the outdoors.

Paley gathered her things. She appeared well rested and unbothered by the change in plans, even the lack of food. She started flirting with Brux again.

Brux acted cordially to her but kept his attention on Van. Wiglaf rubbed his body all over Brux's ankles.

"Good job healing, little guy." Brux bent down and scratched behind Wiglaf's ears.

Van tsked. Even Wiglaf had jumped on the Brux bandwagon.

Brux chuckled.

Van scooped Wiglaf away from him. "You're coming with us, right?" she said to the bunfy.

She tried to stuff Wiglaf into her backpack, but he wriggled and scampered away to a nest he had made during the night. The collection of white fibrous balls on branches formed concentric circles, like a wreath inside a wreath. To Van, it was the cutest thing she had ever seen. "You want me to take your little nest with us? Okay."

"Don't pack that thing." Paley scowled. "It's dirty."

Van ignored Paley, knowing her outburst had nothing to do with Wiglaf's dirty nest. It had to do with Brux paying attention to Van. She had to admit, his attention confused her. Brux had rejected her advances, then blatantly flirted with Paley. Now he seemed to be interested in Van again, which upset Paley. Van didn't know what was going on between the three of them, so she didn't address the matter. Instead, she brushed the dirt from the nest and tucked it into her backpack.

Wiglaf jumped in after it.

Jorie, Brux, and Elmot used spare kindling to make torches and lit them from the fire just before snuffing it out. All of them, except Trey, carried extra, in case the flames burned down to the nub, and they needed more. Then Van and the others followed Elmot as he led them into the hollows of the mountain.

The tunnel walls shimmered with ice. Thick icicles hung from above like great fangs of a monstrous mouth. With the tunnels being wide, Van didn't feel so enclosed. She figured Wiglaf's presence also had something to do with soothing her anxiety.

Occasionally, Van let Wiglaf out to stretch his legs and lick the ice walls. At first, she worried about his tongue getting stuck, but apparently, Wiglaf's bunfy magic warmed his tongue so he could drink. Van waited patiently until he finished and then dashed to rejoin the group. Every time she stopped, Brux hung back, waiting for her. Paley always hung back with him.

As they traveled deeper into the cave, the ice walls created enough light to make the torches no longer necessary.

"The light comes from the principle of geometrized harmonics," Elmot explained. "Remember from when I taught you about the land?" Elmot asked Van. "The ice molecules create triboluminescence by moving against the minerals in the stone walls."

Van only half paid attention to Elmot's summary. She couldn't stop admiring the beauty of the walls. Eventually, she noticed predetermined patterns in the ice crystals. She studied them when Wiglaf stopped to drink. At first, she thought she had imagined the patterns, but with Wiglaf's frequent stops, she discovered messages created within the ice. She was about to tell the others when Jorie interrupted.

"You need to stop it with the bunfy breaks," Jorie huffed.

"Fine!" Van stuffed the critter into her backpack.

Paley gasped and waggled her finger at Van. "Your eyes! They're glowing that weird purple color."

"What do you mean?" Van asked, alarmed.

"They're phosphorescent again," Brux said. "Not flashing. They're staying violet."

"They've never stayed this way before!" Van struggled to see her reflection in the ice.

Jorie stomped over to Brux. "You knew about this and didn't tell me?"

"I promised Van I wouldn't," Brux said.

"Van doesn't like people mentioning her weird glowy eyes," Paley said.

"Let me see." Jorie grabbed Van by the shoulders and looked deep into her eyes. "For the love of the light! Your eyes! That glowy color is a telltale sign the Eternal Light of the Creator is flowing in your veins. Guys, I think Van *is* the Anchoress-in-waiting!"

"I don't want to be the Anchoress-in-waiting." Van didn't need any additional stress.

"Maybe she isn't," Paley said in Van's defense.

"That's why Wiglaf is here," Jorie said, still elated. "He was telling us Van is the Anchoress. It really didn't make sense to me before now. I mean, Van, you've been useless—skill-wise, I mean. No offense. But the Anchoress is supposed to be a powerful warrior. Paley… I still can't figure out why you're here."

"Maybe there're two Anchoress heirs," Brux said, probably thinking of his sister.

Van knew what it meant for her to be the Anchoress-in-waiting. It meant her father had told Merloc the girl he had captured wasn't his daughter. Daisy wasn't the Anchoress heir. Meaning Daisy would no longer be useful to Michael and Merloc. Van shuddered.

"Or there's something we don't know about one of Goustav's heirs," Brux continued, still in denial. "It's possible the—" Brux stopped in mid-sentence as pebbles trickled from above.

Van's feet vibrated.

The cave rumbled, then shook.

"Hold tight!" Jorie shouted. "It's another quake!"

Rocks and dust crashed around them.

Brux covered Van with his body as Trey, Paley, and Elmot dashed away in the other direction.

The deafening noise seemed endless, but the quake lasted for only a couple of minutes.

Van immediately checked Wiglaf.

Two deep-blue eyes nestled in a furry white face peeped from inside her backpack. Wiglaf's ears reached straight up, and he let out a short, squeaky chirp.

Van sighed in relief.

"You okay?" Brux asked, brushing off.

Van nodded. "You?"

Brux noticed Jorie lay partly buried in rubble from the mound of boulders now blocking the tunnel and rushed to her.

"I'm okay, I'm okay." Jorie stood, wiping the dirt and stones off her clothes. She swatted away Brux's help and checked on Zachery with the same fervor that Van had checked on Wiglaf.

"I hope the rest of us got away from the downfall," Jorie said. "Maybe they're on the other side."

Jorie and Brux called through the wall of boulders to their missing teammates.

No one answered.

"They probably can't hear us," Brux said.

"The tunnel's completely blocked," Van said uneasily. "Which way do we go now?"

"The only way we can." Jorie sighed. "We have to go back."

"Without Elmot, we have no map," Brux said. "We'll never find our way out."

Anxiety clutched Van so intensely, she stopped breathing. Trapped in an enclosed space with no way out was one of her major fears. She clutched Wiglaf to her chest and forced herself to take in deep breaths.

"Van." Brux narrowed his eyes at her. "Are you okay?"

Van nodded as Wiglaf purred away, fortifying her until the anxiety receded.

"Don't worry," he said, misreading her apprehension. "We'll get you back to Paley and her gemstone."

Back through the tunnel, Van studied the patterns in the ice crystals again. The longer she stared, the better she could comprehend the markings. She lingered to peer intently at a particular spot on the icy walls.

"Why do you keep stopping?" Jorie asked in frustration.

"The ice… it's talking to me," Van said distractedly. She could feel her eyes glowing.

Brux glanced worriedly at Jorie and asked, "Cabin fever, you think?"

"No, no." Van stopped gazing at the ice and turned to Brux. "I can read the ice crystals."

"And what do these *ice crystals* say?" Brux asked in a placating tone.

Van responded to Brux's skepticism with a scrunched face. "They're showing me how to get through the mountain. It's a *map*!"

"Ho-yeah!" Jorie fist-punched the air. "Another benefit of having the Anchoress on our team."

"What's the matter, Brux?" Van taunted. "Feeling inadequate because you can't read the ice crystals? You're the language expert."

"Ice crystals are the invisible language of the Creator," Brux said, ignoring Van's barb. "The Creator constantly and in many ways tries to speak to us. We just have to be aware and listen."

"Thanks, professor." Van rolled her eyes, fully aware he had tried to change the subject. "Come on. This way."

"Let's hope Elmot will guide Trey and Paley." Jorie gestured a sideways figure eight over her chest and mumbled, "Thank-the-light-and-all-that-is-good."

Since they had lost half of their supplies in the collapse, along with half their team, Jorie decided they couldn't risk the luxury of sleeping and kept them moving.

Van continued to check the map in the ice crystals to make sure they were headed in the right direction. At one point, the markings showed they had passed into Yesod.

Soon afterward, Jorie got cranky. "Let's grab some shut-eye. Just for a couple hours. No more."

Van told them the ice crystals pinpointed their current location as being the dead center of the mountain. She huddled with the two of them and Wiglaf in a dark, ice-free alcove and drifted into a restful sleep.

▬

SOMETHING JOLTED VAN AWAKE.

Innumerable tiny hands snatched Wiglaf off her stomach and dragged her out of her sleeping bag. *Children's hands?* She smelled moldy dirt and heard Brux and Jorie being abruptly awoken as well.

"What the—" Jorie barked.

Someone tied Van's hands roughly behind her back. She glimpsed grubby children just before someone pulled a black hood over her head and plunged her into darkness.

Chapter 36

Day 11: Living World

Tiny hands shoved Van onto a hard, cold seat.

The metal cart rocketed forward. It rattled and shook on the track, tilting around bends like a wild roller-coaster ride. She couldn't decide which was worse, the crazy death drive or the suffocating hood pulled over her head.

Finally, the cart slowed and stopped.

Van's captors yanked off the hood and ordered her out. She took deep breaths, trying to calm her racing heart. Someone from behind untied her hands, but she stood stunned, too mesmerized with the scene before her to turn around.

The enormous cavern functioned as a busy mining community, run by deformed, grotesque little men. They wore shabby pointed red caps, dirty burlap overalls, and tiny round-toed work boots, and most of them had unkempt white beards of varying lengths.

"Gnomes." Brux appeared next to Van, rubbing his wrists.

"We don't have a gift for them," Van said. "Is that why they attacked us during the night?"

Brux shrugged. "Maybe it's just the gnomes' way of saying hello."

"It's customary for visitors to leave an offering for the gnome's leader on the boundary line of their territory before entering," Jorie said.

"I didn't know we were in their territory," Van said. "The ice crystals said nothing about gnomes."

Jorie shook her head. "I should've known as soon as we entered Yesod. We could've left something by our feet before we went to sleep."

The gnome guards shoved them forward with their pickaxes, pitchforks, and sledgehammers raised high. It took two gnomes to carry each of Jorie's and Brux's backpacks, and one for Van's pack. Another gnome held a wicker carrying cage in his hand.

Wiglaf peered out, his ears pressed back against his scrunched, trembling body, and his eyes widened with fright.

Van's rage at the sight made her vow to rid the world of gnomes. "If you so much as lay a finger on him—"

A gnome poked a pitchfork into her back, prodding her forward.

Giant balls of crystals hung from the ceiling, lighting the cavern. The vang-lang-kshang sounds from the machinery rang through the cavern as the gnomes worked the mines. None paid attention as the three large-sized prisoners paraded past them.

"They're mining *gold*," Brux whispered.

"Oh, crap," Jorie muttered. "Just our luck."

Van's stomach flipped. "Why is that bad?"

"Where there's gold, there's Balish," Brux grumbled. "They'll think we came to steal it."

The gnomes brought their prisoners to Hallux, the leader of the gnomes, who dressed and looked like the rest of the bearded males, though plumper. A handful of glowering fellow gnomes surrounded him.

"How did you find the path here, trespassers?" Hallux

demanded. "No one comes this way through the mountain. The path is impossible to navigate and magically protected from stumbling upon by happenstance."

Van mustered her best commanding Anchoress-in-waiting voice and dramatically said, "I am the Anchoress heir, and we need your help. We must retrieve the Coin of Creation to prevent another Great War and stop the Escalation to Dishora."

The incredulous look on Jorie's and Brux's faces was priceless.

"She's lying!" cried one gnome.

"She's a dark sorceress!" hollered another. "That's how she found us!"

"They're here to steal the gold," another wailed. "To get us killed by the Balish!"

"Silence!" Hallux bellowed.

They quieted at once.

"The only one who will know for sure is our seer. Secure them in the cell. I will go call upon her."

They locked Van and the others in a cell carved from the main cavern, where they could view the mining operation through metal bars.

"Good thing my step-mother isn't here to see me doing time," Van joked to lighten the mood. It didn't work. Then a darker thought entered her mind. "They can't hurt Wiglaf, can they? He's a magical creature. Can't he just disappear?"

"Unfortunately, gnomes can hold him here in the physical plane by using a holding spell," Jorie said. "Gnomes aren't highly magical creatures, but can connect to the power of the dirt and stones to make magic. They can't run very fast. Probably know spells that help them catch animals for food. Secretly use it when there's no Balish around."

"Wiglaf will be okay," Brux said. "Harming a magical animal would upset the Elemental Lilla, and her wrath would be great. They don't want that."

Van wrapped her arms around herself to soothe her fear as she thought about her trapped little bunfy being scared and alone.

Jorie paced, fed up with being delayed again. "If these gnomes continue to vex me, I'm going out there and stomping them all to death."

"Fine," Brux said. "Just keep in mind we need the gnomes to come with us *willingly* if we want to navigate through troll territory." He stared at Van. "How are you doing?"

His concern didn't fit the situation. "Tired, but fine. Why?"

"No feelings of lightheadedness?"

"No, why?"

Brux glanced inquisitively at Jorie.

"*Why?*" Van demanded.

"You've been away from Paley's Twin Gemstone for too long now," Brux said. "You should feel sick."

Van had forgotten about the Twin Gemstones. She patted her pocket; the gemstone remained tucked safely inside. Why hadn't she gotten sick? The answer came quickly.

One of the ramshackle carts arrived. The gnomes deposited two human-size bodies in the cavern.

Two.

They removed the prisoners' hoods.

Van heard Jorie murmur, "Where's Trey?"

The gnomes pushed Paley and Elmot across the cavern and threw them into the cell with Van and the others.

"Where's Trey?" Jorie asked again.

"He… he didn't survive the collapse," Elmot informed them as Paley wept.

"*What?*" Van cried, tears already forming in her eyes.

There was a moment of silence.

"He was a good teammate." Brux's voice cracked. "He died a warrior."

Van leaned into him, sobbing. He wrapped his arm around her waist and pulled her close.

Jorie remained strong and gathered the remaining members of team Delta into a healing circle. They bowed their heads and held hands while Jorie said a prayer to the light for their departed teammate.

Then more bad news arrived. The seer needed time to meditate before meeting with Van. According to the guard, she wouldn't be available until after the passing of one solar cycle, meaning tomorrow.

"Dammit!" Jorie dropped to her knees, too emotionally drained over Trey's death to complain about facing another delay.

Despite having Paley's Twin Gemstone back, Van also felt fragile over the loss of their teammate. For a distraction, she asked, "How do they keep track of time down here?"

Brux shrugged; he nestled with Van.

Paley flashed them a disgruntled look.

"Scouts scan the perimeter of their above ground territory," Jorie said, dully, apparently still numb from news of Trey's death. "There are other gnomes who live in villages above ground that tend to their farms."

Van expected her continued closeness with Brux to elicit a comment or two out of Paley, but her friend remained silent. Paley had dark circles under her eyes, her nails were a mess, and her hair, untamed. Van figured after what happened with Trey, Paley didn't have the stamina to confront Brux about being fickle.

Eventually, Paley and the others curled into themselves for solace and sleep.

Brux stayed awake with Van in his arms, whispering words of comfort to her until her eyelids drooped. The moment before Van slipped into the dream realm, she connected to Jacynthia. Tears ran down Van's cheeks when she brought up Trey.

"Adverse circumstances test our will to stay on our true path," Jacynthia said.

We're stuck here for another day. We'll never get to the Coin in time.

"When it appears no progress is made, it threatens our balance. We despair. Rather than be destroyed by difficult times, we must handle them with grace."

Van didn't understand, but knew she would get no better answer. She changed the subject.

Will those evil gnomes hurt Wiglaf? Us?

"Things that appear unattractive or different are not necessarily evil."

Their conversation ended when Van couldn't hold off slipping away from Jacynthia and falling into a deep sleep.

Vivid images of a bright full moon filled her dreams. Moonbeams bathed Van in light, connecting her to their power, and promising to help her fulfill her destiny.

Chapter 37

D ay 12: 12:00 p.m., Living World

THREE TIMES A DAY, a gnome would appear on a precipice near the ceiling of the cavern and cry one of three things: "Welcome of the morn of Thorkin 183!" or "Mid noon is here!" or "The eve of night has arrived!" This was how the gnomes who lived and worked in the cavern knew the time and how they counted calendar days.

Van assumed the time-gnome changed the "Thorkin 183" part daily, and this date correlated with what Van would call the day of the week and the numbered day of the month. Or, according to the Living World's linear lunar calendar, the numbered day in the current cycle. She associated the word *Thorkin* with her calendar's Thursday.

The time-gnome declared, "Mid Noon!" and, despite Brux's strong objections, the gnomes grabbed Van from the cell. They brought her to the gnome's seer, Ildiss, a prophet who advised the gnome tribe.

Ildiss, as a female, had no beard and looked the same as the other female gnomes, except for her clothes. Where the other gnomes wore overalls and work boots or farm dresses, she wore a black jumpsuit and a matching black cape with its pointed hood pulled over her head. A string necklace with various dried-out animal bones hung from her neck.

The necklace made Van's heart pang for Wiglaf. Brux had mentioned Lilla, the Elemental Guardian of All Animals, and Van sent a silent request to her for Wiglaf's safety.

Ildiss sat cross-legged in front of a small pile of radiant rainbow-colored stones. Smoke swirled upward from the glowing stack.

Van suppressed the urge to cough from the cloying incense Ildiss had tossed on top of the stones.

The seer remained silent, didn't acknowledge Van, and continued to rock slowly back and forth with her eyes closed.

Van sat on the ground cross-legged, the same as Ildiss.

"If the Anchoress has been called forth, then the Escalation has begun, the first stage of Dishora has arrived," Ildiss rasped, her tone grave.

Van didn't know what she was supposed to do, so she kept quiet.

Ildiss stopped rocking and lifted her head, though her eyes remained closed.

Gnomes were so unattractive, they unnerved Van. She could barely bring herself to look at Ildiss's gnarled teeth and cherub face, with its thick, coarse skin. Van had never seen anything as disturbing as this creature and hoped never to reencounter anything of the kind.

"The Escalation," breathed Ildiss, "is too early. By at least a generation or so." She opened her beady black eyes. "You seek gold, but not the gold here. You are a pureblooded Lodian… of royal descent… but your quest… your quest is clouded." Ildiss closed her eyes and rocked back and forth again. This time, she also chanted.

The seer abruptly stopped. She removed her hood and aimed her strange black eyes at Van. "Hallux has asked me to determine whether you are the Anchoress-in-waiting, the warrior who carries the Eternal Light of the Creator within."

Van couldn't help focusing on the seer's uncanny black eyes. Ildiss's unwavering stare seemed to lock Van into the prophetic monologue.

"During the Great War, the Balish sought to conquer all lands," Ildiss said. "They would not stop until they had eliminated or enslaved every opposing tribe. Queen Cordelia, the Anchoress of that time, saved our tribe from genocide. She risked her life, using magic to help us burrow deep within the earth to safety, hiding us from the Balish, and thus, we became forever indebted to her and her ancestral line."

Ildiss closed her eyes again and breathed deeply. "People who conspire with demons flirt with the lesser part of themselves, their darkest Selves. This leaves a mark. I can't say what this mark looks like to the human eye. I can tell you this. You will remain powerless until you connect to your ancestral line."

The hair on Van's arms prickled. The scar on her back—was it the mark of a demon? Uxa had told Van she was responsible for fixing her own ancestral line. Had Van's father allowed a demon to mark her at birth? Had he plotted to use Van before he even conceived her? Was this the issue she had to fix in her ancestral line?

Another distressing thought overwhelmed Van. Brux would never be attracted to her with such a disfigurement as her scar. It marked her as ugly, inside and out. Her ancestry, money, and looks would no longer matter. Brux would only see a demon mark and Van as a collaborator with darkness.

Ildiss tilted her head, lifting an ear. "I am being instructed to tell you about your mother."

Van's body went rigid, as if it had solidified into stone. Nothing could've moved her from that spot, at that moment, when she would finally learn about her birth mother.

"I can see the night you were born through my spirit eye." Ildiss kept her gnome eyes closed. "The moon's surface is not clearly visible. Yet my spirit ancestors tell me it was not a Blood Moon. Though you inherited the Anchoress bloodline from your mother, Aelia, you might not have inherited her magical powers."

Ildiss had confirmed Van's worst fear, that she had inherited the

Anchoress bloodline. The seer also implied Van *hadn't* inherited the ability to tap into the same magical power as her ancestors. This matched what Van had overheard Uxa and Fynn talking about almost two weeks ago—except now, Van knew they'd been talking about her, not Daisy. She slumped, weighted by the great responsibilities Ildiss had just placed on her and feeling ill-equipped to handle them.

"Your mother was the Ambassador of Goodwill for Salus Valde. A position that allowed her to travel out of bounds," Ildiss said. "On these ambassador trips, she and your father became *close*. Your father, as her assigned protector, was required to accompany her. As such, the Elementals forbade them to marry."

Van felt stunned by this newest revelation. It meant the Elders had been against her parents' marriage, not only because of her father's commoner status or because he had Balish blood or because having a family was frowned upon by the Grigori, but because the marriage directly opposed the Elementals due to his assigned protector status.

"Your mother's blood had the highest concentration of Elemental blood of all Lodians, and when she chose Michael as your father, their blood mixed inside you. The Lodian part of your blood did not grow stronger with an infusion of another pure Lodian's blood. Instead, it became diluted. Tainted by Michael's Balish blood."

Van lifted her chin. "So what?"

"Diluting a pure Lodian bloodline is blasphemous to the Elementals in its own right," Ildiss said. "But in your case, it reactivated the Anchoress curse that originated in Amaryl's time. A curse tied to Balish blood."

"So, it's true. There is an Anchoress curse." Van needed to know more. "Was Amaryl cursed too? Who cursed us?"

"Silence!" Ildiss eyes shot open, and she peered at Van. "I can only tell you what my spirit ancestors show me. Michael's Balish blood diluted the Elemental portion of yours. This is why you are affected by living in the Earth World. All other Anchoresses were born attuned for life in both worlds. Having less Elemental blood weakens the capabilities of the Anchoress, limiting your ability to connect to the power of the moon and diminishing your capacity to amplify your magic. This and the curse is why Uxa and your father worried you did not inherit the ability to connect to the powers of your bloodline."

"My father and Uxa both know I'm the Anchoress heir?" Van felt enraged. "Why haven't they ever *told* me!"

Van had inherited the Anchoress's bloodline without inheriting its accompanying power. Did this mean she couldn't get the Coin? Or did it mean she couldn't control its power? Or both?

A sick thought entered Van's mind. Had her father married the Anchoress heir on purpose as an insider attack on the Lodians and their regime? Had he destroyed the one hope the Lodians had to protect Salus Valde from the Balish by diluting the bloodline of their most powerful warrior?

"Wait a minute," Van said. "Then why does Uxa need Daisy? Are Daisy and Brux descendants of Goustav?"

Ildiss looked angrily at Van for, again, speaking out of turn.

The seer didn't answer and instead reinstated her constant rocking, but this time, her eyes remained open. "The curse that lay dormant for centuries has returned and was validated the night your mother died giving birth to you. Michael had gone out of bounds that night. He had found a way to sneak into Balish territory without being detected. Your mother discovered he was missing. She knew Michael had illegally gone out of bounds and went searching for him, hoping to stop him from doing something foolish, to bring him home. The Balish caught your mother out of bounds and tortured her with liquid fire. She was eight months pregnant with you."

Van's hand reactively reached behind her, touching her lower back.

Ildiss nodded at Van's unspoken question. "Yes, this is how you got your scar. The liquid fire pierced through your mother's skin and reached you while you were still in the womb."

The seer paused, giving Van time to digest this horrifying reality, and then continued. "Your father found out what happened and rescued your mother from the Balish soldiers. Iphigenia was also there, in the woods of Tipereth, fleeing from the Balish."

By this point, Van was certain Ildiss had invoked memory engrams without touching an object. Ildiss had used her connection to her spirit ancestors to see into the past. Ildiss had the same skill as Van, except the seer had a mastery of this skill that put Van to shame.

"Can you see why Genie fled?" Van asked.

This time Ildiss answered. "Iphigenia was the palace healer at Balefire. She… hurt one of the royals, and the queen did not forgive her. So, Iphigenia fled and happened upon your parents. She saved you, but could not save your mother. This explains why your father felt indebted to Iphigenia, and why he helped her escape to Providence Island."

Genie saved my life? And Van had always thought of Genie as a ditz.

"Your bunfy was originally your mother's. If he hasn't appeared to you until now, then…" Ildiss hesitated. "He had someone else as his charge." Ildiss's beady eyes remained on Van. "Your mother loved you and would have done anything to protect you."

Van's heart swelled with joy. Her mother *loved* her! This awareness came with a corresponding ache over the loss of the life they could've shared if her mother had survived. "Why did my father go out of bounds that night?"

"He went someplace he wasn't supposed to go," Ildiss said.

Those words, seemingly vague, jarred Van's memory. Her father had said the same words to her the day they went quahogging when she asked him how he had gotten his scars. Van understood Ildiss's message that Van was not responsible for her mother's actions or her death. Her mother went willingly out of bounds, chasing after her father.

But her mother never would have been in that situation if her father hadn't snuck out in the middle of the night! *For what?*

"What was so important?" Van muttered, almost to herself.

It seemed likely her father had been plotting with the Balish even back then; maybe it wasn't a coincidence Genie met him that night. Perhaps she was already his mistress. Now Van was even more willing to believe the rumors about her father. That he was a greedy, power-hungry womanizer. Maybe her father and Genie wanted Van to survive because she carried the Anchoress-in-waiting bloodline, a tool they could use later. To get the Coin.

Rage flared inside her.

"Your internal struggle distracts you from your purpose," Ildiss said. "You listen but do not hear. You must use your heart to clear your thoughts, to find your way."

Ildiss closed her eyes for a moment, then continued. "It is the will of the Creator to constantly challenge our inner fortitude. This makes us grow and become stronger. Your father is part of your ancestral line, and you must reconcile your feelings about him to have any hope of coming into your full power." Ildiss peered at Van with intense eyes. "The dark part inside us all constantly struggles for domination. You must choose which to cling to, the light or the dark. This is what makes a person."

With a swift change in demeanor, Ildiss bellowed for the gnome guard to bring forth Hallux.

The gnome leader arrived with his donsy. They gathered inside the seer's nook, crowding around Ildiss, Van, and the fire.

Ildiss spoke to Hallux. "I have communicated with the spirit world, and, in their wisdom, they say this child before me is not the destined savior who rises to fight against evil in Dishora, side by side with the gnomes, and therefore cannot be deemed the true Anchoress."

Hallux ordered, "Take her back to——"

"*However*," Ildiss interrupted.

The surrounding gnomes reaching out to grab Van froze. They stepped back.

"The insight of our spirit ancestors is often beyond comprehension for those of us trapped here in our fleshy prisons. Even those of us whose gifts are vast," Ildiss rasped. "We are to give this child a chance to prove herself worthy of our help. She must present us with an acceptable gift, one that represents life. If not, you may turn her and her friends over to the Balish as nothing more than petty gold thieves."

Van felt stung, slapped in the face by someone she'd thought was on her side. It left her feeling more incompetent than ever. The Anchoress legacy had just been dumped on her, minus the ability to tap into its power, and she still had to complete her mission and find the Coin. Now, she needed to figure out what a gift of "life" meant. *Great.*

While the gnomes led Van across the cavern to the jail, she worried a gift of life meant they planned to kill someone on the team, or Wiglaf.

The ground trembled again.

"Earthquake!" a gnome shouted.

They scattered to take cover. Rocks and dust crashed around them.

With no other recourse, Van curled into a fetal position and covered her head.

Chapter 38

D ay 12: 1:22 p.m., Living World

WHEN THE RUMBLING STOPPED, Van rose from the dust, coughing and staggering. She had survived with minor cuts and bruises, but a roar of agony rang through the hollow.

A female gnome lay on the ground, unconscious.

"Schydel!" Hallux cupped her face in his hands. "Someone help my wife! Please!"

Van seized the opportunity to escape. She saw her teammates milling around the cell. Brux and Jorie tugged at the bent bars, trying to get out. None of them seemed to suffer from any significant injuries, so Van quickly scanned the cavern for Wiglaf. She spotted the wicker cage sitting on the landing area for the carts. The team's backpacks lay strewn on the ground next to the track.

While the gnomes gave their attention to Schydel, Van darted over and tore open the door to the pebble-covered cage. She pulled

307

out the little bunfy, who had kept his white coat clean, despite the flying dust. Though he trembled and tightly pressed his ears against his body, he appeared uninjured.

Van wrapped him in her arms and cradled him like a baby.

Wiglaf stretched his ears upward and chirruped.

Van held Wiglaf with one arm and used her other hand to reach into her backpack and take out the bunfy's nest, hoping it might comfort him.

Hallux's loud moans over his wife's injuries broke into Van's happy reunion with Wiglaf.

Wiglaf turned his tiny head. "Mirpp weep." He stared at the gathering of gnomes around Schydel.

Van glanced at her teammates, still trying to break out of the jail cell, and then back to Wiglaf. "Ugh. Okay." Wiglaf made her feel guilty for neglecting someone in need, so she agreed to his plea and went to Schydel. Van pushed the protesting gnomes aside.

A gnome grabbed Van's arm. "What is *that*?"

"A bunfy. He can make her feel better." Van placed Wiglaf on Schydel's stomach. "It might be enough to pull her through."

The other gnomes stared at Van; some gasped.

Hallux's tiny black eyes opened wide, and he raised his palms upward. "Bless the light! It's the body of a vegetable lamb!"

"No, he's a bunfy," Van said.

"No, no, you simpleton." Hallux shook his head. "The wreath in your hand. We have our offering."

"It's the wreath, right?" Van didn't trust the gnomes and their strange culture. "Not my bunfy?"

Hallux's wife stirred. "By the light! My wife has regained consciousness."

"I think she just had a concussion," Van said, not wanting the gnomes to think Wiglaf had the healing power to revive the dead. If they did, she would never get him back.

Hallux picked up Wiglaf and handed him to Van. She hugged him to her chest and then gave the nest to one of the gnomes, who scurried off to "put it in a safe place."

Hallux bellowed with great joy, "Release the prisoners! They have proved to be our honored guests. We must celebrate our great good fortune. Prepare the Feast of Departure!"

The gnomes cheered.

Van still didn't know what Hallux and the other gnomes were so excited about, as several of them ran across the cavern, dodging the fallen rocks, and opened the jail. A happy gnome bustled by Van, eyeing Wiglaf, and said, "To think we had planned to eat him."

Van squeezed Wiglaf a little tighter.

Her team reunited in the middle of the partly destroyed cavern.

Paley whispered low enough so that none of the busy gnomes scuttling about could hear, "Creepy little things, aren't they?"

"I dunno." Van shrugged. "They're kind of growing on me."

"I hope my maps survived." Elmot scanned the cavern for his backpack.

"Forget your maps," Jorie scoffed. "Where's Zachery?"

"Over here." Van waved for them to follow her.

On the way to the tracks, she told them what had transpired with Ildiss, including the seer's confirmation she carried the Anchoress bloodline.

"So that's why security on the island is so intense," Paley said. "And why the Elders fawn all over you."

Brux's eyebrows pinched together, along with a downward turn to the corners of his mouth. Van knew he still struggled against the idea of her being the Anchoress-in-waiting instead of his sister.

"Brux..." Van stopped. She didn't know what to say to make him feel better. *I'm sure my father isn't torturing your sister too badly*, or *I'm sure Daisy is still alive*. Neither of those would work. So Van didn't say anything, and no one else did either.

Van wondered whether anyone had checked on the old gnome seer since the earthquake, and, after they grabbed their backpacks, she led them to Ildiss's nook.

When they bustled in, Ildiss didn't flinch. She sat as peacefully as ever, cross-legged in front of her smoky fire. She had two gnomes with her. One had a beard and wore overalls. The other was beardless and wore a farmer's dress with round-toed boots.

"I, uh, we came to make sure you were okay," Van stammered. The old gnome with her spirit wisdom intimidated Van.

Ildiss introduced the other gnomes as Nid and Sashee, and then she instructed Van and her team to have a seat and listen well. "My spirit ancestors have counseled us to help you continue your journey. To reach the Caves of Wolfenden, you must pass through the land of trolls. Three guides will accompany you."

Van shivered. She had never told Ildiss about the Caves of Wolfenden or needing gnomes to accompany them.

"Trolls are unfortunate creatures," Ildiss rasped. "They value *things*. Your guides will bring gold—"

"No one ever mentioned needing gold," Brux interjected.

"We don't want to take your gold," Van said. "It's not ours. We didn't earn it."

"It's not our gold, either," Nid said, the bearded gnome standing behind Ildiss. "We're enslaved by the Balish and mine for them."

"Gold has no value, except that which we give it," Ildiss lectured. "Gold itself is not important. It only serves to keep the Balish from annihilating our tribe. We care about one another above all else."

"We gnomes have access to all the gold in the world," Sashee said, the beardless gnome. "But we cannot buy the simple things we need, thanks to the Balish."

"The Balish forbid us to possess the body of a vegetable lamb, a plant you may know of as cotton," Nid said. "The body is the part of the plant that contains seeds. You have given us a wreath with lots of bodies. It will enable us to grow crops in our hidden towns throughout the mountains."

"The Balish don't allow our tribe to own any plant that enables us to create our own clothes," Sashee said. "It is too empowering for a slave race."

"Why do you let the Balish treat you like that?" Paley asked.

"The Balish thought they had wiped our kind out during the Great War," Nid said. "Within several centuries, the Balish discovered our hiding place in the earth and that the gnome tribe had survived. They told us we'd been living on Balish-owned land and would have to pay. We had no protection and no ability to fight such powerful enemies. And so, we became nothing more than a slave race to the Balish."

Ildiss waved her stubby arms. All the chitchat between the earthbound creatures before her must've been too much, and she dismissed them from her nook. "Go. All of you. I must get back to my meditation."

Nid and Sashee walked out of the nook with Van and the others.

"Your journey will begin at first light tomorrow," Nid announced. "Fortified with food, supplies, gold, and guides."

"Now is for cleaning the hollow," Sashee said. "We're getting used to the process. The earthquakes have occurred more and more frequently over the last few years."

Sashee sounded concerned about the quakes. Van was going to ask her about it, when Nid said, "Let us focus on the good, Sashee. Like, preparing for tonight's Feast of Departure."

For the rest of the day, they all helped clean the main cavern. Then Jorie, Brux, and the male gnomes kept disappearing into tunnels and reappearing with round, black circles that resembled flat pieces of coal and long tubes of varying sizes filled with yellow, orange, or red gel.

Van, Paley, and Elmot helped the female gnomes in the kitchen, a designated nook off the main cavern. The room had a counter chiseled from the wall, with a handful of holes carved into the surface and grates over the holes for stovetop cooking. Stone fireplaces had been constructed for baking. Instead of coal for heat or wood to make a fire, the gnomes used mushroom caps for cooking, the black circular stones Van had seen Jorie and Brux carry in.

Van and Paley giggled when the stones generated heat after the gnomes poured yak urine over them.

While in the middle of prepping vegetables, spicing the meats, and kneading dough for bread, Jorie popped into the kitchen, bringing more mushroom caps to replenish the ovens.

"They glow different colors when they're heated," Van said in an animated voice.

"Yeah, ignore the yak urine part," Paley jested.

"Ho-boy!" Jorie said. "The lava sticks don't generate heat. When they're shaken, the lava inside moves and creates a glow so bright that when they're stacked in a teepee, it looks like an actual fire. They last for hours."

Van remembered Jorie's knowledge base included tribal customs. Their team leader seemed thrilled to observe the gnome culture firsthand, now that they posed no threat.

"Who knew gnome traditions could be fun?" Paley asked.

"What you got in there?" Jorie used her nubby finger to point at a boiling pot.

"Peach and thyme–marinated oilbird." Elmot peered into the mixture as he stirred with a long wooden spoon.

When night rolled in, everyone was ready to celebrate.

Before the festivities started, Schydel told Van she wanted to skip the celebration to rest in her nook. The gnome asked Van if she could take Wiglaf with her to ensure her continued healing. Van agreed, thinking it would keep the little guy away from the stomping feet of the many dancing gnomes.

A bonfire made of lava tubes raged in the middle of the cavern. The entire gnome tribe emerged from countless tunnels and crevices to enjoy the feast. Even gnome children, who resembled smaller versions of adult gnomes, complete with wispy beginnings of beards on the boys.

Spit-roasts of fuchsia-bellied lizard and snow-striped eel from various fire pits enticed the revelers. Chilled mead flowed from vast kegs, brought inside from their out-scouts above, some of whom joined in the celebration. Female gnomes brought out freshly made genoise bread infused with oakmoss, and pots of stews. Other gnomes played fiddles, fifes, drums, and flutes in synchronized rhythms.

Van sampled a bit of everything, along with Paley. They tried marinated walnuts and rice, tenderized lime yak stew, and barbecued river crab. All of it was delicious. The team ate like warriors and danced for hours with one another and the gnomes, whom, despite their strange appearance, Van had grown to appreciate.

As the night wore on, and the adults tucked the gnome children snugly in their sleeping nooks, the party quieted down. A core group of gnomes sat in a circle near a small mushroom cap fire with Ildiss, along with Van, Brux, Paley, Jorie, and Elmot. Nid and Sashee lingered there too, but Hallux only briefly stayed, preferring to tend to his recovering wife.

Ildiss seemed much more down to earth, away from her smoky fire in the nook. Van no longer felt repulsed by the seer and grew interested in the old gnome's wisdom.

Ildiss appeared impressed Van had fulfilled the seer's spirit ancestors' request to procure a gift of life. The seer admitted the messages of her spirit ancestors had become more clear to her. Ildiss now believed Van was an Anchoress destined to face the Plague of Evil, the first stage in the Escalation to Dishora. Their conversation turned to the Coin.

"The Coin has many magnificent properties," Ildiss said. "But you will do well to remember all light casts a shadow."

Jorie leaned forward. "Go on."

"A good story always starts at the beginning, so there we will begin," Ildiss said in her raspy voice. "The Creator formed the Coin as a protective device for mortals to use when evil rises to destroy the light. As time moved on, many forgot the Coin's true purpose. They underestimated the object, forgetting to use powerful magic cautiously and with respect. Many learned, tragically, the destructive properties of the Coin."

Everyone in the circle leaned forward, enthralled by the seer's story.

"You see, the Coin's magical powers are immense," Ildiss continued. "Having access to that kind of power can easily corrupt the mind. It is believed only those born of royal bloodlines are worthy enough to access its power without danger. In theory, royals have all they need, making them strong enough to resist the seductive powers of the Coin. Royals do not lack and are therefore less likely to be lured by evil."

Van shivered, despite the heat of the mushroom cap fire.

Ildiss's beady eyes narrowed. "Regarding the Great War, some claim Amaryl was too young to wield so powerful a weapon, and thus, the demons rose into our world, causing the Great War to become the Dark War. It is neither here nor there who used what to defeat the demons. The problem happened afterward when Amaryl began wearing the Coin on a chain around her neck as a constant reminder of her power as Anchoress Queen. It was the first sign of her destructive obsession with the Coin."

The seer turned her black eyes toward Van. "Even the Anchoress can become corrupted by the power of the Coin. If you obtain the item, you will be challenged by your inner nature and true Self. There is a constant struggle between the good part and bad part within our Selves. Without the strength to cling to your inner light, the Coin will corrupt your mind, and you will lose your way."

Ildiss leaned toward Van to emphasize her next words. "Evil tempts those with greed in their hearts. It is skilled at using trickery to create inner conflict, which results in outer fighting. This gives darkness the ability to rise. *Remember this*: If you find yourself surrounded by darkness, you must cling to the light, for therein lies the help of the Creator."

This was the first time Van had ever stayed at a party after she had stopped having fun. Thankfully, after Ildiss's warning, the conversation turned to pleasant topics.

When the last embers of the mushroom cap fire had burned down, the gnomes showed Van and her teammates to their guest sleeping nook. The alcove had small hollows carved into the walls, like mock bunk beds, lined with mattresses made of hay. Exhausted and with little chatter, they nestled in.

Within minutes, Van heard the even breathing of sleeping team-mates. She lay awake thinking about Ildiss's story, the vision Amaryl had shown her, Jacynthia's advice, and the warnings in Manik's text. Van didn't fully understand the warning about the Coin and how it related to her. There was no way she would want to keep the Coin, use its power, or wear it around her neck. She also felt confused about why Amaryl would reveal a vision of her affair with Goustav, rather than other parts of her remarkable life. Nothing made any sense.

Eventually, Van slipped into a disturbed sleep, with nightmares of the earth crumbling beneath her feet. Deeper and deeper she fell, into a dark crevice filled with shadowy, whispering monsters.

Chapter 39

Day 13: Living World

AFTER EATING A HEARTY, gnome-cooked breakfast of truffle scrambled eggs with apricot and walnut–stuffed hearth bread, team Delta headed into troll territory, stocked with food and gold and accompanied by three gnomes: Sashee, Nid, and Wasubel.

Van wondered why the other gnomes made a big to-do about the great "sacrifice" of their three friends, who had volunteered to leave the comfort of their tribe as if traveling with humans were a tremendous chore they would be lucky to survive.

The three gnomes led Van and the others through the tunnels, out of the mountain, and onto rocky, frost-covered terrain, moving fast for creatures with stubby legs.

Van sensed tenseness among her teammates. From the subject no one would talk about—Trey.

"We gnomes have a saying," Sashee said, as if reading Van's

mind. "Loved ones never truly leave us, as long as we remember them in our heart."

This broke the ice, and Van and her teammates spent the morning recounting tales about Trey and how much they missed his talents and quirks. Afterward, the team remained chipper and upbeat, but as the day wore on, the monotony of the trek wore everyone down. Even Wiglaf disappeared back into his magical realm.

"Are we in troll territory yet?" Paley whined.

"It's not something we should look forward to," Brux said.

"Should be," Sashee answered Paley.

"What do you mean by *should be?*" Elmot asked. "Don't you know where we're going?"

"Troll tribes wander," Wasubel said. "We don't know where they'll be. As your guides, we try to avoid them. We have seen no trace of trolls—yet—so we are doing our job."

"Elmot! Check your map," Jorie barked.

Elmot was on it. He hadn't checked his map all day, fearing it would insult the gnome guides.

"Our route is not on any *map*," Wasubel scolded.

"We're taking the most direct path to the Caves of Wolfenden," Nid said. "While trying to avoid trolls."

"If we're lucky, we won't run into any trolls at all," Sashee said.

"They're big, hulking blocks of dumb," Nid said.

"Very awful," Sashee replied.

"They're right. Our route isn't on here." Elmot seemed happier now he had permission to pull out his cherished holographic map. "The map doesn't show troll territory, either. But we're moving in the right direction."

By early evening, the gnomes had led them into a clearing, where the team set up four tents, courtesy of the gnome tribe. The three gnomes shared one tent. Jorie had a tent to herself. Brux and Elmot shared one, as did Paley and Van. Although dusk had barely arrived, they settled in for the night.

"Van," Paley whispered. "Come to the bathroom with me?"

Van had just gotten comfortable in her sleeping bag. She sighed. "Okay."

Paley untied the tent door flap, and they both stepped out into the freezing twilight air.

Van walked a few steps, shivering. Her feet crunched on the frost-crusted ground. "Just go here."

"No. It's too close to the tents." Paley wrapped her arms around her chest and rubbed her knees together.

"Go wherever! Hurry." Van's teeth chattered.

Paley bolted into the trees.

Van heard a thud, then a surprised "Oh!" from Paley, and a squealing, whinnying noise. As Van dashed into the woods, the others rustled in their tents.

Paley lay flat on her back in the snow. She had run into an enormous, yellowish-green hoofed beast, now still screeching and rearing on its hind legs. It had a dragon-like head with a pair of curved horns and a powerful scaled body that snapped a horse's tail. The others arrived in time to witness its massive rider to lose his balance and thump to the ground.

"Congratulations, Paley," Wasubel said. "You just met the Troll King."

The Troll King wore a ridiculous gold crown and, around his bulging wrists, a variety of gold jewelry that looked like necklaces worn by humans. He leaped to his feet and spluttered at them in a guttural language that sounded like he was chewing on rocks.

More trolls wielding clubs rode out of the brush on horselike creatures. The trolls were like the gnomes, in the sense they all looked the same. They were three times the size of an average human, with hairless, square-shaped heads atop thick, stumpy necks. Their flat, crooked teeth protruded from their mouths, along with two fangs rising upward from their lower jaws. Animal skins draped their stocky bodies.

The trolls jumped off their mounts, all of them grunting in agitation.

Thankfully, Brux, the team's languages expert, was fluent in troll.

It turned out the trolls had been following their group for the last couple of miles, waiting for them to settle in for the night before raiding their camp. Paley had blown the trolls' plans when she knocked the Troll King from his qilin, the creature he rode.

"How bad is it?" Elmot asked Brux.

"Uh… not good," Brux said. "When the Troll King falls off his qilin, they consider him to have lost his luck. This means his position is vulnerable to be taken over by another troll."

"Most likely from another clan," Jorie said as the team's authority on different cultures. "Taking the kingship from another clan would elevate that clan's status."

"How are other trolls going to know he fell?" Van asked. "His own clan won't say anything, right?"

"The other trolls will talk," Jorie said. "They'll want a replacement because they've lost confidence in their leader, may even attack him themselves."

"We're in a dangerous situation," Brux said.

Elmot shuddered. "The middle of a troll war is the last place we want to be."

Paley ducked behind Brux. "Are they going to kill me? Tell the Troll King I'm sorry. I didn't mean it."

"Since his kingship is in question, he no longer has the right to decide what to do with us," Jorie said. "We're safe until another king takes over."

"And then we're dead?" Paley asked, biting her cuticle. "Where're our gnome guides? They came prepared for this."

"Sas—" Van stopped mid-word. The gnomes were nowhere to be found. She scanned the landscape. The gnomes could've hidden from the trolls in many places in the trees and the jutting boulders. Their gnome guides possessed skills in troll negotiations. *So, where are they?*

The trolls tied their qilins to nearby trees. They confiscated the group's backpacks and then patted down each of them, relieving them of their weapons.

Jorie winced when one of the trolls manhandled Zachery.

Van and Paley were so small, compared to the trolls' big

calloused hands, that the trolls had missed their Twin Gemstones during the search and everything else the girls had tucked away in their many pockets.

Van relaxed, thinking she was off the hook when the Troll King spluttered gibberish. Two trolls each grabbed Van by an ankle, tipped her upside down, and shook her. Her Twin Gemstone and a lip gloss in a faux gold container fell from her pocket. They shook Paley upside down next. Several packets of contact lenses tumbled to the ground, along with her gemstone. The trolls confiscated the items, satisfying the Troll King.

Brux stepped up and tried to discuss terms of their release with the Troll King, but the king was too preoccupied about an impending attack to listen to the babble of his prisoners.

After unsuccessfully trying to push the entire team into a single tent, the trolls separated Van, Jorie, and Paley into one tent and Elmot and Brux into another. Then the trolls settled around a campfire. They grumbled at one another, not paying attention to their prisoners.

"They're not worried about us running away," Jorie told Van and Paley. "They have guards hidden all over the woods, watching for other troll clans. In the meantime, we'll be okay. At least, until they get hungry. So, let's figure out how to get your gemstones back."

"W-What'd you mean by hungry?" Paley asked, wide-eyed.

"Trolls are like goats," Jorie said. "They'll eat just about anything, but they favor meat."

"No wonder the gnomes are hiding," Van said. "I would've hidden from the trolls too, if I had the chance."

"Don't worry. Trolls aren't smart enough to figure out they can eat us," Jorie said in a bungled attempt to soothe Van and Paley. "There's nothing we can do but wait. Get some rest."

How was Van supposed to rest, knowing the trolls might be discussing a recipe for how to best cook humans?

With the tent being such tight quarters, Van and Paley huddled together in one sleeping bag, both of them trembling, more from being deemed troll foodstuff than from the cold.

Just before Paley fell asleep, she muttered, "I never got to go to the bathroom."

Although Van thought she might never sleep again, because of Jorie's frightening commentary on troll culture, sleep had other plans. It nibbled at Van until she succumbed to its sweet seduction.

Chapter 40

Day 14: 6:28 a.m., Living World

THE TROLL CLAN'S battles kept Van and the others awake all night. It seemed as if every troll strong enough to challenge the king took his shot for the throne and lost.

Morning came, and the trolls settled around the campfire, waiting for an attack from an opposing clan. The all-night fighting made the trolls' stomachs growl, loud enough for Van to hear it in the tent. She knew they were deciding which human to eat first.

Paley moaned, convinced it would be her because the Troll King had pegged her as a troublemaker.

Eager to put her talents to the test, Jorie assured them one of her best skills was hand-to-hand combat. "The trolls are big, but they're dumb and clumsy. I'm fast and deadly."

"And outnumbered ten to one," Van said

Paley quivered and clutched Van's arm.

The trio overheard Brux speaking to the trolls and popped their heads out of their tent to listen. The trolls didn't seem to believe what Brux had told them. Brux whistled, and out of the woods came Nid and Wasubel.

As soon as the Troll King laid eyes on the two gnomes, he waved his chunky, bowed arms and stammered wildly in his native tongue.

"What's he saying?" Elmot asked Brux, loud enough so Van, Paley, and Jorie could hear.

"He said receiving the gnomes as a gift from us proves his luck's returned, and it negates his fall."

The other trolls grumbled.

Jorie whispered to Van and Paley, "The gnomes had to remain hidden until we could present them as a gift."

"What do you mean, present *them* as a gift?" Van's stomach dropped. "The gold is the gift. The gnomes are our guides."

"Shh!" Jorie said, trying to listen in. "It looks like the king's clan isn't convinced his luck has returned."

Wasubel whistled and out from the trees came Sashee. She presented a bulky object wrapped in a thick cloth to the Troll King.

Jorie shook her head. "Too bad. Nid and Wasubel were trying to save Sashee."

"From what?" Paley asked in a strained voice. "Are the trolls keeping the gnomes as pets or something?"

"Or something." Jorie focused her eyes on the scene unfolding before them.

Sashee held the package in the palms of her hands, while Nid and Wasubel untied it. The morning sunlight dazzled off dozens of radiant chips of gold.

The Troll King spluttered rapidly, raising his arms toward the sky.

Brux explained to Elmot, "He's saying Ak, the Troll God, has delivered the gold to him via these vessels, uh… morsels. Anyway, he means the gnomes."

The other trolls grunted, banging their clubs on the ground in approval. The Troll King had regained his throne.

"Does this mean they won't hurt us?" Van whispered to Jorie.

"He accepted our gifts, so it means they'll leave us alone. That's the point of the offering."

One troll went off to notify the other tribes of their king's regained luck. The Troll King greedily clutched the gold as he instructed one of his minions to dig a hole. He dropped the bundle in and the minion buried it.

"Gold is a sign of wealth and power among the trolls," Jorie said. "That's why the Troll King wears gold bracelets and a gold crown, to display his clan's status."

"Why did he bury the gold?" Van asked.

"To hide it, in case an opposing clan attacks the camp," Jorie said.

Other trolls grabbed the three gnomes.

"What are they doing?" Paley asked.

One troll brought out a sharpened spear, and another jabbed the fire with a small branch, making it roar. Two others created a rotisserie with sticks. Without a fight, the gnomes allowed the trolls to skewer them onto the spear, one at a time.

Plop, *slide*. Plop, *slide*. Plop, *slide*.

Van retched.

Paley shrieked and pulled her head back inside the tent.

"What'd you think the gnomes were for?" Jorie muttered.

"Not *that!*" Van slipped back into the tent, so sick she was sure she would never eat again.

"Gnomes are loyal creatures." Jorie closed the flap door. "They're indebted to Cordelia for saving their tribe from genocide. When Ildiss confirmed Cordelia was your ancestor and that you carry the Anchoress bloodline, the gnomes believed it was time for them to repay their debt. They saw it as an honor."

Now Van understood why the gnomes considered it a great sacrifice for Sashee, Nid, and Wasubel to accompany them. For creatures so grotesque in appearance, their courage and generosity awed Van. A need to protect the gnome tribe raged inside her with such feverish intensity, she trembled. Van would never forget their heroic sacrifice. Ever.

At Van's insistence, the three of them held hands and Jorie said a eulogy for the gnomes.

Brux stuck his head in the tent, breaking their circle of reflection and sorrow.

"Sorry to interrupt," he said. "Best you don't come out right now."

The stench of burning gnome flesh wafted into the tent. Van breathed from her mouth to avoid smelling it.

"You negotiated our passing to the Caves, right?" Jorie asked, carrying on as if nothing horrifying had happened.

"The Troll King promised us we would be free to pass without being bothered by any troll clans." Brux stared at Van and Paley. "You two doing okay?"

Both clutched each other's hands and shook their heads.

"It's a custom in the gnome culture," Brux said gently. "If you accept this, it will be easier."

"What's done is done. Time for us to warrior up," Jorie said; however, the pain of the gnomes' sacrifice glistened in her eyes. Refocusing on their mission probably was her way of coping.

"We're on schedule," Jorie said. "We'll go to the Caves, grab the Coin, and be back to Lodestar in plenty of time."

Van packed, still feeling sickened over the incident. She could hear Brux and Elmot taking down their tent. The trolls got riled up.

Jorie leaped out of their tent, and Van and Paley followed.

"What's the problem?" Jorie yelled to Brux.

Brux strode over to them, scowling. "They decided not to let us go."

"But they promised!" Paley shrieked.

"It turns out trolls aren't very good at keeping their word," Brux said.

A troll grabbed Elmot, as other trolls moved in around them.

"I guess the expression *never trust a troll* carries some weight after all." Jorie dodged as a troll tried to grasp her.

"You're just mentioning that now?" Van braced for a fight with a newfound respect for the Troll's Foot Tavern and its severed troll's foot logo.

Elmot struggled, but the troll forced a thick metal collar around his neck and chained him to a tree near the qilins.

Jorie was in her glory with hand-to-hand combat. She rammed an uppercut to a troll's dopey chin, breaking a few of his teeth, following with a roundhouse kick to his abdomen, barely knocking the troll backward.

Brux grabbed a branch from the ground and used it as a club. He smashed the end into the chest of an oncoming troll, then side-swiped the troll's block-head, shattering the branch. The troll barely flinched.

Van twirled a stick she had snatched from the ground and, using one of her koga-clava techniques, smacked the troll on his knees.

It did nothing; the troll grabbed her.

She squirmed and jabbed the stick in the troll's eye.

He howled and clutched his face, releasing Van from his sweaty grip.

She beelined for the Troll King, who sat serenely by the fire, confident of the fight's outcome.

Van plowed into the king, knocking him to the ground. "How's your luck now? You big, dumb piece of—" She was cut off as a troll grabbed her from behind and lifted her in a chokehold.

Jorie and Brux were good fighters, but they were outnumbered. The trolls soon had collars around the necks of Jorie, Brux, Paley, and Elmot and had them chained to trees.

The Troll King lumbered close to Van and took her face in his hands. He stared down into her eyes and mumbled in his marble-mouthed language.

"What's he saying?" she heard Elmot ask Brux.

"Um, he's… upset she knocked him off his seat. Found it very, uh, disrespectful."

"But he's going to let her go? *Right?*" Paley asked hysterically.

"Just spit it out, Brux." Jorie glowered.

Brux took a deep breath and then said, "The Troll King has decided Van's the first one they're going to eat. He says blue eyes are a delicacy. He plans on eating them… *raw.*"

The Troll King dropped his hands and howled a hearty laugh.

Van spat in his face.

"Leave her *alone*!" Brux struggled against the chain binding him to the tree. Pink, bloody scratches formed where the metal collar strained against his neck.

Two trolls rolled a cauldron out of the woods and set it over the fire. Several trolls filled it with large buckets of water.

"Seriously, where are they getting all this stuff?" Van asked as she fought with renewed vigor against the enormous troll holding her.

"*Oh, no!*" Paley gasped.

The Troll King pulled out a dagger.

"No!" Paley and Elmot screamed as they strained against their chains.

Jorie placed her hands on her metal collar and mumbled a quick chant. "Dammit! My magic isn't working. I can't break the lock."

"Take another step, and I'll end you!" Brux growled.

The grinning Troll King raised the blade to Van's eye. The tip of his knife dug into her skin just below the eyeball. Blood trailed down her cheek.

She screamed.

Chapter 41

D ay 14: 11:44 a.m., Living World

"HALT!" yelled a gruff voice from the edge of the woods.

The Troll King swung around, dagger poised to fight the intruder. The trolls sitting around, enjoying the show, shot to their feet and grabbed their clubs.

Out of the woods emerged the strangest creatures Van had ever seen. A disturbing mix of bovine and homo sapien. Their bodies appeared mostly human, except more muscular. Their broad foreheads and elongated faces reminded Van of cows. They had wide noses with large, flared nostrils and a pair of tiny ears on top of their misshapen heads. Slightly smaller than the trolls, they appeared well-groomed in their full leather combat attire. They rode on four-legged, hyper-muscular beasts that looked like a cross between a bison and a camel, each one possibly eight feet tall.

Their appearance frightened Van, yet she'd never felt so happy to see anyone in her life.

Paley shuddered. "What are *those*?"

"Tarcs, riding allocameli," Jorie said. "They're Balish allies."

The trolls attacked. Clubs and fists flew.

Brux frowned. "What are Tarcs doing this far out of Kezef?"

"Zane—the bartender at the Troll's Foot—told us Tarcs would be in the area," Elmot said. "They just saved Van's life."

"A-Are they friends?" Paley asked. "Or do they want to kill us too?"

"We'll have to wait and see," Jorie said. "They don't eat humans if that makes you feel any better." She grimaced as one of the trolls grabbed Zachery and ran into the fight.

The trolls were losing badly to the brutal Tarcs, who swung at them with swords, morning stars, and poleaxes.

When the troll holding Van released her to join the fight, she ran to her teammates and hid behind Brux.

"Get out of here, Van!" he cried. "*Run!*"

"No!" Van fiddled with the metal collar. "How do I get these chains off?"

"Van, get the Twin Gemstones," Jorie commanded.

Van hustled over to the mound where the trolls had piled their belongings, careful to avoid flying weapons and falling bodies, and rummaged around until she found both gemstones.

One troll released the qilins from their binds, and the creatures joined the fight too. The Tarcs struggled against fighting both the trolls and the qilins.

Van ducked as a qilin pounced, tearing a Tarc rider from his beast. A second Tarc rode over and bashed the qilin in the head with a morning star and the creature crashed to the ground. The fallen Tarc twitched, injured but alive. The other qilins saw their dead buddy and scattered into the woods, running away from the fight.

As Van rejoined her team by the trees, she could've sworn she heard Jorie mumble, "Cowards," under her breath. She tucked one gemstone into Paley's pants pocket and kept the other.

Before long, the Tarcs had wiped out the entire troll clan,

including the Troll King. The Tarcs hadn't suffered any significant injuries, except for the rider attacked by the qilin.

Though grateful for the invasion, the Tarcs made Van uneasy. Being allies with the Balish was never a good thing.

The Tarcs dismounted from their allocameli and tied them to the trees.

"Which of you is the leader?" asked the largest and most brutal-looking one. His gold nose ring shimmered in the morning light.

Jorie stretched to her full height. "I am. Jorie Alquest."

"A woman?" The Tarc's taut belly rumbled with a good chuckle. "You must be Lodians."

The other Tarcs snickered.

"We're marketeers' scouts from Hod," Elmot said a little too quickly. "We have papers."

"Oh, you are, are you? With a female as your leader?" The Tarc grinned. "Well, *marketeers' scouts from Hod*, my name is Godreel. I am Lord of the Tarcs."

Jorie dropped to one knee as a show of respect.

Van, Brux, Elmot, and Paley followed suit.

Jorie spoke. "Lord Godreel, we are grateful for your help in freeing us from the trolls. Please allow us to show you our gratitude."

"It is presumptuous to assume we have spared you to set you free," Godreel said in his gravelly voice. The boiling cauldron did not go unnoticed. He nodded to his men, who began searching the slain trolls for anything of value.

The Tarcs collected all the undamaged weaponry. One of them picked up Zachery and another, Brux's dagger. They confiscated the Troll King's gold jewelry, along with some gold coins he had tucked in a leather band around his ankle.

Godreel turned his attention back to Jorie. "But I am interested in your demonstration of gratitude."

"We'll pay gold in exchange for our lives," Jorie said.

"Leader Jorie, I would be happy to take gold off your hands," Godreel drawled. "But you must understand, I cannot take your word. I must see the gold, which I am sure is not on any of you. If it were, I could simply *take* it."

"The gold is hidden nearby. I need your word as a great lord you will accept the gold for our lives. Do we have a deal?" Jorie stood, prompting the others to follow.

"You have a deal, Leader Jorie. As long as you have enough gold to cover *all* your lives."

Godreel grunted to one of his minions, who easily unsnapped the restraint from Jorie's neck using his fingers. She walked to the spot where the Troll King had buried the gold and dug up the cloth sack. Jorie opened it in front of Godreel.

An expression of approval spread across Godreel's bovine-like face. The Tarc Lord had clearly not expected such a valuable offering.

"We are pleased to accept your most generous gift." Godreel motioned to one of his men, who lumbered over to confiscate the gold. "Secure the prisoners."

"What?" Jorie scowled as a Tarc grabbed her. "We had a deal!"

Van dashed into the woods and plowed right into one of Godreel's men. It felt like hitting a tree trunk, and she fell backward with the breath knocked from her. Her nose stung and the cut under her eye throbbed.

The Tarc easily lifted Van by her jacket collar and dragged her back to the others.

"The deal was, Leader Jorie, I spare your lives," Godreel said, pleased with himself. "You did not ask for your *freedom*." He chuckled.

His men chuckled too.

The Tarcs unshackled Brux, Elmot, and Paley from their metal collars and used rope to bind their hands in front.

Jorie and Brux tried to break free, while Godreel watched and sighed.

"Although I do have a fondness for the trolls' style of bondage, chained necks are impractical for our journey. If you continue to struggle, I can no longer guarantee to spare your lives."

"Journey?" Brux stopped his futile struggle. "Where are you taking us?"

"Into slavery, no doubt." Jorie scowled.

Godreel took a round glass disc bordered by yellow metal from his pocket. He elongated it into a tube and handed the looking glass to Jorie.

"Look down the incline, to the black oak tree, if you will," Godreel said.

Jorie peered through the looking glass and passed it to Brux, and then around to each of them.

Van gazed through the lens. In the distance, she saw three bodies dangling from a branch of a large, leafless tree: the thieves of Cortica from the Troll's Foot Tavern. She snapped the looking glass closed and handed it back to Godreel.

"They did not behave," the Tarc lord warned. "Do not let this be you."

Van allowed her hands to be tied without a struggle.

"You are correct, Leader Jorie. Or should I now call you simply… *Jorie?*" Godreel chortled. "Slavery is an important part of our economy. The men are useful as work hands in our fields. The women…" He sauntered close to Paley and perused her lewdly; she visibly shuddered.

"Our numbers are low. Although we have strong women in our tribe, their anatomy allows each to have only one child. We use our female slaves for breeding. If not, then the hardworking men in our tribe use them for housekeeping or…" Godreel eyed Jorie. "Pleasure."

Van wondered whether Jorie's sheer rage would be enough to fuel her escape from her bindings.

Godreel gave Jorie a quick slap to her butt. "This one has good hips! Perhaps she will be best for breeding."

Jorie's anger flared, and she released an animalistic growl so guttural it upset the allocameli tied to the trees. Some of them let out rapid, high-pitched shrieks and struggled against their binds. Others stomped their front hooves and spat.

Godreel grinned at Jorie's outburst and nodded to some of his men, who scurried away to calm the beasts.

Since Van and the others had already been the trolls' prisoners, the Tarcs didn't bother searching them. As puny humans, they posed no threat to the massive Tarcs, anyway.

A Tarc easily lifted Van onto an allocamelus. She felt as if she were sitting on a moving building and became woozy. She thought of the Twin Gemstones, reassured hers was still safely tucked in her pants pocket.

Other Tarcs secured Jorie, Brux, Elmot, and Paley each to their own allocamelus, and each accompanied by a rider. The Tarcs left nothing they considered of value, including the team's backpacks and tents.

With surprising agility, Godreel lifted his massive body onto his allocamelus. The other Tarcs did the same.

They traveled over freezing mountain terrain in the opposite direction of the Caves of Wolfenden. With every step, the allocameli took Van and her team farther away from the Coin. The group talked little and stopped only once to rest and eat.

The sun dropped, and the Tarc lord commanded his underlings to untie the prisoners' hands. He ordered Van and the others to set up camp for the night, for the Tarcs and for themselves.

After they made the site to the Tarc lord's satisfaction, the Tarcs shoved Van, Jorie, and Paley into one tent and Brux and Elmot into another. The Tarcs searched the team's backpacks and then threw the packs into the tents after them, willy-nilly.

"I'm surprised they gave us our stuff." Van rummaged through Brux's backpack, hoping to find some toothpaste.

"And let us sleep in the tents." Paley grabbed a pack. "Oh, look, I got my own backpack."

"The Tarcs are protecting their valuable human merchandise," Jorie explained. She had her own backpack too. "They think we need the items in our packs to keep healthy. They're trying hard to create an impression among the Balish they're a civilized race."

Van snorted. "They have a long way to go."

A hulking mass sat guard outside Van, Paley, and Jorie's tent.

Every time they tried to talk, he would shush them. Finally, he burst his head into their tent and threatened to re-tie their hands and bind their mouths if they didn't quiet down.

Resigned, Jorie ordered Van and Paley to sleep, but not before saying a prayer to the light that tomorrow would bring good fortune.

Van wasn't able to finish the prayer with Jorie. As soon as her head hit the padding of her sleeping bag, she fell asleep.

Chapter 42

Days 15, 16, and 17:
Living World

VAN WOKE EXHAUSTED. The tempting aroma of food being cooked made her stomach growl and gave her an incentive to get up.

Paley stirred and stretched her arms. "Mmm, what's that smell?"

Jorie was already awake. "I've been trying to figure that out. I can't place it."

The Tarc guarding the door grumbled something. He opened the tent flap and ordered them to come outside, one at a time, so he could re-bind their hands.

"Is this really necessary?" Van rolled her eyes as she extended her pink wrists.

The Tarc shoved Van, Jorie, and Paley over to one of the smaller campfires, where Brux and Elmot were already seated on logs.

"They're cooking buffalroo," Brux said to Jorie. "What gives?"

"They're breaking a bunch of laws, far as I can tell," Jorie said.

"Do you think they'll give us some?" Paley asked. "I'm starving."

The Tarcs brought over portions for each of them. At first, Van grimaced at the thought of eating buffalroo. Not only was it meat, but it came from a protected species, one she had never heard of before coming to the Living World. But her rumbling stomach demanded she take a tiny taste. Then Van wolfed the whole thing down.

After breakfast, they moved on.

A silky grayness settled over the sky, and thick, clumpy flakes of snow draped the landscape. They kept a steady pace, getting closer and closer to Kezef—and farther and farther from the Coin.

By late afternoon, Van's lower back and inner thighs ached from riding on the allocamelus for so long. The bindings on her wrists had turned them raw and bloody. The grandfather clock Van had seen in Uxa's office haunted her every thought as it counted down the remaining time for her team to complete their mission. Every passing second pounded like a sledgehammer in her head. Every cell in Van's body screamed for her to turn back toward the Coin.

Turn back. Find a way. Get the Coin. The Coin.

She became numb to the freezing cold and to her aching body. The beautiful snowy landscape tinted to a dull gray. A drowsy weakness overcame her. Did she have her gemstone? Van couldn't remember. She needed sleep. Her eyes closed as she slowly slid off the allocamelus. The animal plodded on, oblivious to the peril of its rider. Clip-*clop*. Clip-*clop*. Clip-*clop*.

━━

VAN DIDN'T OPEN her eyes until the next day. Her head rested on Brux's lap, *again*. She groaned.

The Tarcs had untied all of their hands, and now they huddled together in a clearing. The bovine-like creatures roamed around Van and her team with no fear the puny humans would risk attempting an escape.

"We draped you over an allocamelus like a sack of potatoes for the rest of yesterday's ride," Paley informed Van.

"It's the gemstones," Brux said, anger seeped into his tone. "You're using them correctly, but Paley still saps your energy, has been the whole time. That's how they work."

"Sorry." Paley sulked.

"Or, you may just be sickly by nature," Jorie said.

"Gee, thanks." Van wasn't in the mood for Jorie and her warrior crap.

Brux helped Van to a sitting position. "The good news is the Tarcs will probably throw you back. Too weak for breeding or for doing housework." He grinned, but the smile didn't reach his eyes.

Van forced a chuckle, causing a dull ache in her ribs. She knew Brux was trying to cheer her, but didn't think his joke was funny. She responded with a snicker to conceal the sinking feeling her time in the Living World had almost run out.

The thundering of horses' hooves stampeding toward the camp stopped their conversation cold.

The Tarcs leaped to attention, drawing their weapons.

Sleek black horses broke from the trees, with riders dressed in black. They wore the Balish royal crest.

"Daisy," Brux murmured as he shot to his feet.

My father! Van also jumped up.

If a royal squadron had ventured into this area, it was probably Solana's crew after the Coin. Which would include both Van's father and possibly Daisy—if her father had kept Daisy with him, despite her not being the Anchoress heir.

The black riders drew their swords; the Tarcs fought back.

Van didn't know which were the better fighters, and because of the balaclavas, she couldn't tell which was her father, if any.

Brux dashed through the fight, heading toward the woods in the same direction where the squadron had emerged. Van knew he hoped to find his sister, perhaps hidden nearby.

Paley and Elmot grabbed some backpacks and sprinted away.

"Being caught won't help anyone. C'mon!" Jorie heaved her backpack onto her shoulders. She rushed away, following Elmot and Paley.

Van wanted to run while they had the chance, but… she darted the other way, after Brux.

Jorie stopped running and called ahead, "Elmot! Paley! Keep going." She turned and glanced at Van and Brux. "Dammit!" She changed direction and headed after them.

Brux dodged a sword wielded by a black rider. "Where's my sister? Where's Daisy?" Brux grabbed at the leg of the rider, who kicked out, sending Brux sprawling.

"Brux!" Van screamed, still too far away to help him.

The black rider couldn't use his sword to reach Brux on the ground, so he pulled a dagger from his belt and raised his arm, poised to hurl a fatal blow at Brux.

Van halted before the black rider and looked up at him. "Dad?"

He paused, startled.

With a swoosh, Zachery landed squarely in the black rider's chest. Without a sound, he tumbled from his horse.

"Thanks." Brux scrambled to stand.

Jorie bent over the body and pulled Zachery from the dead man's chest. She lifted his balaclava. "It's not your father, Van."

"I know that. He's much too small. I said it to distract him from killing Brux."

"Nice work." Jorie gave Van an approving nod.

Brux smiled at Van, and then asked Jorie, "Where'd you find Zachery?"

"On the ground, next to a dead Tarc," Jorie said. "Let's get moving."

"I've got to find Daisy."

Brux twisted away from them, about to run into the woods, when Jorie grabbed his sleeve. "Brux, you're gonna get us all killed."

Two Balish soldiers caught sight of the trio. They pulled the reins on their horses and headed straight for them.

"Move it!" Jorie growled.

Van knew they couldn't outrun soldiers on horseback. The three of them were as good as dead. But they ran like hell, anyway.

Van twisted to see the two soldiers closing in on them when a poleax flew and almost severed one of the rider's shoulders.

Several Tarcs on allocameli attacked the soldiers, who stopped their pursuit of Van, Jorie, and Brux to face the battle with the oncoming enemy.

The trio raced away as the two black riders continued their clash with the Tarcs.

When they caught up to Elmot and Paley, Elmot said, "I guess that's what the Tarcs get for breaking the rules by eating buffalroo."

"I don't think that's what's going on, Elmot," Jorie said. "There's some kind of aggressive play going on here. Tarcs and Balish are supposed to be allies."

Once they had successfully escaped the Tarcs and the Balish soldiers, the team slowed their pace.

"My holographic map is gone," Elmot moaned as he rummaged through his backpack.

"Oh, no! We left our backpacks behind," Van said to Brux.

"It's okay. Better to have escaped with our lives than our backpacks."

"I brought yours." Paley pulled Van's backpack from underneath her own.

Van hadn't noticed Paley carried two packs. "Thanks!" Van beamed as she took her backpack from Paley. "That was really cool of you."

"The Tarcs didn't confiscate the map Van gave me, the one of the north." Elmot pulled out a folded parchment. "That, along with my keen ability to use the constellations for navigation, will get us to the Caves. Thank the light."

Jorie made a sideways figure eight over her chest and mumbled, "Thank-the-light-and-all-that-is-good."

Elmot consulted his map and redirected them back toward the Caves of Wolfenden.

Van could tell the gemstones were draining her, now more than ever. Relief filled her when dusk set in, and Jorie ordered them to make camp.

Now without tents, they slept out in the open on the snowy ground. Van lay in her sleeping bag, staring at the three-quarter moon and the twinkling dots in the sky. The stars reminded her of

Wiglaf's tiny paws flashing in the dark as he walked in a circle on her backpack back in her quarters at Uxa's house, and her heart wrenched over missing the little guy. Fatigue encroached on her aching body. She hoped Wiglaf would appear during the night and make her feel better. Van wondered where Brux was sleeping just before her eyelids grew heavy and closed out the starry night.

THE NEXT MORNING dragged on as the team continued their long journey to the Caves of Wolfenden. The grandfather clock Van envisioned in her mind continued to tick away the time, causing her to stress.

By late afternoon, Elmot announced the Caves were only a couple of hours ahead. Though glad they had almost reached their destination, Van tensed in anticipation of what lay ahead there. She silently reviewed what she had learned about how to get the Coin.

It was guarded by the Elemental Loka, who had laid traps throughout a labyrinth of tunnels. There, a terrible beast roamed, ready to kill anyone who trespassed. Van didn't feel overly worried about the Elemental and the traps. However, the monster concerned her. She didn't know what kind of terrifying creature lay in wait for them, but if it was worse than the trolls and the Tarcs, she didn't feel confident they could defeat it.

Their trail abruptly ended at the edge of an enormous canyon. A rickety bridge stretched before the group. The old, weathered wooden slat walkway had a thick rope railing. The drop below made Van queasy.

Paley took a step back. "Uh… you go first," she said to anyone.

"We're lucky the bridge is here," Elmot said. "Otherwise, it would take us three more days of travel."

Elmot's assessment made Van both grateful and terrified.

Brux glanced at Van. "Are you going to faint again?"

"I'm *fine*," she lied.

"Don't look down," Brux said. "You can do this, okay?"

His advice didn't help. Van remained petrified.

Paley clutched onto Brux's elbow. "Let's cross together. You'll keep me safe."

Van replaced her fear with resentment. How could Paley continue to flirt with Brux, knowing Van had feelings for him? Van and Brux weren't *officially* together, but something was going on between them.

"Can't." Jorie took several cautious steps onto the planks. "It's not strong enough to support both of you at the same time."

"We can't risk it." Brux detached Paley from his arm. "Sorry, Paley."

Jorie went first. "Don't follow until I'm halfway across." She bravely inched her way onto the flimsy bridge.

Van crossed her fingers and imagined Trey's spirit watching over them, helping them safely pass.

Elmot went next, followed by Brux.

"I'm going next." Paley cut in front of Van.

Van's stomach lurched when Paley's sudden move pushed her close to the cliff's drop-off. *Paley doesn't care if I fall over the side!*

Paley's actions—cutting Van off, flirting with Brux—proved she didn't value her friendship with Van. Even after everything Van had done for her over the years.

I took Paley into my life as if she were family. She pays me back by not caring whether I live or die?

Fueled by fury, Van stomped onto the bridge before Paley made it halfway across.

"You're too close," Jorie hollered. "Go back!"

"Van, the bridge is rotted," Brux cried. "It can't support the weight of both of you!"

Van ignored them. She assumed they were overreacting. The bridge seemed sturdy enough to support both of their light bodies, and she needed to have words with Paley.

The planks wobbled under her feet.

Van's anxiety skyrocketed as she gripped the rope railing.

If Paley can do it, so can I. "Don't look down. Don't look down," Van chanted under her breath as she regained her balance.

Paley turned and faced Van's direction. "You idiot. Go back!"

How dare *Paley call me an idiot! Who does she think she is?*

"No! You go back!" Van yelled, knowing her statement made no sense. "You're pathetic, chasing after Brux like a fool."

Paley made her way toward Van. "No. *You're* the pathetic one, always *taking*, never giving back. You appreciate nothing!"

Jorie screamed, "Spread out!"

"Shut up!" Paley twisted and yelled back to the others on the landing. "Together, we don't even weigh as much as one of you!"

The bridge swayed, and Van's head spun. She clutched the handrails in a death grip.

A terrifying crack filled the cavern.

The rotted slat beneath Van's foot sunk and then collapsed. The planks supporting Van's weight gave way.

Paley blanched and dashed toward her teammates.

Van screamed as her body dropped, then jerked. Her backpack had caught on the edge of a broken plank, stopping her descent.

She swayed, dangling precariously. Van frantically grasped for a secure slat less than an inch out of her reach.

"Van!" Brux cried.

As Paley made her way to safety, Brux brushed past her, stumbling along the bridge as it continued to sway and creak.

"Brux, no!" Jorie knelt on the ground at the end of the bridge and hastily rummaged through her backpack for a coil of rope. "First rule in an emergency is to keep yourself safe. Let me tie you to the rope."

He paid no attention and continued working his way toward Van.

Crrrrrack!

A plank gave out under Brux's foot.

Van's stomach knotted as she watched him regain his balance. Then the planks supporting her creaked, and she slipped lower.

"Help!" Van's legs thrashed about in her futile attempt to gain footing.

Jorie moved tentatively onto the bridge, grasping the rope.

Elmot and Paley watched, wide-eyed and gripping each other for support.

"Hurry," Van whimpered. The plank wouldn't hold her much longer.

Brux was only feet away when a strained creak came from the ropes suspending the bridge.

It sent chills down Van's spine.

Jorie stopped a quarter of the way onto the bridge. "Brux! There's too much weight! Come back and grab the rope!"

"Brux," Van said calmly, resigned to her imminent death. "Go back. The bridge… it's going to collapse."

"Not a chance." He inched closer to Van, knelt down, and grabbed the strap of her backpack. "I got you."

Brux lifted Van onto the slats; the bridge groaned.

A deafening screech reverberated throughout the chasm.

The bridge shuddered and the rope handrails, unable to bear their weight, untwined around them.

Van gripped a plank to save herself as the support ropes let go, and the bridge split in two.

They plummeted.

Van hung tightly to the planks as she swung in a wide arc toward the stone cavern wall.

Brux didn't have time to grab hold and tumbled past her.

Van smacked the side of the cavern several times, knocking her breath away, and nearly lost her grip. All she could think of was Brux. Through her peripheral vision, she saw a bulky object whizz by and feared it might be Jorie, but it was only Jorie's backpack, which she'd left too close to the edge of the bridge.

Cursing echoed downward.

Van looked up to see Jorie dangling from the slats.

She heard grunts from below, and her heart soared. She looked down and saw Brux hanging onto a frayed rope.

An angry stretching sound howled from the strained ropes that tethered the dangling bridge.

Van gripped the plank tighter.

"Get rid of any extra weight," Brux yelled from below. "Van, drop your backpack." He began climbing upward.

Paralyzed with fear, Van couldn't move, let alone remove her backpack.

"It's okay," Brux said soothingly, close to Van now. "Just start climbing."

Sheer terror turned her to stone. "N-No. I-I can't move."

"I'm right behind you. I'm with you. I won't let anything happen to you," Brux coaxed in a strained voice. "I promise."

The overtaxed ropes screeched louder.

Van had to get going, or they'd both plummet to their deaths. She couldn't do that to Brux. She fought against her paralyzed muscles, unclasped her trembling hand, and began to climb.

"There you go," Brux said, sounding relieved. "Just like that."

Van looked upward and saw Jorie reach land.

Adrenaline, along with Brux's coaxing, gave Van the will to make it to the top. Once there, she stumbled several shaky steps away from the cliff's edge, dropped to her knees, and fell flat onto her stomach, weeping and exhausted. Someone removed her back-pack and spoke to her, but the ringing in her ears blocked out their words. Van lay face-down, hugging the frost-coated ground, thankful she'd survived.

The near-death experience on the bridge had bonded Van to her teammates, making her feel as if she were part of something bigger than herself. Brux and Jorie had risked their lives to save her. For that, Van couldn't put her gratitude into words, even as Jorie screamed at her for putting the team in danger.

Paley and Elmot fussed over her too. Concern shined in their eyes. Van had never experienced such sincere caring before, from either her hypercritical step-mother or her emotionally distant father. Her heart swelled with affection at the thought of Brux and how he risked his life to save her. Van wished he would think of her as more than a friend. He had turned out to be a fantastic guy and a great warrior.

Once back on their trek, Van and Paley seemed to get along after Van's near death. However, Jorie declared they had unresolved issues. She ordered them to "work it out" by sending them on a hunt for edible berries during their break, while the others tried to catch some wild game.

After some polite conversation, Paley opened up and accused Van of wanting to keep her "in her place," socially below Van.

"You can't stand me being treated as an equal to you," Paley said. "Or boys being interested in me, instead of you. I'm no longer boosting your self-esteem."

Van's joy over surviving her brush with death vanished. Stunned Paley felt that way about her, Van said in retaliation, "So? You just used me on the island for your own social survival. And because I bought you things. You were never a true friend to me."

Before they had resolved their issues, Jorie called the team back. She, Elmot, and Brux had caught nothing, so they had to eat the berries harvested by Van and Paley.

Jorie checked the berries before doling out portions. She scowled. "Don't you idiots know how to tell edible berries from poisonous ones?"

"Yes." Van lifted her chin in the air, sick of people criticizing her. "I learned the edible berry rule in school. White and yellow, kill a fellow. Purple and blue, good for you. Red, could be good, could be dead."

Jorie picked through the berries and tossed several away. "Then why are yellow berries here?"

Van glared at Paley.

Paley shrugged. "I guess I wasn't privileged enough to get that lesson in school."

"Enough. Let's eat." Jorie handed out the berries to everyone.

The group ate in silence while Van and Paley glowered at each other.

Time ticked away as Jorie moved them onward, with only three backpacks among them, limited supplies and food, and Van and Paley in the middle of the worst fight of their lives.

The team traveled with little conversation. Eventually, the setting sun cast a glow over the landscape, highlighting an enormous layer of granite slabs encasing a mountain. As they moved closer to the heaps of granite, Elmot got more and more excited.

Finally, they were close enough for Elmot to jump onto a block.

"My fellow teammates, may I present," he extended his arm toward a massive crevasse in the mound, "the Caves of Wolfenden!"

Chapter 43

D ay 18: Living World

"THAT'S THE ENTRANCE?" Van worried about squishing herself between tightly packed slabs of granite.

"I won't fit through that fissure," Jorie said. "Neither will Brux. Elmot! Find another way in!"

"Well," Elmot hesitated. "I have good news and bad news."

"Shoot," Jorie barked.

"The bad news is the details in my maps end here," Elmot said. "Even the holographic map didn't show beyond the outer granite part of the mountain."

"Makes sense," Brux said. "No one has made it to the Coin and back, so how could anyone map the Caves?"

"The good news," Elmot continued, "is I know enough about tunnels to navigate through here without a map."

"Ho-yeah!" Jorie yelped.

"It's late. I think we should rest before tackling the Caves," Brux said.

Van couldn't help but think he'd mentioned it for her benefit. Her exhaustion from the drain of the Twin Gemstones must be apparent from her appearance.

"Elmot, are there any caves for shelter nearby?" Brux asked.

Elmot sulked. "I don't recall any from the holographic map."

"It's not worth the risk of scouting around." Jorie pointed to a natural granite lean-to jutting from the mountain of stone. "We can camp here for a few hours."

Before it got too dark, Van and Paley hastened to collect dry sticks without talking to each other. Elmot followed, scouting for a particular type of tree. Jorie and Brux searched the ground for "good rocks."

Elmot found a birch tree and peeled some bark from its trunk. It had bulbous, reddish-brown blotches inside.

"Tinder for the fire," Elmot said through chattering teeth. "The inside fungus easily catches a spark. We don't want to get frostbite."

Brux arranged the sticks into a pyramid.

Jorie held a "handstone," a small, flat stone in one hand and a "striking quartz" in the other. She began banging the two rocks together on top of the birch peel.

Van reached into her pants pocket and pulled out a matchbook. "Here. Use my matches."

Jorie looked as if she wanted to throttle Van. She grabbed the matches and grumbled, "Thanks."

Paley tsked at Van. "Why didn't you tell anyone you had matches?"

"Nobody asked," Van snapped.

"Shut it. Both of you," Jorie barked. She lit the campfire.

Based on his knowledge of geology and speleology, along with information he had gained from his holographic map, Elmot conjectured the Caves of Wolfenden made up a network of winding tunnels underneath the mountain, which was most likely the labyrinth Zane had mentioned at the Troll's Foot Tavern.

"There's probably a cavern in the deepest part of the underground cave network," he said. "If there is, then it's the most logical place for the Coin to be hidden."

Van, Elmot, and Paley grabbed sleeping bags from inside their backpacks and inflated them. The count was three sleeping bags for five people.

"I'll share one with Bruuux," Paley cooed as if she were joking.

Van knew it was no joke. It revealed things were still not right between her and Paley.

No one wanted to share a sleeping bag.

At that moment, Van needed to rest more than she hated Paley. She volunteered to share a sleeping bag with Paley so she could go to sleep; the others could waste their time squabbling. Paley, who must have been just as tired, agreed.

Brux and Elmot refused to sleep in one bag together, and Jorie refused to share a bag with either Brux or Elmot.

"Why don't you rotate while one takes watch?" Van yawned as she crawled into her sleeping bag, trying her best not to touch Paley, which was impossible being wrapped together. She fell asleep before finding out how her teammates had solved their sleeping arrangement crisis.

━━

Jorie woke at dawn and roused everyone.

Van couldn't tell who had slept where or whether anyone had kept watch. But Jorie, Brux, and Elmot had dark circles under their eyes, and they appeared cranky. To make matters worse, the temperature had dropped to near freezing. They were starving, and Trey was no longer around to hunt for them. No one else in the group had hunting training, and with the land around the caves barren of animals and edible plant life, the group deemed searching for food to be futile.

Jorie commanded all of them to search their pockets so she could take an inventory of their supplies.

Van patted her cargo pants and felt a lump in one of her many pockets: the stash of salted auroch sticks she had swiped from Roguey. Without hesitation, she offered the auroch sticks.

"Sorry," she said. "I forgot Roguey had given me these." She didn't want to admit she had kept food from the group.

Paley opened her mouth to comment.

Jorie cut her off. "Just be grateful we have food." She portioned out small shares to each of them.

As Van nibbled, her anxiety reared its ugly head. They would soon go deep underground, to a place with no exits and no turning back. "Elmot, are you sure you can get us out?"

"Absolutely." He tapped his head. "Got all the information we need stored up here."

To conserve their matches, Jorie and Brux lit makeshift torches from the campfire before putting it out and carried some extra unlit torches for later. Jorie cast a simple spell on the torches to extend their burning time. Then Elmot led them over mounds of enormous granite blocks, uphill and slippery, and into a cave made from a large fissure. Their torches threw light inside the tunnel.

At every bend, Elmot formed a pile of stones, showing the direction back to their original point of entry. The tunnels grew narrower the deeper they went underground, and the walls and ceilings had a thin, sooty coating. The temperature got cooler, and the smell of damp stone stuffed up Van's nose; her apprehension set in.

"Elmot, how do you know where we're going?" she asked.

"I'm checking the ground for an incline and mapping our path in my head," he replied. "I have a talent for recognizing the various compositions of the rocks. There are designs in the stratified stone."

"Like how I can read ice crystals?" Van asked.

Paley tsked. "It's not always about you."

Elmot cut in before Van could retort. "Not quite the same thing," he said kindly. "I'm memorizing the shapes and the different minerals mixed with the clay and sand."

To calm her nerves, Van asked Elmot to point out the various minerals and their patterns.

"Here, the sooty coating is manganese." Elmot went on about the plates and chips in the walls and the ceiling; what he could see, and what he hoped to see. "Look at the golden attapulgite." He pointed. "We should come across crystal celestite… There." He pointed again. "That beautiful blue is azurite. Coming across some gypsum would be great…"

Van couldn't grasp any of what Elmot said. Instead, she tried memorizing every twist and turn, so if her anxiety became unbearable, she could flee back to the surface. Then Van gave up. She was in too far now. The only way out was through.

To her relief, the tunnel opened into an expansive chamber. Their torches lit the cavity, exposing soot-striped pillars, a dusty mosaic-tiled floor, and a cracked reflecting pool empty of water. A plain, round fountain stood intact, and a trickle filled its base with fresh mountain water. The dilapidated condition and the layers of dust suggested the once-beautiful temple had been abandoned centuries ago. Engraved writings of a long-forgotten civilization covered the high, smooth walls.

Van craned her neck and studied the ancient script, hoping she could read it. She couldn't.

"Whoa. Who used to live here?" Brux asked Jorie, the team's cultures expert.

"I-I don't know." Jorie glanced around the temple. Her eyes settled on the wall. "You're the languages expert. Can you read it?"

"It's not one I've seen before." Brux scrutinized the writing. "It looks like a derivative of the language of the ancients. I think I can figure it out."

"I need to rest for a minute." Van threw her butt down on a cracked stone bench.

"They were the Ming I." Brux wrinkled his brow. "They're telling a story about… their *end*."

"What does it say?" Van slipped off her hiking boots and rubbed her feet.

Paley sat on another bench, nowhere near Van, and did the same.

"Do they say why no one ever mapped this place before?" Elmot took in the sights of the temple.

"They were a peaceful, light-worshipping tribe," Brux said. "Then came a time when darkness reigned in the external world."

"Humph," Jorie said. "Sounds familiar."

"The only light remaining lay inside themselves... their Wise One directed them to quietly nourish themselves from within, to nurture their light. If they reacted to their lack of progress with anger and negativity, they would extinguish their inner light and block the aid of the Creator." Brux silently perused the words, then continued. "They didn't listen. Instead of finding grace, they fought against the darkness, which gave it power. They shined their inner light, rather than conceal it. The dark forces consumed them, and they suffered great misfortune."

"What does all that mean?" Paley stretched out her legs and wiggling her toes.

Brux shrugged.

"It means what it means." Jorie walked over to the fountain, more interested in inspecting the chamber. "This is a good place to rest. The fountain has fresh mountain water, and there's a fire pit we can use."

Elmot held up his hand. "I feel a slight breeze. They must've worked out a ventilation system. Still, I recommend keeping the fire to a minimum."

"Too bad we don't have any proper food," Paley complained.

"Maybe..." Elmot walked to the far end of the temple and looked into an aqueduct in the floor. "Does anyone have a hook or a compass?"

"A compass won't work, Elmot. You should know that." Jorie frowned. "The earth in this area is full of iron ore."

"I have a compass." Van rifled through her backpack. "What do you need it for if it won't work?"

"This is a stream." Elmot pointed to the flowing water in the duct. "Fresh water means fish."

She handed Elmot the compass, confused.

He took apart the compass and removed its needles. "Since none of us has a hook." He bent the arrow needle into a J-shape, then unraveled a string from a ball of twine he had packed. Elmot attached the string to the needle and made a fishing line. He put a tiny piece of dried auroch meat on the hook and lowered it into the stream.

Within an hour, the team had settled around a small fire. The air filled with the aroma of roasting fish.

Brux sat on the crumbling stone bench next to Van, where she quietly ate from stoneware they'd found in the temple. He had watched her all evening, if it was evening. They couldn't tell time in the caves. She knew he had something on his mind.

"Van, I'm worried about you," he said. "Are you ready to face the challenges of the Elemental?"

"Not really," Van said honestly. "I still can't believe I'm—" She couldn't bring herself to say *Anchoress*.

"I want you to know… I read something in Manik's text."

Van lost her appetite. She placed her bowl on the floor next to the bench.

"The Elemental will challenge your strength against what the text described as the first plague. The Plague of Evil."

"Yeah, we know that from Ildiss." Despite the chill in the temple, Van felt sweaty and warm from stress.

"No, well, what I'm trying to tell you…" Brux fidgeted. "What the text described guarding the labyrinth, it's… a Minotaur."

"You mean like a Tarc?" Van asked.

"No," Jorie said from across the room, listening to their conversation. "The Tarcs are mostly human. The Minotaur is all beast. Be prepared. The Minotaur's appearance will shock you. It looks nothing like a Tarc."

"Great." Van threw her hands in the air. "Just great. Wonderful!" She wiped her sweaty forehead with the back of her hand. "So, the Tarcs were a warm-up act."

Brux narrowed his eyes at her.

"Why can't it be a bunfy?" Van said. "Why's it have to be a monster?"

"I'm not letting you do this alone." He stared at her. "Van, are the gemstones making you sick?"

"Just tired." She rose with effort, dragging her weary body to one of the sleeping bags. "And I'm *not* sharing a sleeping bag tonight. Stupid Minotaur." Without another word, Van tucked in and pulled the sleeping bag over her head.

Just before she drifted off, her mind filled with a soft amaranthine glow. The blurry outline of a figure emerged.

Jacynthia! Van called out in her dream state.

"Greetings, my little warrior." Jacynthia's mouth tipped into a soft smile, creasing her face.

Jacynthia, how can I be the Anchoress if I didn't inherit access to my ancestral magic?

"I cannot answer your question."

Why not?

"I do not understand it."

Van sighed in frustration. She changed the question. *How can I defeat the Minotaur that roams the labyrinths?*

"Have no fear. Fear gives away your power."

How can I not have fear? Van's anxiety grew, despite her peaceful vision.

"All knowledge is already known but can only be transferred with truths. The path of truth is always the path of least resistance. Humans create their own evil through their incorrect actions. Be secure, knowing there is no evil, for evil has no power, other than that which you give it."

But I have to conquer a Plague of Evil. How am I supposed to do that?

"By confronting evil, knowing it has no power."

How do I know it has no power?

"By connecting to your spiritual Self."

But what weapon do I use to defeat evil?

"Everyone is provided with what they need to fulfill their spiritual destiny."

I still don't understand—

"Goodnight, my little warrior. Good luck."

Jacynthia flickered, faded, and was gone. In the next instant, Van slipped into a deep sleep.

Chapter 44

D ay 19: Living World

Jorie had risen first, as usual, and roused everyone. They could no longer see the sky, so nobody knew the time.

They took turns washing in the icy mountain water.

"Finally!" Paley said as she cleaned up, using fresh water from the fountain. Then she changed clothes and declared, "Ready to go." Today she wore brown contact lenses.

Balish brown!

This enraged Van, but not as much as what dangled from Paley's ears. "My earrings!" Van grabbed Paley's wrist. "Those are my mother's earrings!"

"What?" Paley wrenched her wrist from Van's grip. "Solana gave them to me when I told her I was the Anchoress-in-waiting. *They're mine!*"

"No, they're not," Van growled. "They're *mine!*"

"I was waiting for a chance to clean up before I wore them," Paley said.

Van lunged at her and tried to tear the earrings from her ears. "Give 'em back."

Brux leaped between the girls, holding them apart. "Paley, I saw Solana take them from Van's stuff in Araquiel. We all did."

"Of course *you* would say that," Paley spat. "Trying to protect your precious *Van*."

"The journey has finally started to wear on them." Elmot backed away from the fight, wide-eyed.

"This has been a long time coming," Paley snarled.

"I think it's one of Loka's tests." Brux remained in between them, struggling to keep Van and Paley apart.

"If this is a test, Van isn't passing it," Elmot cried. "She won't be able to get the Coin!"

"This isn't a test," Van snarled. "Paley's a *jerk*!"

Jorie moved in. "Stop attaching to the dark part of your Selves. Like each other. That's an order."

Van ignored Jorie. Her mother's earrings dangling from Paley's ears fueled her uncontrollable rage. She charged at Paley again, but Brux held her back. How *dare* Paley steal her jewelry!

"Solana gave them to me because she *likes* me," Paley screeched. "She's *nice*! You don't understand her because you're *stupid*!"

"I'll show you who's stupid!" Van positioned into combat stance, fists raised. She wanted those earrings back. She didn't care how she got them.

Jorie eyed them both, swore under her breath, then held her palms outward and chanted, "Negative energy go away. By my words you cannot stay. Ground them with the earth as well, and reclaim their space with this spell." Jorie lowered her hands. "Paley, give them back."

Paley opened her mouth to protest, then reluctantly took off the shimmering silver earrings and handed them to Van, who quickly tucked them into her pants pocket.

The gesture broke the anger between the two, and Van said to

Paley, "These earrings mean a lot to me. They're all I have left of my mother."

Paley softened at Van's words, and her eyes teared up. "I'm sorry. I didn't mean to be such a jerk. I should've known Solana lied to me."

"It's okay." Van wept. Things between her and Paley weren't okay, but Jorie's spell had given her clarity and peace.

"Solana used the earrings to cause you two to fight," Brux said.

Jorie nodded. "It's what evil does. Tempts people with things they desire to create chaos and cause fighting within their ranks."

"That was *great*," Elmot said, in awe of Jorie's spell, and then frowned. "But I hope the spell didn't drain your energy." He nervously brushed imaginary dirt from his pants.

"Doubt it," Jorie said. "It was a simple spell. I cast it right, and for a good reason. Should work for an hour or so."

Frightened by what had happened, Van couldn't believe how close she'd come to connecting to the dark part of her Self. She had felt out of control and was thankful for Jorie's magical intervention. Van's experience with Paley had been so profound, had resonated so deeply to her core, it caused her to have an epiphany.

Everything Van had learned on her journey came smashing together. Jacynthia's counsel, her meeting with Ildiss, Amaryl's warnings, Manik's advice, giving away the boundless bowl to an impoverished family in Agerorsa, Brux's rejection at Ox's Bunkhouse, her father's mistakes, her mother's magical bloodline, accepting the gnomes and their culture, encountering trolls and the Tarcs. Her fight with Paley.

Van now understood her challenge. Surviving the journey to retrieve the Coin wasn't only about facing her father, Solana, or the Minotaur. It was about being able to stand up to all kinds of evil, including fear, greed, materialism, and prejudice.

Evil would always try to knock her off her path. Try to disconnect her from her light.

Evil in all of its forms was the plague of humanity. This was what Van's journey had groomed her to combat as the Anchoress.

This was the Plague of Evil.

Chapter 45

D ay 20: Living World

THE NEXT DAY Van's epiphany stayed fresh in her mind, helping to fortify her as the team spent the day wandering through an endless system of caves. It was enough to drive anyone mad.

The tunnel walls and ceiling enclosed them, allowing just a few feet of space in any direction. Knowing only the torches' light kept Van from plunging into absolute darkness made her uneasy. The air seemed thin, making it a struggle to breathe, although the tightness in her chest could be from anxiety, covertly creeping into her body. Van walked tensely, dreading when her claustrophobia would reappear, encroaching on her newfound enlightenment. To her surprise, though, the claustrophobia never came.

Every time Elmot insisted they had reached the deepest part of the caves, the floor around the next bend sloped again, and they went even deeper.

"We're going to die in here," Paley moaned.

The group answered with grunts.

Van's stomach growled, the muscles in her legs ached, and her feet throbbed. She was getting shaky from lack of food and exhaustion.

The team stopped to eat a ration of their dwindling food supply and grabbed a quick nap.

Then they moved on.

Chapter 46

D ay 21: Living World

"Is this ever going to end?" Van complained. They were so deep underground, she kept expecting a Minotaur to jump out at any second.

"What time is it?" Paley asked grumpily.

"Keep moving. That's what time it is," Jorie snapped.

"Are we close to the Coin?" Van asked.

"Probably not, since Elmot is leading us in circles," Brux said.

"We haven't come across any of my stone piles," Elmot responded stiffly. "We're going the right way."

"Then hurry up and get us to the Coin," Brux said to Elmot. "Before we all die from fatigue."

"You want to take the lead? Fine!" Elmot stepped aside and extended his arm for Brux to take his torch.

"I'll do a better job," Brux roared as he snatched the torch from Elmot.

"Our supplies are running seriously low," Paley added with a quiver in her voice. "We're burning our last torches, and we don't have any matches left. Never mind that there's no food. *No food!*"

"Shut up, you guys, and keep moving." Jorie led the team, holding the other of their two torches. "Keep alert. This is all part of Loka's tests."

"Elmot, not knowing his way, is one of Loka's tests?" Brux asked snidely.

Elmot grabbed the torch back from Brux. "Jorie, step aside." He whooshed past her. "I'm the only one among us who can get us there and back wit—"

Before Elmot could finish his sentence, he completely disappeared into the ground. The light from his torch sank below the earth, leaving them in near darkness.

Brux jumped to action, but Jorie blocked him, almost dropping the one torch they had left. "It's no use," she said. "He's gone. It's a bottomless pit. There's no coming out of the black mud."

"*Hell no!*" In a flash, Van dropped her backpack to the ground, snatched a rope from inside, and maneuvered around the wrestling match between Jorie and Brux. She held onto one end and tossed the rope into the mud, hoping it was long enough to reach Elmot.

"Stay away from the mud!" Jorie screeched. "It'll suck you in!" She released Brux, ran over and grasped Van, pulling her away from the slick, black puddle.

"Jorie's right." Brux also clasped Van. "The mud. It's alive. It'll take you."

Van resisted. The torchlight flickered wildly in the scuffle.

"No!" Van lost her grip on the rope as she struggled against Jorie and Brux.

Paley crashed to her knees and grabbed the end of the rope before it slipped all the way into the blackness. She wrapped the end around her wrist and held tight.

"Paley, no!" Jorie released Van, dropped the torch, and dashed for Paley.

The rope tugged. "I got him!" Paley twisted, facing the others with a smile.

"Let go!" Brux yelled as he sprang toward her.

The rope yanked Paley's arm again, this time stronger.

Paley's smile faded, and her expression turned to fear. The rope jerked again, causing her to lose her balance.

Jorie and Brux had just grasped Paley as the unnatural force pulled from the other side, and they lost their grip.

"Help—" Paley's scream became silenced as the black mud consumed her.

"Paley!" Without thinking, and before Brux or Jorie could stop her, Van dove headfirst into the mud.

Liquid black engulfed her.

The defining silence made her inner ears throb. Van kept her eyes open, but they didn't hurt, and she could breathe. She raised her weighted arms, using all her might to reach into the inky blackness.

Her hand came in contact with a body.

Paley! Van gripped the sleeve of her friend's jacket.

Paley didn't respond to her touch.

Van couldn't tell whether they were sinking, but figured they were. She tried to speak; her words didn't carry through the blackness. She reached out with her other hand to find Elmot and felt nothing.

Someone, some*thing*, whispered in her ear. A chill shimmied down her spine.

Murmuring voices came at Van from every direction.

Give up... nobody cares about you... you are worthless... your existence is meaningless... nobody loves you, deep down you know this... you're tired, just let go... embrace the darkness... it's the right thing to do...

She felt a tug on her grip as she sank lower than Paley. Although drained from the blackness siphoning her energy, Van tightened her grasp.

The voices told Van she belonged there, in the darkness. If she let go, all her dreams would come true. She would know family. She would know love.

Maybe the voices were right. What was the point of life? It

seemed kind of meaningless. Perhaps she belonged there. At least in this place, she would be loved.

Van's grasp on Paley's jacket let her know her friend had also sunk lower; they were level with each other.

Convinced her existence was pointless, Van told herself she should just let go. Of Paley. Of her life. And let the darkness consume her. Doing so would bring her peace. Brux, Jorie, Genie, her father, they would get on fine without her. No one would miss her. Letting go was the right thing to do.

The voices told her so.

Other words slipped into Van's consciousness. "When surrounded by darkness, cling to the light." *Cling to the light.*

Van came to her senses, angry at the voices for trying to trick her. But unlike the lost civilization in the temple, instead of lashing out, she turned inward and forced herself to focus on her light.

Memories flooded her thoughts. The day her father had taken her quahogging… the majestic beauty of Providence Island… lazy summer days on the beach with Paley. She thought of Brux and Wiglaf. Her heart surged with wonder and love. Van countered every horrible whisper with a positive thought.

She began to rise.

But Paley continued to sink, causing Van's grip to loosen.

Van turned her thoughts to their friendship. How Paley would sneak in through her bedroom window for a sleepover. Them riding in a buggy over sand dunes on a sunny island day, or hanging out in the hallways at Canterbury Bells… getting pampered at the Naked Ape… Memories of her friendship with Paley filled Van with *love*.

They both rose.

Although Van could breathe while submerged, as soon as she broke the surface, she gasped for air.

Paley did the same.

Van realized they both had been suffocating in the black mud without knowing it.

Their noisy reentrance caught the attention of Brux and Jorie, who were wrestling by the tunnel wall.

He and Jorie released their hold on each other.

"Van!" Brux cried. "You're alive!" He scrambled to help Van crawl out of the black mud, tears glistened in his eyes.

Jorie dashed to help Paley. "That nitwit almost jumped in after you two. I tried to stop him."

Van and Paley hugged in relief, despite being covered in oily black mud.

"Elmot?" Brux asked.

Van and Paley lowered their heads in sorrow.

"There's no way he's alive now." Van shook her head. "He went in before us. Another few seconds and we would've suffocated to death."

Jorie bowed her head. "How did you get out?" She picked up her still-lit torch from the ground. "No one has ever survived the black mud before."

Van and Paley tried to explain about the whispers that seeped into their minds and caused their brains to rot, but neither could do it justice. Van felt sure someone who hadn't experienced it would never fully understand the lure of the whispering voices.

Paley no longer had her backpack. She had wriggled out of it while in the black mud, hoping to give herself the ability to ascend toward the surface, away from the ensnaring call of the eerie whispers.

Brux volunteered to carry Van's pack.

Jorie gave Van and Paley the okay to use the rest of their drinking water to wash the black goo off their skin, afraid it might harm them if left on.

Afterward, the surviving members of team Delta held a brief memorial service.

Van's guilt twisted in her gut over her and Paley escaping the black mud while Elmot couldn't. It made Elmot's death that much sadder for her.

Jorie remained stoic, but Van could tell she hadn't forgiven herself for her error in judgment about the black mud. Their delay in rescue had cost Elmot his life.

Van's heart ached for Jorie's pain and over the loss of another friend. She found it disturbingly ironic that Elmot had devoted his life to navigation, yet couldn't find his way out of the mud. This thought made her tears flow uncontrollably. She feared they might never stop. That grief would consume her the same way the black mud had consumed Elmot.

But they had no time to continue with their grief.

After the service, the team moved cautiously onward, down the sloping tunnel, deeper into the Caves of Wolfenden.

Chapter 47

D ay 22: Living World

THE GRANDFATHER CLOCK had chimed in Van's mind again last night, waking her from sleep. She knew another day had passed. The window to retrieve the Coin was closing fast.

The team spent the better part of their waking hours winding through the dark tunnels, the same as on previous days, except today Van glimpsed the Minotaur before anyone else. She stopped short.

"What's wrong?" Brux asked.

"T-The Minotaur." Van gasped.

Paley ducked behind Brux.

"Where?" Jorie swooshed her torch in an arc. "Where?"

"I don't see anything." Brux squinted through the darkness. "Are you sure?"

"I swear I saw it, over there." Van pointed to the entrance of an adjacent tunnel.

"I'm not going that way," Paley said.

"Follow me." Jorie guided them through a tunnel leading away from the Minotaur.

With Elmot gone, all they could do was follow the slant in the cavern floor to find the center of the labyrinth that held the Coin. When the ground remained flat, they took a chance and hoped for the best.

They trudged on for what seemed like an entire day until the tunnel widened into a small cavern. The walls, laden with mica, amplified the torch, illuminating the cavity. A plethora of fiery-red flowers burst from around a bubbling spring. A rich, intoxicating scent filled the air.

Jorie placed the torch between a crook in the wall and Brux filled the two remaining wineskins with fresh water. Van and Paley used the spring to wash off the remaining dregs of black goo.

"They're so beautiful." Paley touched one of the flower's delicate petals.

Van gaped, awed by the gorgeous array.

"I wonder how they grow here. There's no light," Brux said. "They seem unnatural to me. Be careful, Paley."

Jorie guzzled water, then used her sleeve to wipe her mouth. "They're four-petaled lotus flowers." She nudged Paley with the wineskin. "Their genus is aquatic. Maybe the mica in the walls gives them enough light to grow here."

Paley took a quick sip, then handed the pouch back to Jorie and continued examining the flowers.

Jorie sat down on a nearby rock and took another squirt of water from the wineskin, when Paley shrieked, "Oh, my gosh! I found it!"

"Found what?" Van said skeptically.

"I found—" Paley turned around, glowing. Between her thumb and index finger, she held a small gold coin the same size and color as the center of a lotus flower. "*The Coin!*"

"Let me see." Jorie reached to grab the disc.

Paley closed her hand into a tight fist. "It's *mine*! I found it. This means *I'm* the Anchoress, not Van."

"Give me the coin." Jorie extended her palm to Paley. "I need to check it, to make sure it's the real thing. That's all."

"*I* found it!" Paley said, not budging.

Jorie stood unyielding. "Don't make me take it from you."

Paley's brow furrowed. She grudgingly handed it over.

Jorie inspected the coin, turning it front to back, then shook her head. "I don't know." She handed it to Brux. "What do you think?"

Brux studied the coin. "Uh… I don't know." He handed it to Van. "You look."

Van took the coin. It appeared similar to the coin necklace Van had seen in Amaryl's vision, but lacked the finer details. Plus, they hadn't yet faced the challenge of the Minotaur. And where was Loka, the Elemental Guardian of the Coin?

However, if Van's step-mother had taught her anything over the years, it was how to tell real gold jewelry from fakes. And this coin was pure gold. It would be worth a fortune, even if it wasn't *the* Coin. Van's fingers twitched, thinking of the things she could buy. That ring she wanted, the expensive one Genie wouldn't let her get. The newest line of haute couture clothes. Pocketbooks, shoes, boots in every style and color…

A voice penetrated Van's awareness. "Evil tempts those with greed in their hearts." Ildiss had initially said it, but the words came in the voice of Jacynthia, strong enough to shake Van loose from her obsessive thoughts.

"It's not the Coin." Van held it out for Paley to take.

Paley swiped the coin from Van's hand. "Oh! You're just jealous. You can't stand the fact *I'm* special too."

"Put it back," Van demanded. "It's not ours."

Paley defiantly stuffed the coin into her pocket.

Though annoyed, Van realized Paley had attached to the lowest part of her Self: greed.

Was Paley always like this? Is this how I am? Is this why we became friends on the island?

No matter. The difference was Van had learned to overcome her darker Self during this journey. Paley obviously hadn't. The challenges the team faced brought out Van's best. For Paley, they brought out her worst.

"I agree with Van," Jorie said. "We need to leave things the way we found them."

Brux's eyes darted around the cavern. "This doesn't feel right."

The lotus flowers wilted and shriveled.

Van stiffened as her nostrils picked up a rancid stench.

A gruff, snorting sound echoed into the cavern from the tunnel.

Van pivoted toward the opening and saw it.

Glaring black eyes peered from the head of a bull, with horns thick and twisted. Its male torso looked like an experiment with steroids gone terribly wrong. Its lower half became a bull again, complete with hooves and a long tail that swished and snapped. It let out a deafening roar as it stomped into the cavern.

Paley screamed and took off in the opposite direction, followed by Jorie.

Van stood like an idiot, rooted to the ground in shock, until Brux grabbed her.

The Minotaur's unnatural body moved awkwardly, which slowed it down.

Van and the others sped through the tunnels until they could run no more.

"We should be okay." The torch Jorie carried flickered back and forth with each breath. "We've outrun it, for now."

Van leaned against the tunnel wall, catching her breath.

A rancid odor filled the air.

"It must know shortcuts through the tunnels!" Brux cried.

A blaring roar shook the tunnel walls as the Minotaur entered through a perpendicular opening a few feet away. It went directly for Paley.

She shrieked as its disturbingly human hands grabbed her. It lifted Paley high and threw her against the tunnel wall.

Jorie wedged the torch between two rocks and whipped out Zachery. She sliced the monster.

It batted Jorie aside as if she were a rag doll and let out a roar so loud it caused more debris to fall.

Van backed away, shaking. How on earth was she supposed to defeat this thing?

Brux unsheathed his dagger. He slashed the Minotaur, barely piercing its skin, making it angrier.

It swatted at Brux, who ducked and leaped out of range, but instead of going after him, it turned and went for Paley again, who remained unconscious.

Paley! Van pulled herself from her trance and rushed at the Minotaur. She flew using a koga-clava kick. As her foot crashed into the back of the Minotaur's knee, pain shot up Van's leg as if she had hit a stone wall. She thumped to the ground and heard a crunch as she landed on her hip.

The monster twisted and reached in her direction.

Before the Minotaur clutched Van, Jorie sank Zachery into its back.

Its nostrils flared as it bellowed, then turned and swiped its arm, smashing Jorie against the wall. More dust and rubble loosened, followed by rocks and stones.

The tunnel was collapsing.

"Van!" Brux yelled, his voice muffled by the crashing boulders.

Van pulled her aching body from the ground and ran from the rockslide. She took shelter in a nook until the collapse subsided, then she cautiously stepped out. She stood in complete darkness, but she could see clearly, as if her eyes had turned into a self-generating flashlight. Van felt a slight tingling in her body, like a switch had turned on an electrical connection to the magic in her bloodline. As the Anchoress, she had abilities beyond the norm and could use her flashlight eyes as a protective mechanism. She knew, in this moment, her eyes glowed violet.

The rockslide had wholly blocked the passageway. Brux, Jorie, and Paley were nowhere in sight. She didn't know where the Minotaur was, but she guessed the boulders had crushed it.

She crept over to the barrier and saw flesh—a human arm—sticking out of the bottom edge of the rubble. Van quickly scooped away the rocks.

"Jorie…" Van's voice quavered.

Jorie lay motionless, splotched in blood. Her legs were bent at unnatural angles, and her chest appeared mortally indented with no rhythmic breathing.

"Jorie!" With manic intensity, Van cleared away every stone and speck of dirt from her friend. "Jorie!"

Van clasped Jorie's head and gently turned it upward. "Jorie."

She brushed dirt from Jorie's cheeks; it turned to smudges as Van's tears dropped. She placed two fingers on Jorie's neck to feel her carotid for a pulse. There was none. "Jorie…" Van wept and cradled her friend's head in her arms.

She glimpsed Zachery's handle and pulled it from the rubble. "I'll take good care of him, your labrys. I will." She brushed away her tears. She needed to be strong for Jorie. "You can count on me."

Van heard a slight toppling of stones coming from the mound. Worried about the rest of her friends, she stood and called out, "Brux?"

Eerie silence answered.

"Paley?"

A tiny pebble tumbled from the middle of the rubble.

The hairs stood on the nape of Van's neck. She took a step backward.

A grotesque distortion of a massive human hand burst from the debris, followed by the Minotaur's horned head and colossal body. It saw Van and snorted. It traipsed toward her; the boulders in its path spilled aside like dust.

Van raced off.

The Minotaur stomped after her so hard, its hooves shook the ground.

Van twisted to calculate her lead. She stumbled and fell. A wrenching pain shot through her ankle. She scrambled to her feet and tried to get away, but her sprained ankle gave out. With this injury, she couldn't outrun the creature. She hobbled to the entrance of a nearby tunnel and hid in a natural hollow, hoping the Minotaur would pass her by.

No such luck.

When the Minotaur stopped at the tunnel's entryway, it sniffed, let out a grunt, and headed straight for Van.

The Minotaur also seemed to have flashlight eyes, and apparently a heightened sense of smell.

Van fled. Into a dead end. Trapped.

"No!" Van hacked at the dirt wall using Zachery, to no avail.

She heard snorts and the shuffling of hooves coming from behind her.

She turned to meet her fate.

The Minotaur took up most of the space in the narrow tunnel as it came plodding toward her.

Van panicked and hurled Zachery at the beast.

The labrys smacked into its chest sideways and bounced off the monster's tough skin like a pebble. It roared in annoyance and steadily lumbered forward.

That was dumb. Now I don't have a weapon.

"Everyone is provided with what they need." Jacynthia's words came to Van.

I need an army to combat this monster. And I don't have that in my pocket!

The Minotaur loomed close enough for Van to feel its rancid breath on her face. She cringed.

My pocket! She plunged her hand into her pocket and pulled out her mother's earrings. Remembering some animals liked shiny objects, she hoped the Minotaur was one of them.

As the Minotaur reached for Van, she dangled the earrings at it like a cat's toy.

It stopped, startled, then let out a livid roar and swiped at Van.

She ducked, avoiding the beast, clasping her mother's earrings so tightly, they stuck together, fitting like pieces to a puzzle.

The earrings burst into a silvery orb of light. The orb spun in Van's palm, making beautifully haunting music composed from the purest notes of peace and love.

The Minotaur dropped to its knees. Its black eyes met Van's. Tears ran down its bull-shaped cheeks as it reached out a trembling hand toward the orb.

With the beast subdued, Van could've smashed its head with a rock and taken off. Instead, her heart went out to the sad creature. She handed it the orb. A pang of regret hit her for giving away her mother's earrings, but, deep down, she knew didn't need them anymore. On this journey, she had discovered her mother had loved her, and that gift far surpassed anything material.

The creature accepted the offering, jumped up, and scurried away.

Van noticed it limping. Its leg trailed blood from an injury caused by the cave-in.

Before turning the corner, it twisted around to catch Van's attention and waved its arm. It wanted her to follow.

Van scooped up Zachery, tucked it in her belt, and hurried after the Minotaur. It led her to an opening that broke into four passageways.

The beast went down the tunnel to the far right. The dark, scary tunnel.

The other passageways beckoned, crammed with riches. One to the left contained mounds of gold and silver coins; another was filled with heaps of diamond and ruby jewelry, haute couture dresses, shoes, and designer pocketbooks.

But Van found it most difficult to turn away from the third tunnel. A portal to her bedroom at Mt. Hope Manor.

She heard a scuffle in the dark tunnel and became concerned the wounded Minotaur might need help. She decided her bedroom could wait and hurried down the tunnel after it.

Intuitively, she knew the grandfather clock in Uxa's office had struck midnight.

Another day had passed.

Chapter 48

Day 23: Living World

VAN HOPED Brux and Paley were okay as she followed the Minotaur through winding tunnels, going deeper and deeper into the bowels of the labyrinth.

It led her onto a precipice in an enormous chasm. The site looked like a snapshot from her geology textbook at school. Glowing flowstone covered the walls, and stalactites hung in beautiful formations from above. A river rumbled far below.

Glowing minerals in the cave walls dimly lit the cavern and, along with Van's flashlight eyes, allowed her to see clearly. Still, she blinked to clarify her vision. At first, she thought the Minotaur had walked across the chasm on air. Then she realized it had scuffled along a narrow strip of ground suspended across the wide opening. Light emanating from the orb revealed a camouflaged dirt bridge.

The other side of the chasm appeared so far away it made Van queasy. Her fear of heights raged, but she crept to the edge anyway and peeked down. Bad idea. Now anxiety paralyzed her.

But she had come too far to fail. Van took a deep, calming breath and swallowed her fear. Determined to follow the Minotaur, she placed a shaky foot onto the narrow strip a hair wider than her boot. Stalagmites reached upward from below, like nails in a coffin, mocking her, making sure she knew how far she would drop with one wrong step.

She watched as the lumbering Minotaur easily made its way across, its hooves unchallenged by the narrow width of the dirt bridge.

Van had to hurry if she didn't want to lose track of the Minotaur on the other side, unsure whether it would wait. She took another deep breath and repeated over and over, "I got this… I got this…"

She took a step, then another, and another. It was like walking a tightrope, a skill she had learned in her special classes. However, in her classes, the suspension hung three feet above the gym floor, not over an abyss. Still, she could do this.

Her injured ankle gave out, and she wobbled. Her arms flew to the side, and she caught her balance.

She breathed evenly. "I got this."

Then fog rolled in.

Van stopped and held steady as her vision became obscured.

A patch cleared in the fog ahead.

The bridge had widened. Paley stood there. She held the Coin. The real Coin.

"You were *wrong*," Paley said. "I have the Coin."

Van knew Paley spoke the truth.

"You can't have it. It's *mine.*" Paley wobbled.

Van wanted to say, "Be careful," but didn't. She felt nothing but hatred toward Paley and her greed.

Paley screeched as she lost her balance and tumbled. Her hands clutched the dirt bridge as her body dangled over the side, hanging in the air. "Van! Help!"

The Coin precariously balanced on the ledge, next to Paley's hand.

The bridge crumbled.

Van had time to save only one.

She dashed forward and bent down. Van grasped Paley's hand just before the dirt supporting her friend's grip broke away.

The Coin plummeted into the depths of the cavern.

The fog cleared.

It took Van a moment to realize she stood on the bridge in the same place as before the hallucination.

It was one of Loka's tests. Van shook her head to clear it. *I guess I passed.* She continued across the bridge in time to see the Minotaur disappear down one of several tunnels.

The tunnel led into a small cavern. Millions of shimmering glass shards covered the walls. *It's a mix of anhydrite and gypsum,* Van recalled learning from Elmot. A lake had formed in a natural cradle of bloodstone on the opposite side of the cavern. Reflections of the breathtaking crystal walls sparkled in its water.

Van had entered the heart of the caves. She knew this because in the center of the chasm sat a woman.

Seated serenely on an elaborate gold throne imprinted with phases of the moon, the woman wore red and gold robes and a crown of stars. She had long hair the color of ripe wheat, and her eyes reflected the same deep blue-green as the lake water behind her. A woven basket full of pomegranates lay uneaten by her feet. As Van approached, the woman's terracotta lips curved into a smile.

"Welcome, young one. I am Lady Loka, the Elemental Guardian of the Coin." Her voice held a motherly quality, rich with ancient wisdom.

"Um, h-hi," Van said, astonished by such ethereal beauty.

The Minotaur took its place beside Lady Loka and her grand throne, still holding the musical orb. Next to the Elemental, its animal features softened, making it look more human than bull.

"You are early, my child. But you have proved yourself worthy." Lady Loka paused. She and the Minotaur stared at Van, unblinking.

Van felt pressured to say something. "I-I'm sorry if I'm early.

The Alignment—Luxta—is ending, and I have to get back to Salus Valde." She sounded like a babbling fool. It would be a miracle if Lady Loka let her take the Coin.

"Many people worship the light," Lady Loka said. "And at the same time, choose to make themselves slaves to materialism. They carry out unspeakable acts in the name of the Creator to possess *things*. They do not know money and objects have no power in their own right. Our worship of material things gives them power. To combat this obsession of materialism, spirit must rise above greed."

Am I still being tested? "Agreed," Van said, hoping she would pass.

"Darkness cannot harm you unless you attach to it by giving it attention, which gives it energy. This means humanity's choices bring about evil on the physical plane and, for that reason, evil is preventable." Lady Loka paused again. "I am satisfied you have learned the cure for this Plague of Evil. That you understand the Elemental Law of Abundance, the Creator provides everyone with what they need to fulfill their spiritual destiny. When this is known, there is no need to align with darkness by giving in to fear, greed, materialism, or prejudice, and, therefore, no consequence of evil." Lady Loka gave Van a nod. "You have overcome this flaw of human nature and have passed my tests."

Van gasped, not from Lady Loka's speech, but at the Minotaur. It… *he* was now almost entirely human.

Lady Loka followed Van's gaze to the Minotaur and beamed. "He attacked your friend because she took the decoy coin, demonstrating her inability to resist the temptation of greed. For this, I am truly sorry. He only did what was in his nature. A nature bound to him by a curse cast by my jealous sister, Lilla. The Minotaur was once a handsome prince, with whom both my sister and I had fallen in love. He chose me. So my sister, out of vengeance, cast a spell, turning him into a beast. Lilla created the labyrinth around my Station of the Coin and sent him to wander endlessly in vain, searching for the correct path to me. We would be forever close, yet never together."

The story made Van's chest tighten. Her eyes welled up.

"From here, I constantly heard him moving about. My voice

resonated through the labyrinth. I kept telling him he could reach me by crossing the camouflaged bridge in the chasm. So simple. However, his bull ears muddled my words. He could hear my voice, but did not understand. For centuries, I had to listen to his moans and cries as he heard my calls. Over time, my tears accumulated into the lake you see behind me. Only someone who possesses the power of creation could undo my vengeful sister's curse. Someone able to access the power of the light. Someone such as the Anchoress."

For the first time, Van saw her Anchoress legacy as a benefit, rather than a burden. A warm, swirling sense of happiness filled her, knowing she had helped Lady Loka and her prince in such a meaningful way.

"Instead of using violence against the Minotaur, you gave him a gift of something precious to you, demonstrating your lack of corruption. The orb you so generously gave to him illuminated the bridge, and the orb's music reversed my sister's curse. As you have noticed, the Minotaur is turning back into his human form. Soon, he will become the handsome prince he once was, though our victory will be bittersweet. Being in human form, he will rapidly become his true age and turn to dust. Returning to the earth as all mortals do."

Lady Loka's unbearable sorrow caused a stream of tears to warm Van's cheeks.

"As I have said, you have proved yourself worthy and, therefore, may retrieve the Coin of Creation. It is hidden in my Lake of Tears, but I must warn you. Failure will result in your death. The choice is yours."

Van knew why Lady Loka had given her this warning. The earrings reversing Lilla's curse weren't Van's. They were her mother's. Van's father, Uxa, Ildiss, and now Lady Loka were uncertain of Van's ability to connect to the magic of her Anchoress bloodline.

Van thought differently. She had felt the power in her blood when her eyes lit the darkness. She had passed Lady Loka's tests and survived the mission so far.

She marched to the edge of the lake.

A feeling of grief emanated from the calm blue-green water and flooded Van. She shook it off and engaged her brain. The Coin lay hidden in its depths. Van had to figure out where to start and what to do. She decided to begin her search at the bottom of the lake. She stripped down to her ribbed tank top and panties.

As soon as her toe touched the water, its smooth, glassy surface grew rough and rumbled with waves. She took several steps back as the water broke and a gigantic serpent ascended from its depths. Mud slid from its sleek body, clouding the blue-green water. Its scales glittered with green and red flakes, the same color as the enormous bloodstone basin.

"The ground serpent is very protective of his lake." Lady Loka rose from her throne. She held her now-handsome prince's hand as she watched Van.

The serpent moved as gracefully as a silk scarf floating in the wind. Its forked tongue flicked at Van. For brief a second, she thought it had come across the lake to offer her a friendly greeting, but then she remembered Lady Loka's warning about retrieving the Coin. Van knew she would have to fight for it.

The serpent let out a blaring shriek. Its long jaw opened, exposing deadly fangs. It snapped at Van while the rest of its body remained concealed in the lake.

She leaped aside and rolled on the ground, losing Zachery. There were no sticks around for her to twirl. They'd be useless against the serpent, anyway. According to the Law of Abundance, she didn't need Zachery or sticks. The Creator provided her with what she needed to fulfill her spiritual destiny. So, what did she *have*?

She dodged as the serpent made another lunge. This time, it caught its fang in Van's tank top, scraping the skin on her back.

It raised its head, lifting Van into the air, where she dangled uselessly.

The monster flailed its head, attempting to flick her into its mouth.

She flapped her arms to keep from swinging and dropped a few inches as the material of her tank top gave out. She plunged to the ground, landing next to the lake.

As she hit, she heard a sickening crack and felt a sharp pain in her shoulder.

The serpent made another deadly swipe.

Van rolled away, certain the fall fractured her body in several places. She scrambled onto her bare feet, and ran, hoping the serpent couldn't leave the water.

"Dammit!" Van watched as the serpent slithered out of the lake in pursuit of her.

Her injuries slowed her. Van knew she wouldn't be able to outmaneuver it, so she stopped and grabbed the nearest thing—a rock—and hurled it at the serpent's head.

It shrieked.

"You're making him angry," Lady Loka said.

Lady Loka's words provided a hint. *Fighting the serpent gives it power.* Van needed to take away its power. How? Connect to her ancestral line, as Zane and Ildiss had said?

Van's father fought evil creatures every day. How did he do it? Van remembered the chant she had found in her father's study, the one Brux told her could kill demons. Maybe Brux had been wrong, and it wasn't for demons. Her father had done a lot of research on how to get the Coin. Perhaps the chant could defeat this serpent.

Van ran from the serpent on raw bare feet. Her weak ankle gave out, and she stumbled. The serpent moved in for the kill.

Van had nothing to lose, so she gave the chant a try. "Thrice around the circle's bound, evil sink into the ground." It didn't work. Van rolled and dodged the serpent's snapping snout. She changed the word *evil* to *serpent* and repeated it.

The third time Van shouted the chant, the serpent froze. With a poof, its body collapsed to dust, sending its scales scattering across the cavern floor. Hundreds of thousands of them. All the same color. But to Van's discerning eye, one looked different.

She picked it up.

"Congratulations, my young Anchoress." Lady Loka smiled. She continued to hold hands with her prince, who had markedly aged. "You have successfully retrieved the Coin of Creation."

Van rubbed it between her fingers to remove the reddish-green, slimy coating from its years in the lake. She crinkled her brow. It still looked nothing like Amaryl's shining gold Coin.

"It's sealed with a protective, skin-tight covering. The covering masks the Coin as an aged bronze stip, giving it the appearance of little value. The Coin is now yours, to do with it what you will. Keep in mind, young one, your lessons do not end here. Your journey has just begun."

"What'd you mean? My mission was to retrieve the Coin. Once I bring it back to Lodestar, I'm done."

"It is time for me to bid you farewell. Your retrieval of the Coin has brought my time here to an end."

Van raised her eyebrows, unsure whether she had accidentally killed Lady Loka by retrieving the Coin, or if the Elemental was merely returning to Mt. Altithronia.

"Goodbye and good luck," Lady Loka said as she and her elderly prince floated toward the ceiling and then faded away.

The cavern grumbled furiously, bringing it and the surrounding labyrinth to its final collapse.

The rip in the back of her tank top caused it to sag and slip off her shoulder. Van rushed over to her clothes. All she had time to grab were her pants. After tugging them on, she tucked the Coin into her pocket and sprinted to the nearest tunnel. She swooped down and snatched Zachery on her way out of the chamber, barely escaping the falling boulders.

She dashed down a shuddering tunnel, using her flashlight eyes to guide her, ignoring the stabbing pains from her injuries. Her bare feet flared with every pounding step.

A sense of pride filled Van for having passed Lady Loka's tests and retrieving the Coin of Creation. For the first time in her long journey, she felt confident about being able to access the power in her Anchoress bloodline.

The ground shifted violently.

Rubble crashed around her, collapsing the tunnel and burying Van in a mound of rocks and stone.

Chapter 49

Day 24: Morning hours, Living World

Van wasn't dead. She hadn't even lost consciousness. An invisible shield protected Van from the avalanche encasing her. She panicked.

I'm buried alive! How am I going to get out?

An ominous creak came from the protective bubble.

It's collapsing!

Van closed her eyes and took several calming breaths. She reached deep to grasp her inner light and said, "This is my space, given to me by the Creator. Nothing can harm me unless I let it, and I do not let it. I am safe."

She had added a new twist to the protective mantra she'd learned in her meditation class at school. The words acted to reclaim lost energy and allowed her to be fully present in her physical body, giving her control over what happened in the space around her.

The creaking stopped. The invisible force regained its strength.

A feeling of groundedness and tranquility filled Van.

The Coin! She slapped her hand against the pocket where she had hastily slipped it. The Coin was still there. As her elbow accidentally hit the edge of the bubble, it expanded, easily pushing aside the surrounding rocks.

Curious, Van stood. The bubble stretched upward as it continued to surround her, and the debris slid away to make space. She took a step forward, and the bubble moved with her, pushing aside the rocks and boulders like a bulldozer. She took another step, then another, and then burst out of the collapsed area.

Van reached out to touch the bubble. She couldn't feel anything.

Her feet vibrated from the unstable land, prompting her to get moving. She dashed through the winding tunnels, wincing as her bare feet hit the ground. She maneuvered around the fallen debris from the previous quakes and followed the open pathways.

One of the Coin's inherent magical properties was to bring luck, and it worked. Van had to stop short as she nearly crashed into Brux and Paley.

Brux wrapped his arms around Van. Paley clutched her in a vice-like hug.

"Your back is bleeding." Brux scrutinized the scrape, easily seen through her gaping tank top.

"I'm so sorry, Van. I don't know what came over me." Paley gave Van the decoy coin. "It does bad things to me. I don't want it anymore."

Van couldn't risk anyone else picking up the solid gold decoy coin and suffering its adverse effects, in case there were any. She slipped it into her pocket.

Before Brux fully inspected Van for injuries, she broke the sad news to them about Jorie's death caused by the tunnel collapse.

Brux kept a stiff upper lip. Paley sobbed.

"You saved Zachery. Jorie would be happy about that." Brux's voice cracked.

He said a prayer for Jorie's spirit to have a safe journey as it made its way to the light and back into the arms of the Creator. Then, all three held one another and cried.

Brux was uninjured, mostly, but Paley felt drained and sweaty from a wound on her thigh caused by the Minotaur. Brux had made a tourniquet out of a piece of rope to keep her from bleeding out.

Now, though battered from her struggle with the serpent and still exhausted from the gemstones, Van proudly showed her injuries to a worried, hovering Brux.

He tended to her wounds as best he could, given their limited supplies. He tied the back of her tank top together and even destroyed their one remaining backpack to make Van a pair of temporary shoes out of its material.

Then, they stuffed some of the backpack's items into their pockets. Brux tucked Zachery into his belt and used their only torch to light the way, although they didn't know where they were going. Van and Brux took turns supporting Paley as she hobbled, putting weight on her good leg.

Along the way, Van filled them in on Lady Loka, the Minotaur, who had turned out to be a handsome prince, and the deadly ground serpent that hid the Coin. Van didn't tell them about the mysterious invisible bubble that had saved her life. It sounded too ridiculous for them to believe her.

"Mission accomplished," Brux said.

Paley cheered meekly.

"Not yet," Van said, acutely aware time was slipping away. They needed to get the Coin back to Uxa to stop the Balish invasion of Salus Valde before midnight of the next full moon.

"I don't think Solana is after the Coin for its magical power. That's a Lodian belief unsupported by the Balish Council," Brux said. "It's unusual for a female heir to be allowed to take the throne. I think her only aim is to take over Salus Valde so she can prove her worth to the Council."

"She knows from reading Manik's text the Coin can't be used against other humans," Van agreed. "How does she plan to use it, then?"

"Solana doesn't want the Lodians to have it," Brux said. "In our hands, it gives us the power to defeat demons, satisfying the Elemental ruling that our Grigori can protect the Living World. Manik's law will remain in place, and the Elementals won't allow Solana to attack Salus Valde."

"So, she's running around searching for the Coin, all to impress her father?" Van hated to admit it, but she could relate to that.

Their conversation ended, and they trudged on through maze-like tunnels that Van swore had been forged from the rocks of hell. Every so often, they came across Elmot's stone piles, but the vibrations from the earthquakes had scattered them, so they held no clues about navigation. The trio wandered through tunnel after tunnel, coming across rockslides and dead ends.

"This is hopeless." Paley unhooked her arm from around Van's shoulders and slid to the ground, drained.

"We have to keep trying." Brux held the torch high and pointed to one of several openings. "I don't think we've tried this one yet."

"We already went that way," Paley said wearily.

"Are you sure?" Brux asked. "Van, do you remember?"

"Um." She had no idea. She needed rest too, but also wanted to escape the endless tunnels. *Figures.* She'd survived retrieving the Coin, only to end up dying while she tried to find her way out of the caves. Just her luck.

Luck! She pulled the Coin from her pocket. One of its inherent magical properties was to bring the holder luck. Maybe it worked better without the protective coating. Using pressure, Van rubbed the Coin between her thumb and forefinger. The covering shifted, revealing the startling gold Coin beneath. Five triangles on the Coin's face intertwined to form an ancient sacred symbol, exactly like Amaryl's Coin.

"Van!" Brux strode over to her. "What are you doing? Don't use it."

"I'm not. I just wanted to see if opening it would bring us magical luck."

The tunnels rumbled again.

"This area is dangerously unstable," Brux said. "We have to find a way out."

The vibration caused Van's finger to brush against the exposed Coin. She felt dizzy… detached. *Oh no!* She tried to hold herself in the present and couldn't.

Van heard Brux cry her name in the distance as she was pulled back to another time…

Van caught the fresh scent of pine.

Amaryl fled through the woods of Tipereth clutching a newborn baby in her arms. Rowen, Romet and his wife Regina Lake, rushed along with her.

Regina, Amaryl and Zurial's first cousin and closest friend, Romet, and Rowen had accompanied Amaryl to Balefire Palace for the birth of Zurial's child.

A time of joy had turned to one of terror as Goustav and his followers massacred all opposition in the palace. Amaryl could not use the Coin against them without causing damage to her soul, so she used it for direction to escape.

Amaryl touched her neck and gasped. "I have lost the Coin!"

She stopped and handed Zurial's baby, Mehal, to Regina. Amaryl dropped and frantically ran her hands over the ground. "It is gone." She stood and clutched her husband's shoulders. "I must go back. I need to retrace my steps and find it."

"We do not need the Coin," Rowen said. "We can find our way back to Lodestar without it."

"Goustav will come after Manik's baby," Romet said. "We must keep going."

"We never should have taken Mehal," Regina said as the baby fussed in her arms. "The little one has put us in danger."

"Amaryl, my love." Rowen clasped his hands around hers. "Your obsession with the Coin will kill us all. We must let it go. The Elementals can retrieve it from the forest later."

"You go ahead. I am going back." Amaryl turned away from him.

"I will not leave your side," Rowen said to his wife, then he twisted toward Romet and Regina. "Go. Save yourselves and the baby."

They didn't argue and sprinted away deeper into the woods.

Amaryl retraced her steps through the trees, inspecting every inch of the path for her shiny gold Coin.

Rowen followed, his sword drawn.

"The Coin is close. I can feel it." Amaryl took small steps as she studied the ground.

Branches snapped and cracked as something came crashing toward them with unnatural speed.

Amaryl and Rowen turned to face it, knowing it could not be outrun.

Rowen protectively stepped in front of Amaryl, his sword raised.

A beast slid from the shadows of the forest as if darkness itself had taken on the shape of a wolf-like creature. Terrible and growling, its red eyes glared. Its deadly fangs dripped with saliva as it snarled and spit. Its massive clawed paws impatiently gouged into the earth, as if it longed for something to rip apart.

The shadow beast leaped forward, its red eyes locked on Amaryl.

Rowen and his sword were no match for the hellish creature. Its claws effortlessly tore through his tunic, ripping apart his soft human skin.

Amaryl screamed in horror as her heart broke from sorrow. Thoughts flashed through her mind. Of her never returning the Coin to the Elementals after the Dark War ended... using the Coin for her personal gain... taking the baby Mehal... refusing to leave the Coin in the woods for retrieval by the Elementals...

She realized too late that greed had consumed her... that she had succumbed to the Coin's corruption.

Her folly had resulted in the death of her husband. She should have listened to the others and not turned back. Amaryl's crushing regret made it difficult for her to breathe.

The shadow beast, now done with Rowen, turned its attention to Amaryl.

Flecks of Rowen's bloody flesh dripped from its fangs. It snarled and advanced toward Amaryl.

She feared not even the light could protect her from such a creature. Resigned to her fate, she stared into its vile red eyes.

It pounced to claim its prey.

A flash of fiery rope encircled the creature mid-flight, binding the maddened beast and anchoring it to the ground.

Amaryl rushed to her husband's dead body, not even glancing at her rescuer. She wept, then wiped her eyes and turned to greet her savior.

Her stomach dropped.

Before her stood Prince Goustav, surrounded by a handful of his bloodthirsty men on horseback.

The familiar unwilling physical attraction to Goustav stirred within her, despite her venomous hatred of him. Revulsion, not gratitude, churned inside her.

"Looking for something?" Goustav casually flipped the Coin and caught it in his palm.

Amaryl's frustration grew as he lustfully gazed at her body.

His lips tilted into an arrogant smile.

Amaryl tried to resist the lure of the tiny gold object, but longing for the Coin soon replaced her repulsion for Goustav. Her mind spun with crafty ways of getting it back. She didn't want the Coin. She needed *it.*

Goustav stopped flipping the Coin and slipped it into his tunic pocket.

He sauntered over to Rowen's mutilated body. "So sorry about your husband." He nudged the lifeless body with the toe of his boot. Not sorry at all.

With that careless gesture, something snapped inside Amaryl. The love she felt for her husband surged inside her and released Amaryl from her fixation on the Coin.

"Where is the baby Mehal?" Goustav asked.

"Safe." She would never help this man find the baby.

Where is the baby?" Goustav asked more forcefully.

Two of his men grabbed Amaryl and held her by the arms.

Several of Goustav's men broke through the brush on horseback. One of them carried baby Mehal and said, "They left him alone in the woods, my king. We found him not far down the path."

The sting of betrayal burned in Amaryl's gut. Romet and Regina must have left Mehal behind to ensure they would get away, figuring Goustav would not pursue them if they gave up the baby.

Satisfied, Goustav pulled out the Coin and began flipping it again. "We seem to be finding many things in these woods. The Coin… the baby… the Lodian queen." Flip… flip. "What would you do to get this back, my pet?" Flip… flip. "It can be yours once again. I will gladly give it to you."

Amaryl held steady, remaining stoic.

The hideous shadow beast continued to strain against its fiery constraints, growling and snapping. Never taking its deadly eyes off Amaryl.

"I will give you everything you could ever hope for, anything you desire," said Goustav. "Once Manik hands me his throne, which he will, I will officially take

my place as king, raise my brother's son, and rule with mercy and greatness. With you at my side, my Balish queen."

He stopped flipping the Coin and closed it in his fist.

Amaryl lifted her eyes to meet his.

"There is no longer any reason for you to deny me this, now that you are widowed. Come, it is time for you to show respect to your future husband and king. Kneel to me."

Amaryl's outward demeanor remained serene. Inside, grief and bitterness rose, mixing to create intense fury. Amaryl strolled toward Goustav as if to kneel. Instead, she spat in his face.

"I will never kneel to you!" Amaryl's lips twisted with rage as she spoke in ancient tongues, conjuring a spell. She cursed Goustav's bloodline, making him unable to conceive children, and vowed he would live a doomed half-life, one of loneliness and pain.

Goustav sniggered and wiped her spittle from his face.

His men guffawed along with him.

"You are upset now, my pet. That is understandable. Women are of weak constitution, after all. There is plenty of time for us to get to know each other better. With the death of your husband, you are now free to be my bride."

Amaryl's inner storm raged. She thought of her baby hidden away on Providence Island, being cared for by the Grigori. She had taken great pains to conceal her pregnancy from the Balish. If… no, when Goustav discovered their daughter, Astrid, the Anchoress heir, she feared how he would react.

With her baby in danger, Amaryl knew what she must do.

"Take her back to Balefire, put her in my chambers. I will take care of the shadow beast." Goustav turned his back on Amaryl to collect his prized war staff from his horse.

Amaryl pulled a hidden dagger from inside her robes and lunged at Goustav.

By pure warrior's instinct, Goustav must have sensed an impending attack. He swung around, ready for battle, his deadly war staff raised, perhaps even suspecting the shadow beast had somehow broken free.

Amaryl, in a frenzied intent to kill Goustav, accidentally plunged into the sharp tip of his war staff. Her eyes widened in surprise as the staff punctured her delicate skin, glided into her chest, and went straight through her heart.

Goustav and Amaryl stood face-to-face one last time.

Blood dribbled from the sides of Amaryl's mouth.

A flicker of pain and remorse flashed in Goustav's eyes; the same sense of regret surged within Amaryl.

The horrible shadow beast struggled against its bindings, making one last attempt to break free, snapping and growling until the light faded from Amaryl's eyes. Then, after her death, it quieted and sank into the earth, back to the bowels of darkness from which it had come.

VAN SNAPPED TO THE PRESENT. Her eyes sprang open, and she shot upright.

"Holy crap!" What the hell was that thing? A piece of darkness, for sure, but it was so… *personal*. Van trembled. She never wanted to encounter the shadow beast in real life.

Besides that, she was such a dope! One of the Coin's magical properties was revealing the correct path. *Duh!* She smacked herself on the forehead.

Brux frowned. "Do you feel okay?"

Brux and Paley had become used to Van's fainting spells and had patiently waited for her to regain consciousness.

"You were out for a while this time," Paley said.

"Memory engram, right?" Brux asked.

Van nodded. "I know how to get us out of here." She hopped to her feet, unafraid to use the magical properties of the Coin anymore. As long as she heeded Amaryl's warning and used the Coin responsibly, she'd be okay.

"I'm going to use the Coin to get us out of the caves *only*, and not for a second longer," Van said.

Her teammates agreed. She picked up the Coin from ground, fully removed its protective coating, and tucked the covering into her pocket. Then she cupped hands, shook the Coin, and slapped it onto the back of her left hand as if playing heads or tails. The lines of the pentagram faded, leaving one isosceles triangle that pointed in the best direction.

The three of them marched onward. Until they came to a fork.

Van took out the Coin, ready to shake it again when she noticed it had automatically turned in her palm to show the correct way.

She didn't need to shake the Coin like game dice after all. Her cheeks reddened with the blush of a fool.

As Van led them through the tunnels, she relayed Amaryl's story to Brux and Paley.

"Amaryl used the Coin to find Manik's baby, Mehal, so she could steal him, keeping him from Goustav," Brux said. "I guess the Coin gives only physical direction, not inner direction."

"Manik hid the Coin the way he did, not just because the Anchoress has to be worthy enough to wield its power," Van said. "But she has to be strong enough to put it back when she's done with it. Using its power too often, even its inherent magical abilities, can corrupt the user. This was Amaryl's message."

"She gave value to an object," Brux said. "More than she valued herself or the safety of those she loved. Manik was right. We create our own evil through incorrect actions."

"I saw Amaryl curse Goustav." Van shivered down to her bones. "She made him unable to have children and doomed him to a life filled with loneliness and pain."

"So he never had an heir," Brux said. "Puts that rumor to rest."

"What about that horrible shadow wolf-thingy? What's that all about?" Paley asked weakly, as if she were barely hanging on to consciousness. Brux propped her up, and Paley plugged along as best she could.

"I don't know." Van shuddered. "And I never want to find out."

Within a couple of hours, they made it to the outer granite caves. They rounded a corner, and faint light from the evening sky flooded the tunnel.

Van reattached the Coin's protective covering and tucked it into her pocket.

Brux snuffed out the torch.

Paley seemed unusually quiet and extremely pale.

"Are you all right?" Van peered at her friend.

"Yeah, I'm fine. Let's get out of here." Paley attempted to walk toward the light on her own, took a few steps, weaved, and then dropped to the ground, unconscious.

Van and Brux rushed to her.

"I think she has internal injuries." Brux knelt beside Paley. "She needs medical care."

"The closest town is Araquiel," Van said, her nerves on edge.

"We can get to Araquiel *and* make it back to Lodestar in time." Brux tenderly picked up Paley and draped her over his shoulder.

"Especially if I use the Coin to guide us," Van said. Using the Coin to find medical help for Paley, or to determine the fastest way back to Lodestar were both correct uses.

They headed toward the long-awaited exit.

With high hopes, Van and Brux stepped from the dark cave into the dusky evening light.

A familiar sultry voice greeted them. "Well, well, well. If it isn't the little Anchoress and her ragtag crew."

Solana stood, hands on hips, flanked by a squadron of Royal Balish Soldiers.

Her lips curled into a cunning smile. "I've been waiting for you."

Chapter 50

Day 24: Evening, Living World

"Nice shoes." Solana glanced at Van's feet, still covered with torn pieces of the backpack.

Seeing Solana was like a punch in the stomach.

The Balish princess answered their unspoken question. "Your hairbrush. I cast a locator spell using your hair. I've been tracking you since the border checkpoint."

Van surveyed the soldiers, searching for her father.

Brux laid Paley on the ground, careful not to make any sudden movements that would alarm the edgy soldiers. One moved in and relieved Brux of his dagger and Zachery.

"Don't look so surprised," Solana said. "That's when I saw Vanessa's eyes flash, giving me confirmation she is Michael's daughter, the Anchoress-in-waiting. You should've joined me then. Your journey would've been much easier."

"We would never accept your help," Brux growled.

"Really?" Solana drawled. "What made you head north at the Salus Valde-Tipereth border? Me. Even with the map, you tried to head south like team Echo." Solana snorted in disgust and then faced Van. "Michael and I knew Uxa would send you to retrieve the Coin after we killed my brother."

"You just admitted to bringing demons here." Van pointed her finger at Solana. "It wasn't the fault of the Grigori!"

Solana shrugged in acknowledgment and continued. "It was inevitable we would find you. And I did at the border checkpoint. When you refused to join me, I let you escape. Then I closed the border, so you had to go north from Araquiel. I even sent the double-crossing Tarcs to rescue your pathetic group from the trolls in Fomalhaut. Without my help, you bumbling idiots would have never retrieved the Coin." She stretched out her hand. "Now, give it to me."

"Let me talk to my father!" Van squirmed as a soldier grabbed her. "Where is he?"

"Where's Daisy?" Brux also struggled against a couple of soldiers.

Solana flashed her palm.

The soldiers stood down.

Solana's golden eyes turned to Brux. "Of course. You're Daisy's brother. Poor, simple Daisy. My cousin Merloc is taking care of her, holding her prisoner in the dungeons at Balefire. As you know, he can be quite… *merciless.* The rest of her pathetic team didn't survive his interrogation, I'm told. But he took a fancy to Daisy and kept her alive. I'm sure the two of them are having *fun.*"

Brux snarled and lunged for Solana.

Four of her soldiers tackled him.

Solana watched. Her lips curved upward in a smile.

"A-And my father?" Van shook from fear and anger.

"Let me tell you about your father." Solana started her predatory pacing. "He spent all his time fighting demons in the Earth World. For what? There's no cure for terrigens' greed. They will never learn. Breeding like a virus, thriving on violence and war. They exude energy so negative it creates demons. It wasn't hard for me to convince him terrigens are a *disease*, a threat to our world, and, by extension, so are the Lodians for protecting them. Especially the Grigori."

"I-I don't understand," Van said.

"Of course, you don't! You're dimwitted, just as your father tells me." Solana stopped pacing and faced Van. "He brought demons here under my command because he shares my vision of clean, peaceful worlds. Both of us believe a decimation of terrigens is in order."

"The negativity created by slaughtering terrigens will cause the destruction of both worlds." Brux fumed. "Demons will gain the energy to rise. It will cause Dishora!"

"Pfft. A Lodian belief."

"Is that why you want the Coin?" Van asked. "To get rid of the terrigens?"

Brux clenched his fists.

"I am a skilled sorceress," Solana bragged. "That, along with my militia, gives me enough power to take control of Salus Valde and the Earth World. Unfortunately, I couldn't kill my brother or repeal Manik's law without using demons, which triggered the retrieval of the Coin."

"Getting the Coin… it was nothing more than a repercussion from your plans to take over the kingdom?" Brux said, his jaw agape.

"Devon was difficult to kill," Solana said. "My mother, out of love for her *son*, used her sorcery to bind herself to Devon with a protection spell. When I discovered this, I saw it as an opportunity to take over Salus Valde. You see, this spell of my mother's kept my brother out of harm's way. No matter which way I tried to get rid of him, luck, chance, circumstance would intervene and save his life. Which is why I couldn't use my magic to simply drop a boulder on his head. My mother had connected to the universal energy of love to create protective magic for my brother. Love's source is the light. So, I had to use the light's opposing force to break it. Darkness. Demon help. It was the only way."

"That's where my father came in," Van murmured.

"So when Devon died, my mother died along with him. I was simply protecting my right to have what I deserve."

"Your brother deserved to be murdered?" Brux said through gritted teeth.

"I went to great lengths to make sure my brother's death didn't look like fratricide, so I could successfully position myself as the Balish heir. By taking over Salus Valde, I would earn my place on the throne, something I needed to do as the first female heir to the Balish kingdom. This would prevent my male relatives, like my cousin Merloc and my brother Ferox, from challenging my right to the throne, from trying to take my power simply because I had the poor taste of being born female. Nobody takes my power!"

"You thought Devon was taking your power by being between you and the throne?" Van asked. "You *killed* your own brother?"

"*I* am the firstborn, not Devon!" Solana beat her fist against her chest. "The throne is rightfully mine. When I allow Michael to rule Salus Valde, he will give me access to the portal, and I will have the Grigori decommissioned. Uxa and the rest will be out of a job. Only one thing prevents me from completing my plan. Give me the Coin!"

"Let's put the Coin aside and fight warrior to soldier," Brux growled. "We'll see who's more powerful."

"I am," Solana said. "I don't need the Coin to prove it."

"You must know the Coin's power can't be used against people," Van said. "Why do you want it, then? Unless you don't care about the consequences—"

"*I* don't want the Coin, you imbecile," Solana said impatiently. "The demons didn't help us for the fun of it, although powerful demons *do* like killing people. We made a deal with the master demon and must surrender the Coin as payment. Then the master demon will destroy it."

Van realized the master demon and Solana had similar agendas. The master demon would get the Coin so it can destroy an item of light, one that can kill demons. While Solana gets rid of an ancient relic that would continue Manik's law, preventing her takeover of Salus Valde.

Solana calmly faced Van. "I will make you an offer. Give me the Coin, and I will protect the terrigens and let you go."

Ever since Van's required field trips off island, she had disliked the mainlanders—the *terrigens*—even before she knew they generated demons. Solana was right about the people of the Earth World. They would never comprehend the Law of Abundance. Van could relate to her father's point of view. Still, she couldn't condone the mass murder of terrigens.

"If we don't pay our debt, the master demon will consume our souls," Solana said. "Your father and I will suffer a fate worse than death."

"Van! You're not actually..." Brux said in an incredulous tone.

Van considered Brux naive to believe they could defeat an entire squadron of Royal Balish Soldiers, and Paley hovered near death. Making a deal was the best option. Amaryl had made a deal to bring peace to the lands by allowing her sister to marry Manik. Now, as the Anchoress, Van had a duty to act in her people's best interests and to save her father's soul. Maybe the Coin should be destroyed. After learning about Amaryl's story, Van surmised the Coin had too much power for mortals to use responsibly. If they lived in harmony, no one would ever need to use the Coin, anyway.

"I want to talk to my father." Van needed to make sure her father would be a just and fair ruler before she gave up the Coin. "I want him to tell me the terrigens will be safe, and no harm will come to the people of Salus Valde under his rule."

"Van!" Brux cried. "Are you crazy? Solana is lying! She—"

Solana's vicious laugh cut Brux off.

It set off Van's internal alarm. "My father's not here, is he? What have you done with him?"

"You will see your father soon enough." Solana waved her hand at one of her men. "I didn't want it to come to this."

The soldier hustled forward and placed a small metal box dotted with holes at Solana's feet.

"Well, maybe I did," Solana drawled.

Van heard a weak chirrup come from the box. A surge of terror coursed through her. "No." Van jerked her head back and forth in denial.

"I could have you searched." Solana grinned. "But I can't take the Coin from you. You must give it to me willingly. My ancestor Manik hid the Coin so well that for you to have retrieved it, you had to be aligned to the good part within your Self. It means the Coin is connected to the power of the light. I have not yet found a spell to make myself immortal, so its vibration is too high for someone who conspires with demons. You must surrender the Coin to me, and by doing so, you will surrender your light. This will neutralize the Coin's vibration so I can touch it. Then I will hand over the Coin to the master demon."

Brux opened his mouth to say something.

Solana raised her palm to stop him.

"No tricks," Solana said.

Wiglaf mewled as a soldier pulled him from the metal pet carrier.

Van's little bunfy trembled. She had never felt so helpless in her life. Her eyes widened as Solana pulled a long, thin blade from her sleek, knee-high boot.

Van shook, unable to breathe. "N-No."

"Our little chat has been lovely," Solana said. "However, we must move on. This is your last chance to disconnect from your light and give me the Coin."

Van recalled Manik's text warning her not to surrender her light, and she didn't care.

She had decided to give Solana the Coin, when Solana said, "Too late."

Her blade oozed red with Wiglaf's blood.

The high-pitched screams of the bunfy being skinned alive sounded like those of a tortured child. The sound of evil tearing through innocence. For Van, nothing would ever be right in the world again. She dropped to her knees, gagging.

Brux's hand quivered as he grasped Van by the elbow. He gently pulled her to her feet and whispered in a strained voice, "Lilla will seek revenge over the wrongful death of one of her magical animals. Solana will pay for this.”

A flash of red and white flew as Solana tossed the bunfy skin at Van’s feet. She chucked the carcass aside.

Bile rose in the back of Van’s throat.

Solana strolled to where Paley lay unconscious. “Now… neutralize the Coin and it hand over.” She held the point of her bloody blade to Paley’s jugular. “Or watch your friend *die*.”

After seeing Solana kill Wiglaf, Van knew she would also kill Paley. “*Stop!*”

Van reached into her pocket. She had no time to fumble around, trying to determine the real Coin by touch, so she pulled out her pocket’s contents. Two coins. One, shiny gold; the other a dull, aged b-stip. Van turned out her palm and held the two coins for Solana to choose.

Solana slid her lethal blade into her boot, blood and all, and meandered over to Van, her chin in the air. “People *always* bend to my will.”

Without hesitation, Solana snatched the gold coin. She squinted, holding the coin between the thumb and forefinger of her gloved hand, and raised it in the waning evening light for a better look.

Van held her breath.

Solana broke into a slow, satisfied grin. “Thanks for retrieving it for me.” She tucked the coin into the hip pocket of her obscenely tight black pants. The spark of excitement in her golden eyes clouded. “Kill them!” she said so emphatically spit flew from her mouth.

Van, still in shock over losing Wiglaf, barely noticed as two soldiers grabbed her. They shook her. Back and forth. Back and forth…

What’s that earsplitting noise?

“Landslide!” yelled a soldier.

Van cringed and raised her arms to protect her head as stones and dust came tumbling down.

Chapter 51

D ay 24: Late night, Living World

The soldiers scattered.

A mass of boulders, rocks, and granite roared downward as if the mountain had imploded.

Van grasped through the falling dust, reaching for Brux, and felt a wooden handle. She reflexively wrapped her fingers around it and pulled back, clutching Zachery.

She glimpsed Brux making a dash for Paley, as a black mass hurtled toward Van, knocking her backward into the cave.

Van thumped to the ground, winded.

She smelled jasmine as her throat tightened, making it hard for her to breathe.

Solana straddled Van. She wrapped her hands around Van's neck, strangling her.

"It seems your luck's run out," Solana drawled.

Van yanked Solana's hair to pull Solana off of her.

The cracked ground underneath them shuddered and then gave way.

She and Solana crashed to the bottom of a cavern, splitting apart.

A sharp pain ran through Van's chest. It hurt to breathe, probably from more cracked ribs. She rolled onto her feet, saw Zachery several yards away, and snatched the labrys, ready to face Solana.

The two circled each other, crouched in defensive stances.

Solana tried to hide a limp. "You want the Coin back?" Solana snarled, her pretty face now ugly to Van. "This isn't Providence Island. Nothing will be handed to you here. You'll have to earn it!"

"How do you know about Providence Island?" Van strained to hold Zachery in one hand. It was much heavier than it looked.

"Your father told me, idiot." Solana lunged for Van.

Van leaped away from Solana's reach, ignoring the pain in her sprained ankle, and carefully dodging the surrounding sinkholes.

"You make me sick," Solana taunted. "Your bloodline gives you the power to rule your people, and you're too stupid to use it. You're a princess. *Royalty*. You have a right to your throne, just like I do."

Van snarled. "You don't know me." Her ribs howled in pain as she used both hands to swing Zachery in a wide arc at Solana.

Solana easily dodged the swipe. "*You* barely know you." She swung her fist at Van, catching her on the chin.

Van spat blood. "I know I'm the Anchoress." She swiped Zachery and nicked Solana's injured leg with its blade.

Solana cried out in pain and thudded to the ground. "Your mother handed that to you," she said, gritting her teeth from pain and anger. "It's just another thing you didn't earn."

Solana attempted to stand. Van kicked her back down. They teetered dangerously close to the edge of an enormous sinkhole on the cavern floor.

Van straddled Solana and held the labrys's handle across Solana's throat.

"The Lodian Consilium is holding you back," Solana said in a strained voice. "Forcing you to hide your power because they *fear* it."

"Let's see how you like it." Van pushed the handle deeper into

Solana's throat. "Tell me where my father is! Why won't he see me?"

"Your father hates you. Hates all Lodians." Solana's lip curled. "He blames you for killing your mother. If you hadn't been born, Aelia would've survived. That's what he always said."

"What do you mean, *said?*" Van gripped the handle tighter.

"Oops. Picked up on the past tense, did we?" Solana's words came out in a croak, yet she kept grinning. "Your father is *dead.*"

Van's body went numb, loosening her grip. Brux had been right all along. No wonder she hadn't seen her father on their journey.

Solana took advantage of Van's stunned reaction. Not as injured as she had pretended, Solana easily flipped Van over the side of the sinkhole.

Van instinctively swung Zachery, digging its blade into the side of the cliff.

She continued to slide downward, dangling from Zachery. Van jerked as the blade caught on an outcropped rock. Then she maneuvered herself onto a nearby ledge.

"The master demon appeared to your father in the Earth World, letting him know it was time to enact our plan by stealing Manik's text," Solana yelled over the side of the sinkhole. "He went through with it because you're so *incompetent.* Useless. Weak. Nobody wants you. Just give up. Jump." The wily sorceress stomped her foot, causing the sinkhole to shake.

Van wobbled and clutched the wall. Once steady, she checked to make sure she still had the Coin. Her pocket was empty! Did she lose it during her fall into the cavern? Van tried to locate the Coin intuitively but couldn't. Apparently, her locator instinct had turned off after she had retrieved it.

"The mighty and powerful Anchoress. Dumb enough to surrender your light when you gave me the Coin." Solana's voice carried down to Van. "Not so powerful now, are you?" Solana dropped an item over the side.

Manik's text whizzed past Van.

"You're next." Solana stomped her foot again.

The ledge beneath Van's feet crumbled. She flattened herself against the wall.

"Your father brokered a deal with demons on my behalf." Solana cruelly chuckled. "Then I worked with the master demon behind his back. Your father died for me the night he lured my brother into the woods. Now you will too. There's no escape. Fall!" She stomped her foot again.

Van gripped the wall to hold herself steady on the shaking ledge. Hearing Solana casually speak about how she murdered Van's father sickened Van.

"He had to be killed during the attack," Solana continued. "He knew too much from reading Manik's text, and he was Uxa's right-hand man. This made him too powerful."

"You were paranoid he would betray you," Van cried. "The same way you betrayed him!"

"I never planned on sharing my rule, especially not Salus Valde," Solana bellowed. "Michael knew how to fight demons, so he didn't die right away. He became mortally wounded. Your father lived long enough to carry out my plan of destroying the text. You know, the one that confirms Goustav has an heir. But he screwed up, putting the text directly into Lodian hands. My worst nightmare."

Now, it made sense to Van why Solana had kept Manik's text in Araquiel, despite needing Van to retrieve the Coin. The Balish princess had worked too hard to get it. She wasn't about to give it away. Solana had confidence Van could retrieve the Coin using her intuition, along with Solana's secret help.

"You said Goustav doesn't have an heir," Van hollered.

"My, you are dimwitted." Solana stomped her foot again, harder this time.

The ledge trembled and dislodged an arrowhead at Van's feet. It pointed to a small accumulation of dirt, as if Trey had given her a hint from the beyond. Curious, Van bent down, brushed away the pile, and found... *the Coin!* It must've fallen out of her pocket when she climbed onto the ledge.

It had powerful magical abilities, and Van had magical warrior blood, but she didn't know how to access either to create magic.

Maybe it would've helped if she had paid more attention in school. With a pang, she remembered Elmot and his mock topography class. Hadn't he told her these caves comprised a network of interconnected tunnels?

She ran her hand along the dirt wall of the sinkhole and realized it wasn't as thick as she had thought.

One portion gave out. Van pushed again and again.

Solana stomped her foot one more time, and the ledge beneath Van's feet gave way, just as she stepped into an opening on the side of the cliff.

She followed the tunnel, which dripped with moisture from a huge cenote above.

As Van made her way through the passage, she processed Solana's confession.

Solana and the master demon had recruited Van's father and used him to construct the perfect plan. Her father knew demons were coming to kill Prince Devon and trusted Solana would use her magic to control them. When the demons attacked him, he figured Solana was wrong about her magic being powerful enough to control demons. In reality, once Van's father had stolen the text, Solana no longer needed him.

Van recalled her vision in the bushes outside Mt. Hope Manor. When she saw her father toss Manik's text into the fire, he had said, "Let us hope… no Lodian… ever lays a hand on this." By burning Manik's text, he'd ensured Solana would have no competition in retrieving the Coin, and so anti-Manikists wouldn't get traction by having evidence confirming Goustav's heir. Her father had believed in Solana's agenda and destroyed Manik's text to protect Solana's throne.

Van felt sick to her stomach by this truth. She continued to follow the tunnel, which led only one way back to the surface of the cavern.

She emerged on the far side, across from Solana, who peered over the side of the sinkhole, checking to make sure Van had dropped to her death. Solana had her back to Van. Big mistake.

Lesson 101 in her special classes. Never turn your back on the enemy.

Van tiptoed toward Solana. Then paused. Could she really push a human being off a cliff?

A crow flew overhead, landed on Solana's shoulder, and chattered into her ear as if telling her a secret. Solana abruptly turned toward Van, seething. She slid two fingers into those skintight pants, pulled out the decoy coin, and flung it to the ground.

The crow flew away.

Solana's nostrils flared in anger. "I want the *real* Coin!"

The crow must be her familiar, spying from the sky and revealing secrets like a tattletale. Van took out the Coin, hoping to intimidate Solana.

Solana threw Van a lopsided grin. "Even if you knew how to access its magical power, you can't use it against me."

"Don't you see how you're playing into the master demon's hands?" Van tucked the Coin back into her pocket. "The master demon wanted you to destroy Manik's text, an instruction manual on how to kill demons. It also wants the Coin destroyed, an item of light that can eliminate demons. You're being coerced to create more violence in the Earth World. Killing terrigens will give demons more energy to breed and the strength to rise. This master demon is using you to bring about Dishora!"

"There you go, spouting those Lodian beliefs again." Solana shook her head in disgust. "Just because I dabble in dark magic doesn't mean I like demons," she said, affronted. "Once I take over Salus Valde, I will prevent Solmor, the rise of demons generated from the terrigens. I'll assign the duties of the Grigori to my militia so they can keep demons under control in the Earth World. Fewer terrigens equal fewer demons. Decimating the terrigens will take power *away* from the master demon and, given the strength of this demon, it needs to be done."

It unnerved Van to see Solana so threatened by the master demon's power. Solana was all about control, and this master demon had a lot of control over Solana. Until she made her payment.

"Our Grigori will stop you," Van said.

"Lodians won't stand a chance against my Balish army in a war for Salus Valde. That's why Uxa is so desperate to keep Manik's law intact."

"How can you be sure this master demon will destroy the Coin?" Van asked, changing tactics. "The Coin will amplify the dark part of the demon's Self. It will turn the Coin into an item of darkness. This demon will then have the power to destroy the light of all the worlds. It will be unstoppable!"

"Nice try, but sorry. Nope," Solana said. "Demons can't connect to the Coin's power because demons do not have a Self, you dimwit. Even with the Coin neutralized, it's still an item of light made by the Creator. The Coin will do nothing but bring out the master demon's true nature of darkness. It will become enraged and seek to destroy the Coin, not use it."

"My father would never have helped you with that plan," Van said, certain of Solana's insanity.

"Enough! *Give me the Coin.*" She paused, then Solana's eyes grew distant. "Screw it." She lowered her head and stretched out her arms, palms down, and began chanting.

Van recognized the ancient language, but Solana mumbled too fast for Van to catch any of the words.

Spots of dirt on the cavern floor swirled.

Van smelled sulfur.

Chapter 52

Day 25: Early morning, Living World

"Now, you'll meet the same fate as your father," Solana said.

Lumps rose from the ground, taking the form of overlarge humanoid mud creatures. They looked like the monsters from the Native Island Legends storybook Van had seen in her father's study.

She sprinted toward a tunnel opening.

An earth demon rose in her path.

It swatted Van with its club-like arm, knocking the breath out of her. She crashed to the ground. Zachery skittered away.

The demon lifted its behemoth foot to crush Van.

She rolled and kicked the demon, knocking out its leg.

It crashed to the ground and shattered.

From the pieces grew more demons.

Van darted and dodged the creatures, chanting the words she had used to defeat the serpent. They had no effect.

"If you use the Coin to kill my demons, it will harm me. The demons and I are magically bound," Solana said. "This act will make you unworthy. You'll attach to the dark part of your Self and become corrupted like your ancestor, Amaryl."

Van assumed Solana was lying, but the dire situation required the immediate use of her koga-clava skill, not the Coin. She kept the mud-demons at bay, but each time she took one out, its pieces multiplied into more demons. More and more sprouted everywhere. Van's injuries worked against her, and she felt weakened from being away from Paley's gemstone. She doubted how much longer she would last.

Then fire shot from the creatures' mouths. They aimed their blowtorch breath at Van.

"What the—?" she muttered.

Solana cackled, enjoying the show.

Van took cover by wedging herself behind a group of boulders and quickly collected her thoughts. *The Creator provides everything we need. What do I have? Again, the Coin.* Yet Van couldn't risk using the Coin against Solana. That would count as using the Coin's power against another person. How could she use it to fight Solana's demons?

Think!

"I needed you alive long enough to retrieve the Coin," Solana said. "Now you truly are useless."

The horde of mud creatures bashed themselves against the boulders as others blew their fiery breath.

Van couldn't hide much longer. The demons' fire had caused the stones to retain heat, cooking her alive.

She unwrapped the Coin, hoping Amaryl wouldn't pick this moment to send her another memory engram. Not a good idea to black out during an attack by an evil sorceress and her mud demons. Van took the risk and held the uncovered Coin in her palm, using it to find the best path out of this mess. It pointed back to Van.

Great. She gripped the Coin in frustration and silently asked for Amaryl's help.

"You sound scared," Van shouted, lying. She opened her hand.

The Coin disappeared into her palm. *What? That's no help! Thanks a lot, Amaryl.*

Van struggled to recall her advice. What had Jacynthia and Lady Loka said? Evil has no power? Solana had generated the demons by connecting her dark magic to the power of the earth. Elmot had said the opposing element to earth is water. *The cenote!*

Van raised her eyes to the immense collection of water above her. It loomed too high for her to reach.

"Not as scared as your mother on the night she was tortured to death," Solana jeered. "People told me she sobbed and begged for her life."

Solana kept trying to disrupt Van's ancestral connection, hoping Van wouldn't tap into the power of the Coin. It made Van more determined to succeed.

Van turned inward and attached to her light. She accepted her right to exist as the Anchoress and then sensed the loving presence of her mother and then others. She connected to a spiritual pulse cascading back through her entire ancestral line of Anchoresses, allowing her to harness their collective power.

The blood magic in Van's veins came to life. Her right palm raised almost on its own and aimed at the collection of water high above her.

She felt a vibration in her palm as the Coin illuminated and a ray of light shot from her hand, hitting the cenote.

It exploded.

A tidal wave came crashing down, flooding the cavern.

Van crouched and covered her head with her arms. She expected to drown, but no water touched her. She opened her eyes and found herself surrounded by the invisible bubble again, this time protecting her from the rush of water.

The tidal wave passed.

The Coin's light had ritualized the water, causing the demons to disintegrate back into the earth. Solana was nowhere in sight.

Van felt a thud as Solana hurled herself at Van from behind.

Soaking wet, Solana had stripped off her jacket and gloves to get rid of the water weight.

They rolled on the ground, grappling.

Solana pinned Van and wrapped her hands around Van's neck. "Give. Me. The. Coin," Solana said, pounding Van's head against the ground with each word.

Van bent her knee and used it as a wedge to push Solana, breaking them apart.

They both stood, panting.

"You can't use the Coin against me," Solana said. "And without its power, you'll never win."

Solana was right. Van could never win against her without using the Coin. Van felt too drained from the Twin Gemstones, too injured from her battles, and too exhausted from her journey. She imagined Paley dying from her injuries, Brux being tortured and killed, and the Balish taking over Providence Island. All because Van couldn't perform her duties as Anchoress.

Her only choice was to use the Coin.

Despite Van's attachment to the good part of her Self, which had made her worthy enough to retrieve the Coin, she still felt her soul being pulled in two different directions, one toward the light, the other toward darkness. Was she more like her angelic mother or her anarchist father? Her mother would've created a binding peace pact with Solana. Her father would've used the Coin to demolish his enemy.

"You're proving to be a worthy foe. I'll give you that," Solana said with a change of attitude.

When Van destroyed Solana's demons, it must have made the Balish princess think twice about Van's abilities.

"Your father would want you to follow in his footsteps," Solana continued. "I can give you everything that would've been his. Fame, power, land, money, protection. I'll preserve Providence Island and Salus Valde and give you all the credit. I'll give you your *throne.*"

Solana paused and scrutinized Van.

"I'll make sure Brux and Paley get home safely. Without medical care, Paley will die in a few hours. You'll be a hero," Solana coaxed. "If you keep the Coin, what? You'll have to give it to Uxa, and she'll take all the credit, all the power, all the glory. You'll be left with nothing."

Van watched Solana, taking in everything the Balish princess said.

"We'll rule as sisters. Twin princesses." Solana's smile came from a place of confidence. "You'll have family, my family. You'll inherit the position your father wanted to occupy. And you'll be safe, which is what your mother wanted." Solana's expression had the look of a winner's relief, and she couldn't stop talking. "My mother didn't know your mother carried the Anchoress bloodline when she killed her. I'm glad you survived. We're going to make a powerful team."

With great clarity, Van understood what to do. She called the Coin from her palm. Its gold radiated like the brightest star in the galaxy.

"Here." Van flip-tossed the Coin to Solana.

Solana caught the Coin in her bare hand. A huge grin spread across her face.

Then her grin faltered. Her mouth opened into a scream, just before Solana exploded into a thousand screeching shadows in the shape of black crows.

Chapter 53

Day 25: Afternoon, Living World

THERE WAS nothing left of Solana.

Except for the shreds of her black uniform scattered across the ground.

Gleaming in the spot where Solana had stood was the Coin. Next to it lay the bloody patch.

The wet ground squished as Van walked over to the Coin. She scooped it up and stuffed it into her pants pocket.

She turned to leave, then hesitated. Why had Solana kept her father's patch? Was it a valued memento? Had Solana and her father been... *lovers*?

Van went back and hovered over the patch. Ildiss, the gnomes' seer, had told Van her powers would remain compromised until she connected to her ancestral line. The bartender Zane had told Van her ancestral line would remain broken unless she reconciled her feelings about her mother, which she had done. But Van hadn't reconciled her feelings about her father.

By touching the patch, Van would learn the truth. She knew plenty about her father already. Did she want to know more?

She sighed. The patch remained there for a reason. How much worse could it get?

She stood alone in the in the cavern. Now was the time. She bent down and placed the tips of her fingers on the patch. Her vision blurred and then faded…

"The trail leads this way." Michael wore the black uniform of a Balish palace guard.

The sky was dark, nighttime. A thick scent of pine came from the trees surrounding them.

Luck was with Michael when Prince Devon gathered a squadron to chase the thief who had stolen Manik's text. The prince had come across Michael, a newly appointed palace guard, in Balefire and recruited him on the spot. As the only tracker in the impromptu squadron, the prince allowed Michael to lead the search party.

The prince didn't know Michael wasn't a palace guard or that he had lied about aspiring to become a tracker in the Balish military. Michael already knew how to track from being a Grigori. Michael, a Lodian spy, tracked no one.

"The thief is headed north, toward the Tipereth border," Michael said. Not quite a lie. Since the thief they searched for was Michael.

Michael had worked undercover in Balefire for the last few months. This position gave him access to the Balish palace's artifacts in the Hall of Records, the place that stored ancient documents. Allowing him to search for information about Goustav and the Dark War, including Manik's text.

"Headed toward the Old Mound?" Prince Devon raised his brow.

"I am not familiar with that place, my prince," Michael lied. He intentionally led the squadron toward the ancient temple so he could slip away and escape back to Providence Island through the temple's secret portal.

"Didn't pay attention in history, Rogziel?" The prince grinned. "It's a deserted temple dating back to the Dark War. No Bale would ever venture there. It's rumored to be haunted."

Yet Michael knew the history of the temple. His wife, Aelia, had died there. Michael ran his fingers along the scars on his jaw and neck. His heart ached with pain as he remembered that night fifteen years ago…

HE HAD CROSSED the boundary out of Salus Valde, searching for a way to counter the Anchoress curse, one that doomed the Anchoress to die giving birth. His months of research led him to the Temple of the Cross, known by the Balish as the Old Mound.

The Elementals had built the temple in Amaryl's honor as her resting place. They had used Amaryl's blood to construct it on the exact spot where she had died. A place Michael thought held clues to the counter-curse hidden in the cryptic ancient writing on the temple's walls. He had searched for a counter-curse ever since he had learned of his wife's pregnancy. Time had run out. Aelia would soon give birth. He had to act.

That night, Aelia discovered him gone and went searching for him, to protect him, to tell him the curse was ridiculous and to come home. But as Aelia entered the temple, Queen Brigid caught her.

The queen had gone there to search for her husband's latest mistress. The Old Mound was King Nequus's favorite meeting place, and he had spawned rumors about the temple being haunted, so no one would go there and catch him being unfaithful.

Queen Brigid had found out about her husband's upcoming rendezvous with his mistress that night. However, the king's spies told him his wife would be at the temple to catch him in the act, so he didn't go.

Aelia had arrived at the temple, searching for Michael, who had already left to go back to the Hall of Records. The queen mistook Aelia for King Nequus's lover, became infuriated over her pregnancy, and tortured Aelia.

Michael had heard his wife's screams and rushed back to the temple. He killed the queen's men, causing the queen to flee.

Fortunately, Iphigenia had been running through the woods that night. As the palace healer at Balefire, she had done her best to please the monarchy but had angered Queen Brigid, who wanted Iphigenia's head.

If it weren't for Iphigenia, Van would've died. But the healer couldn't save Aelia.

"It's too much strain," Iphigenia said. "Too much for Aelia to survive both the injuries from Queen Brigid's torture and childbirth. I'm so sorry."

Michael knew it didn't matter how the Anchoress died in childbirth. It only mattered that she had died. The curse had returned.

The image blurred for a few seconds and then became clear again…

VAN'S FATHER knelt sobbing at the foot of a weepy, purple-pink leafed tree.

His grief, so intense, he could barely breathe.

It brought him too much pain to keep Aelia's belongings after her death. So, Uxa had arranged for him to travel outside the boundary, under the guise of collecting needed ingredients for the Lodians' potent medicines. He went to the trista trees where he buried his deceased wife's possessions under a tree. People believed this brought healing to those suffering from grief.

His overwhelming guilt over being unable to protect Aelia had destroyed him. He could not go back in time and save Aelia, but he would do whatever it took to protect his helpless baby, Vanessa.

Life is for those who can be saved. And it was his fault Van needed protecting. Van was born disadvantaged because of his Balish blood. It reactivated the Anchoress curse that had lain dormant for centuries and probably blocked her ability to access her ancestral blood magic.

Michael would never forgive his selfishness. He had known Aelia was the Anchoress-in-waiting when they married, but didn't know about the Anchoress curse until Aelia became pregnant. And then it was too late.

He never should've married Aelia. His heart swelled with love, remembering his beloved wife. She had never believed in the curse or cared about the rules for Anchoress-protector relationships. The HG and the Elders called her immature, irresponsible. Aelia didn't listen, and she paid with her life.

Michael's stomach churned every time he looked at Van. His daughter served as a constant reminder of his failure to protect Aelia. Yet, Van was all he had left. He would do anything to redeem himself, to protect her. Including searching for a counter-curse so Van wouldn't meet the same fate as her mother—to die during childbirth.

. . .

THE VISION abruptly returned to Michael in the woods with Prince Devon and his squadron…

Michael sensed someone on the path ahead and stopped.

Prince Devon, also aware, held up his hand, silently halting his men. The squadron raised their torches high, but the denseness of the forest dimmed the light.

The ground beneath Michael's feet vibrated briefly.

Prince Devon shouted into the darkness. "In the name of the Royal Balish Militia, I command you to show yourself!"

The wind swirled, rustling the tree branches, picking up leaves and dirt from the ground.

Michael, vulnerable without his Grigori killing tools, squinted, desperate to see something, anything, through the darkness.

He smelled sulfur.

The earth rumbled in spots as the mud took form and rose.

"Take cover!" Michael cried.

None of the soldiers listened.

The wind picked up. Their torches flickered, and then extinguished. The night's blackness enveloped them.

"Show yourself, thief!" Prince Devon barely finished the last word when mud demons attacked their squadron.

Michael fought the demons as best he could and escaped the ongoing battle. Alone, he stumbled through the woods, mortally injured.

The partly hidden archway of the Temple of the Cross appeared through the trees. Michael staggered inside. He dragged himself along the cave-like entrance and into the underground main room of the temple.

His bunfy had waited there, and, on noticing the condition of his charge, bounced up and down in great distress.

"Hey, little friend. Slight change of plans." Michael placed his palm on the outer edge of the circular design on the back wall. Blood dripped from his hand, staining the etched stone.

The portal whirled to life.

"C'mon." He stepped into the swirling black disc.

His bunfy hopped in with him.

Michael staggered out of the private portal and into his study at Mt. Hope Manor. The trip took seconds, but the bunfy, using his magical ability to travel, had arrived ahead of him. The little animal bounced back and forth on his hind legs and nervously rubbed his front paws together. His bunfy stopped fidgeting and chirruped as soon as Michael stepped into the room.

"Shhh. There is little time." Michael took a gasping breath to fortify himself against his injuries.

His bunfy quieted and stared at his charge. His long ears were straight and alert, ready for instruction.

"Get... Genie... hurry."

His bunfy zoomed away.

Michael struggled to remove a woman's locket from around his neck and then clutched it in his hand. In his other hand, he held the ancient book he had stolen from Balefire. Manik's text.

Blood seeped from Michael's wounds, darkening his already black uniform. Still, he lumbered to the burning fireplace. "Important... important..."

When he reached the fireplace, Michael mumbled deliriously to his bunfy, which he forgot was no longer there. "Let us hope... no Lodian... ever lays a hand on this."

Michael and Uxa both knew the increasing demon problem in the Earth World meant it was only a matter of time before demons found a way into their world. So, Uxa had taught him the language of the ancients, allowing him to read ancient documents while undercover in Balefire. He'd intended to memorize the map in Manik's text and use it to retrieve the Coin in Van's place, using Goustav's heir. His daughter most likely wouldn't survive such a journey.

Then, as he read Manik's text while on duty in Balefire, he discovered Amaryl and Goustav had a baby. Van was both the Anchoress heir and Goustav's heir. He also found out the magical weapon Goustav used during the Dark War wasn't the Coin. It was Amaryl.

A Class III demon had killed Tilly Hopewell, a girl who reminded him of Van. Young, unskilled, naive. And of what Van's duties as the Anchoress heir might require his daughter to face. When the winged demon appeared, he knew the Escalation had begun, sending him straight back to Manik's text.

As proven tonight, demons had reached their world. Michael was right. The first stage of Dishora had arrived. The Anchoress would be called forth to retrieve her Coin and fight demons. With Van being both heirs, Uxa would send her to get the Coin.

He'd planned to safeguard Van on her journey, but with the map being so complex, he had to steal the text. This went terribly wrong. Now, dying, he would not be there to protect his daughter.

He could do only one last thing to help her. Without the text, Uxa would never know Van was Goustav's only heir, and she would continue her search. The search would be futile, and Uxa would eventually find another way to stop the Escalation and prevent Dishora.

Michael's priority was to protect Van.

He dropped the worn, hand-bound book into the fire, then lost consciousness…

Van remained in complete blackness when she heard a woman's voice…

"Michael? Michael? Can you hear me?"

Genie's blurred face came into focus, racked with worry but still exquisite in its beauty.

"What happened?" Genie cried. "Why are you dressed in a Balish palace guard uniform?"

A groan gurgled from Michael's throat as he attempted to speak.

"What's a portal doing in your study?" she shrieked, wide-eyed.

His voice came, strained and low. "Give… this… to Van." He grasped his wife's hand. So soft, so delicate. In it, he placed the locket.

Genie lifted the bloodied necklace to get a better look. "This gaudy thing? Why?"

"It was her mother's. Genie… promise me you'll give it to her." Michael noticed a strand of her silky white-blond hair had fallen out of place.

"Tell me what's going on!"

He struggled to sit up, but Genie held him down.

"Keep still! You're more injured than I thought. I need my healing kit." She attempted to rise.

"No!" Michael grasped her silk bathrobe and pulled her to him. The blood on his hand seeped through the delicate material, staining the white lace and light yellow fabric a brilliant red. "It's too late for me… I can't be saved… can't be found here…"

"What are you talking about? Don't be foolish. Let me go."

Michael let out a weak groan. "Must… get back… to the portal."

"How is this possible?" Genie stared at the swirling disc.

Michael struggled to get up.

"No!" She pushed him back down. "You stay put. I'll be right back."

She tried to stand, but Michael had her bathrobe clutched tightly. He used his dead weight to hold her down and raised himself to a semi-upright position. "Erase all evidence I was here. Tell no one... no one... promise me, Genie. Forget you ever saw the portal, forget you ever saw me... promise!"

Genie flinched as his last word sprayed her face with spittle and blood. She gently nodded. She didn't wipe her face.

Satisfied, Michael released her bathrobe and sank back onto the blood-streaked floor.

Genie seized her chance and dashed from the room.

As soon as she was gone, Michael gathered his remaining strength and stood.

He glanced at the fireplace one last time to make sure the text had kept burning. Then he lugged his body toward the wall that normally displayed an artistic stone carving but had now transformed into an activated, swirling portal. He had only a few more seconds until the portal timed out.

He turned to face his bunfy, who silently watched the scene unfold from a corner.

"I am truly sorry, little friend, but it's the only way... please... watch over Van."

The bunfy nodded, accepting his new instructions. Then he seemed to realize what the request meant, and he shook his tiny head. His long ears drooped. His eyes brimmed with tears.

The bunfy leaped onto Michael's chest to prevent Michael from reentering the portal. To do so without the attunement key, which Michael no longer had, meant certain death.

Michael stepped backward into the portal.

As he disappeared into the swirling blackness, his last fading sight was of the dislodged bunfy scrunched into a ball on the floor. A piece of bloody material torn from the chest of Michael's uniform dangled from the bunfy's tiny mouth.

Chapter 54

Day 25: Evening, Living World

VAN REGAINED consciousness with her head in Brux's lap. Her cheeks were damp.

"I wasn't sure if it was a memory engram, or you got hit on the head," Brux said softly.

Van bawled. Her eyes gushed tears.

Brux cradled her in his arms.

He told Van he had dragged Paley into the cave above in time to see her and Solana both plummet into this cavern. He had searched for Van through the interconnecting tunnels and found her there, unconscious. Brux didn't think any of Solana's soldiers had survived the landslide.

After Brux finished his update, Van processed what she had learned from her father's memory engram. Most important, both of her parents had died over love for their family. Her mother, out of concern for her father's safety, and her father, to protect Van.

Michael had acted under Uxa's orders until Van's safety had become threatened. Then he had taken matters into his own hands by stealing Manik's text, not expecting to get killed. When her father became mortally wounded, he did the best he could, given the circumstances.

Her father knew he wouldn't live to protect Van on her journey, so Manik's text had to be destroyed. That way, Uxa would not learn Van was both heirs. Michael thought Uxa would leave Van alone, deeming her too weak to retrieve the Coin, and would continue searching for one of Goustav's heirs to do her bidding.

Van gazed at the patch. It must have slipped from the binding in the text during her fight with Solana, and Solana hadn't noticed it. Van's father never worked with Solana. He'd never had an affair with the Balish princess or Uxa or anyone. He wasn't money-grubbing or power-hungry. Her father wasn't a traitor. He had chosen to cling to the light.

He was good.

Van sat up and the words spilled out of her mouth as she told Brux what she had learned, starting with her father's innocence.

"Amaryl tried to tell you," Brux said. "That was the purpose of the vision of her in the garden with Goustav. That you were the heir to both bloodlines." He sighed.

"When Amaryl showed me the vision of her cursing Goustav, she—she tried to tell me she was the one who had cursed me," Van said between sobs. "In a fit of rage, she couldn't see by cursing Goustav's blood, she had cursed her own daughter and—and all the other Anchoresses from that point onward."

"Over the centuries, all the Anchoresses married pure-blooded Lodians, those with the highest percentage of Elemental blood, to weed out Goustav's Balish blood," Brux added. "So the curse became dormant. Then your father comes along with his Balish blood, and this new infusion reactivated Amaryl's curse."

Van bobbed her head. She used the back of her wrist to wipe her tear-stained cheeks. "He had put his family in danger with his tainted blood—and then—then wasn't able to protect Aelia," she whimpered. "He could never f-forgive himself for it. That's why—"

She sniffled. "Why he seemed so emotionally distant to me. *He loved me.*"

Her father's tainted blood had inadvertently led to Aelia's death via the curse. He never blamed Van. He blamed himself. And every day he had to live with that pain.

Van ran her fingers over the scar on her lower back. Her sobs subsided.

"Are you hurt?" Brux asked. "Let me see."

Before Van could push him away, he pulled up the back of her shirt.

He caressed her scar. His fingers felt coarse.

Brux lifted his eyes to hers. "That's from Queen Brigid?"

Van nodded. "It's there to remind me I'm a survivor."

He moved his hand away from the scar and cupped the back of Van's head. "You're beautiful." Brux leaned in and pressed his lips to hers in a soft, lingering kiss.

The fireworks of Jaychund seemed to go off inside Van. She smiled.

Brux lightly ran a finger over her cheek. "We should get going." He rose and extended his hand to Van.

She took it.

"Brux." She didn't want to lose control and start blubbering again, so she blurted it. "I'm sorry about Daisy being captured."

Brux's eyes glazed for a second, and then he said, "I'm going to rescue her. You can count on it."

They headed back to the spot where Brux had Paley safely tucked away.

Saddened about her father not having faith in her, Van said, "My father stole Manik's text to help me. Instead, what he did sent me on this mission, unwittingly playing right into Solana's and the master demon's plans."

"Van, if it ever came down to it, your father knew you could use your intuition to find the Coin," Brux said. "He believed in you."

Van shrugged, unsure whether this was true. "How much do you think Uxa knew? She told me my father's soul was in danger." She felt certain both Uxa and Solana had used her ignorance about her father against her to advance their own agendas.

"I'm not sure." Brux frowned.

"She must know about the portal in my father's study," Van said.

"It's a private portal," Brux said, enthralled. "It must operate differently than the public portal. Maybe the attunement is done by using a special code or some kind of key."

"Um." Van bit her lip, unsure how to tell him about her final confrontation with Solana.

"Van, what is it?"

"When I stood face-to-face with Solana, I remembered Manik's warning about people not using the Coin against each other. I tried to work out how to best defeat her." She paused to get her emotions in check.

"You were facing a kill or be killed situation," Brux said. "Solana knew from reading Manik's text that you were also Goustav's heir, which we didn't know because that part had been burned out. It was another reason the Balish discredited the text and locked it away."

"That's what the traveling peddler, Len, meant when he told us something in Manik's text gives the Lodians power. Not only is the Lodians' Anchoress the heir to the Balish kingdom, but the Coin gives her the power to take it. If she chooses to use it that way." Van added the last bit as a warm-up to her confession.

"Once you retrieved the Coin, it would be proof the Anchoress bloodline had survived the Dark War," he said. "And if that part of Manik's text was true, then so were his other writings."

Van remained quiet and let Brux finish his thoughts.

"Solana's grand plan included eliminating all threats to her throne, including the death of the Anchoress and Goustav's heir—you."

"Manik warned us to use the Coin only against true evil." Van swallowed and braced herself. Then she confessed *how* she had defeated Solana. "I called the Coin from my palm, not only without surrendering my light, but I charged it with even more light, raising its vibration. I knew Solana would die when she touched the Coin with her bare hand."

"Solana must've forgotten she'd removed her gloves after getting wet," Brux said.

"I misused the Coin." Van wondered if Brux had missed the point. "I attached to the dark part of my Self. Now, on top of the Anchoress curse, I'll have to suffer the consequences of my actions."

Van had finally reconciled her feelings for her father, but it was too late. Her soul had already been damaged.

"I should've been there to protect you." Brux shook his head angrily. "I'll never forgive myself for that." He wrapped a comforting arm around Van.

She gratefully leaned into him.

"Solana was truly evil," Brux said. "She murdered people and Wiglaf. She conspired with a demon to destroy the Coin of Creation. You prevented that. It's what being a good Anchoress is all about."

Van remained subdued. She needed absolution more than she needed analysis.

Brux understood. "I'm proud of you." He gave her a squeeze and a smile.

"Manik advised the Anchoress not to surrender her light." Van tried to convince herself her actions were correct. "The only way out was to use the Coin."

Was Brux right? Did Solana count as true evil? Solana, though unquestionably evil, wasn't a demon, so Van was unsure.

But Van was sure about the profound shift that occurred inside herself the moment Solana revealed Queen Brigid had killed Van's mother, Aelia. A fierce protective instinct for Van's ancestral line had taken over.

"The Moor family is rotten and dark," Van said. Solana's mother had nearly ended the Anchoress bloodline. "They shouldn't be ruling the kingdom."

Solana's desire for power led to her callous indifference toward family and death. She had murdered her twin brother and killed her own mother and Van's father. And she had tried to kill Van.

During their confrontation, Van had peered into Solana's soul. She had glimpsed a dark thread and knew the master demon had already claimed a piece of Solana's soul. Ildiss had told Van conspiring with demons left a mark. This mark appeared not on the skin, but on the soul.

Solana's dark thread had wound so tightly around greed and a desire for power, no chance of redemption remained for her.

This was when Van knew she had to use the Coin against Solana.

Solana had chosen to cling to darkness, and she had lost.

Some people cannot be saved.

Chapter 55

D ays 26, 27: Living World

When Van and Brux found their way to Paley, she was conscious, but not doing well. Although she could walk with help, her pulse fluttered weakly.

Van's ribs ached with every breath and with each step, her sprained ankle howled in pain. Paley switched between using Van and Brux as her crutch until she became too exhausted to walk anymore. Then Brux draped Paley over his shoulder again.

They had all suffered injuries. However, Paley's being the most severe, slowed them down.

They didn't need the Coin to find their way to Araquiel, but Van used it anyway to locate the fastest route. They had only four days left to get the Coin back to Uxa at Lodestar. Or the Balish would repeal Manik's law and invade Salus Valde, even without Solana.

It took them a day and a half to reach Araquiel. When they

arrived, Balish soldiers still mobbed the town. The surviving three members of team Delta hid on the outskirts and planned their next move.

Van eyed Paley, who lay on the ground, semi-conscious. "I think the luck of the Coin is keeping Paley alive."

"Let's hope the Coin has enough luck to go around." Brux had dark circles under his eyes from exhaustion. "There's no way we can make it through Araquiel without getting questioned, not with all these soldiers around."

Brux's comment triggered Van's memory. The Law of Abundance. She brightened. "We already have what we need to make it through the town, and it's not luck."

"What?"

"Friends." Van took out the Coin and held it in her palm. "Show me the safest way to the Troll's Foot Tavern."

They used the Coin to weave their way to the edge of town, back to the dirt street with the single stone building, without being noticed by the Balish soldiers. The familiar parchment reading "Closed for renovations" remained nailed to the door.

Brux knocked.

The little horizontal slat in the door slid open. Van smiled as she recognized the sparkling blue eyes peering out.

Noam whooshed open the door. "Quick! Get inside!" He scanned the street for onlookers.

Zane stood just inside the door. "Van! I was hoping to see you again."

He gave her a big hug. Brux scowled.

"Zaney, go get Healer Hollycap," Noam said. "Go."

Zane dashed away.

Noam led Brux and Van down a back hallway to a small, dim room and pointed to a worn cot.

Brux laid Paley down, while Van brushed away the overhanging cobwebs.

Noam looked over Paley, who had become unconscious again. "You got here just in time." His expression grave. "Looks like this one's circling the drain."

"Will she be all right?" Van asked.

Noam sighed. "That'll be the healer's call." He closed off Paley behind a curtain. The motion caused dust to shake loose.

Van snapped the back of her wrist to her nostrils, hoping to stifle a painful sneeze, but the movement itself caused a sharp pain through her ribs. Then she sneezed anyway.

"Ouch," she said meekly.

Noam turned his eyes toward Van. "Hollycap will need to look you over next. None of you'll be okay if you stay in town. Balish soldiers cut up Roguey's gut real good. Interrogated him, looking for spies, Manikists, and Anti-Manik Rebels. He didn't tell 'em a thing." Noam beamed proudly. "If he had, none of us would be here right now."

"Is he okay?" Van and Brux both asked.

"Holly says he'll recover."

"We need to get moving as soon as we can," Van said.

Before Noam could answer, Zane returned with a bob-haired, apple-cheeked healer who immediately went behind the curtain to examine Paley.

Brux, Zane, and Noam left the room to give Paley privacy.

The healer pulled an ampule from her bag and put a few drops of tincture in Paley's mouth. "Potent. Lodian-made," Hollycap said to Van. "Best stuff on the market to treat internal injuries. Bought it meself at the marketplace in Hod."

The healer pulled a needle and thread from her travel bag and stitched a wound on Paley's forehead. Then motioned for Van to help her remove Paley's tattered pants. "She's got some things in her pockets."

Van reached into Paley's pants pockets and found her Twin Gemstone, along with several pairs of spare contact lenses. She grinned.

Hollycap stitched up Paley's thigh. Next, she pulled out a salve and rubbed it over the stitches and then wrapped the leg in gauze. "Should fix her up well enough."

"How long until Paley is strong enough to travel?" Van asked.

Hollycap gave Van a once-over. "Not just your friend here. You and the boy too. Both of you need a look-see."

The healer sat Van in a wooden fold-up chair next to the cot and examined her cuts and scrapes. She treated Van's abrasions with a soothing balm and then focused on her collarbone, ribs, and ankle.

"Ankle is sprained, ribs are cracked." Hollycap wrapped both in strips of sturdy canvas. "You have a headache?" She stared into Van's eyes.

"Yes," Van replied without nodding, afraid the slightest movement would set off pain.

Hollycap raised her fingers in front of Van's face. "Follow my fingers with your eyes." The healer moved her fingers back and forth. "You may have a psi spasm."

"A what?" Van raised her eyebrows. The movement triggered a throbbing ache throughout her scalp.

"A mild case of brain bruising," Hollycap replied. "Enough time has passed since your injury. Don't need to keep you awake. You got a scraped and bruised body too." She gave Van several drops of pain-relieving medicine under her tongue. "May make you sleepy."

Elated, Van wanted nothing more than a few good hours of rest, and then to hit the road again.

"Now, the boy."

Van turned to Paley, still lying unconscious. "I'll be right back." She followed Healer Hollycap into the adjacent room, where Brux sat in a fold-up chair next to the cot.

Noam stood next to him.

"Is Paley well enough to travel?" Brux asked as Hollycap looked him over.

"Not yet." She applied a salve to his abrasions and placed several drops of liquid under his tongue.

"Paley and I have to stay together," Van said, thinking of the Twin Gemstones.

"How long?" Brux asked the healer.

Hollycap considered the situation for a moment. "Your friend in the other room won't be well enough for travel 'til the day after tomorrow. Then, I think it best you get going, given the military situation happening in town."

"Okay, then." Noam clapped his hands. "Let's figure out the best way to get these kids back to Lodestar." He left the room. Hollycap followed.

Brux stood to leave. Van grabbed his arm and pulled him back into the room.

"What about using the private portal in my father's study?"

"We don't know how to attune ourselves for transport," Brux said. "We need a code or a key to use it. And the Temple of the Cross is in the southern woods of Tipereth. That's much farther away from here than Lodestar." Brux noticed Van's pout. "It was a good idea, though."

Brux went to the main room to ask Noam how to best smuggle them out of town, and Van walked back to Paley's room. Her friend continued to sleep soundly. Or remained unconscious. Van couldn't tell. She nabbed some blankets and sheets from a nearby linen closet and snuggled into a nest she made on the floor next to Paley's cot.

Van yawned. The pain medicine had kicked in. She wished Wiglaf were there to make them feel better. Then her heart tore, causing more pain than her physical injuries as she remembered what had happened to her poor little bunfy.

She barely wiped the tears from her cheeks before slipping into a deep, medicated sleep.

Chapter 56

Days 28, 29: Living World

By nightfall the next day, Paley claimed to be well enough for travel.

Van doubted this was true. She barely felt ready for the road herself, and her injuries weren't as severe as Paley's.

But everyone at the Troll's Foot knew if Van, Brux, and Paley didn't get moving, they wouldn't reach Lodestar before midnight of the next full moon, an impending deadline now less than two days away.

Zane brought them a pouch full of coins and each a fresh change of clothes.

Van wept tears of joy when Zane handed her a pair of hand-sewn, leather walking shoes. She couldn't care less they were used hand-me-downs.

As they washed and changed, Van told Paley what had happened while she lay unconscious. She wasn't sure Paley believed their tales about Solana until Paley changed her eye color to a warm blue.

"I'm so glad the spares I carried in my pocket survived the journey." Paley smiled.

Van, Brux, and Paley ate an excellent meal of fire-baked yams and something Zane called, "Wild mundo legs." To Van, they looked like charbroiled chicken legs. When they felt satiated, they said their goodbyes.

Van offered to donate Zachery to the Manikist movement as repayment for their help.

Noam's eyes glistened as he accepted the gift. "I'll proudly display it in the Troll's Foot Tavern for everyone to admire."

Van sensed Jorie's spirit smiling, happy over Van's generosity, and proud Zachery would have a home where he'd be held in high esteem.

Noam, Hollycap, Zane, Jeb, and some others gathered with Van, Brux, and Paley as Brux said a prayer to the light for their lost teammates, including team Echo and Wiglaf, and one for Daisy, being held in the dungeons of Balefire.

Brux tolerated Zane's lingering hug with Van. Then the trio set off for Kezef, hidden in Roguey's modified hay wagon, driven by Jeb.

At the Fomalhaut-Kezef checkpoint, Jeb explained he had special permission to deliver much-needed hay to a farm in northern Kezef. The soldiers ran their swords through the hay but didn't discover the secret compartment below. With the help of the underground Manikist network, Jeb's paperwork was in order and the lie, successful.

The concealed travelers napped through the brisk night, keeping warm by being squashed together. Van found the rocking motion and Brux's body heat soothing and comforting. She slept the whole way.

By morning, Jeb had driven into Kezef as far as he dared. He needed to return to Araquiel to avoid suspicion.

Once out of the wagon, Van consulted the Coin for the best way back to Lodestar. Van, Brux, and Paley slipped on their mittens, bundled up in their jackets, and then moved on.

They walked under a near-full moon, which glowed brightly through a thin layer of clouds drifting across her face as if trying to hide her beauty from the unworthy mortals below. Van smiled at the enchanting image, feeling fortified.

The Coin led them to a village called Lone Rock, where they planned to stop briefly, in desperate need of food and rest. Their deadline loomed, and time was ticking away.

They checked into the only bunkhouse in the small town, which had a large shared room for sleeping. After washing in the community bath chamber, they went downstairs to the bunkhouse's busy eatery for dinner. They overheard some locals talking about Balish troops gathering along the Salus Valde border, preparing for an invasion.

"Forget taking naps, we have to keep going." Van crammed a piece of deep-fried jasmine bread into her mouth.

"No," Paley said. "I need rest." She still hadn't fully recovered from her injuries.

Paley looked peaked, and Brux dreaded the thought of having to carry her again, so they decided to take a quick nap.

Brux and Van had an unspoken agreement to continue keeping their budding relationship a secret from Paley, especially now, not wanting to upset their friend and cause her more distress.

Van didn't feel safe napping in a shared room and wanted to sleep close to Paley and Brux.

He pushed three cots side by side, close together. That way, Van and Paley could get some solid rest, knowing he napped in the middle.

Van pressed her back as close to Brux's as humanly possible without waking him. She needed to feel his warm body next to hers, to be lulled by the soft, rhythmic in and out of his breathing. She couldn't fall asleep any other way.

Chapter 57

Day 30: Living World

THE SUN'S morning rays reached in through the window, waking Van. She shook Brux and Paley.

"Let's get going," she said. "We overslept!"

They each gobbled down a quick egg wrap for breakfast as they hurried to the supply store.

Through a mouthful of egg, Brux said, "We can use the money Zane gave us to buy horses and a bit of food. It's the only way to make it back to Lodestar in time."

"I like it. How much do horses cost?" Paley asked. "Do we have enough?"

"Let's find out," Van said.

Brux walked to a nearby barn, while Van and Paley purchased a bare minimum of dried food sticks and one wineskin filled with water at the local supply house.

Brux returned with two stunning horses, one black and the other brown with a white nose, both of them saddled. "We had enough money for two."

The girls rode on the brown horse, Brux took the black one, and they trotted away from Lone Rock.

At mid-day, they stopped near a small pond to rest the horses and take a break.

Van slid from her horse, helped Paley down, and then stretched her aching back.

The trio devoured apple-infused dried mundo strips from their food supply, while the horses lapped up the fresh pond water and grazed in the meadow.

The sun shone in the sky directly overhead.

"It's high noon," Brux guessed. "We've got about twelve hours to reach Lodestar."

The weary travelers gathered their two horses and continued onward across Kezef, toward Salus Valde.

Blackness had crept into the sky hours ago when the trio crossed the unguarded Kezef-Altithronia border.

Van figured it was close to midnight but hadn't yet heard the faithful chimes from Uxa's odd grandfather clock ring in her mind.

"This is part of Blackwood Forest," Brux said. "The TAVs should start up again here."

"On it." Van reached in her pocket to grab the Coin, while Brux and Paley unsaddled the horses and set them free in the lush grass fields of Altithronia.

They didn't have Jorie's magical skills to make a TAV work, so Van consulted the Coin to find the best *working* TAV to Salus Valde.

Within minutes, they stood in front of a giant oak with a large knobby knot in its trunk. They piled into the TAV and eagerly studied the illuminated curved map on the wall.

Brux pointed to a tree icon on the panel map. "This TAV will land us on the wedge-shaped piece of Tipereth bordering northern Salus Valde. It's about an hour's walk to Lodestar and doesn't look like a checkpoint. Hopefully, no guards will roam the border there."

The TAV delivered them so close to the Salus Valde border, they could see the boundary signs.

Along with the five Balish soldiers, who stared as three disheveled kids walked out of a tree.

Van heard Uxa's grandfather clock chime in her head as the clock struck midnight.

They were out of time.

They had failed.

She had failed.

The Balish soldiers closed in.

Chapter 58

Midnight: Living World

Van and Paley were each nabbed by a soldier.

Brux struggled against the remaining soldiers, but it was a losing battle of three to one.

"We're doomed," Paley groaned.

A low, blood-curdling growl grabbed everyone's attention.

The hair prickled on the back of Van's neck as she scanned the woods.

The forest remained still, except for the soft rustling leaves from the gentle night wind.

Twigs snapped as something barreled toward them.

The brush parted.

Horrible red eyes emerged from the blackness.

A guttural growl rolled out from the shadow.

"W-What in the bloody name of darkness?" muttered one soldier.

It was as if the darkest shadow had come to life. Although this, this… *thing* was darker than dark. Blacker than black.

Van recognized the same monstrous wolf-like creature she had seen in Amaryl's vision. The one that had killed Amaryl's husband, Rowen. The beast that had never stopped hunting Amaryl had now come for Van.

The shadow-wolf hunched and sprang at Van, its teeth bared.

The soldier holding Van pushed her aside.

The beast swatted him down before he drew his sword.

Brux came hurtling in, hip-checking the beast.

Van screamed, remembering how the shadow creature had ripped apart Rowen.

Brux tumbled across the ground, entwined with the beast.

The terrified Balish soldiers slashed their swords at the creature, allowing Brux to break from its hold.

Van rushed to Brux to see if he had gotten severely wounded, but before she got to him, he picked up the dead soldier's abandoned sword and dashed back into the fight.

"Brux, no!" Van cried.

Another soldier yelped and went down as the beast tore him apart. The other three continued swiping their swords.

Even as they held it off, the creature watched Van, alert for the first clear path to her.

When she took out the Coin, the beast grew more enraged and tore through another soldier.

Van fumbled and dropped it.

She fell to her hands and knees, searching the leaf-covered ground. She couldn't find the Coin.

"Why are you crawling on the ground?" Paley shook from fear. "We have to help Brux."

"I have to find the Coin." Van frantically ran her fingers through the leaves, dirt, and grass.

"Brux!" Paley yelled. "Fighting this thing is a losing battle. *Come on.*"

Breathing heavily and splotched with blood, Brux kept his eyes on the beast. "If we run, it will follow. It has to die."

The beast tore through another soldier, leaving only one.

"Van, do something! Hurry!" Paley shouted in terror. "Brux will come if you call him."

"The Coin." Van frantically searched the ground. "I have to find the Coin." Then she paused. She remembered Amaryl's vision, her ancestor's obsession over the Coin, and how it had led to her husband's death.

Van shot to her feet. "Brux!"

Brux and the soldier fought side by side against the creature, slashing and stabbing their swords.

The shadow-wolf swatted Brux. He screamed and went down.

Numb, Van didn't care about the Coin or the mission or Paley. Only about Brux. She realized life without him wouldn't be worth living. She knew of only one way to stop the beast before it killed him.

The beast wanted her. Van had to give herself to it.

She stepped forward and almost crushed Wiglaf.

He had the Coin in his mouth and stood upright, bouncing from foot to foot.

"Wiglaf!" Van cried in surprise. "You're alive! How is this possible?"

"Holy crow!" Paley shrieked. "It's a miracle!"

"I don't think so," Van said. "Solana tricked us by killing a simi-lar-looking bunfy, not Wiglaf."

"Now the shadow-wolf will eat Wiglaf." Paley whimpered. "Oh, why did he come back?"

Van grabbed the Coin, thinking Wiglaf wanted her to figure out how to use it, but Wiglaf nudged Van's shins and scurried across the Salus Valde border. He sat on his hind legs and spoke urgently in animal talk.

Van pushed Paley toward Wiglaf. "You go. I'll get Brux." She inched over to Brux, who appeared to have only minor wounds and was up and fighting.

The beast saw Van and fought with renewed vigor to reach her.

"Van, get away from here! Are you insane?" Brux screamed as he slashed his sword at the beast.

"We need to get across the border," Van said. "Come on. Trust me."

The remaining soldier tackled the beast, giving Brux the break he needed to sprint away.

As he and Van crossed the border into Salus Valde, the shadow-wolf massacred the last soldier.

Its vile red eyes turned to Van, and it raced directly at her, snarling and chomping.

Brux stepped in front of Van, panting, his sword raised. "Van, go!"

"You were right. We can't outrun it." Van accepted her fate by standing firm.

Paley made a move to run, then changed her mind and stayed with Van. They wrapped their arms around each other, trembling.

The beast sprang forward.

With a loud thud, mid-pounce, it hit an invisible wall marking the Salus Valde border.

It slid to the ground, but continued clawing and snapping.

The creature repeatedly threw itself against the wall. Its claws tearing, its awful red eyes never wavering from Van.

"It can't cross into Salus Valde." Brux lowered his sword. "Van, how did you know?"

"Wiglaf told me. He's alive." Van's eyes darted her surroundings, searching for her bunfy. She heard a chirrup by her feet and looked down to see him.

Brux flashed a smile at Wiglaf, then said, "Let's get moving. There might still be time to hold off the invasion."

Paley remained still. "What—the hell—is that thing?" She couldn't take her eyes off the creature as it attempted to bite and claw its way through the invisible wall.

"I'm not sure, but we're safe now. Let's go." Van tugged Paley's sleeve, spurring her friend to action.

The three of them dashed through the woods.

Fynn and another man stood anxiously waiting outside the main entrance to Lodestar.

"Only three of you?" Fynn asked, though overjoyed by their return. "We had a sentinel round-the-clock here for the past week."

Fynn ushered them through the lobby, up the main staircase, and into Uxa's office. Wiglaf scuttled in after them.

It was fifty-three minutes past midnight.

The trio spoke in a rush, words and emotions gushed forth, all of them eager to tell their story.

Uxa let them pour out their tale as she rose from her chair and glided to the front of her desk.

"My warriors." Uxa held up her hands to quiet them. "Take a breath. You made it back in time. I am happy about the success of your mission and offer my sincerest condolences over the loss of your teammates. Brux, I am sorry to hear about Daisy's capture. And Van, your father."

Van couldn't help it. The reality sank in. Her father was dead. Tears streamed down her cheeks.

Paley gave Van a hug.

Brux put a comforting arm around Van's shoulder and left it there.

Paley noticed and furrowed her brow.

Van used her knuckles to wipe her tears. She bent down and picked up Wiglaf.

Brux stayed close but didn't put his arm back around her. Most likely he knew it would bother Paley, which would then upset Van.

"The Elemental meeting with the Balish Council is happening now," Uxa said. "Their top members will go to the Celestial Tower to view the Coin shortly."

"The Council waited for us to get back?" Brux stood, bloody and sweaty and had a smudge of dirt on his nose.

Van thought he had never looked more handsome.

"Of course not," Uxa said. "It is easy to create a filibuster among politicians. Then I told the Council I needed to check the Celestial Tower to make sure the Coin was secure for viewing, whenever they were ready."

Van raised her brow. "You told the Council we had the Coin before you knew we had it? Awesome."

Uxa's chest puffed in pride. "Congratulations! You have all, indisputably, earned your place."

The three of them beamed.

Uxa stretched her palm to Van. "The Coin, please."

Van hesitated. She had no desire to give Uxa the Coin. "Uh, I have some questions first."

Paley groaned. "C'mon, Van. I want to go *home!*"

"Fynn," Uxa said. "If you would escort Brux to the medical wing. Stop in the parents' waiting area on the way back. Tell the parents I will speak to them once the Council meeting has concluded. Tactfully pull away Brux's father and take him to see his son." Uxa turned to Paley. "Fynn will escort you back to Providence Island, where you will be tended to in the medical area of the complex. You will both be debriefed once your injuries are properly treated."

"I don't want to leave without Van," Paley said.

Van noticed the pallor of her friend's face and the desperate need for sleep in her eyes. Paley needed additional medical care right away. "It's okay," Van said. "I'll see you soon."

Uxa turned to Van. "Are your injuries stable enough for us to talk before I send you to the complex? I would like to speak with you privately."

Van nodded as she stroked Wiglaf.

The bunfy purred.

"Please hand Fynn your Twin Gemstone," Uxa said to Van.

Van placed Wiglaf on the floor, then reached into her pocket, pulled out the gemstone, and handed it to Fynn.

"Wait," Brux said, apparently still in hyper-protective mode. "We can't separate Van from her gemstone."

"Brux," Uxa said calmly. "Fynn needs it to take Paley back through the portal, only a few floors below us. He will re-attune the gemstones once he gets there. Van and Paley will be fine."

Brux barely relaxed his stance.

Van and Paley hugged their goodbyes, as did Van and Brux.

"See you soon," he whispered to Van.

Her heart whirled in delight.
Then Fynn led Brux and Paley out of the room.
As the door snapped shut behind them, Van felt strangely alone.

Chapter 59

D ay 31: Lodestar Station, Living World

UXA WAITED EXPECTANTLY for Van to ask her questions, but Van didn't know where to begin.

"Would you care to use the ladies room?" Uxa asked. "To freshen up?"

"Nah," Van said. "I'm good. Thanks."

"Are you able to walk without pain?"

Van nodded. "A healer treated me in Araquiel."

"Come with me." Uxa guided Van from her office down a long, white marble hallway. Van glanced at the floor to make sure Wiglaf followed them. He raised his tiny whiskered nose at Van, giving her a reassuring glance as he scampered down the corridor, keeping pace with them.

"Where are we going?" Van asked.

"To the Celestial Tower. A magically protected room designed to hold the Coin." Uxa's sky-blue cape flowed from her brisk pace. "On the way, you can tell me more about your journey."

Van's experiences spilled forth as if she couldn't speak fast enough. She told Uxa about Solana's guilt and her father's innocence, about Amaryl's cryptic messages from beyond, and about Lady Loka and her Lake of Tears.

"You beat Solana," Uxa stated proudly. "Our reservation program seems to work well." Uxa flashed a grin, then became solemn again. "With Solana gone, her younger brother, Ferox, is next in line for the Balish throne. Ferox is a good and fair prince. This is seen as a weakness by Balish society. Other Balish royals desire to rule the kingdom, including Ferox's cousin Merloc. There may be a battle for the throne."

Van wondered whether Uxa had hinted about using the Coin to prevent the Balish royals from squabbling over their kingdom, so she described finding Manik's text in her father's study. She explained Manik's warning about evil being created by our actions, and, therefore, can be prevented and what she learned about correctly using the Coin's power.

Uxa didn't seem surprised Van had found Manik's text. Again, Uxa asked Van if her father had given her anything the night he died.

Van's thoughts flashed to the necklace her father had given Genie and wondered why Uxa wanted it so much. "My father didn't give me anything."

As Uxa led Van up a tight winding stairway, Van grew pensive.

"We have one thousand one hundred and twenty-two steps," Uxa said. "Ask."

"D-Did you know my father was dead the whole time?"

Uxa's expression became stern. "When I told you your father's soul was in jeopardy, I believed it." Her eyes became glossy, and she averted her gaze away from Van.

Van wondered whether Uxa felt sad or guilty.

They remained silent the rest of the way to the top floor.

Uxa opened a heavy white marble door. Van and Wiglaf followed her into the Celestial Tower, a cylindrical room with a funnel-like ceiling made from elongated, elaborately braced windows. Moonbeams spilled into the chamber, falling on four statues, two women and two men, in various poses, dressed in togas and sweeping robes. The statues, evenly spaced and facing outward, surrounded a mosaic on the floor depicting two serpents forming a figure eight by swallowing each other's tail.

"She is Gaea Mater, the Guardian of the Earth." Uxa pointed out the highlighted statue facing north. One of the statue's hands lightly gripped the arm of the throne; the other was raised, palm up, with her thumb and forefinger lifted as if holding a small object. "If you place the Coin in her fingers, she will guard it."

Van's eyes narrowed as she scrutinized this newest guardian of the Coin. Gaea Mater sat securely on a stone throne designed with two trees forming the back of her chair. The side of her throne facing Van was engraved in a pattern of halved pomegranates filled with seeds. Gaea Mater wore a toga and a crown of wheat. At her feet lay a stone cornucopia of fruit and flowers.

The statue reminded Van of Lady Loka, which comforted her. Still, she struggled with her desire to keep the Coin. It was her Coin. She had earned it, and it was way better than her All-Grades Trophy. Yet she knew she had to give it up. Keeping it meant corruption and ultimately her downfall, as had happened to Amaryl.

"Do not worry," Uxa said. "The Coin will be safe here."

Van turned and faced Uxa. "I was the first one called into the meeting before the briefing because you knew I was the Anchoress-in-waiting. Why didn't you tell me?"

"Ah." Uxa nodded, as if she now understood Van's hesitation. "I could not tell you. Discovering the truth within yourself was part of your journey. A person does not know how brightly she can shine until she is challenged by that which is dark."

"It would've been a hundred times easier if you had just told me!" Van said.

"Hearing and listening are two different things."

Van crossed her arms. She still wasn't buying it.

Uxa sighed. "Telling you would have made you feel like a victim of your circumstances. It would have disempowered you, which would have led you toward self-sabotaging behavior. For you to connect to your abilities, you had to acknowledge and accept your power. A person cannot transform when she does not recognize the part within herself that needs to change."

The truth of Uxa's reasoning resonated deeply within Van.

"You would have been told, eventually," Uxa said. "The Anchoress-in-waiting is made aware of her position, the curse, and the guidelines for her marriage after she turns of age at eighteen. In the end, it is your choice what to do with this information. As it was your mother's and father's. They broke the rules assigned to them. As a result, they were banished to live on Providence Island, and your father was demoted. As you know, Amaryl also made poor choices."

"Let's hope I don't make the same mistakes, right?" Van said, finishing Uxa's thought.

Uxa placed a comforting hand on Van's arm. "Thanks to you, the Balish invasion will be put on hold by satisfying the Elemental ruling. Your friends, family, Lodian culture—all are safe. Your mother and father would be proud."

"But what about Daisy?" Van thought Professor Lake wouldn't be pleased after discovering his daughter had been captured by Merloc. "Why did you send her team out if you knew I was the Anchoress-in-waiting? You must've known only I could get the Coin."

"Ah." Uxa raised her brow. "During your father's undercover research in Balefire, he told me he discovered Goustav had an heir who could also retrieve the Coin. There were many people whom I thought could be his descendants. The most likely candidates were on both of your teams." Uxa contemplated for a few seconds before speaking. "From what you have uncovered on your journey, I now know you are Goustav's only heir."

The hair on the back of Van's arms prickled, indicating Uxa was lying to her. If Van's intuition was right, it meant Uxa *had* known only Van could retrieve the Coin, and Uxa had intentionally sent Daisy's team out as a decoy.

Startled by this negative thought, Van feared the idea might've resulted from having attached to the dark part of her Self when she used the Coin against Solana. She inwardly shook away the disturbing notion. Of course, Uxa was being truthful about not knowing Van was both heirs.

Uxa continued, unaware of Van's inner turmoil. "After Amaryl cursed Goustav, he had no other children besides Astrid, his child with Amaryl. Since then, only one child, a female, has been born to that ancestral line."

"Because of Amaryl's curse?" Van asked.

Uxa gave a curt nod. "I believe so. It is easy to conclude Regina and Romet Lake adopted Astrid after Amaryl's and Rowen's deaths. They are Brux's and Daisy's ancestors."

"That's why so many people thought Daisy was the Anchoress-in-waiting." Van fidgeted thinking about poor Daisy trapped in the dungeons of Balefire, scared and alone. "I want to stay and help Brux rescue his sister." Plus, she felt empty without Brux. They had made plans to see each other, but if Van stayed in Salus Valde, it would be easier, and they could be together more often.

"Your concern for Brux is only natural," Uxa said. "As you might have already guessed, he is your assigned protector."

Stunned, Van had *no idea*. Even worse, Brux, being her assigned protector, made him undatable. Numbness spread through her body. *Of all the boys in both the worlds, why did the Elementals pick Brux?*

"I will award him his position shortly," Uxa said. "Brux misdirected his innate drive to be a protector toward Daisy. The consilium will not allow him to search for his sister. His only concern, now, is to protect you."

Van became acutely aware this newest arrangement would be unacceptable to Brux. Assigned protector or not, he had a bond with his sister that wouldn't easily be put to rest.

"The consilium will reassign Brux's father to work in the complex," Uxa informed Van. "I will arrange for the Lakes to live on Providence Island. Brux will transfer to Canterbury Bells and be placed in the reservation program with you."

Van's stomach twisted with anguish. She would be forever close to Brux, yet they could never be together. She would live in torment, the same as Lady Loka, when Lilla trapped her prince in the labyrinth. With a sinking feeling, Van realized this catapulted her onto the same trajectory as her mother and Amaryl. She had thought her testing was done. She was wrong.

"You must return to Providence Island as soon as possible. You are not safe here at Lodestar," Uxa said.

"Solana knew about the island. I'm probably not safe there, either." Van waited for Uxa's reaction.

Uxa's serene confidence faltered. "The spy," she said, as if it caused her pain. "It wasn't your father." She cast her eyes downward.

Van scrutinized Uxa's moment of silence. Was Uxa trying to figure out who was the actual spy or who to frame next? But again, Van didn't want to attach to her dark Self and inwardly brushed away the idea of Uxa being a traitor.

"I am certain the spy is not a Grigori or one of the Elders," Uxa said. "You are safest on the island. No one can get there from our world without going through the portal, and our Grigori track all transports. The Elders, Brux, and the Grigori stationed on the island will watch over you. For those select Grigori who know your identity, their main oath is to protect the Anchoress heir."

A pang of sorrow wrenched Van's heart as she thought of her father. He had fulfilled this oath to the fullest. It cost him his life.

"Do not worry," Uxa said, misreading Van's concern. "The island protects you, your line. The same way the Celestial Tower protects the Coin."

"Is that why my classmates pretended to like me?" Van asked. "You told their parents I was someone special and for them to become friends with me?" She felt queasy knowing Pernilla had spoken the truth.

"Yes," Uxa said bluntly. "I instructed the adults on the island to be overprotective of you. They, along with island security, were told you are to be safeguarded as someone who is important to the tribe. But the only people who know the real reason for your protection are the Elders and select Grigori."

"The real reason?" Van asked. "You mean, my Anchoress bloodline?"

Uxa turned to face Van. "Being the Anchoress allows you to connect to the power of the moon, the Elemental part of your blood, and your ancestral line to create magic. The Coin amplifies this power. The Coin does not carry the power. You do."

Van gulped. "That's a lot of power." And a responsibility she didn't feel ready to handle.

"For your own protection," Uxa warned, "we must keep your identity a secret from the Balish until you are fully trained. Your retrieval of the Coin confirmed the existence of our Anchoress. The Balish Council will send assassins to kill you. The Moors will seek revenge for the death of Solana. Providence Island is the safest place for you to stay hidden."

"I'm not afraid of the Moors," Van said. "Or any Bale."

Uxa's eyes darkened. "The Balish are not the only reason it is unsafe for you to stay."

Van could feel the other reason in her bones. "It's because of that—that shadow-wolf, isn't it?" That creature, she feared.

"It is called the Quasher," Uxa said, unnerved. "The Alignment is the only time of year you are protected from the beast. During this thirty-day window, the Quasher cannot track or find the Anchoress. With the Alignment over, although you are safe from the beast in Salus Valde, it is not worth the risk of having you stay here."

Van trembled, thinking about the Quasher. "Why does it want *me*?"

"The Anchoress has the highest percentage of Elemental blood of any Lodian, making you close to the divine, yet still mortal. Your inner light shines more brightly than any other. Light attracts darkness. The Quasher is your natural opposing force, formed by nature at the same time you were created. Nature balances every positive force with a destructive one."

Van shuddered. She didn't like that rule of nature.

Uxa continued. "The Elementals immediately contained the Quasher upon its creation, giving the Anchoress protection during the full year. The Elementals removed this safeguard during Amaryl's time. I instructed you to return by midnight, not solely because of the Elemental ruling but because the Alignment is the only time when the Quasher is contained."

Van understood.

The Elementals had released the Quasher as Amaryl's punishment for breaking the purity of the Anchoress bloodline by having a child with the Balish Prince Goustav. This act would affect all future Anchoresses-in-waiting. The Elementals had warned Amaryl to protect the purity of the Anchoress bloodline, and she hadn't listened. Van's ancestor had acted rashly and immaturely, which led to her corruption by the Coin.

Van's mother had been fool-hearted too. She had done the same thing as Amaryl, had a baby with someone of Balish blood. Van's mother's punishment for diluting the Anchoress bloodline was the reactivation of the curse, which caused her to die in childbirth.

The brunt of their reckless behavior fell directly on Van.

She grasped why it was necessary for her return to Providence Island. But Uxa seemed to have already decided Van was destined to be irresponsible, acting with the same irrationality as her mother and Amaryl.

"You cannot return here safely until the next Alignment," Uxa said, a welcome interruption to Van's thoughts. "I suggest you use the time in between wisely. Build your skills, absorb your power. Much rests on your shoulders now that you have come out of waiting."

Van worried Uxa was right about her inability to live up to the Anchoress's duties. She had fallen for Brux and remained unsure whether she had misused the Coin to kill Solana. Van confessed the latter worry to Uxa.

"Solana attached to her dark Self and therefore could not handle the high vibration of the Coin," Uxa said. "The path she chose for herself rendered her unworthy. That is what destroyed her, not you. Stopping Solana's attack on Salus Valde halted the Escalation and prevented Dishora. As the Anchoress, you did your job."

Van hoped Uxa was right.

The time had come for Van to complete her mission. She had one more difficult task to do. Give up the Coin.

Van wasn't sure if she could trust Uxa, but she heeded Amaryl's and Manik's warnings about holding onto the Coin after being done using it. Van couldn't risk not following the rules. The Celestial Tower was a holding place for the Coin. It would be safe there.

Van pulled out the Coin, took a deep breath, and then, using all of her will, placed the Coin in the fingers of Gaea Mater.

The mosaic on the floor came to life. Snakes flowed in a continuous pattern of swallowing each other's tails. The statue creaked as it turned toward the inner circle, then stopped, as did the mosaic.

Van stepped back from the Coin. She felt a pang in her heart as though she were abandoning a member of her family.

Uxa gripped Van's shoulders, turning her, so they stood face-to-face. "I must caution you not to speak of that which must be kept secret. You cannot tell anyone the truth about your summer project."

Van's shoulders slumped. Her exhausted body felt abused and neglected, which contributed to her feeling upset. She would get no credit for overcoming incredible obstacles to retrieve the Coin of Creation, a major feat. She inwardly cringed, knowing Solana's words had rung true.

"Make sure neither you nor Paley discuss your mission with anyone, anywhere," Uxa warned. "Not with your step-mother. Not with Ken. Your life depends upon it."

Van nodded, surprised she had forgotten about Ken. Their relationship seemed like a lifetime ago. Now, he remained only a faded memory of someone who used to be important to her.

Fynn rushed through the doorway. "The Balish Council members are coming!"

"Go," Uxa urged.

Van didn't budge. "I'll go, but only if you promise to clear my father's name."

Uxa agreed.

"'Til the next Alignment," Van said.

"'Til then," Uxa said with a smile.

Chapter 60

Day 31: Return to the Earth World

VAN, Fynn, and Wiglaf hurried down the winding staircase, while Uxa exited through a different door.

Her mind spinning, Van thought of everything that had happened during the last thirty days. Information she gathered on her journey had freed her from the guilt of believing she had caused her mother's death. But she was now burdened with the guilt of having killed Solana. Regardless of what Uxa and Brux had told her about Solana, Van feared Solana's death held consequences for her. Van had finally earned her place in her community. However, the cost had been a piece of her soul.

Was Van's folly part of the Anchoress curse? Amaryl had been in denial, believing her baby was her husband's, but deep down she knew the baby was Goustav's. The regret that flashed in Amaryl's eyes the moment before her death told Van this was true. Amaryl knew she had unintentionally cursed Astrid, her own child, thereby cursing the entire Anchoress line.

Van's father felt guilty his blood had reactivated Amaryl's ancient curse. For this sole reason, he had gone out of bounds the night Aelia died, the night Van was born.

Although Van no longer dreamed of marrying Ken and having eight kids, she saw herself having children in the future. If she didn't want to die while giving birth to her first child, then she needed to continue her father's search for a counter-curse.

Fynn walked with Van and Wiglaf through the deserted Lodestar Station.

"Uxa cleared the station for your departure," he said.

Van remained in deep in thought as Fynn led her to the portal.

By harming another person, Van had attached to her dark Self, which was amplified by using the power of the Coin. The restless pull of darkness tugged within her, causing a constant inner struggle for her to cling to her light. Her gut twisted with the fear she might lose the battle and tip toward darkness. The thought haunted her.

She found consolation in Solana's defeat, knowing the Balish princess wouldn't cause any more trouble. Now Van would monitor Solana's brother, Ferox, the newest heir to the Balish kingdom. When Van returned, she would check him for a dark thread. If she saw one…

The sight of Twinkle Toes interrupted her thoughts. The stuffed animal sat on the landing by the portal, waiting for her. Van had forgotten about it. She no longer had any interest in a child's toy. It would do nothing but clutter her bedroom.

"Keep it." Van handed the stuffed animal to Fynn. She didn't need a physical memento of her father's love anymore. His love for her was now firmly rooted in her heart.

Van bent down and picked up Wiglaf, who hovered by her feet, and hugged him to her chest.

"Bunfys don't need to be attuned for travel," Fynn said. "He can magically transport himself anywhere. He'll follow you if he wants to go, but you need to put him down so I can attune you."

Van nodded. She gave Wiglaf one last squeeze and placed him back on the floor. "See you back home."

"Mweep erp!" Wiglaf responded, his ears raised straight and tall.

Fynn pointed to a yellow dot on the floor of the landing. "Stand in this spot. I'm going to the control room, so I can attune you and activate the portal."

Van stood on the dot wondering why he continued to stare at her.

"Uh, Vanessa." Fynn shifted his weight, looking uncomfortable. "Good job getting the Coin." He turned and disappeared into the nearby control room.

Van knew Fynn, her biggest critic before the journey, found it difficult to give her a compliment. She grinned and placed her attention back to the portal.

Things weren't as settled as Uxa wanted Van to believe. If the spy in Lodestar wasn't Van's father, who was it? Uxa? She had an ulterior motive for wanting the Coin—power. If Uxa was the spy, it meant she had attached to the dark part of her Self, and if she accessed the power of the Coin, it would amplify the darkness within, causing her to become more corrupted and dangerous.

And why did Van's father feel it crucial to get that necklace to Van as one of his last acts in life? As a keepsake from her mother? Van doubted it. If that were the case, Uxa wouldn't be so interested in it.

Genie never gave Van the necklace, but Michael had told Genie to erase all evidence he had returned to Mt. Hope Manor. It dawned on Van that Genie had been in her father's study before Uxa had arrived with the Grigori. The bleach smell had resulted from Genie cleaning Van's father's blood.

The thought of Genie scrubbing the floor, removing all traces of her husband's death, made Van queasy. This act must've confused and flustered Genie. And Genie felt jealous of Aelia, so she might've thrown out the necklace. But Genie was more ditz than anything and probably hid the necklace from Uxa, then forgot where she put it. So where was the necklace now?

The three other statues in the Celestial Tower also bothered Van. Were they holders too? For what? Translating singular and plural words proved difficult in the ancient language. Manik's text had referred to the Coin as an Item of Creation. Had Van mistranslated the passage? Were there other Items of Creation?

Determination set inside Van, to come back during the next Alignment for answers. In the meantime, when not training, she would search for that necklace.

A wave of light swept over Van from above. Then the portal came to life, its silvery blackness swirling. Van wanted to spend more time in the Living World, but for now, leaving was the correct path.

As she transported back to Providence Island, she resolved no matter how strong the pull toward darkness grew inside her Self, she would cling to her inner light. Ildiss and Uxa had both spoken about choosing between the path of light and that of darkness. For Van, there was no question of choice. When presented with a decision between good or evil, from now on she would always choose the good.

Her skin prickled with the feeling of unsettled darkness moving about in the universe. The master demon Solana had contacted using her dark magic was strong enough to help Solana carry out her evil plan. With that kind of power, why hadn't this demon risen to the Living World yet? It wanted the Coin destroyed, which meant it must need more strength, something it would have gained from a war between the Lodians and the Balish. Thankfully, Van had saved the Coin from destruction, preventing such a war.

But the master demon had sampled the light of the Living World through Solana's demons and remained out there, hiding somewhere in the Earth World, waiting for another chance to rise.

In a never-ending battle, as darkness always seeks to destroy the light.

Read the first chapter of
book 2, Plague of Death

To Vanessa Cross's benefit, her sixteen-year-old heart had hardened over the past year, which made it easy for Van to shoo Wiglaf off of her bed.

"Beat it," she said to the furry, white bunfy curled up, sleeping beside her.

As Van wriggled upright, the critter raised his head, followed by his long ears.

"Urrrp. Eeep," he said in mild protest. He shifted his tiny body, stood on all fours, and blinked his warm-blue, round eyes at Van, looking sleepy.

His adorable whiskered face triggered a comforting swirl in the center of Van's chest. She tensed and brushed the feeling aside.

"Move it, pal." Van used her thumb to motion for him to get off the bed. "Time's a ticking. Don't want to waste the day."

She threw aside her orange and gold-laced curtains. The muted brightness of the clear June sky told her it was slightly past dawn. Her eyes moved down the expansive lawn to the edge of the forest surrounding Mt. Hope Manor. The brilliant green leaves barely fluttered in the mild breeze.

"It's a glorious morning for surfing," Van declared as she admired the majestic beauty of the oak, pine, and beech trees that blanketed a good portion of the small, hour-glass shaped island off the coast of Massachusetts.

The bunfy stretched his front legs and arched his back in a cute way that raised his butt and coiled tail.

Van watched as Wiglaf took his sweet time kneading the mattress.

"This proves you aren't a hundred percent bunny." She restrained herself from scooping him up in her arms and giving him a loving hug. It wouldn't do for a Giorgi warrior, albeit even a junior one, to show affection. Emotions equated to weakness.

Van patiently watched as Wiglaf finished his morning stretch.

"Definitely the Living World's version of a rabbit." She caught herself smiling at the critter. "Or maybe a cat."

The parallel world, separated from Van's Earth World by an invisible membrane-like veil, contained a variety of unusual animals. Van, unfortunately, discovered this last year after the Elders had sent her on a mission to retrieve a magical relic called the Coin of Creation. Some creatures she'd encountered on that journey were harmless like Wiglaf. Others were terrifying like…

Van's smile turned into a scowl. Her skin prickled as she unwittingly clenched her fists.

"Hey!" Paley threw open the door and strutted into Van's third-floor bedroom. "Get up."

Van leaped out of bed, poised and ready for battle.

Wiglaf disappeared in a snap, back to his magical realm.

"Paley!" Van calmed after recognizing the intruder as her best friend since kindergarten.

"Whoa. Take it easy, warrior queen." Paley held up her palms, expressing wide-eyed faux fear. "It's time for our morning surf. Get moving."

Van leaned in and squinted at Paley's eyes. "Are those lightning bolts?"

"So?" Paley flipped her wavy, dyed-blond hair over her shoulder, a nervous tic she had picked up since suffering trauma during their journey to the Living World last summer. "They look amazing, right?"

Paley's habit of wearing crazy colored contact lenses never grew old. Today her irises were deep green, with streaks of yellow lightning bolts shooting from the pupils.

"Yeah. Great," Van said with as much enthusiasm as she could muster. She thought they made Paley look like a crazy person, but didn't want to diminish her friend's fragile self-confidence.

Excited by the prospect of catching the ever elusive perfect wave, the girls hurried down the stairs and out of the manor before Van's step-mother, Genie, woke and started interrogating them with annoying questions like, "What're you girls up to today?" or "How's your summer training going?"

The girls scurried down Sandy Cove Lane in the direction of the crossroads, an intersection of Providence Island's seven main roads.

"Blackrock?" Van shifted her eyes toward Paley.

"Blackrock? Since when?"

"Whitecap Beach is for wimps." Van raised her chin and ran her hand over her silky white-blond hair, smoothing it behind her ear.

"Blackrock is off-limits," Paley said. "Jagged rocks, dangerous surf—"

"Surfing helps strengthen our core. Makes us better warriors. We need more of a challenge."

"Dangerous… off-limits… I'm in!" Paley's eyes sparkled.

Van used to fear her own shadow, unwilling to walk on the wild side. Once she recovered the Coin of Creation, a door opened she couldn't close. Being able to retrieve the Coin proved Van had inherited the magical Anchoress bloodline from her Lodian mother, Aelia. She also inherited a sense of duty from her Balish father, Michael. Over the past year, Van had absorbed the magnitude of her responsibilities as the Anchoress heir. The designated savior of the worlds. She developed an intense, almost obsessive, desire to protect her people, the Lodians.

Being the Anchoress also meant Van had the highest concentration of Elemental blood of any person alive. That, along with an innate ability to channel the energy of the moon, allowed her to access powerful warrior magic. So far, she could only get this power while in the Living World.

As long as she remained trapped on Providence Island in the Earth World, she could do nothing but train and wait for the Alignment. Or Luxta, as the ancients called it. The annual thirty-day window when Van could safely travel to the Living World.

"I need the challenge of Blackrock." Van wanted to stay in peak physical condition. Keep her reflexes and mind alert, ready for threats.

She trained every day, usually twice a day. Sometimes formally in her classes, other times she would offer to lead a session outside regular classroom hours. She only invited her peers in the special classes called the reservation program. They, like Van, were the students selected to become Grigori warriors. But, mostly, Van liked to train alone.

"You're taking this whole thing too far," Paley said.

"You're a warrior, or you're not," Van snapped. "You want to go to the Living World with me or not? Make up your mind. The Alignment begins tomorrow." She stormed ahead onto a path in the woods.

"We have to talk about this situation between you and Brux," Paley shouted to Van's hastily departing form.

Van rolled her eyes. Of course boy-obsessed Paley would mention Van's ex-boyfriend. Brux had anguished because of Van. His sister Daisy was lost in the Living World, kidnapped by the Balish Prince Merloc, the Merciless, probably being tortured daily, if not already dead.

After completing their mission last summer, the Elders forced Brux and his father to leave their home in Salus Valde, the Lodian region of the Living World, so that Brux could fulfill his duties as Van's assigned protector. Until Van came into her full power, the allusive demigods, the Elementals, appointed a specific warrior to look after her.

Usually, Van would be delighted for the guy she wanted as her boyfriend to be re-assigned to Providence Island. However, the Elementals didn't allow the Anchoress and her assigned protector to become romantically involved. Their reasoning: the protector cannot protect if he's distracted by love.

Van's blood duty required her to follow the ancient traditions, put in place to protect the Anchoress and the Lodian people. She was required to marry a pureblooded Lodian and have a child to pass down the Anchoress bloodline. Brux would've been a perfect choice.

She shook her head. *I'm much too young to be thinking about such things.*

Besides, Brux remained angry at Van for causing him and his father to move to the island. The assigned protector stipulations forced Brux to stay there to "protect" Van rather than run off to the Living World to rescue his beloved sister. Professor Lake, Brux's father, was an adult, making it illegal for him to go outside the boundary of Salus Valde. So neither could search for Daisy, causing frustration in them both.

"V-Van," Paley said huffing, out-of-breath from her quick jog to catch up with her friend. "You haven't opened up at all about last summer. You can talk to me."

"You and me." Van kept her attention on the path ahead. "We're different."

"It's okay to feel sad about losing your dad," Paley said.

Van stopped short and glared at Paley.

"My dad?" Van's cheeks flared. "How about my mother? How about Jorie, Trey, Elmot?" The latter three had been on Van's team to retrieve the Coin. Van wanted to include another person who had died because of her, but she couldn't bring herself to push the name through her pursed lips.

"Solana," Paley said softly. "You avoided mentioning Solana. Again."

Hearing her name made Van's stomach clench.

Van straightened her spine as she continued walking, and said, "Strong warriors have to sacrifice for the greater good of their people." With renewed determination, she pressed on through the woods.

The path ended, dropping Van and Paley onto Whitecap Beach. They ignored the ongoing beach volleyball game, or at least Van did.

"Brux isn't there, but I see Ken," Paley whispered. "And Pernilla."

Van glanced at the players, then scowled for doing so.

"I don't care where my ex-boyfriends are." She headed straight to her family's beach hut. "Or who they're with." If she couldn't have Brux, the love of her life, then she didn't want anyone. Dating and boys. They were both *out*.

In the Cross family's beach hut, Van and Paley wriggled into their wetsuits.

"Ugh." Lately, Van had trouble fitting into hers.

"Maybe it shrunk," Paley offered.

Van glared at the suggestion.

"I have an extra one in the bin if you need a size bigger." Paley zipped her suit.

"No, it's just," Van struggled with all her might to stretch the rubber suit, "I've packed on extra muscle from all my training." Though she had a sinking feeling, there might be something to her step-mother's criticism. Van's compulsive overeating had caused her to gain weight. She sucked in her stomach, and with some effort, zipped it. "I'm good."

Once sealed into their wetsuits, the girls flung beach towels over their shoulders, grabbed surfing boots and surfboards, and headed away from the beach hut.

There was no direct route to Blackrock, other than an access road used by island security, so they slipped back into the woods and followed the winding, sandy path to the off-limits beach.

Blackrock was deserted, as expected. The beach's sharp rocks and wild currents petrified Van. Over the past year, she had made great strides to confront and overcome her fears. Paley had no fear, though, when it came to showing off for the island boys. Too bad none were around.

Paley dipped her toe in the water, knowing it wouldn't be a comfortable temperature this early in the summer. "Yikes!" She yanked back her foot. "Need these." She sat down on the sand and slipped on her surfing boots.

Van frowned. She chucked her boots onto the sand. "There's nothing like the feel of the board under bare feet."

Van splashed into the water and then stretched out on top of her board.

Paley scrambled to follow.

They paddled until reaching a suitable distance, then stopped and sat upright, straddling their boards. They idly soaked in the early summer sun while waiting to catch a swell back to shore.

Paley grinned, at home bobbing up and down in rhythm with the waves. "Look!" She pointed to the horizon at a rise Van would call a tidal wave. "Here comes a good one!"

Van gathered her nerve. "Let's go!" She laid on top of her board and paddled like crazy, catching the rise.

Her body and board rose along with the wave. At the crucial moment, Van placed her hands on the board, elbows up, arched her back, and moved her feet into position. She crouched, arms wide, weight on her back foot, heart pounding. Her leg muscles cried under the familiar strain as she found her balance and stood. *I got this!*

The adrenaline high achieved from being in sync with the perfect wave hummed through Van's being. Her body, the board, the water—all came together and worked in harmony.

"Woo-hoo!" Van controlled the wave. It didn't control her. Overconfident, Van made the mistake of glancing back to see if Paley had also caught the wave.

The slight movement threw Van off balance. She wobbled. Every muscle in her core tightened as she struggled to regain command of the board.

Van's mind whirled in a panic. Her arms flailed. Instead of focusing on controlling her breath and concentrating on getting back her balance, she focused on how dangerous the undercurrents were at Blackrock and the jagged rocks that would rip her apart if she were to fall.

The dark, depthless water snapped at her like the jaws of a giant monster.

Van's feet, legs, and arms wouldn't cooperate, and she crashed into the deadly sea.

Enjoyed *Shock of Fate*? Let's stay connected!

Be the first to know about updates, releases, and exclusive content! Sign up for my newsletter at:

DLArmillei.com

Follow the *Anchoress* Series @anchoressseries
Dive deeper into the adventure and connect with other fans of *Anchoress*!

FACEBOOK GROUP:
https://www.facebook.com/groups/anchoressseries/

INSTAGRAM:
https://www.instagram.com/anchoressseries/

TIKTOK:
https://www.tiktok.com/@anchoressseries

Connect with D.L. Armillei @DLArmillei
Learn more about her, her writing journey, and upcoming projects:

FACEBOOK PAGE:
https://www.facebook.com/DLArmillei/

INSTAGRAM:
https://www.instagram.com/dlarmillei/

X (TWITTER):
https://x.com/DLArmillei

BOOKBUB:
https://www.bookbub.com/profile/d-l-armillei

GOODREADS:

https://www.goodreads.com/DLArmillei

Amazon Author Profile:
https://www.amazon.com/D.-L.-Armillei/e/B06XD25WT4/

Thank you for being part of this journey. Your support keeps the magic alive!

About the Author

D. L. Armillei (Donna) is a *USA Today* and international bestselling author who began her storytelling journey at just four years old. Unable to read or write at the time, she presented her mother with a "story" in "cursive," hoping to hear it read aloud. Instead, her mother lovingly tucked the pages away, promising they'd read it together once Donna learned to write for real.

Today, Donna crafts immersive, imaginative stories with emotional depth. Her flagship *Anchoress* series—a young adult epic fantasy—invites readers into a richly layered world of adventure, spiritual self-discovery, and empowerment.

A Massachusetts native, Donna now splits her time between living in her home state and Florida.